# CROWN OF GHOSTS

(Lost Kings Mc #19)

## AUTUMN JONES LAKE

# COPYRIGHT

**Crown of Ghosts (Lost Kings MC #19)**
Copyright 2021 Autumn Jones Lake
All rights reserved
Photographer: Wander Aguiar Photography
Cover Designer: Lori Jackson
Model: Wander Aguiar
Edited by: Creating Ink
Proofread by: Julie Barney
Digital ISBN #978-1-943950-62-1
Paperback ISBN# 978-1-943950-73-7

No part of this publication may be reproduced, distributed, or transmitted in any form or by any means, including photocopying, recording, or other electronic or mechanical methods, without the prior written permission of the publisher, except in the case of brief quotations embodied in critical reviews and certain other noncommercial uses permitted by copyright law. Please do not participate in or encourage piracy of copyrighted materials in violation of the author's rights. Purchase only authorized editions.

*Crown of Ghosts* is a complete work of fiction. Names, characters, places, and incidents either are the product of the author's imagination or are used fictitiously. Any resemblance to actual persons, living or dead, business establishments, events, or locales is entirely coincidental. The Lost Kings MC Series is a registered trademark of Ahead of the Pack, LLC.

## ALSO BY AUTUMN JONES LAKE

### THE LOST KINGS MC™ SERIES

Slow Burn (Lost Kings MC #1)
Corrupting Cinderella (Lost Kings MC #2)
Three Kings, One Night (Lost Kings MC #2.5)
Strength From Loyalty (Lost Kings MC #3)
Tattered on My Sleeve (Lost Kings MC #4)
White Heat (Lost Kings MC #5)
Between Embers (Lost Kings MC #5.5)
More Than Miles (Lost Kings MC #6)
White Knuckles (Lost Kings MC #7)
Beyond Reckless (Lost Kings MC #8)
Beyond Reason (Lost Kings MC #9)
One Empire Night (Lost Kings MC #9.5)
After Burn (Lost Kings MC #10)
After Glow (Lost Kings MC #11)
Zero Hour (Lost Kings MC #11.5)
Zero Tolerance (Lost Kings MC #12)
Zero Regret (Lost Kings MC #13)
Zero Apologies (Lost Kings MC #14)
White Lies (Lost Kings MC #15)
Swagger and Sass (A Lost Kings MC Novella)
Rhythm of the Road (Lost Kings MC #16)
Lyrics on the Wind (Lost Kings MC #17)
Diamond in the Dust (Lost Kings MC #18)
Crown of Ghosts (Lost Kings MC #19)
Throne of Scars (Lost Kings MC #20)
Reckless Truths (Lost Kings MC #21)
...and many more to come!

## Books in the Lost Kings MC World

### *The Hollywood Demons Series*

Kickstart My Heart
Blow My Fuse
Wheels of Fire

Bullets & Bonfires
Warnings & Wildfires
*Renegade Path* formerly known as: Cards of Love: Knight of Swords

### Paranormal Romance

Catnip & Cauldrons
Onyx Night
Onyx Shadows
Feral Escape

# CROWN OF GHOSTS
## Lost Kings MC #19

***It's a long road to redemption...***
I sacrificed fifteen years for a crime I didn't even commit.
In my absence, the world kept on turning.
The one dream I held onto burned to ashes.
Everything's changed, except my love for the Lost Kings Motorcycle Club.
As soon as I met her, the darkness recedes.
A new dream takes shape.
Her touch restores me.
Her broken soul is mine to fix.
But I can't shake the déjà vu sensation every time we touch.
History wants a repeat and all I want is peace.

*Crown of Ghosts is Grinder's first book and can be read as a stand alone. For the full, rich backstory on all the characters you'll meet, reading the series is encouraged.*

# GLOSSARY OF CHARACTERS AND TERMINOLOGY

## The Lost Kings MC™ World © Autumn Jones Lake

Grinder's story can be read as a standalone. He's never had a book or short story written about him before. We've seen and heard about him through other people's eyes throughout the series (see what I did there, *people* not characters!) But Crown of Ghosts is the first book where we are in his head.

The series has had some shakeups in the last few books. I've updated the glossary to reflect certain events. Obviously, I can't cover every detail here or we'd be reading a million word glossary instead of a few pages!

*The following may contain spoilers* if you are not caught up on the series or have skipped books.

*If* you're starting the series here—welcome! Grinder is an OG member of the Lost Kings MC so his story is a great place to jump into the Lost Kings MC world!

If you've been part of the LOKI family for a while—welcome back!

Please note, this glossary only pertains to *my* romantic fictionalized motorcycle club world. It should not be construed as applicable to any other fictional club or a real-life motorcycle club.

## THE LOST KINGS MC: UPSTATE, NY ("Empire," NY)

**President:** Rochlan "Rock" North. Leader of the Upstate NY charter of the Lost Kings MC.

**Sergeant-at-Arms:** Wyatt "Wrath" Ramsey. Protector or enforcer for the club.

**Vice President:** Blake "Murphy" O'Callaghan. Murphy was the road captain up until *White Lies (Lost Kings MC #15)*

**Treasurer:** Marcel "Teller" Whelan. Handles the money and investments for the club.

**Road Captain:** Dixon "Dex" Watts (newly appointed to the position in *White Lies*)

**Grayson "Grinder" Lock:** The former sergeant-at-arms of the New York charter. We saw a little about his relationship as Rock's mentor in *Wheels of Fire (Hollywood Deoms #3)*. We first "met" him in *Corrupting Cinderella (Lost Kings MC #2)* and have seen him a few other times throughout the series, most recently in *Zero Regret (Lost Kings MC #11.)* He has been mentioned throughout the series by the brothers as they looked forward to his release from prison.

## THE LOST KINGS MC: DOWNSTATE, NY ("UNION" NY)

- **President:** Angus "Zero" or "Z" Frazier. As of *Zero Apologies (Lost Kings MC #14)*, Z is the president of the Downstate, NY charter of the Lost Kings MC.
- **Vice President:** Logan "Rooster" Randall
- **Sergeant-at-Arms:** Steer
- **Treasurer:** Hustler
- **Road Captain:** Jensen "Jigsaw" Kilgore

## THE LOST KINGS MC: PORT EVERHART, VA

- President: Cypress "Ice" Caldwell
- Vice President: Farmer
- Sergeant-at-Arms: Pants
- Treasurer: T-Bone
- Road Captain: Wings

## THE LOST KINGS MC: DEADBRANCH, TN

- President: Digger
- SAA: Squiggy

*We haven't met anyone else...yet!*

## OTHER LOST KINGS MC MEMBERS

**Cronin "Sparky" Petek**: Sparky is the mad genius/hippie stoner behind the Lost Kings MC's pot-growing business. He is rarely seen outside of the basement, as he prefers the company of his plants.

**Elias "Bricks" Serrano**: We have seen Bricks and his girlfriend Winter throughout the series. He's one of the few members who does not live at the clubhouse.

**Sam "Stash" Black**: Lives in the basement with Sparky and helps with the plants.

**Thomas "Ravage" Kane**: We've gotten to know Rav and his snarky humor a little bit better in each book. Ravage is a general member who helps out wherever he is needed.

**Sway**: Former president of the downstate charter of the Lost Kings MC. We've seen Sway and his wife Tawny off and on in the series since *Strength From Loyalty*, usually annoying Rock in some fashion.

**Hoot**: We've seen glimpses of him since *Slow Burn* when he was a lowly prospect. He finally got his full patch, but still gets a lot of the grunt work.

**Birch**: We also met him as a prospect. He's been voted as a full-patch member but shares in a lot of the grunt work with Hoot.

**Priest**: The Lost Kings MC's national president. We first met him and his wife, Valentina, in *After Burn*.

**Malik**: Soon-to-be prospect for the Lost Kings MC. Helps out at Crystal Ball. Owns the Lucky Duck pawnshop in Ironworks.

## THE LADIES OF THE LOST KINGS MC

**Hope Kendall North, Esq.**: Nicknamed *First Lady* by Murphy in *Corrupting Cinderella (Lost Kings MC #2)*, Hope is the object of Rock's love and obsession. Their daughter is named Grace after Rock's mother.

**Trinity Hurst Ramsey**: Wrath's angel. Former caretaker of the club. She now has her own photography and graphic design business. She is married to Wrath, fiercely loyal to the club, and best friends with Hope.

**Heidi "Little Hammer" O'Callaghan**: Murphy's wife and Teller's little sister. Heidi just graduated from college and works at Empire Med. Murphy officially adopted her daughter, Alexa Jade.

**Charlotte Clark, Esq**: Teller's sunshine. Often credited with taming the brooding treasurer of the Lost Kings, Teller.

**Lilly Frazier**: Z's brave and devoted siren. The new queen of the Lost Kings MC's downstate charter. One of Hope's best friends. Z and Lilly's son is named Chance.

**Shelby Morgan**: Rooster's sassy little chickadee. Country music singer from Texas. We first met Shelby in *Swagger and Sass*.

**Serena Cargill**: Former downstate club girl. At one time, she was broken-hearted over Murphy. We first met her in *Strength From Loyalty*, got to know her better in *White Heat* and *More Than Miles*. She has appeared here and there in the series since then. Mistreated by Shadow, the former VP of the downstate charter, we have not "seen" her since *Zero Regret*.

**Swan:** Lost Kings MC club girl and dancer at Crystal Ball. Swan has found a new calling as the yoga teacher for the old ladies of the Lost Kings MC and is slowly moving away from dancing at Crystal Ball.

**Willow:** Bartender at Crystal Ball, but once or twice we've caught her sneaking in or out of the basement with Sparky.

**Tawny:** Sway's ol' lady. The former "Queen B" of the downstate charter of the Lost Kings MC.

**Anya Regal:** Porn princess of the Lost Kings MC, Virginia charter.

**Stella:** Pornographic film actress. The downstate charter is the sole investor in her production company. Ex-girlfriend of Z. Current...*something* of Sway. Her *Sex in Every City* series sometimes requires members of LOKI to work as bouncers on her film sets.

**Shonda**: Club girl from the Lost Kings, MC Virginia charter.

## OTHER RECURRING CHARACTERS RELEVANT TO THIS STORY

**Russell "Chaser" Adams:** President of the Devil Demons MC in Western NY. (*The Hollywood Demons* series contains his story.)

**Mallory "Little Dove" DeLova-Adams**: Chaser's wife. Daughter of mafia boss Anatoly DeLova.

Angelina Adams: Mallory and Chaser's daughter

**Linden "Stump" Adams**: Chaser's father. Former president of the Devil Demons MC.

**Sullivan Wallace**: Jake's brother, and the owner of Strike Back Fitness. He's a significant character in *Bullets and Bonfires* and has his own book, *Warnings and Wildfires*.

**Remington "Ruthless" Holt:** Owns "The Castle" with his best friend, Griff. It's an underground fighting ring Murphy used to participate in. We've seen him most recently in *Lyrics on the Wind*. He is the caretaker of his younger sister, Molly and runs a bar that his grandparents left him, where the Lost Kings have recently had some interesting events happen.

**Griffin "Stonewall" Royal:** Remy's best friend and business partner.

**Eraser**: Owns Zips, a racetrack near the Lost Kings MC territory. Married to Ella. Most recently seen in *White Lies*.

**Roman "Vapor" Hawkins:** The book *Cards of Love: Knight of Swords* is his story. We first met him and his wife, Juliet, in *After Burn*.

**Jake Wallace**: One of Wrath's business partners in Furious Fitness. Jake has appeared off and on throughout the series since *Tattered on my Sleeve*. He sometimes holds self-defense classes for the ladies.

**The mysterious "Quill"** who we met in *Diamond in the Dust* and is Chaser's half-brother.

**Anatoly DeLova:** Mallory's father. Leader of Russian mafia. Sometime business associate of the Lost Kings MC.

**Dawson Roads:** Famous (fictional) country music singer in the Lost Kings MC world. He's been mentioned here and there since *One Empire Night*, but we didn't "meet" him until *Rhythm of the Road*.

**Carter Clark**: Charlotte's goofy, often inappropriate, younger brother.

**Loco:** Business associate of the Lost Kings MC. He covers the Ironworks area of the Lost Kings MC's territory. He has appeared throughout the series and become a strong LOKI ally.

## OTHER MCS: FRIENDLY CLUBS:

**Devil Demons MC:** Based in Western NY. Long-time friend of the Lost Kings MC. Their clubs are intertwined and share a lot of history. More of this is explored in the *Hollywood Demons* series.

**Wolf Knights MC**: Mostly an ally of the Lost Kings. Runs Slater County but has had a number of shake-ups in the last few years. Whisper is their current president. Claimed to be dissolving their charter and turning Slater County over to the Lost Kings but we haven't seen them fully exit the area yet.

**Iron Bulls MC** (From the *Iron Bulls MC* series by Phoenyx Slaughter): Southwestern outlaw club. Meets up and does business with LOKI once in a while.

**Savage Dragons MC** (From the *Iron Bulls MC* series by Phoenyx Slaughter): Texas outlaw club.

## ENEMY CLUBS:

**Vipers MC:** Used to run Ironworks until the Lost Kings took over that territory. Still active in other parts of the country.

**South of Satan MC:** Vermont MC who has stirred up trouble for LOKI in the past.

## LOST KINGS MC TERMINOLOGY

**LOKI:** Short for LOst KIngs

**War room:** Where the Lost Kings hold "church."

**Property patch**: When a member takes a woman as his old lady (wife status), he gives her a vest with a property patch. In my series, the vest has a "Property of Lost Kings MC" patch and the member's road name on the back. The officers also place their patches on the ol' lady's vest as a sign that they always have her back. Her man's patch or club symbol is placed over the heart. Rock's patch is a crown. Wrath's is a star. Murphy's is a four-leaf clover. Teller's is a dollar sign. Z's is the letter Z. Rooster's is a rooster wearing a crown. As a joke, Wrath gave Rock and Hope a "product of" patch for baby Grace. Maybe it will catch on as more kids are born into the club? We'll see.

## PLACES IN THE LOST KINGS MC WORLD

I use a mix of real and imaginary names to describe the places in my series. Again, I bend and shape geography to my needs as this is a *fictional world that I have created.*

**Empire, NY:** The territory run by the Lost Kings MC upstate charter. This is a fictional version of Albany, NY, the capital of New York State. Many of the Lost Kings MC's businesses are located in and around Empire.

**Slater, NY**: Loosely based on Schenectady County. Until recently it was the Wolf Knights MC's territory.

**Ironworks, NY:** Loosely based on Rensselaer County (Troy, NY).

In the beginning of the series, it was run by the Vipers MC. It is now considered territory of the Lost Kings MC.

**Union, NY**: A fictional area two hours south of Empire, NY, where the "downstate" charter is located.

**Crystal Ball:** The strip club owned by the Lost Kings MC and one of their legitimate businesses. They often refer to it simply as "CB." Located in Empire County.

**Furious Fitness:** The gym Wrath owns. Often just referred to as "Furious." Located not far from Crystal Ball.

**Strike Back:** Owned by Sullivan Wallace but members of the Lost Kings MC have worked there in the past.

**Johnson County/Johnsonville:** Fictional area where Heidi grew up. About an hour west of "Empire." Where Strike Back Gym, The Castle, and Zips are located. Possibly the new home of a Lost Kings MC support club? We'll see!

**Zips:** Racetrack owned by Eraser where all the illegal gambling/racing in the area happens.

**The Castle:** Formerly a juvenile detention center. The building is now used to house the underground fighting ring run by Remy and Griff. Murphy used to fight here. Other LOKI members also blow off steam in the cage here from time to time. Located in the middle of nowhere, NY, it once-upon-a-time housed Griff, Vapor, and possibly Teller during their "troubled youth" days.

**Kodack, NY:** Another *fictional* NY area located in Western New York. Somewhere near Buffalo, perhaps. This territory is run by the Devil Demons MC.

**Empire Medical Center**: Local hospital where all the Kings receive medical treatment. Heidi also works there now.

## OTHER MC TERMINOLOGY

*Most terminology was obtained through research. However, I have also used some artistic license in applying these terms to my romanticized, fictional version of an outlaw motorcycle club. This is not an exhaustive list.*

**Cage**: A car, truck, van—basically anything other than a motorcycle.

**Church**: Club meetings all full-patch members must attend. Led by the president of the club, but officers will update the members on the areas they oversee. (Some clubs refer to the meeting room where they hold church as the "chapel." My club refers to it as their "war room."

**Citizen**: Anyone not a hardcore biker or belonging to an outlaw club. "Citizen wife" would refer to a spouse kept entirely separate from the club.

**Cut:** Leather vest worn by outlaw bikers and adorned with patches and artwork displaying the club's unique colors. The Lost Kings' colors are blue and gray. Their logo is a skull with a crown. The *Respect Few, Fear None* patch is earned by doing time for the club without snitching. *Brother's Keeper* patches are earned by killing for the club. *Loyal Brother* is for a brother who's spent more than five years with the club.

**Colors**: The "uniform" of an outlaw motorcycle gang. A leather vest, with the three-piece club patch on the back, and various other patches relating to their role in the club.

**Fly colors**: To ride on a motorcycle wearing colors.

**Muffler bunny or "bunnies"**: A girl who hangs around to provide sexual favors to members. Old ladies in my series will sometimes refer to them as "friends of the club," depending on the girl in question. Some clubs refer to them as club whores, patch whores, or cut sluts. These terms are not regularly used in my series. Sometimes simply referred to as a "club girl."

**Nomad:** A club member who does not belong to any specific charter, yet has privileges in all charters.

**Old lady/ol' lady**: Wife or steady girlfriend of a club member.

**Patched in**: When a new member is approved for full membership.

**Patch holder**: A member who has been vetted through performing duties for the club as a prospect or probate and has earned his three-piece patch.

**Road name**: Nickname. Usually given by the other members.

**Run:** A club-sanctioned outing, sometimes with other chapters and/or clubs. Can also refer to a club business run.

I'm sure I'm forgetting something! But that should get you started!

# PROLOGUE

## Grinder

*Thirteen years ago.*
*Pine Correctional Facility, Upstate New York*

Time waits for no man. It spins ahead, out of our control, no matter how hard we wish it would slow. For some, it seems to go by too fast. For others, it drags on and on, while you slowly rot away.

Prison steals time better than any thief.

It had stolen two years from me so far.

Rock stared at the papers in his hand, then stuffed them in a large yellow envelope before tucking it under his mattress on the lower bunk. "I hate leaving you behind."

The raw anguish in his voice punched me in the gut.

"It's not right," he continued.

"It is what it is," I grumbled. "I'm sorry I got you into this."

He'd be checking out of the correctional facility we've called home for the last couple of years any day now.

But I'd bought myself an extended stay. I'd had no other options. It was kill or be killed. My body was littered with the scars of survival. I did what I had to do to keep us alive and didn't regret my choices.

Now the time had come.

One of us had to stay.

One of us had to leave.

"Use your head. I don't want to see you in here again," I warned him. "You feel me?"

"I'll do my best."

"Do better than that." My words needed to be a hammer to pound this into his thick skull. "Keep Wrath and Zero out of trouble. You've got the cunning and skills. They'll follow your lead."

His mouth twisted in a wry smile. "So cunning, I ended up in here?"

Rock was smart. I had faith he could run the club the way it was meant to be run.

He was also still a smart-*ass*. Prison hadn't stolen that from him yet. "That was Ruger's doing, and you're gonna set that right once you're out and can make a plan to dethrone that disloyal fuck." I lowered my voice. "Marcel and Blake are good kids. Watch out for them. Especially Marcel. Keep his ass out of juvie, for fuck's sake."

"Wrath's got him on a tighter leash since he got out. He's not lettin' either of 'em run errands for Ruger."

"Good. They'll be brothers for life if you mold them right. Owe their loyalty to you 'til the day they die."

He cocked his head and gave me a sideways glance. "The way you molded me as a kid?"

A flash of guilt pummeled me. "No one else was lookin' out for ya. Your fucking father was too busy whoring around and starting fights."

He scrubbed his hands over his face. "Fuck."

"You're gonna be fine. Turn the club around. Carve out the dead weight." I squeezed my hands into fists. "Get us out of guns—the brotherhood was never supposed to be about unlimited power and piles of cash. Ruger's forgotten the meaning of loyalty—letting brothers starve while he's feasting. He ain't fit to wear that president's patch."

"Amen to that."

"Build whatever alliances you can with other clubs. That's the only way we're gonna keep law enforcement at bay. Get us away from the fucking cartel before they chop off all our heads."

"Christ, brother. That's a tall order."

"You can do it. I have faith in you."

He nodded slowly and ran his hand over the back of his neck. I could see the wheels turning; he was already searching for the right path. "Wrath said Sparky's got a few ideas. *If* we can find the right facility."

I choked on a laugh. "Fucking Cronin. That little shit's a smart kid. He's ready to wear a full-piece patch."

Rock side-eyed me then laughed. "Yeah."

"Keep Dixon close," I continued. "He's got your mindset. Well, except he doesn't fuck every woman that walks by—"

"I don't—"

"Yeah, yeah." I waved my hand in his face, dismissing his protest. "I know you took a break for Carla. But you're a free man now—in more ways than one. You'll be back at it."

"Fuck off," he growled.

"Try to find yourself a *good* woman." I continued my lecture, ignoring his attitude. I couldn't risk him doing something reckless and winding up back inside, and a good woman would have the power to anchor him. "Find someone *loyal*, for fuck's sake. Not a bitch who's gonna undermine you at every turn. You need someone who can understand and love the club. A girl who will help you shape it into a *family*."

He slowly turned his head and stared at me. "Sway's poison. He needs to go too." Interesting, how he connected Sway's wife to my warning so quickly.

"Then make it intolerable for him to stay. With Ruger gone, the rest of the trash will take itself out." I ran through a mental list of brothers we'd be able to count on. "You'll have a small crew. But that's okay. Expand slowly. Vet each prospect thoroughly. Not everyone's fit to wear our patch."

"Ain't that the truth," he muttered.

"When the time is right, gut Ruger. Bury his carcass somewhere he'll never be found." I let myself fantasize about doing the kill myself for a few seconds. Nice and clean with a bullet to the head? Or slow, methodical wet work? "And after it's done, you slip that tacky fucking ring off his hand. Wear it to pay me a visit so I can celebrate."

He scoffed. "It's not even club colors."

"I don't give a fuck. Don't let him go to the grave with it."

"I won't," he promised.

Three years later, he kept that promise. It didn't make the agonizing years ahead any easier. But it gave me hope that one day I'd be free and able to reclaim my life.

# CHAPTER ONE
## Grinder

Fifteen years of my life wasted.

Fifteen years of eating shitty food, being watched every second, and being told what to do and when to do it.

Thirteen years pacing an eight-by-six cell.

Two years pacing my much more spacious eight-by-fourteen cell.

Fought every second to stay alive.

The constant vigilance wore me down and turned me into an animal I no longer recognized.

I came through the gates the sergeant-at-arms of the Lost Kings MC New York charter. Planned to do my four years and get the hell out. But those first few years behind bars, the club kept giving me "assignments." I did what my club asked of me and paid the price with years added to my sentence.

Eventually, I ended up ruling through fear and intimidation.

I *should* be happy to finally get the hell out. Go back to my life.

Except I don't have a life anymore.

My wife barely responded to my letters.

I have no children to reunite with.

No job or job prospects.

Officially, I can't associate with my club for another year. Even if they want me back.

I'm not the same man who walked into this prison.

And I'm not so sure I like the man I've turned into.

"Don't fuck it up, Grayson," Carl, the only guard I can tolerate, says as he walks me to the front gate. "Don't want to see you on this side again."

"Trust me, I don't plan on it."

I'd traded in my snazzy prison-issue green pants and shirt for a pair of jeans and a thick flannel shirt Rock made sure to provide for my release. If I never see another pair of scrub-like clothes again, it'll be too soon.

The few things I'd gone inside with fit in a plastic bag. A wallet full of outdated information. A set of keys that don't unlock anything anymore. Tucked under my arm, I have a large envelope with my medical records and information about when and where to meet with my parole officer.

Carl walks me to the door, even though technically his job is finished, and holds out his hand.

Surprised, I take it and he gives me a quick shake. "I mean it. Good luck."

"Thanks."

I've dreamed about this day for years. Stepping out into the blinding sunshine. Tasting freedom again.

The reality is, it's winter in upstate New York. The sky's gray and overcast.

Still, the weak sunlight and cool breeze feel damn good on my pasty skin.

The crisp air fills my lungs with peace.

Fat, wet snowflakes fall to the ground, creating a slushy mess, and I'm glad to have the black work boots instead of my former prison-issued canvas slip-ons.

Freedom tastes like brisk, soggy air, and I inhale a deep gulp.

I don't want to take anything for granted this time.

I've had fifteen years to pinpoint all the mistakes I've made.

The black SUV parked at the curb has to be someone from the club. Cautiously, I make my way to it. When I'm maybe five feet away, the driver's side door opens and Rock steps out.

He's no longer the boy I mentored and brought into the club. Now, he's the president. Never expected him to personally pick me up. Figured he'd send Murphy or Teller, just as he'd sent them to visit me every month for years.

"Grinder." He pulls me in for a tight, brotherly hug.

At first, my body stiffens. I stand there in his embrace without moving or breathing. Human contact has been rare and unpleasant over the last fifteen years. Even though I'm a hundred percent sure Rock's not planning to sink a knife between my ribs, the hypervigilance I developed in prison won't melt as fast as the falling snowflakes.

"It's good to finally see you on the outside, Gray," he says. "Missed you, brother."

Slowly, I will my arms to return the embrace.

We hang on probably longer than necessary, but I'm too choked up to speak or let go.

Never had any kids of my own. Even if he's less than a decade younger than me, Rock's as close as I'll probably ever get to having a son.

"Good to be outside," I finally respond, pulling away. "You didn't have to pick me up yourself."

"Of course I did." He waves at the SUV and opens the door. "Let's get you out of here."

I expect him to turn onto the Thruway and head north toward Empire, but he takes the back roads leading into the outskirts of Empire County instead. I watch the scenery in amazement.

So much has changed.

"What the fuck is that?" I press my finger against the cool glass and stare at an alien, futuristic field of black, shiny panels three or four feet off the ground.

"Community solar farm."

"A *what*?"

The quick explanation he rattles off flies over my head. Information overload.

"Where you headed?" I ask.

"Our main clubhouse. You've never even seen the place."

Shit, that's right. When I went inside, our clubhouse was a sorry little building next to the strip club the MC owned.

"Jeez, figured you'd at *least* take me to Crystal Ball first," I mutter.

He chuckles and glances over. "We can arrange something."

The last damn thing I need is a parade of strippers begging to bounce around in my lap. "I don't suppose you managed to track down Rose and let her know I was getting out?" I fail miserably at pushing the hope out of my voice and sounding casual.

The smile slides off his face. "I called. She hasn't responded."

"Figured." While time's pretty much stood still for me, I'm sure Rosie's moved on and forgotten all about her inmate ex.

Back in the day, when a brother was released from prison, the club held a big party, complete with plenty of sweet butts, club girls, and strippers to "tend" to him as the first get-out-of-jail fuck.

But I can't muster up any interest.

Not until I see Rosie.

No matter how much I've suffered over the years, the small spark of hope that there's still a chance for us has refused to be snuffed out.

"Tell me what you've been up to?" I ask to calm my rising anxiety. "Z said you got married. This the girl you told me about?"

"Yes." His smile returns. "Hope and I have a baby girl now too."

That hits me right in the gut with joy for my brother and regret for myself.

"What'd you name her?" I ask, even though I bet I know the answer.

"Grace."

After his mother. "Beautiful."

"She is. Hope's waiting at the clubhouse. She's looking forward to finally meeting you."

"Really?" I'm surprised he bothered to mention me to his wife.

How involved with the club does he allow her to be? I told him to find someone who'd *love* the club, not learn its secrets.

"Just the club and family are there now. Later…"

"I can fuck as many bunnies as my dick will stay up for?" I sneer.

He snorts and shakes his head. "Whatever you want. Murphy's got your bike set up for you if you wanna risk going for a ride."

I flex my fingers, imagining smooth leather gloves surrounding my hands, legs hugging the machine, the blur of the pavement under my feet, battling the wind to stay in my saddle. The essence of freedom.

I roll my right shoulder. The ache shoots through my bicep to my wrist. *Can I even ride?*

"Roads aren't great." I gesture toward the slushy asphalt we're speeding through.

"There'll be plenty of time."

*Time, right.* I want to make the most of it now that I'm free.

"Wrath's wife there too?" I ask. "I still can't believe he tricked some poor girl into marrying him."

Rock's laughter fills the cabin. "No trickery. Trinity's a good girl. She's good for him."

Trinity, huh? Is that a road name or her real name? "Yeah, but is he good for *her*?"

"They're right for each other," he answers with confidence.

Well, shit. Good for Wrath. Always worried the angry fucker would end up in a cell next to me.

"I don't think I can deal with Murphy married to Heidi. She's still about five years old in my head."

"Teller learned to live with it. You will too."

Teller, shit—I've missed that mouthy little fucker. He hasn't been out to visit as regularly as he used to. "He's claimed an ol' lady too?"

This time, Rock's slower to answer. "Charlotte's exactly what he needs."

"She can put up with that mouth of his?"

"She handles him fine."

"I'm having trouble believing Z settled down with one girl." Z mentioned he had a wife *and* son last time he visited. Never thought I'd see the day.

"You'll like Lilly."

"Last time Dex came out to see me, he said Rooster's been out on the road following his girl around." Although he wasn't even patched-in to the club when I went inside, Rooster's a loyal brother who's visited me more than once. "Looking forward to meeting him on this side of the fence."

"He's solid. He really helped Z transition to running Downstate. He and Shelby should be here tomorrow."

Fifteen years and it seems as if all my brothers have settled down.

Fifteen years and everything has changed.

Except me.

## CHAPTER TWO
### Grinder

WHAT THE FUCK HAS THE CLUB BEEN DOING TO EARN MONEY ALL THESE *years?*

The "new" clubhouse is more like a high-end retreat hidden away in the woods. Someplace rich celebrities would go to detox and kick their addictions. Learn yoga and talk to their spirit animals or shit like that.

Not a motorcycle club.

We weren't this loaded fifteen years ago. If anything, the club struggled under the weight of lawyer fees, fines, and payoffs.

"Jesus Christ. This is something else," I mutter as Rock stops his SUV in the parking area in front of the hotel dressed up as a log cabin. Never seen a biker clubhouse that looked like *this*.

"It's served us well," he says, cryptic as ever.

"How many banks you rob to build it?" I mutter.

He huffs a laugh. "Got lucky when we found the place. It suited all our various demands." He gestures toward the woods. "Lots of property to grow with us as our needs…*change.*"

Vague answer.

I'm still gawking at the log castle like a fucking teenager when

Rock opens my door. At the same time, the front door to the clubhouse opens and Wrath fills it.

"Hey, old man," he says, bounding down the steps to meet me. He's been calling me *old man* since he was an angry sixteen-year-old, and now it brings back a flood of affectionate memories.

"Get over here, you big beast," I call out.

He laughs and quickens his steps, embracing me in a hug that knocks the wind out of me.

"Damn, son." I pull away and slap his shoulder. "You're a bigger brute than ever."

"Thanks," he says, thumping me on the back one last time. "So good to see you outside, finally."

"Come on," Rock urges.

I follow them up the short set of stairs and into the clubhouse.

Inside's even more impressive. High ceilings, gleaming hardwood floors, exposed wood beams, and leather furniture fill the wide space.

And family.

Brothers with their wives and children. Everyone whole and peaceful.

The first one to approach me has to be Rock's wife. The way she looks at him gives it away. In her arms, she carries a sleepy-eyed little girl.

Rock settles his hands on her shoulders. "This is Hope. Hope, this is Grinder. He looked out for me. Mentored me." He swallows hard and stares me straight in the eyes. "Brought me into the club."

Notice he left out the part where I helped him get tossed into prison alongside me. And don't I have some lingering guilt about *that*.

"Welcome home, Grinder," Hope says, her gaze skipping to Rock, who nods. "I've heard so many good things about you. We're all happy you're here."

She appears too sweet and innocent to be a lawyer, much less the wife of an MC president, but her words are firm and sincere. She holds out her free hand and I take it briefly.

"Knew it would take someone special to settle Rock down," I say.

Her eyes widen, but then she laughs, jostling her daughter.

"Look at you." I reach out to touch her cheek, stopping midway and dropping my hand to my side.

The girl blinks and rubs her eyes, then smiles when she sees her dad, holding out her arms for him to take her.

"Grace," he says, "this is your Uncle Grinder."

She swivels her head and stares at me with wide, unblinking blue eyes before resting her head against Rock's chest. Rock sets his hand on my shoulder and steers me toward the group assembled in the living room.

Z's on his feet and wrapping his arms around me before I have a chance to react. "Good to have you home, brother."

I pull away, keeping my hands on his shoulders. "God damn, that president patch looks good on you, Zero. Proud of you, son."

He grins, familiar dimples appearing, and ducks his head. "Can't lie, Grinder—I wasn't thrilled being taken away from home." He gestures toward the clubhouse. "But we're making it work." He slaps Rock's shoulder.

"Club's stronger than ever," Rock agrees.

No one's given me the details on how that all went down. I gathered it had something to do with our national president playing God. Priest always did have a knack for sticking his nosy ass where it didn't belong.

Teller latches onto me next. "Good to finally see you outside, Grinder."

There I go gettin' choked up again. It meant a lot to me that Teller and Murphy visited me often. I'm not sure how to express that without breaking down, so I pat his back. God damn, he seems even bigger outside the prison walls—nothing like the sullen, mouthy teenager he was when I went inside. "Good to see you too, son."

He pulls a tall, pretty redhead to his side. "This is my fiancée, Charlotte."

"I'm so happy to finally meet you," Charlotte says.

Murphy joins our widening circle, one arm wrapped around a girl who absolutely can*not* be little Heidi. "Jesus Christ," I breathe out. "You've grown up."

She blushes and ducks her head, so now I *know* it's Heidi.

"You even remember who I am?" I ask.

"Of course I remember you," she says, opening her arms and giving me a big hug. "Welcome home, Grinder." She's soft and light in my arms. Smells like strawberries and soap. Not that I'm trying to be a creep, sniffing a brother's wife—someone I knew when she was a little girl—but it's been a while since anything pleasant tickled my nose. I inhale deeply and release her. Heidi beams and rests her hand on my arm while Murphy lifts a miniature version of Heidi into his arms.

"This is Alexa," Murphy says. "Wanna say hi to Uncle Grinder?"

"Hi!" the little girl chirps, waving her fingers at me.

"Well, don't you look just like your momma did." Shit, this is weird. Heidi couldn't have been more than five or six when I went inside. Jesus, time's a rotten thief. Now she's got a kid of her own?

Heidi chuckles. "You think so?"

"Absolutely."

"She's not quite the holy terror Heidi was," Teller says, patting his sister's shoulder. "Not yet, anyway."

Heidi grins up at him. "Give her time."

Murphy sets his daughter down and she scampers over to Hope. My gaze lands on Murphy's still crisp-looking VP patch. "Congratulations." Even as a kid, he was reserved and thoughtful. A good choice to advise Rock and move the brotherhood forward. "That VP patch suits you, Murphy."

His smile slips. "Thanks, Grinder."

Dex muscles his way in next to Murphy. "So glad you're out, Grinder." His arms jerk at his sides and he cocks his head, silently asking if a hug's okay. Time's only sharpened his observant and perceptive nature, it seems.

I pull him in for a quick embrace and pat his back. "Real happy to be out, son."

Ravage had barely patched-in when I went inside, but he still approaches with a respectful handshake and welcome.

Sparky was only a prospect, but he's a hard kid to forget. "We've been working on raising the vibrations in the house for your arrival."

He presses his palms toward the ceiling. "Much healing and restorative energy for you, sir."

My gaze slides to Rock, who answers with a quick just-go-with-it headshake and shrug.

"I'll accept all the good vibrations you got for me, Sparky. Thank you."

Stash side-eyes his buddy before shaking my hand. "Got all sorts of hotties lined up for ya, Grinder."

That's the last damn thing I'm worried about. "Appreciate it."

Bricks is even stockier than I remember—a solid armful as I return his tight embrace. "Welcome home, brother."

Wrath pats my back. "Trinity, Lilly, and Swan have been cooking all day. You hungry?"

My stomach rumbles at the mention of food. Although, after the garbage I've been eating, I'm not sure how my body will react to anything not coming out of a package. "Sure."

The herd of us move down a long, wide hallway.

"We need to give you an official tour," Rock says.

"Now that Wrath mentioned it, I'm kinda set on the food thing." I clutch my stomach to emphasize my point.

"You got it, brother."

Stash and Teller push open wide, swinging doors, holding them for everyone to pass. Inside, two long, rectangular dining tables take up the dining room. Smaller round tables fill the unused space. To the right, along the back wall, a bar and coffee station are set up.

"You want a drink?" Murphy asks.

"No, but real coffee would be nice." I eye the dining tables anxiously.

"Coming right up."

Rock casts a quick glance my way, then snaps his fingers. "Let's turn this table to make it easier to get around."

Rav, Stash, and Sparky go about moving one of the long tables so the people seated on the left side will have their backs to the wall instead of out in the open. If anything, it makes it *harder* for everyone to navigate, and I suspect Rock's order has more to do with providing me with the comfort of putting *my* back against the wall—something you learn to do early on in prison if you want to survive.

I'm both appreciative and annoyed by the gesture.

Rock takes his place at the head of the table with his girl. He pats the spot to his right and motions me closer.

"You don't need to go to special trouble for me, Rock," I grumble as I pass him.

He studies me for a few beats. "Enjoy it while it lasts."

I bark out a laugh and slap his arm. That works. I can tolerate the fussing for a day or two. Then I want to get back to normal. Whatever that is.

A door at the back of the room swings open. A tall blonde with curves to grab a man's attention glides across the room, right into Wrath's arms. He kisses her forehead and leans down to whisper in her ear.

Ah, now I understand how Wrath ended up settling down.

Finished with their short conversation, she beams a bright smile my way and rounds the table with him to come to my side. "Welcome home, Grinder."

Wrath slips his arm over her shoulders. "Grinder, this is my wife, Trinity."

"We're all so happy you're finally free." She reaches for my hand and I accept a quick shake.

A boulder of exhaustion rolls over me. So many new people. Reuniting with brothers. Adjusting to new space.

I drop into my seat.

While everyone chatters around me, Trinity squats next to my chair, resting her arm on the table.

"I didn't want to make anything too rich for your first meal on the outside," she says softly, careful not to draw attention to our conversation. "We're having chicken thighs with ginger rice. Ginger's supposed to be good for the stomach." She rests her hand on her belly. "There's a ginger-scallion sauce on the side. But I can make you chicken breasts if you'd prefer something leaner."

My mouth waters at her description. Real food. Actual spices. No bland, starchy crap. My heart's lodged in my throat. She's put a lot of thought into the meal and my comfort. But it's her discretion that really claws into my heart. The last fifteen years have been an exercise in enduring one humiliation after another. Feels nice to be treated with dignity.

"Or I can make cheeseburgers," she says when I don't answer right away. "Or a—"

"You don't have to go to extra trouble for me."

"It's no trouble," she insists.

"I'm already drooling over the ginger-scallion chicken," I assure her.

A warm smile curves her lips. "Good."

I rest my hand over hers. "Thank you."

"You're welcome. We've got fresh pineapple and other fruit for dessert too."

Jesus, I'd forgotten how much I miss actual fruit. "That sounds great." I hesitate, not wanting to make extra work for her. "You think I could have a side of pineapple with dinner?"

"Absolutely." One corner of her mouth twitches, and she lifts her chin toward the end of the table where the younger guys have gathered. "Good call. They're likely to gobble it all down if you don't get to it first."

"You telling Grinder stories about us, Trinity?" Ravage shouts.

"Nope!" She laughs as she stands. "Not me."

Stash jumps out of his chair. "Whatever she says—"

"Is probably true!" Dex finishes for him.

I chuckle at their antics.

"Let me know if you want anything else." Trinity pats my hand. "We're pretty well stocked but someone can always run down to Ward's and get whatever you need."

"I will."

"Thanks, Trinny," Rock says as she passes him.

Murphy sets a mug of coffee on the table in front of me, and Heidi adds a small pitcher of cream and a shaker of sugar. Real cream and sugar. It's like I've hit the jackpot.

"Thanks."

Z approaches with his arm around a busty brunette, a little boy the spittin' image of Z skipping next to them.

"Grinder, this is my wife, Lilly. Lilly, this is Grinder."

She takes my hand between both of her soft ones and gently squeezes. "I've heard so much about you. It's good to finally meet." She tilts her head toward the hallway. "Sorry I wasn't out there when you arrived. I've been helping Trinity—"

"No apologies necessary, sweetheart." I nod toward the kitchen. "Sounds like you're whipping up a feast in there."

Z swings the little boy up into his arms. "This little dude is Chance."

"Well, damn, you've grown since I last saw a picture of you."

Chance flashes a quick, dimpled smile, then wriggles out of his dad's arms.

When everyone's finally seated at the table and big bowls of rice and platters of heavenly scented chicken are being passed around, Rock stands and taps his glass.

"Ah, fuck," I mutter. I can't deal with anyone gettin' all maudlin on me.

"Tonight we're welcoming our brother home. Grinder's sacrificed for this club. He lives and breathes our code of love, loyalty, and brotherhood. This is a time for celebration."

Everyone cheers or thumps their hands against the table. Embarrassed, I duck my head. "Thank you."

"Let's eat!" Murphy shouts.

The guys hassle him for being the chubby kid worried about stuffing his face. But if I remember Murphy's nature accurately, he did it to take the attention off of me. Sure enough, when I glance at him, he flashes a quick smile and winks.

Warm ginger aromas fill my nose, triggering a grumble in my stomach. I cut into the tender chicken and take my first bite of freedom.

*Fuck me.* I barely hold back a moan as the spicy layers of flavor burst over my tongue. I struggle not to pick up one of the large serving spoons and shovel the rice, vegetables, and chicken in my mouth.

*Pace yourself.*

No one's gonna steal my plate or mess with my food. It's not going anywhere. I've got all the time in the world. Don't need to act like a savage in front of all my brothers.

Next, I close my eyes and savor the cool, tart burst of pineapple. Then I return to the chicken. So many different flavors. Little blasts of heaven on my tongue. I'd long ago forgotten the simple pleasure of real food prepared by someone who actually gives a damn.

AFTER DINNER, ROCK CALLS EVERYONE IN FOR CHURCH.

I follow the guys, staring at everything. Still can't wrap my head around this clubhouse. Wrath points out a few things—laundry, bathroom, yoga studio.

"I think I'm gonna need a map," I grumble. "And why the hell do bikers need a yoga room?"

"Excellent question." Stash slings his arm around my shoulders. "You see, it used to be *our* champagne room. Poles, mirrors, comfy couches—girls would visit and put on a show for us." He throws a stink eye at Wrath. "Then *someone* decided the wives should use the space for their *yoga* practice instead. And we're not even allowed to watch!"

Wrath smirks, clearly not giving a fuck about the accusation. "You're gettin' a whole new clubhouse to host your degenerate parties."

"The new clubhouse is gonna be off the chain!" Stash pats my back. "You have to come down to Crystal Ball with us. Dex and Z have done amazing things with the place. You won't recognize it."

What changes does a strip club need? Ah, fuck everything else has changed—why not Crystal Ball too? "I'm sure."

"It'll be easier for you to get some action away from the homestead." He throws another pissy scowl at Wrath, who still doesn't seem to care that his bikerness is being called into question by a brother.

Wrath casually shoves Stash into the wall and turns his serious stare on me. "We want this to feel more like a *home* now. A bunch of us built houses on the property. We've got kids here. It's less risky to have the wild parties they wanna throw somewhere else. Gives us a place to house out-of-town visitors, too."

I nod, agreeing with his logic. "Just how much property is there?"

"A lot."

Teller bumps up along my other side. "We hunt the property in the fall. My house is right down the hill but we broke a trail from my place to the back of the club's property. Got a few tree stands scattered around." He lifts his chin at Wrath. "We put in a food plot to fatten up the wildlife. Sasquatch over there nailed a beautiful eight-pointer last season."

Damn, I haven't been out in the woods in years. Pretty sure handling a rifle violates my parole. And I'm not doing one damn thing to jeopardize my freedom. Thankfully, hunting season's way off.

Wrath picks up an imaginary weapon, aims, and fires. "Never knew what hit him."

Sparky turns around. "You're so *mean*. Poor lil' buck was out there trying to live his best life and get some deer pussy." He points an accusatory finger at Wrath and Teller. "And you two come along and fuck up his game."

Teller cocks his head and runs his hand over his chin in the same dickish way he did as a teenager. "I don't recall you complaining when you were cooking up that big batch of venison chili."

Sparky rubs his stomach. "That was *so* good. We need to make that again."

"You could, I don't know," Wrath says slowly, infusing as much sarcasm as possible into his words, "get your ass out in the woods with us."

Sparky's eyes bug. "Me?" he sputters. "Nope."

"That's what I thought." Wrath shakes his head while Sparky skips away.

"He keeps you busy, huh?" I ask.

"Nah. He's down in the basement most of the time. It's good for him to be up here interacting with other humans for a change."

I squint at him. "I don't remember this...*paternal* side of you, Wrath."

"Aw, fuck." He wipes his hands on his chest and down his sides. "It's Rock's fault. Must be fucking contagious."

Teller snorts. "Paternal my ass. Wrath threatens to beat us to death with our own limbs at least once a day."

"Now *that* sounds familiar." I grin and pat Wrath's shoulder.

He bares his teeth at me in response.

When we reach the main room, Murphy pushes open a wide, wooden door. Inside, I recognize the old, scarred table and the chairs. Especially the president's chair.

I stare at the setup for a moment, allowing the ghosts of my past to settle around me.

Wrath directs me to his chair—which used to be mine—but I wave him off and take the seat next to him instead.

"Brave man," Dex says. "No one else has the balls to sit next to Wrath."

As an answer, Wrath holds up his arm, reaches past me and shoves his middle finger in Dex's face.

"What?" Dex shrugs. "It's a compliment. Sort of."

Once everyone settles down, Rock knocks his knuckles against the table. "First, we need to officially welcome Grinder back to the table." He turns to me and slaps the worn wood top. "Missed you here, brother."

I hold up my hands. Everyone needs to understand from the get-go that I don't expect special treatment. "As long as I stay outside, I'm happy."

A thundering chorus welcoming me home echoes through the room.

After a minute or so, Rock sits forward, silencing the brothers.

"What can we do to help?" Rock asks.

"Technically, I'm not even supposed to be here...I have to meet with my parole officer—"

"That's handled," Rock informs me.

"What?"

"Parole," Z interjects from the opposite end of the table. "We know someone. As long as you don't have major violations, you shouldn't have any issues."

"Well, aren't you a crafty son of a bitch."

Z grins even wider. "Damn right, brother. We've been itching to get this stuff in place for you."

"As far as a suitable place to live…" Rock slides a piece of paper my way. "We have an apartment for you in Johnsonville."

"It's conveniently located near your job," Wrath explains, handing over another piece of paper with directions to *Strike Back Studio*.

My mind's having trouble catching up to all this unexpected information. I frown, staring at the unfamiliar address in front of me. "What job?"

Z sits forward, drawing my attention again. "Parole says you gotta be employed within a certain timeframe."

"My friend owns this place." Wrath taps the paper. "Sully isn't affiliated with anyone and he's not connected to the club in an easily traceable way. He's flexible. Show up, see what he needs. He'll sign off on whatever parole requires. Provide you with a steady paycheck."

I narrow my eyes at him. "I ain't taking charity from some stranger."

"It's *not* charity," Wrath insists. "Money'll be coming from the club —just in a round-about way."

"You've more than earned it," Dex adds.

That's debatable. But I don't feel like arguing. "Don't suppose the job offers health insurance?" I'm aiming for a joking tone, but I fail. I flex my fingers and roll my shoulder. My whole body tightens at the painful sensation, but I keep my face as neutral as possible. "Need to see a doctor. Got jumped by a couple guys not that long ago. The physical therapy I got inside was less than useful." Prison medical wasn't exactly concerned with whether I'd be able to ride again.

"Whatever you need, we'll get it covered," Rock assures me.

Can't remember the last time I shed any tears. Didn't think I was still capable of it. But my eyes burn and my nose stings. I stare down at my hands in my lap for a few seconds to collect myself before speaking. "Thanks."

Rock must sense I'm overwhelmed. He nods at me, then turns the attention to him again with a quick clap of his hands. "All right. Figured you'd want a low-key evening with the family. That's why the rest of Downstate isn't here yet." He doesn't wait for me to answer. Doesn't need me to. He's right. What I want most is peace and quiet. Hell, I might find a sleeping bag and drag it out into the woods, just to reacquaint myself with the night sky.

"Tomorrow, the rest of Downstate will start arriving," Rock says, gesturing toward Z's end of the table. "So prepare yourself."

"That include Sway?" I ask Z. "Or is he sulking since you took over?" God damn, it makes me happy to know Z kicked that arrogant piece of shit out of the president's chair.

"Not sure yet," Z smirks.

A sharp bark of laughter bursts out of me. "Shocked that fucker's still alive. Figured Tawny woulda gutted him by now."

"No such luck," Rock says. "Couple of brothers from Virginia are planning to visit at some point too." Rock curls his hands around the edge of the table. "Priest made some noises about riding up here and paying us a visit."

I groan and rub my fingers over the tension gathering between my eyes. Our national president stopping by to thank me for my sacrifices isn't what I need right now.

"One other thing," Z says. "With Downstate comes a bunch of—"

"Porn stars!" Ravage yells and punches his fists in the air.

"Nice." I nod, although I don't really give a shit. What the fuck am I gonna talk about with girls less than half my age? Seems damn unappealing. "That's the club's new business venture?"

Rock and Z share a look. Makes sense. They're not gonna want me poking into all the club's details until they're sure my alliances are in the right place. Can't blame 'em.

"It's Downstate's main business," Z answers. "Rooster handles a lot of the technical stuff for it."

Technical. Shit. There's something I won't be able to help out with. From what I understand, technology has moved light years ahead since I went inside. What inmates had access to wasn't up-to-date. "Maybe he can teach me some new tricks."

"Definitely," Z says. "I can help with whatever you need too."

"Thanks, kid." Don't care how old he is, that he's wearing a president's patch, or that he has his own family now. Z will always be a kid to me.

They all are.

# CHAPTER THREE
## Grinder

This is what Rock and I talked about the club turning into so many years ago.

Family.

Not by blood.

By choice.

Bound by loyalty. Honor. Respect. Love. Brotherhood.

The ol' ladies are damn fine women too.

In one way or another, they remind me of Rose. Especially Z's girl, Lilly, with her long, dark hair and easy smile.

The clubhouse is full of noise. Brothers in a cheerful, upbeat mood.

Glad I could provide a reason to celebrate.

I choose a seat in the corner of the massive L-shaped couch taking up two walls in the back of the room. Here, I can watch the party without worrying about anyone sneaking up behind me.

Murphy drops down to my left, pulling Heidi into his lap. Wrath's big frame dominates the space on my right.

Earlier, Sparky unfolded something he called a 'Tibetan mattress' in the center of the room. Looks like a thick, square hippie blanket to me. He has several glass bongs arranged in front of him, and he's giving three barely dressed girls a class on different strains of pot, from what I can tell. Even though the guys assured me my parole officer wouldn't cause trouble, I'm not sure how much second-hand pot smoke I want to inhale.

"Do you need anything else?" Trinity asks, setting her hand on my forearm.

Can't help but admire her knack for being attentive without being annoying. "I'm good. Thanks, sweetheart."

She joins Wrath, who immediately wraps his arm around her. Rock and his wife move in next to Wrath. Can't make out their conversation—not that I'm trying to eavesdrop.

The unattached brothers around us loudly discuss which girls might visit the clubhouse this weekend.

I lean to my left and tap Murphy's shoulder. "I don't suppose there's a sleeping bag around I can borrow?"

He frowns. "It's like forty degrees and falling."

Fuck, I wish I'd gotten out earlier in the year. My urge to be outside as much as possible won't go away.

"We have an enclosed porch," Trinity offers as if she knew exactly what was going through my head. "It has a wood stove." She blushes. "We sleep out there sometimes. It's like sleeping under the stars—without all the mosquitoes and the threat of bears."

Rock leans forward and catches my eye. "We have a guest room. Grace mostly sleeps through the night these days," he says, wobbling his hand from side to side.

"You're welcome to it," Hope adds.

Wrath nudges me with his elbow. "We have a guest room, too, if you don't want to risk the Gracie alarm clock or the porch."

"Grinder's not a stuffed animal. No need to fight over him, kids," Z snarks from his perch farther down the couch.

"Why you still here, Rock?" I lift my chin. "Hoping to watch me get laid?"

He shakes his head. "No, thanks. I can do without."

"These parties already annoyed you when we went inside."

"They still do." He shrugs. "But it's your first night home."

*Home.* Maybe if everyone keeps saying it enough, it'll start to feel like it.

Hope wraps her arms around him and rests her cheek against his chest. Something about her seems too pure or innocent to be hanging around here, but she doesn't seem to notice anything but Rock. I like her. Loyal woman. Glad Rock finally found one.

A lifetime ago, I'd had one of my own. At least, I *thought* she'd be loyal. Hard to ask a good woman to sit through fifteen years of incarceration.

"Do you need anything, Grinder?" Hope asks.

*The last fifteen years of my life back.*

I cough into my elbow. "Water?"

"Sure." She lifts her gaze to Rock and he shakes his head. Trinity follows Hope over to the bar.

"Sweet girls," I say after they're gone.

As if old ladies vacating the area was a signal, a girl who doesn't look old enough to drive brushes up against my leg. Eh, I feel ancient around everyone in the room.

"Hi. Grinder, right?" she asks in a soft voice.

"Not now, darlin'," I answer without giving her another look.

She handles the rejection well. Saunters away and cozies up to someone else.

Rock raises an eyebrow at me.

"If you laugh, I'll fucking gut you," I warn him.

He holds up his hands.

Not that I need to explain myself to anyone, but I say, "I need to see Rose first."

"Brother." He shakes his head. "I understand."

"Do you?" I take in his rigid posture and the way his gaze keeps straying to the bar. "Yeah, you probably do."

Wrath laughs. "It's good to have you with us—where you belong.."

I don't feel like I belong here—or anywhere—but I appreciate the sentiment. Especially coming from Wrath.

"Feels good to be free." Now, I just need to figure out how to earn my place in a world I no longer recognize.

The girls return and Hope hands me a bottle of water.

"Thanks, sweetheart." I uncap the bottle and take a long sip. Even cool water that doesn't have a metallic tinge feels like a treat. I screw the cap back on and tuck the bottle next to my side. Not like anyone's gonna steal it from me but it's habit to guard my resources now.

"Trinity," I say. "I should've said so earlier, but that was the best damn dinner I've had in a very long time." That doesn't seem strong enough to convey what I feel, but it's the most I can come up with.

Her cheeks flush. "I'm so happy you liked it." She flicks an affectionate glance around the room. "I'd say I'll pack leftovers for you, except there are none. But anytime you want me to make it, just let me know."

Unlikely that I'll ask a brother's wife to cook for me, but it's a nice offer.

"We're supposed to make waffles tomorrow," Heidi says.

Trinity nods. "Dex and Swan picked up everything you'd ever want to stick on a waffle."

"Sounds more like dessert than breakfast," Wrath grumbles.

Trinity playfully presses her hand against his mouth. "Easy, Reverend Sugar-Free. Let Grinder enjoy his first days of freedom before you go preaching the gospel of the no-sugar lifestyle to him."

A sharp bark of laughter bursts out of me. "For real? You drank soda by the gallon when you were a kid."

Wrath shrugs. "Gettin' too old to put garbage in my body. Feel a million times better without all the sugar and—"

"Oh Christ," Murphy moans. "Here we go."

"Fuck off." Wrath scowls. "You said you felt better too."

"I do." Murphy pats his stomach. "I'm not as rigid as you, though." Murphy flashes a sly grin. "Then again, I'm not as old as you, either."

"And yet"—Wrath takes a dramatic pause—"I could run circles around you."

"Sure you can, Sasquatch."

Wrath growls a few things under his breath. Can't help but enjoy their good-natured ribbing.

"Uh-oh, Grinder," Hope says. "It sounds like Wrath's planning to pull you into his Furious Fitness cult."

As if my body understands the conversation, a sharp pain shoots from my shoulder to my bicep. I bite back a groan and adjust my position on the couch.

"Like you're not a card-carrying member." Wrath grins at her then turns to me. "We'll need to get you down there to visit."

Pain stabs through my shoulder again. I clutch it, rubbing my thumb into the spot where it throbs the most. "Looking forward to seeing what you've built."

He studies me for a few beats. "Let's find a doc for you first."

I'm not sure what to make of this mind reading, compassionate version of Wrath.

The conversation shifts to what I gather is Trinity's photography business. More brothers stop by to shoot the breeze or welcome me home. A few more girls rub up against my leg. Can't say I'm a fan of random strangers touching me, female or not.

While I appreciate the respect from my brothers, all the attention saps my energy and patience. The need to escape clamps down on my body. But where the fuck am I gonna go?

Wrath reaches over and taps my leg. "Trin and I are heading to our place. Wanna come with?"

*Thank fuck.* "That offer of the porch still open?" I need peace and distance from all the noise, smoke, and people.

"Yeah. Absolutely." He nudges Trinity off his lap and they both stand.

"Ready?" She flashes a bright smile that helps me feel less shitty about invading their home.

"Looking forward to the fresh air." I gesture toward the front door.

As if they'd been waiting for the signal to leave, Rock and Hope also stand.

"We have an extra bedroom. You don't have to sleep on the porch," Trinity says as we move through the crowd. "You know what? I'll set up both and you can come in and out as you please."

"Thanks, Trinny," Rock says.

"No problem." She leans in closer to me. "We're farthest away from the clubhouse so you won't hear much of this at our place."

"That's what I'm after. Some quiet."

She tugs on my arm. "You got it."

We lose Rock and Hope somewhere in the middle of the room. Thankfully, Wrath keeps right on moving. Trinity and I stick with him. I'll have to catch up with Rock tomorrow. I'm dying to sprint out the door.

A chill slithers over my skin outside, but I stop to stare at the sky anyway. Clouds conceal some of the stars. The outside floodlights around the clubhouse make it hard to see much. It's still beautiful.

*I'm free.*

"Stargazing is one of my favorite things to do up here," Trinity says in a hushed voice. "We cleared a lot of trees by our house. You'll have a nice view."

I swear, the way she says it makes me think she understands exactly how I feel.

Wrath takes her hand and I follow them into the woods. Tiny lights illuminate a wide trail through the trees.

"My dad always said the worst thing about being inside was not seeing the sky whenever he wanted," Trinity says softly.

Ah, that explains how she seems to know so much. "Got that right."

"Everyone…we're all happy you're free, Grinder."

"So am I, sweetheart." Like a wave hitting the shore, a memory bounces to the surface of my mind. "Trinity? You're Bishop Hurst's daughter?" She has to be the same girl. She'd be about the right age.

"Yup, that was my dad," she says softly.

Well, damn. Funny how she ended up with Wrath. I let out a sad laugh. "Bishop was an ornery bugger."

"Look who's talking," Wrath mutters.

"But he was a good man," I say to Trinity, ignoring Wrath. "Didn't deserve what happened to him."

"Thank you," Trinity whispers.

It's unnerving having Wrath be so quiet while Trinity and I keep talking. "You all right, big guy?"

"Yup." He slows his steps and pats my back. A fancy log cabin appears to our right.

"This it?" I ask.

"Nope, that's Rock and Hope's place." Wrath chuckles. "You know how anti-social I am. Needed to be far, far away from everyone else."

"Poor Murphy," Trinity laughs. "Wrath made him move his building site twice."

"Murphy's got a home here too?"

Wrath snakes his arm out in front of him. "This path loops around. Z's in the middle of construction right now."

"Teller has his ranch down the hill," Trinity says. "Rooster bought a place between here and Downstate. Bricks is still at Rock's old house."

"Everyone else pretty much lives at the clubhouse." Wrath jerks his thumb over his shoulder.

We turn off the wide path to a narrower one, still lit by bright lights low to the ground. "This Ramsey Lane?" I ask.

"This is it."

"Jesus," I breathe out.

"Big guy needs a big home." Wrath grins as he lopes up to the front door.

"Can't argue with that logic."

Inside is a wide-open floorplan—nothing to make a man feel caged in.

I'm too tired to take in much more. Wrath jogs up the stairs while Trinity shows me to the spare bedroom, the bathroom, and where to find a few things in the kitchen. Wrath returns as we're heading toward the enclosed porch.

*Porch* doesn't quite describe it. It's more like another living room, with walls of glass. Trinity touches a control panel on the wall and there's a gentle whirring sound. I peer up at eight wide skylights with shades retracting. The night sky is visible beyond the glass. "Heat's here, too, if you want to turn it up or down."

"Doubt I'll need to mess with it."

"We eat breakfast out here a lot," Trinity says, nodding to the table for two. There's a couch and a couple of chairs, although I can't picture Wrath ever sitting still long enough to enjoy them.

"Here, brother." Wrath holds out a stack of clothing. "This should hold you until we can get a little shopping done."

Shit, how'd I forget I don't have any clothes other than the ones on my back? "Thanks."

Together, they set up a cot big enough for two. Certainly nicer than the thin, rock-hard piece of junk New York State Corrections considered a mattress. Trinity stacks a pile of soft, downy blankets on the foot of the bed. A crisp, clean scent unfurls from the bedding. Freedom smells so good everywhere I turn.

I glance at the kitchen. "You sure I won't be in your way?"

"Not at all." Wrath slips his arm around Trinity's shoulders. "I'm beat. We're headed upstairs."

"We'll try not to wake you in the morning," Trinity says.

"I'm sure I'll be up with the sun. They keep you on a tight schedule inside."

After they leave, I pad down the hallway to the bathroom, feeling like an intruder the whole way.

For a guest bathroom, it's fancy. A large, stone walk-in shower with water shooting from several directions. No one barks the time or yells at me to hurry up. I spend so long enjoying the steady stream of warm water, I almost fall asleep under the spray.

Trinity's left out a toothbrush and every sort of toiletry I might possibly need, along with several fluffy towels on the counter.

Once I'm finally nestled under the covers out on the porch, I finally peer up at the sky. Darkness surrounds the house, providing me with a clear view through the panels of glass. Dark blue velvet sky. Soft white moonlight peeking out from the clouds. Twinkling spots of light.

*So many stars.*

I've longed for this exact moment for years. Some days, I never thought it would come. Thought I'd die behind those cinder block walls and never know freedom again.

I stroke the empty space next to me. Where Rose would've been. Loneliness settles over me like a scratchy blanket.

As soon as I get myself sorted, I need to see her. If she's truly moved on, let her say it to my face. I deserve that much.

Tucking one hand behind my head, I stare up at the sky until my eyelids start to droop.

The rest of my life might be in shambles, but at least I finally have peace.

## CHAPTER FOUR
### Grinder

"Teeooo, teeeooo, whoit whoit whoit."

Songbirds. Rich, flutelike little voices carrying through the crisp, morning air.

Followed by silence.

Pure, unadulterated *silence*.

No screaming, yelling, rattling of keys, or clinking of metal. No dragging of chains against the concrete floors. No guards shouting.

I blink open my eyes and stare at the unfamiliar ceiling.

Inhale the crisp air.

Best sleep I've had in years.

I groan as I roll over and push the pile of warm blankets aside. Forgot how nice minor comforts could be. Scrubbing my hands over my face, I stare out the window at the sunlight bursting through the trees. I sit up and walk over to the glass, admiring the view that wasn't visible last night. Forest. Green pine trees and naked branches. A few elaborate birdhouses on tall poles right outside the window. Bright red cardinals flitting in and out.

"So you're the soundtrack that woke me." My mouth curves up. Best morning music I've had in a long time.

Inside, I find a neatly handwritten note in purple ink.

*G-*

*We're at the clubhouse. End of our walkway and take a left. The path will bring you straight there. You'll pass Rock's house on the left on your way.*

*Trinity*

I swallow hard, appreciating the opportunity to have a few moments to myself before everyone's in my face again. A lot of faith they have to allow an ex-con to wander around alone in their fancy house.

Now that I'm not tired and overwhelmed, I stare at the finely crafted timber and log home. Vaulted ceilings and lots of light. I run my fingers over the cool granite counter. Take in the high-end appliances.

Who knew the big brawler Rock carried to the clubhouse one afternoon would end up with such refined taste? Wrath was so hostile and angry, but underneath, I always knew he was a good kid. I spent a lot of time worrying he'd end up dead or in prison.

But he turned out okay.

Still smiling, I scoop up the clothes Wrath left for me last night and head to the bathroom to change.

When I'm ready, I follow the brief directions and find my way to the clubhouse.

Feeling like a burglar, I approach the front door. One hand's on the knob and one's poised to knock.

Gravel crunches behind me. "Morning, Grinder."

I turn and find Dex walking out of one of the garages. He crosses the parking lot quickly and bounds up the steps, slapping my back in greeting. "How was your first night home?"

"Best damn sleep I've had in years."

Something close to pity shines in his eyes, souring my good mood.

An irritated grunt leaves my throat, wiping the look off Dex's face. He reaches past me and opens the front door. "They're probably all in the dining room."

He follows me inside. I stop, trying to orient myself in the large space. Dex jogs upstairs without offering directions and for that I'm thankful. I may have been overwhelmed yesterday, but I'm not some senile old man.

Soft, twangy notes drift down the hallway. A guitar. Too pure to be coming from the radio.

Curious, I follow the music, pushing through the wide double doors into the dining room.

A woman with long blond curls is sitting in a chair with an acoustic guitar in her lap, strumming and singing.

I'm too stunned to move or breathe. What an angelic voice.

Is this the kind of girl the club attracts now, or is she someone's ol' lady? I can't remember everyone I met last night. And as much as I have no interest in getting to know any woman yet, this one would've been hard to forget.

My gaze drops to the little kids scattered on the floor at the singer's feet. Even tiny Grace seems enchanted by the music, her big eyes keenly fixed on the singer. The woman's not singing them some Old MacDonald bullshit, either. It's something more grown-up and complicated about being saved from drowning.

Trinity spots me and waves. "Morning, Grinder."

I make my way over to where she's seated with Heidi, Hope, Lilly, and Charlotte. At least, I think I remembered all their names.

When the girl finishes her song, the kids clap and jump around, begging for more.

"Give Aunt Shelby a break." Heidi reaches for Alexa, pulling her into her lap.

"Come here, Chance. Say good morning to Uncle Grinder." Lilly gestures to me.

Chance—such a cute little shit—races over to me. "Morning!"

"Hey, little guy." Shit, he already reminds me an awful lot of Z.

"Morning" Alexa chirps from her mother's lap.

The blonde approaches me slowly.

"Hello," she says in a soft Texan drawl.

I nod to the guitar in her hands. "You're fantastic. You should be a singer."

She blushes and ducks her head. "Thank you. That's very sweet."

The girls give each other nervous looks, like they know something I don't know and are afraid of offending me.

Heidi squeezes Shelby's hand. "Shelby's a country singer. She just finished touring—"

"Pssh." Shelby waves off Heidi's explanation.

I'm getting the feeling Heidi's trying to hint that Shelby's someone I should've heard of. "Sorry, I'm not exactly up on—"

"Rooster's my old man," Shelby says, smoothing over the awkward moment with pure class. "We arrived real late last night. I'm sorry we missed ya."

"That's all right, sweetheart. I wasn't up for a lot of socializing."

"Can't blame ya." She flashes a warm, serene smile and gestures toward the hallway I just came from. "Rooster's real keen to see ya. I reckon they're down in the war room?" She raises an eyebrow and turns toward the other girls.

"Or in the garage," Trinity says.

"Actually, I wanted to find Z first."

Lilly stands and threads her arm through mine. "I think he's in the office. I'll walk down with you."

Chance skips around us the whole way, and I can't help smiling at his antics. The gesture feels foreign on my face.

"He must keep you on your toes," I say to Lilly.

"Oh, you have no idea." She laughs and reaches out to knock on one of the doors in the living room.

It opens and Murphy's ginger beard comes into view. He grins, wide and easy. "Morning. How'd you sleep?"

"Good."

"Hey." Z pushes Murphy aside and squeezes my shoulder.

"I'll leave you guys to it." Lilly pats my arm and takes Chance's hand.

"Hang on, siren." Z steps past me to talk to Lilly and his son.

Murphy shakes his head. "What's up?" He opens the door wider and motions for me to come in.

Z returns to us. "We'll be having breakfast after church," he says to me.

Last night had more to do with welcoming me home than anything else. Not sure the club will want me to sit down with them for anything too official yet, but I nod anyway.

"I need to talk to you," I say to Z.

"Heidi still down in the dining room?" Murphy asks.

"She was a minute ago."

"Cool." He slaps my back. "I'll see you in a few, Grinder."

"Didn't mean to kick him out," I say to Z after the door closes.

"Don't sweat it. I do it all the time." He plops down at the desk Murphy had been leaning against. "This is my old desk." He grins the same devilish smile that used to get him attention from all the ladies back in the day. "What's on your mind?"

"You still able to find addresses and track people down?"

He turns toward a slim black machine on the desktop. "Hell yeah. Who you need to find?"

"Rosie."

The cheerful expression slides off his face.

"I don't want to hear it, Angus."

He holds his hands in the air. "I didn't say anything, brother."

"I need to see her…to talk to her."

"Is that why you scared all the eager bunnies away last night?" His tone's almost accusatory, and I don't care for it one fucking bit.

"Fuck off," I growl.

"Grinder—"

"Can you get me her address or not?"

"Yeah, yeah. I'll get you the address. Just tell me why you want to see her?"

Ah, I get it. He's worried. "I ain't gonna hurt Rosie," I assure him.

"She did ya pretty fuckin' dirty. Talking you into that plea deal, then never coming to visit."

"Thanks for the recap." Fucking hell. Is all my business common knowledge? "It's not your concern," I snap.

"What's going on?" The door swings open, almost bumping me, and I jump out of the way.

"Easy." Rock holds his hand up. "Sorry, Grinder." His gaze swings from Z to me and back. "What's going on?" he asks again.

"I asked him to get Rosie's address, and the fucker's throwing me attitude." I shoot a glare at Z who's busy fiddling with the laptop now. I'm probably gettin' more pissed off than I should, but I can't help it. Rosie's off-limits to everyone. Even my brothers. "Don't give a fuck what patch you're wearing now, Prez. Stay outta my personal business."

"All right. Simmer down." Rock uses one of those *whoa* hand gestures like you might try to calm a wild stallion with, and it's having the opposite effect on me. "Z will get you the address."

"Here." Z bumps my hand. "This should be it."

I glance down and take the piece of folded-over paper he's offering me.

"Thank you." I snatch it away from him. I should apologize. By all rights, Z should kick my ass for showing him so much disrespect.

"You want one of us to go with you?" Rock offers.

"No." Even though it hurts like hell to say the words out loud, I explain, "I need to talk to my wife."

Both of them drop their gazes to the floor.

I get it.

Rosie divorced me years ago.

Doesn't mean I'm not gonna try.

"We good now?" Rock asks after several uncomfortable seconds tick by.

"Yeah, Prez. I'm good." That came out more sarcastically than I meant it to, but I don't follow up with anything else.

"Good. Let's all sit down at the table." He gestures toward the war room.

I lumber past him. "Gee, Prez, how often you call everyone for church around here?"

"As often as I feel like it." His tone has a bit of bite this time. A warning to watch myself. He's gotta make it clear he won't tolerate disrespect from anyone. Not even me.

I shouldn't be letting the thought of seeing Rosie rattle me this much. There were days inside where I fought like an animal to stay alive. I'm no fuckin' pansy. Gettin' twisted up over a woman—*any* woman—isn't worth disrespecting the brotherhood.

Inside the war room, it's more crowded than yesterday. *Great.*

Steer grabs me first, shaking my hand. "Good to see ya, brother," he says.

A lump forms in my throat. "How you been? Thank you for all the letters you sent. They always gave me something to look forward to."

"Glad you're back. Can't wait for you to visit Downstate and see what we've built."

"Give him time to settle in," Wrath says.

I force a smile. "There's plenty of me to go around, boys."

Rooster approaches next. One corner of his mouth hitches up. "Grinder, we finally meet on this side."

I pull him in for a quick hug and he slaps my back a few times. Whether he realizes it or not, the few visits he made to me meant something. Plus, there's no baggage of pre-prison history between us. I step back, keeping my hands on his shoulders for a second. "Met your girl earlier. Got a beautiful voice."

He ducks his head but smiles even wider. "Yeah, I'm real proud of her."

"Shelby's the bomb," Hustler says, muscling into our conversation. "Rooster don't wanna brag, but we spent the summer on tour with her. She's a big deal—the next Taylor Swift."

I stare at him.

Rooster chuckles. "She'd like to be the next Dolly Parton, for sure."

Now *that* name I know.

Jigsaw joins us and shakes my hand. "Congratulations, brother."

"All right." Z's voice rises above the noise in the room. "Find a seat."

While he said it casually, it seems most of the guys have a usual spot. Wrath pats the seat next to him and again, I take it. At least today I'm slightly more comfortable with my back to the door.

Baby steps.

AFTER CHURCH, ROCK ASKS ME TO STAY. NOT REALLY SURE WHERE HE thinks I'd be running off to, or how I'd get there since I don't have a vehicle.

Z, Wrath, Murphy, Teller, and Dex also remain, except Z joins us at our end of the table.

"Didn't want to do this in front of everyone else," Murphy says. "But Heidi asked around and got you the name of a physical therapist. They can see you tomorrow. Just need to bring whatever medical records you've got."

I stare at him, then Rock.

"You'll have to go as self-pay since you're not on anyone's insurance yet." Rock reaches for a cabinet on his right and slides a drawer open, pulling out a thick envelope that I assume is full of cash.

"I'm not taking charity, Rock." I cross my arms over my chest and fight off the burning humiliation. "You know me better than that."

No one at the table moves or even breathes.

Rock sits back and glares at me.

"It's *not* charity," Teller says. "It's club earnings you're entitled to."

"We all know I've barely been a member for years," I argue. "Inside...it's a whole different world."

"A brother inside is still a brother," Rock says. "You taught me that."

"We take care of our own, Grinder," Z adds.

I turn toward Z. "And the club took care of me. Always kept dollars in my account. Appreciate that. Made things easier for me more than you'll ever know. But I'm a free man and need to earn my way."

"Bro, you've been out for a *day*," Wrath says.

"You think I can't tell time, son?" I snap.

He clenches his jaw. "We want to help make the transition easier on you. That's all."

Why is this so hard to accept? The whole point of the club and the brotherhood was to take care of each other during hard times. But I guess I never saw myself on the receiving end of that help. "I need to work."

"You will." Rock laughs. "Trust me. We've got plenty for you to do."

"Good. That's all I ask."

"But you'll take this money now and get yourself sorted." Rock's expression turns cold and steely. That's new to me. I'm sure it serves him well as president. "This isn't a request."

I swallow. Never figured it'd be so hard to tolerate Rock as my president, giving me orders. "Listen—"

He sits up and slaps the table. "If our roles were reversed, what would you do? Tell me."

*This little fucker.*

"That's what I thought." He smirks and leans back. "You'd make sure I was taken care of whether I liked it or not. Stop making this harder."

"Thank you." I reach for the envelope and stuff it in my pocket. "Gotta be careful how I spend it or I'll draw attention."

"For now, just worry about the medical bills," Dex suggests.

"I can set up some accounts for you," Teller offers.

One corner of my mouth turns up. "You always were a genius with money."

Teller shrugs and slides his gaze toward Rock. "I do okay."

Rock flashes a tight smile in return. "You do more than okay, knucklehead."

Wrath exhales a long, noisy, annoyed breath. "We done with the circle jerk?"

"It's okay, buddy. You're good at stuff too." Z scratches the side of his head. "Give me a second and I'll think of something."

Murphy busts up laughing and reaches over to tap his knuckles against Z's.

"Careful, Ginger Yeti," Wrath rumbles. "I haven't decided how I want to torture you at Furious yet today."

Murphy crosses his arms over his chest and flashes his best do-your-worst smirk. "I ain't scared of you."

I cough-laugh into my fist. *That* wasn't the case when I went inside.

Rock raps his knuckles against the table. "We're not done yet."

Wrath turns toward me, all serious now. "Brother, you can stay at our place as long as you like."

Murphy raises his hand. "Our place is always open to you, too, if you get tired of watching Wrath run around in his underwear."

"Joke's on you." Wrath smirks. "I don't wear underwear around the house."

Z cringes. "For fuck's sake. Why'd you have to plant *that* image in my head?"

Rock casts a glance around the table. "Can we stay on track, please?"

"You've got your 'official' address for parole but we want you to have a place of your own here." Wrath points to the ceiling.

"Well, shit." I glance at the door. "I still haven't even seen the upstairs yet."

"You'll be next door to me," Dex says.

"So you'll have plenty of peace and quiet," Z quips.

Dex shoots a glare at Z. "You say that like standards are a bad thing."

"That's because he didn't know what they were until he met Lilly," Teller adds with a devilish grin.

Z giggles like a kid. "Ain't even gonna bother denying it."

"Oh, brother," I mutter.

"They can keep it up all day." Rock knocks his knuckles against the table and stands. "Before we go, I need to give you something."

Longing unfurls in my chest as Rock reaches into a closet and pulls out a handful of black leather that can only be one thing. It's stiff and new. Not the cut I wore before my incarceration. Rock knows me well. I don't want to reclaim that old life. I want to start a new one, fresh from the bitter memories of the past.

Our skull in the center patch is slightly different than I remember. More detailed, the blues and grays of our colors more vibrant.

"We'll get you the rest of your patches," Z says softly. "And your bottom rocker."

"But we wanted you to have that now," Rock adds. "I know you can't wear it outside of the clubhouse for now—"

"Doesn't matter." I clutch the leather in my hands. "Thank you."

Wrath rests his hand on my shoulder. "Let's go."

"Is everyone trailing along?" I ask, turning to stare at each brother.

"Sure." Teller taps my arm. "Why not? Family field trip."

"Upstairs?" Murphy raises an eyebrow.

"It's *my* old room," Wrath says.

"Trinity and Lilly fixed it up," Z adds.

"Go on." Rock pats my back. "I need to check in with Sparky."

"I'll be out in the garage." Murphy nudges my arm. "Come see me when you're done?"

"Sure."

Teller and Dex end up following him. Thank fuck. I don't need everyone watching me like I'm a kid at camp getting his bunk assignment.

Wrath leads the way up the stairs. The landing's wide enough to accommodate an old motorcycle. "That Lucky's?" I ask.

"Yeah." Z rests his hand on the seat. "Seemed like the right place for it."

I glance around at the high ceilings and sturdy wood beams. "He would've liked this place a lot."

They both nod and I suffer a pang of guilt. They've had lots of time to move on from the past while I've been sitting in limbo, nursing my pain for years.

Photographs line the wall up the stairs. Each one another phantom punch to the gut. Lucky and me outside Crystal Ball. Brothers at their patch-in parties. The old clubhouse. Birthdays. Biker rallies. Parties. They seem to be in chronological order. Lost Kings MC history, frozen in time. Closer to the top of the stairs are wedding photos. Hope's in a green dress and Rock's in a suit, posed against an autumn backdrop. I stop and tap one of the photos.

"You two get married up at Fletcher Park?" I ask Wrath.

His mouth curves into a smile, like it's one of his favorite memories. "Sure did."

I scowl at another photo. "Where the hell did Heidi and Murphy get married? That's one hell of an ugly chapel. And why does he look like a shaved ape?"

Z chuckles. "After all the crap they went through, neither of them gave a shit about the trivial stuff."

"Where's yours?" I ask Z.

"He skunked us and eloped," Wrath says.

Z taps another photo of what has to be more than several charters crowded in together in front of a bar with Z and Lilly at the center. "Here's the wedding party they sprung on us." He taps the frame again. "That's the downstate clubhouse."

I study the picture again, seeking familiar faces. "Jesus Christ, is that Priest?"

"On his official ball-busting tour," Z confirms.

"Fuck me, Valentina hasn't aged a day," I mutter. "Good to see they're still together."

My gaze moves to the next one. Rooster, Shelby, Jigsaw, Wrath, Steer, and a bunch of brothers I don't recognize in front of what looks like another log cabin in the mountains. "Virginia," Wrath explains.

I squint closer. "That Ice?"

"He's the prez down there now," Wrath says.

"Well, fuck me." I sweep my gaze over the wall again. A profound sense of loss settles over me. "Lot of things I've missed. History to catch up on."

Z gently clasps my shoulder. "You've got all the time in the world now, brother."

⚜

MURPHY MIGHT BE VP NOW BUT FROM WHAT I'VE GATHERED, HE STILL spends a lot of time on road captain duties. After my tour upstairs, I meet him and Dex in the garage farthest from the clubhouse—apparently the property has *three* heated garages where cars and bikes are worked on. I can't get over all the details they've added to make this little slice of paradise a blend of MC and family space.

"Sorry it's still so shitty out, brother," Dex says, as if I hold him personally responsible for the weather.

"We set up two rides for you." Murphy places his hands on the handlebars of the Harley Softail standard. Painted shades of dark blue and silver, it looks awfully similar to the one I had before I went inside, but newer.

"Nice." I run my hand over the seat; a tug in my shoulder makes my jaw clench. Shitty weather or not, I don't think I could handle this machine right now. Good thing I was released in the winter, giving me an acceptable excuse not to ride.

"Whose is it?" I ask.

"Yours." He holds up his hands before I have a chance to protest. "Take it up with Rock, old man. I just do what I'm told."

"Bullshit," I grumble.

Ignoring my crankiness, Murphy walks over to a shiny black Ford F-150 with silver stripes down the sides and slaps the hood. "This is all set up for you to use while the weather's bad."

"Whose is it?"

"Mine. But I'm loaning it to you."

I cock my head. "I ain't taking charity, son."

Murphy rolls his eyes. "It's not charity, old man."

I stare at him, and he finally throws his hands up. "It's my *old* truck. I didn't feel like selling it when I upgraded, but now it's sitting here collecting dust. You'll be doing me a favor by running it."

*Doing him a favor.* What a load of bullshit. But I appreciate him understanding my need not to feel like a parasite. "High roller, huh? Hanging onto *two* trucks?"

"Fucking hoarder is what he is," Dex jokes. "He's got Heidi's old SUV parked down at her brother's."

"She's actually running that in the winter." Murphy grins. "Got the Hellcat stored down at Teller's now."

I glance at the truck again. "You sure I'm not putting anyone out by using this?"

He raises his right hand. "Swear."

"I'll pay you when I start—"

"Fuck that," he growls. "I don't want anything for it, Grinder."

I work my jaw from side to side, and Murphy holds up his hands again. "Fine. When you're ready, we'll work out something."

"Thank you."

Now that we've come to a vehicle arrangement, I haul myself inside the truck, settling into the soft leather seat. Murphy hops in on the other side.

"This is more like a luxury car than a truck," I say, running my hands over the leather-wrapped steering wheel.

"It's still a workhorse." Murphy grins. "But I like my creature comforts." He presses his finger to the screen in the center of the dashboard.

"What the fuck is this? A damn spaceship?" Where'd all the knobs and buttons go?

He gives me a thin smile and doesn't even crack any *old man* jokes, which somehow makes me feel worse. Fifteen years locked away from the world is a lot of time. Technology—well, everything—kept on going without my knowledge or consent. The realization of how much I've missed springs up and slaps me at the most unexpected times.

"GPS." He taps a neon blue square on the screen. "Input any address you need and this will direct you there."

"Shit." What addresses do I even remember? I tap one in and Murphy chuckles. "Crystal Ball's still where I left it, right?"

"Yeah, it's still there."

It's the last place I feel like visiting, but there's no reason for Murphy to get up in my business more than he already has. I close out the screen. "We'll see where the day takes me."

"Sounds good, brother." He opens his door, then stops himself. "Here, let me sync your phone to the Bluetooth before you get on the road."

He might as well. I haven't gotten used to the flat little rectangle Z swore up and down was actually a phone. I'd been expecting some little silver flip thing. Rock assured me the club still had plenty of those around to use as burners but for my personal line, they'd upgraded me to a "smart" phone. Whatever the fuck that means.

Murphy finishes fucking around and suddenly the cab of the truck echoes with a loud ringing.

I duck and cover my head like a bomb's about to drop. "What the motherfuck?"

Murphy wags his phone at me and points to the screen. "Answer it."

My gaze drops to the green "accept call" button on the screen and I punch it—harder than necessary. "What?"

"That's all you need to do, brother." Murphy's voice bursts through the truck's speakers. He disconnects the call and points to the steering wheel. "You can answer from that button there too."

"I don't want to talk to anyone while I'm driving."

"That's probably best." He holds up his hands. "You need anything, call me. My number's programmed into your phone." He nods to the screen. "The addresses for Furious Fitness and Strike Back Studio are both in there if you want to visit either one." He smirks at me. "And you seem to remember where Crystal Ball is."

I flip him off.

"Rock's old address is in there too. He runs his custom shop out of the garage. I think he'll be there later if you want to stop by and spread some of your cheer."

*Little prick.*

He taps his chin a few times. "I put the address for Downstate's clubhouse in, too, but I doubt you'll feel like driving all the way there."

"That safe?" I point to the screen. "Having all those addresses in that thing?"

"Probably not. When you're situated, we can erase everything." He nods to the screen again. "This place is under 'yoga retreat' so you'll be able to find your way back."

"Yoga retreat…Cute." I gesture toward the open door. "We done here? Or are you planning to come with me and play babysitter?"

"No, sir." He jumps out of the cab and salutes me. "Drive safe."

Now I feel shitty for snapping at him. I grip the steering wheel, biting back my pride. "Thank you, Murphy. Appreciate it."

"No problem, Grinder. Just glad you're back and whole."

*Whole.*

I may have made it out of prison with my life. Maybe on the outside I appear to be in one piece. But whole?

Not even close.

## CHAPTER FIVE

### Serena

*Never try to run from your past. It will always catch up to you.*

Gee, thanks. Great advice.

I quit scrolling through Instagram motivational quotes and tuck my phone in my pocket. Lunchtime. I push my chair away from my desk, stand, and stretch.

I'm starving. The cheap, hole-in-the-wall restaurant next to Empire Med is supposed to have Swedish meatballs on the menu today. I'm dying for a huge plate of buttery egg noodles smothered in tiny meatballs and savory cream sauce. I can almost smell the garlic and taste the sweet lingonberry jam they serve on the side.

My phone buzzes in my pocket and I pull it out. *Amanda.*

Sighing, I answer. "What's up? I'm at work."

"Shouldn't you be at lunch?"

"I was heading there now." Against my better judgment, I sink into my chair again.

"There's a party up at the Lost Kings compound this weekend. We *have* to go."

*No way in hell.* "Pass."

"Come on," she whines. "You haven't gone to a club party with me in for-evvvvv-er."

"Yes. For good reason." I never want to see another biker again as long as I live.

Unfortunately, quite a few come into the clinic, recovering from various injuries. I cringe every single time, praying I won't run into someone affiliated with the Lost Kings. Someone who will recognize me. Remember who I used to be.

That desperate party girl is dead and buried. No resurrection happening. I've worked too hard to distance myself from my club girl days and I'll be damned if I'm dragged back to a clubhouse now when my life is finally on track.

"Please," Amanda begs.

"No." I'm proud of my firm voice. Old Serena would've caved by now.

"Come on. Shadow won't be there." She lowers her voice. "Lala told me no one's seen him since he tried to stab Z."

*Shit.* Z. One of the few people who ever stood up for me. I never properly thanked him for rescuing me from Shadow.

"Things are totally different with Z running the downstate club. Sway and Tawny are almost never around," Amanda says in her staccato, let-me-convince-you voice. "But it doesn't matter. This party's upstate. You always liked it there better anyway."

Where I made an ass out of myself over and over, chasing after Murphy. *No thanks.*

"Come on," she pleads. "Jigsaw asks me how you're doing all the time."

My lips curve. Once I got past the scary exterior, Jiggy had been like a playful older brother. He and his best friend, Rooster, were always nice to me.

"All the time, huh?" I laugh. "How often do you talk to him?"

"Not that often, but the last time I was there, he did ask about you."

That's nice and all, but I've made too much progress to backslide now. "Well, tell him I said hi."

"Seriously?" she whines. "You're really going to make me go alone?"

"Go with Lala."

"She's out of town."

*Great, I wasn't even her first choice of party partner.*

"I really have to go, Amanda. I'll call you later." I end the call before she tries any more convincing arguments on me.

This time, I shut off my phone before shoving it in my pocket. I grab my wool coat, peering closely at the sleeve, and sigh. Is that a threadbare patch on the elbow? Damn, that doesn't look very professional. Too bad it was the best the local thrift shop had to offer. Once a few more paychecks are deposited in my account, maybe I'll be able to afford something without holes.

*Swedish meatballs, here I come.*

I open my office door and almost run smack into my boss.

"Oh! Serena, I was just looking for you." Slightly flustered, Trish steps back and pats her cloud of dark, springy curls.

My stomach clenches. I recognize that determined look on her face. Dreams of meatballs and noodles fly away as my resolve crumbles. I'm too new at my job to say no to whatever she's about to ask.

"I have a new patient for you," Trish says.

Disappointed about my thwarted lunch plan, I accept the file she holds out to me and paste on an eager, team-spirit smile. "Sure."

"Older male. Shoulder injury. Had some treatment…well, you'll see."

*Patient reports pain, stiffness, and loss of motion in right shoulder.* I scan the SOAP notes but with Trish watching me so closely, I'm too nervous for the information to sink in. "Is he here now?"

"Unfortunately, yes. He was referred by Doctor Michaels, and I hate to say no to him." Her eyes take on a dreamy quality at the mention of her doctor crush.

I study the file again, this time concentrating on the words in front of me. "Uh, there seem to be a lot of details missing. Who treated him last?" There should be a lot more information about his progress throughout the course of whatever treatment he's received.

Her face puckers like she's trying to locate the source of a fart. "He got treatment in *prison*," she whispers.

"Oh." I've encountered plenty of monsters who've never seen the inside of a cell, so an ex-con doesn't scare me. If anything, I'm more eager to assist. While he might not have had the best care before, maybe I'll be able to help him heal and return to a productive life.

"You'll take him?"

"Sure."

"You're a saint," she praises before spinning on her heel and marching away.

Feeling more positive about the situation, I duck inside my office and hang up my holey coat and peek at myself in the mirror on the back of my door to tame any frizzy hairs.

Armed with my clipboard, file, and polished ponytail, I walk down the hallway.

I stop dead as my gaze lands on the silver fox in the waiting area.

*So not what I expected.*

Thick, black hair streaked with silver. Neat and tidy gray beard. Tight, rigid posture. Intelligent eyes, constantly scanning the room. His gaze strays to the door, like he's about to bolt.

I clear my throat. "Grayson Lock?"

His gaze swings my way, and I'm nailed to the floor when our eyes meet. Haunted. Hard.

I step back, clutching my clipboard to my chest as if it will protect me.

He unfolds himself from the faux-leather chair.

He's so tall, easily over six feet. Lean but muscled. There's an obvious stiffness on his right side, but otherwise, his movements seem fluid, if not cautious.

"I'm Serena Cargill. I'll be treating you today."

I'm met with stony silence.

*Huh.* I'm sure he expected someone older. Or a male physical therapist. Too bad. I harden my voice and wipe the smile off my face. "Leave your coat here and follow me."

He eyes our coatrack warily.

"Or bring it with you if you prefer," I suggest.

Finally, he slips the coat on a hanger and leaves it. My heart throws itself against my ribs as he steps close, towering over me. I've always had a weakness for tall men.

He raises an eyebrow, silently pointing out that I'm standing there staring at him like a hormonal schoolgirl.

"Right this way." I duck my head and march through the clinic, leading him to a private area. The quick walk helps me regain my composure.

"Let's see what we're dealing with." I set my clipboard on a desk and ask him to sit on a stool in front of me.

He remains quiet as I prod at his muscles. Grits his teeth when I manipulate his arm.

I try not to stare at his swollen biceps covered in faded tattoos. He obviously doesn't sit in front of the television pounding beers every night.

*He just got out of prison. He probably worked out to stay alive.*

My gaze snags on the faded skull and crown tattoo on his forearm. A skull wearing a crown is a pretty common design. It's the words underneath that make my blood run cold.

*Lost Kings MC.*

Your past always catches up to you.

## Grinder

I don't like doctors.

I prefer the company of people who don't judge and aren't stuck up.

I like honesty.

Physical therapy isn't quite the same as a doctor's office visit. No one grabs my balls and asks me to cough. Or looks at my ink and gives me a suspicious eyebrow raise when I answer "no" to their "do you smoke, abuse alcohol or drugs" questions.

The moment Serena touches me, my reservations about the appointment recede.

Such soft hands. Probing, strong fingers, though. I bite the inside of my cheek so I don't scream when she hits a certain spot.

For a brief moment, her body freezes. Her gaze locks on the Lost Kings tattoo on my arm. Is it fear in her eyes? Or the scorn I expected all along?

Whatever it is, it disappears.

She slips into clinical mode.

The longer she studies me, the more my muscles bunch in annoyance. Why'd I bother? Physical therapy didn't do me any good in prison. What made me think it could help now?

Besides, this...this *girl* is supposed to be my therapist?

She looks like she belongs in a bikini on a Florida beach, not in shapeless pants and a preppy polo shirt with a clipboard in her hands. Is she even old enough to *be* a physical therapist? Or was I assigned someone's teenaged assistant, or intern, or whatever they call 'em nowadays?

"Mr. Lock, why don't you tell me what your goals are for physical therapy?"

*God, her voice.* Relaxing and calm. Every word that passes her lips is like a balm soothing my jagged nerves.

"What are you hoping to achieve from our sessions?" she adds when I don't respond.

I flex my fingers, pretending to twist a throttle. "I'd like to be ready to ride my motorcycle by spring."

A slight wrinkle forms between her eyes. Yeah, yeah, she probably wants to lecture me about how unsafe it is to ride. Injuries. Risk of death. *Blah, blah, blah.*

"As your therapist, I'm obligated to mention how dangerous riding can be."

*There it is.*

I open my mouth to tell her she can shove the lecture up her pretty little ass.

"But riding's a great way to feel alive," she continues, closing her eyes as if she's savoring the wind in her face. "A little motorcycle therapy always clears the mind."

Damn, she nailed the reason I love it so much. I haven't known a lot of women riders. Somehow, I can't picture her commanding a big machine. "You ride?"

"Me?" Her eyebrows crawl halfway up her forehead. "Only on the back. But not in a long time."

I can definitely picture her on the back of *my* bike.

Now my dick has something he'd like to add to our list of goals.

"Why spring?" she asks.

Club rules—you have to ride a minimum number of hours every year. Exceptions exist, of course. Rock would give me a pass, no doubt. He'd consider this injury related to "club business" since it happened while I was serving time for the club.

Am I going to explain that to the pretty stranger? Hell no. "Something to look forward to when the weather's nicer."

"Well, I can't make any guarantees. But we'll try."

I like how she says *we*—as if she has some sort of stake in this, too, and I'm not random patient number one-oh-one on her list. "Thank you."

She rolls my shirtsleeve down and picks up my file again.

As she studies the pages, I study her expression. Serious. Bright, inquisitive eyes—dark blue, like the night sky I'd missed so much inside.

A slight frown wrinkles her brow. Bet she got to the part about my injuries coming from a fight in prison.

Great. She'll assume I'm some lowlife criminal and won't want to help me. Maybe do the bare minimum like the joker I saw at the prison.

Coming here was a waste of my time.

"Hmm. I wish these were more detailed," she murmurs.

Big surprise. Sounds like the prison therapist put as much effort into my notes as he did my therapy.

My gaze travels over her again. Fresh-faced. Doesn't look like she bothers with makeup. Pretty Cupid-bow lips. Her long hair's gathered in a neat, shiny ponytail. A few loose wisps frame her oval face.

Why the fuck am I hellbent on studying her like someone's going to quiz me on my way out the door? Pretty faces are everywhere. If I need female companionship, there's plenty of that to be found at the clubhouse.

Once I figure out where I stand with Rosie.

"On a scale of one to ten, how much pain are you in right now?" she asks.

"A three."

She scowls.

"Maybe a four."

Besides the desire to ride once spring arrives, Wrath went to the trouble of lining up a job. I'm no freeloader. If I'm collecting a paycheck, I plan to do the work. And to do the work, I'll need this shoulder to be functional.

I continue observing her careful movements. My greedy eyes suck up every inch of her as I try to guess her story. Looks like the quiet, good girl type. I always had a weakness for the innocent-looking ones.

*This is a medical appointment. She's supposed to help fix my shoulder, not my lonely dick.*

No amount of internal warnings stop the heat prickling my skin. Parts of me I thought had died yawn and wake right the fuck up each time her body brushes against mine.

This is ridiculous. And inappropriate as fuck.

She manipulates my shoulder again and I clench my jaw. No more soft, gentle, erection-inducing touches. She means business now.

My left hand curls into a fist.

*Knees in the breeze. Starry nights. Freedom.* Concentrate on anything other than the pain shooting from my shoulder to my wrist.

*Fuck*, this is more like a seven or eight on her little pain scale.

"Relax, Grayson," she says softly.

*Relax.* She's joking, right?

Any sign of weakness would've gotten me killed in prison. And while my body may have left, my mind is still stuck behind those walls.

"I'm not used to relaxing," I mutter. Even before prison, I never sat still for long. Always had to be moving and hustling.

A faint smile ghosts her lips. "I can see that." She gently squeezes my bicep. And, like a damn teenager, I can't help flexing the muscle.

Her lips part and her gaze travels over my body with more than professional curiosity. Or at least, that's how the story in my head plays. I worked hard for every muscle and inch of definition. Half the battle inside was just *looking* scary enough to keep people from messing with you. Now, at least I can enjoy an appreciative glance from an attractive woman.

"How much PT have you had since the injury?" she asks.

"Not much. It didn't get treated right away. Then, when I finally saw someone, the guy gave me a few stretching exercises to do on my own and sent me on my way."

"Hmm."

Fuck, those sexy humming noises she makes every time she takes in new information are driving me crazy.

Her gaze flicks to the papers in her hands again. "Did you *do* the exercises?"

"Sure did. Didn't seem like enough, though, so I added in some others to build strength."

There's the crease between her eyes again. She doesn't like that. "Overdoing it can be counterproductive."

I brush off her light, scolding tone. "The exercises he gave me wouldn't have tired out a toddler."

A hint of a smile plays at the corners of her mouth. "I won't go easy on you if you promise to follow my instructions."

"I will if *you* don't go easy on me because you think I'm old and frail."

She sweeps her gaze over me again. "You're definitely not frail, Grayson."

Fuck, I love the way my name sounds coming out of her mouth.

"Or old," she adds. "Now, let me try a few tests and see what we're working with."

My body tenses again.

"All right," she says in a firm voice. "Extend your arm to the side for me." She holds her arm parallel to the floor to demonstrate, and I imitate the position.

"Try to hold it there while I push down." She clamps her hands on my forearm and pushes. Hard. Strong girl.

Agony shoots through my arm. But I last longer than I should through sheer stubbornness. My curse-filled rants remain in my head as she performs increasingly difficult strength tests. Showing her my weakness is pissing me the fuck off.

"All right. Relax." She leans over the small desk in the corner. I study her long legs hidden by the hideous baggy pants. Generous hips, but she's a little on the thin side. Maybe she works long hours and doesn't have time to cook. Does she go home to a man who appreciates her? Takes care of her? Protects her from pervy patients like me?

She said she's ridden on the back of a bike before. With who? A boyfriend? A husband? Her father?

Jesus Christ, I'm losing my fucking mind.

I spend the rest of the time she's writing in my chart staring at the ceiling.

"Okay." She turns and gestures to the table behind me. "Would you mind laying facedown? I want to perform a different set of tests."

Don't care for that. Seems too vulnerable. Then again, I could easily bench press her, so I'm not exactly in danger.

She's patient, almost serene—her name fits—as I take my sweet time arranging myself on the table.

Soft, gentle fingers probe the muscles around my shoulder, down to my shoulder blade, along my spine. No clue what she's trying to figure out, but I hope it takes her a while. My body relaxes under her touch. She's got a much kinder manner than the jerk in prison who'd handled me like I was spoiled meat.

A pleasant shiver races over my skin as she traces a line from my shoulder to the base of my skull.

"Mmm." I sigh, my body relaxing another notch into the table.

"Does that hurt?" she asks.

"Yes, but not in a bad way like the shoulder."

"You carry a lot of tension here," she says in a low voice. "Deep breath. In and out."

I try to follow her breathing instructions.

Her touch transforms into something firmer, pressing in circular motions. Soothing. More like a massage than an examination. I continue the deep breathing and finally, my body fully relaxes.

I don't even tense up when she starts prodding my shoulder again—until she pokes a certain spot. "Fuu—ow." I flinch but, trapped on my stomach, I can't escape without knocking her on her ass.

"Is it tender here?" She jabs the spot again.

"Like a hot poker. Quit it," I growl.

She ignores me and continues her exploration. I shift and twitch but she's relentless. If it didn't hurt so damn much, I'd respect her tenacity.

Finally, her pokey little hands of steel retreat.

"Do you need help sitting up?" she asks.

Torture time must be over.

"No." I roll to my side and push myself upright.

"All right, I think I've tormented you enough today."

"Got that right," I grumble, clasping my shoulder with my left hand.

"They ruled out a rotator cuff tear at the time of the injury," she says, proving she actually read what little was in my chart.

"Yeah."

"That's good. We'll start with two times per week." She glances at my chart again. "I don't see any insurance information—"

"It's fine. I'm paying out of pocket."

"Oh, well..."

"It's not an issue," I say with more force than necessary. Don't need her thinking I'm some scrub who can't pay his bills.

"If you wouldn't mind wearing something maybe without sleeves next time..."

*That* might be a problem. Got some ink inside that I'm not exactly eager to show anyone. Instead of coming here, I should've searched for a place to cover them or burn 'em off.

"If you're comfortable," she adds.

I grunt a non-committal noise and slide off the table. "Are we done?"

Not deterred by my tone, she outlines what she wants me to do at home and what we'll do at our next session, all without looking at me.

Finally, she takes a breath. "I'll walk you up front so we can schedule your next appointment."

As she reaches for the door, our eyes lock.

The dark blue color holds me hostage. Inside the shining depths, it's easy to see she's not a teenager. Today, she helps others heal their injuries. But she's had her share of pain. Things that still haunt her.

Maybe I've lost my mind, but damn, if I'm not ready to hunt down her ghosts and slay every one of them.

## CHAPTER SIX

### Serena

Don't focus on the rearview mirror. You're not going that way.

Life isn't meant to be traveled backwards. And yet somehow, tonight, I'm about to undo all the hard work I've done over the past year.

I've lost my mind.

And for what? To see one of my patients outside of our therapy appointments, which could possibly get me fired?

The party is being thrown to celebrate Grayson's release from prison. Every single muffler bunny who shows up will be vying for his attention, hoping to give him comfort and welcome him home in order to prove their loyalty to the club. So at best, I'll witness him getting a blow job from one of the club girls. At worst, I'll find out he's married or already has an old lady. Bonus misery points for discovering he's married and cheats on his wife.

"I'm so excited you decided to come with me!" Amanda shouts in my ear. She grabs my shoulder and jumps up and down, forcing me to smear black liner into the corner of my eye.

"Knock it off," I mumble, dabbing at the stray black smudge with a Q-tip.

"Sorry." She picks up a brush and fusses with her newly layered and feathered hair. The style is straight out of the Seventies. Reminds me of the cut my mother favored. She'd had a passion for everything from that decade—the music, hairstyles, clothes, *and* drugs.

"What made you go for the Farrah Fawcett hair?" I ask.

"Who?" She pats the little blond, feathered wings above her ears. "It's cute, right? Kinda retro?"

"It's kinda something," I mutter.

She punches my shoulder.

"Sorry, yes." Who am I to judge when the only hairstyles I choose are "up" or "down"? "It frames your face nicely."

"Thank you." She fusses with the big, bouncy curls. "It's totally on trend."

"It is," I agree. I've certainly seen enough videos on social media featuring similar styles. My heavy hair would never hold the look, so I've scrolled on by. Besides, makeup is my passion, not hair.

"I love this color," Amanda murmurs, picking up one of my new plum-berry glosses. "Did the company send it to you?"

"Yes, but I haven't had a chance to review it yet." *So please don't steal it.*

"Oooh! I'll be your model. You can snap a photo before we leave. I don't mind if you post it."

I study her for a moment. The deep berry color will probably look fantastic on her tanned skin. It'll be a nice contrast to my paler complexion. "Thanks. I'd like to expand and use different models occasionally."

"Anytime." She pauses and sweeps her gaze over me. "You're the brand, though. People follow to see *you* wear the stuff."

"I know. A little variety once in a while would be great." I pass her a lip liner that should match the gloss.

"Totally." She bumps me out of the way and leans into my mirror to line her lips. I need a bigger mirror. *One day.*

When she's finished, she poses and blows a few fake kisses my way. I flick on two of my ring lights and adjust them to a flattering angle, then pull out my cell phone. "Can you give me a natural smile?"

"What? You don't like my dick-sucking-lips pose?" She acts out the scenario.

"Well, my audience is women, not dirty old men, so no."

She giggles and I grab a few nice shots. "Perfect," I praise, checking the photos.

"I bet you have more creepy male lurkers than you realize," she says, peering over my shoulder at the photos.

"If they really enjoy watching a stranger compare shades of lipstick, more power to 'em, I guess." I shrug. Whatever helps my burgeoning makeup influencer empire grow.

"Seriously. Didn't you hear about that country singer who got abducted by one of her Instagram stalkers or something? It was scary."

"Maybe. I haven't had time to pay attention to a lot of news lately."

"Girl, what am I gonna do with you?"

I expertly dodge the question by asking, "Ready to go?"

"Is *that* what you're wearing?" Amanda curls her lip in disgust as she sweeps her gaze over my outfit. "To a clubhouse party? No one's gonna let you ride the D dressed like that."

*That's the whole point.*

I may have changed my mind about attending the party, but I'll be damned if I'm digging out my club-whoring clothes or stupid too-high heels that are impossible to walk in at the clubhouse's rustic property. Nope. I no longer pick my outfits according to what will please the male gaze. I wear what makes *me* happy. And tonight, that's my favorite skinny jeans, a long, cozy, cable-knit sweater with a cowl neck and little pockets in the front, and a pair of knee-high boots. No freeze-my-ass-off short skirts to show off my legs or invite people to touch me. No belly-button-baring tops. No cleavage on display.

I choose to wear makeup, though. I'm not a savage.

When it's obvious I'm not changing into something more revealing, Amanda sighs. "Well, the olive-green color is pretty on you. It makes your eyes sparkle."

"Thanks." I grab my coat with the hole in the elbow and toss it over my arm. "Ready?"

"Yessss." She heaves a dramatic sigh. "I'm *so* ready. I need to let loose. And since you're apparently still boycotting dick, I'm happy to take your share."

I chuckle. "Well, you're headed to the right place."

"Are you sure you want to drive?" she asks as she carefully clomps down the stairs.

Another reason to avoid heels—navigating stairs is so much easier without them.

"I don't mind." Plus, that way I won't be stranded if she wants to spend the night. I'm not staying over or sleeping in anyone else's bed. *Period.*

The temperature must've dropped fifteen degrees since I got home from work. I shrug into my coat and we hurry to my little Mazda hatchback, throwing ourselves inside and slamming the doors shut.

*Please let the heater work tonight.*

The engine turns over. After a few tense, questioning moments, actual warm air flows from the vents.

"Phew. I was worried it might be a chilly ride."

Amanda chuckles. "My sunroof is stuck. If we get another big snow storm, I'm screwed."

We have to pass Empire Med on our way to the clubhouse. My darkened clinic sits next door to the massive, sprawling brick hospital. Amanda stares at the medical complex as we pass. "How's work going? Do you still like your job?"

"I really do," I answer without hesitation. "It's hard and some of my patients are difficult, but I love helping them make progress and heal."

"So, it was worth finishing school? You don't regret all that time you wasted on studying?" A mixture of disbelief and disgust creeps into her tone.

"Not for a second. It wasn't a waste." I pause, considering how to express my thoughts without hurting her feelings. Amanda dropped out of college in her first semester. She bounces around from one low-paying job to another, living off boyfriends and sometimes her parents. "I wish I'd gotten serious about school sooner and finished on time. I could've been a lot farther along now."

"Farther along in what?"

I glance over at her. "In life? My job? Maybe drive a nicer car. Live in a decent neighborhood. Own a house instead of renting." I take a breath and try to focus on the positive. "But I'm getting there. I'm untangling all my bills and student loan debt and slowly paying everything down." Turns out creditors *really* don't like it when you stop paying your bills and move around a bunch so they have to track you down. And I discovered the hard way that student loans will haunt you to the ever-loving grave.

She reaches over and pats my leg. "I'm proud of you. Personally, I'm still holding out for a rich husband to take care of me."

"I'd rather take care of myself."

"When'd you get so bitter?"

"I'm not bitter," I say with more calm than I actually have in this moment. "I'm *realistic*."

"I don't want to get married now anyway," she scoffs. "Tonight, I wanna hook up with Ravage, so hands off."

"He's all yours."

"I told you Jigsaw's been asking about you. He should be there." She lowers her voice to a *wink-wink-nudge-nudge* tone and elbows my side.

My lips curve up. While I'm fond of Jiggy, I don't want to hook up with him. Or anyone.

Except Grayson.

*No. He's my patient. That's it. No making out, no blow jobs, and definitely no sex tonight. The boycott remains in effect.*

And yet, the only reason I agreed to go was to hopefully see him outside of work. Why? His stoic strength? The way I caught him watching me when he thought I wasn't paying attention?

I just want him to see me when I look nice instead of all gross in my work clothes and no makeup. That's all.

Oh, God. Am I stalking him? I haven't even been licensed that long, and I'm already stalking my patients. This is terrible.

"Serena?"

"Huh?"

"The light's green."

"Oh. Shit." I step on the accelerator harder than necessary. My car sputters, then rockets forward.

"Easy. No one was behind us," Amanda breathes out.

"Sorry."

"Steer was happy when I told him you were coming with me."

"Wait." I frown and glance over at her. "Why'd you call Steer about a party at the *upstate* clubhouse?"

"Well, I wasn't about to call Wrath. I don't need his scary bitch wife kicking my ass."

"Trinity's not a bitch." She *is* intimidating, though.

"Pfft." She snorts. "Okay."

Birch is manning the gate to the property when we arrive. While we're waiting for him to let the cars ahead of us through, Amanda flips her visor down and fluffs her hair in the mirror.

I slide my window down as Birch approaches. He smiles when he recognizes me. "Serena. It's been a minute. What's up?"

*Oh, just enjoying a backslide and lapse in judgment by showing up here.* "Not much. How've you been?"

"Can't complain." He gestures toward the driveway. "Full house tonight. Welcome home party for an older brother."

Amanda leans across the seat, practically crawling in my lap, and wiggles her fingers at him. "We heard. That's why we're here."

"Hey, Amanda." He lifts his chin at her. "Got a few clubs coming up this weekend. Brothers from different charters."

A flutter of fear stirs in my belly. Maybe I shouldn't be here.

"Sounds good." Amanda winks at him.

"Go on." Birch waves us through.

"Variety of dick." Amanda slides back into her seat. "A dick buffet. I like it."

I choke on a laugh and press my foot to the accelerator, gliding past the gate. "An abundance of dick was never a problem here."

Amanda snort-giggles and stamps her feet on the floor. "So true."

"Driveway's a lot smoother," I say as I steer the car up the hill. "Keep an eye out for a spot. I don't want to get boxed in."

"Don't park all the way down here and make me walk up the hill," she whines.

We compromise and I pull into a spot on the grass under a tree near the top of the driveway.

"Ugh. My heel's stuck," Amanda shrieks. "Serena!"

"I'm coming." I hustle around the back of the car and help her pull her foot loose. She huffs and limps her way to solid ground with her hands clutched around my arm.

Music thumps from the clubhouse, and a tingle of the old, familiar excitement runs through me. Followed by fear. Amanda said Shadow wouldn't be here but what about Sway? Or even worse, Tawny? She'd have no problem announcing to Grayson that I used to be a club whore. Surely they'd make an appearance at a welcome home party?

At the front door, Stash waves us inside with a welcoming smile and enthusiastic greeting.

I step to the side, out of the way of the flow of traffic, and survey the large, crowded space. The lights are low, but it's bright enough to recognize familiar faces. Rock and his wife circulate through the crowd. *Weird.* Other girls said they stopped showing up to these parties a while ago. Then again, I guess as president, Rock would need to be here.

"I don't see Murphy," Amanda shouts in my ear.

I roll my eyes. "I wasn't looking for him." Sometimes I think Amanda had a bigger crush on him than I ever did.

"Too many patched ol' ladies here tonight." Amanda checks the room again and pouts. "Not the dirty party I was promised."

I quickly scan the room. She's not wrong. Lots of "property of" patches on display. At one time, I swore a property patch would be the ultimate romantic gift. Declaring to all the brothers that *this* woman was off-limits. It meant that you truly belonged somewhere and to someone.

"Ugh." Amanda elbows me. "Ravage told me they're opening a second clubhouse in Empire just so we don't have to suffer through these boring mom and dad fiestas." She rocks her hips in a slow circle. "Get down to business without the judgy looks from the ol' ladies."

"Give it time," I mutter, searching the room again. Still no sign of Grayson. This party was supposed to be *for* him, right? Maybe he already found his bunny for the night and went upstairs.

"Serena?" a husky female voice says behind me.

My whole body freezes.

I turn and breathe a sigh of relief. "Lilly. Hey."

She yanks me in for a warm hug. Stunned, I stand there like a mannequin for a few seconds before finally returning the embrace.

"How have you been?" she asks, pulling away. Her curious eyes study me like I'm a bird who wandered too far from the nest and finally returned.

"Good." I tuck my hair behind my ear and find some steel for my spine. "I hear Z's still running Downstate?"

"He is."

As if Z heard us talking about him, he walks up behind Lilly and slings his arm around her shoulders. He pulls her to his side and kisses her cheek before flashing a genuine smile my way. "Hey, Serena."

"Hi, Z." I wring my hands together in front of me. I've practiced this in my head a few times but I'm not sure I can get the words out. "I never, uh, thanked you for, uh, protecting me from Shadow," I say in a rush, before my courage slips away. "Thank you."

His face softens for a second before a cold glint enters his eyes. "Don't thank me. And don't worry about him. He won't show his face here."

I'm not sure how to respond, so I just nod quickly. The fact he and his wife even acknowledged my presence is too strange to process. Z's an MC president. Stooping to talk to a lowly club girl seems abnormal.

*Former* club girl.

But before I left, Lilly had been really nice to me. She'd given me a few responsibilities around the clubhouse and I'd helped her figure out how to deal with some of the pushier club girls. She'd been kind and hadn't judged when Shadow roughed me up.

I open my mouth but can't work up the courage to ask them about

Grayson directly. What would I say? *"My new patient has a Lost Kings MC tat. So here I am to play psycho-stalker."* That wouldn't sound bonkers or anything.

Rooster bumps Z's shoulder and leans over to say something against his ear. Z nods.

"See you later, Serena." Lilly waves at me as Z pulls her away.

"Long time, Serena." Rooster dips his chin in acknowledgment. He squeezes a short, curvy blonde to his side. "This is my ol' lady, Shelby. I don't think you two ever met."

She looks familiar but I don't think it's from hanging out at the clubhouse together. "Hi, Shelby."

She tucks closer to Rooster. Can't blame her. She probably assumes I've banged him at some point.

*I hate this. Why'd I come back here?*

"Serena. That's a pretty name," she says in a soft Southern drawl I can barely make out above the noise.

"Thanks." I study her again. Is she already wearing Rooster's property patch? *Wow, guess I have been out of the loop for a while.*

"Serena." Jigsaw's gravelly voice draws my attention.

"Jiggy!" I smile up at him and he leans in to give me a quick hello hug.

His severe expression transforms into a smile as he pulls away. "Haven't seen you in a while. You doing okay?"

The concern in his voice wraps around my throat and squeezes. "I'm good," I croak. "I finished school." He'd always encouraged me to stay in school and get my degree.

"Good." He smiles even wider. "Glad to hear it."

"Hey, Jiggy," Amanda says. "I'm good, too, in case you were wondering."

He flashes a tight smile without taking his eyes off me. "I know."

"How are *you*?" I tap his arm with the back of my hand. "I heard you've been out on the road a lot."

"I was." He tilts his head toward Rooster and Shelby. "I helped him out while Shelby was on tour—"

"Serena? What are you doing here?" I instantly recognize the raspy voice. My heart races.

Firm fingers wrap around my upper arm, gently tugging. I peer into Grayson's surprised stare, concern etched in every line of his face. My lips part but I can't form an answer.

*He's here.*

*He found me.*

"Grinder, you two know each other?" Jigsaw asks.

*Grinder.* His road name. It fits. I can easily picture him grinding his enemies to dust with his powerful hands. Especially with the way he's currently scowling at Jigsaw.

"Yeah, we know each other," he answers in a gruff tone. He slips a possessive arm around my shoulders and pulls me against his side. "She's with me."

# CHAPTER SEVEN
## Grinder

I've had plenty to keep me occupied since my therapy appointment. But for some reason, my thoughts have returned to Serena like clockwork. My brain recognizes it's probably because she's the first woman to touch or comfort me in so long. The rest of me doesn't give a fuck about logic.

I met with my parole officer and, as the guys predicted, he didn't seem to give a shit. Told him about the job and apartment. Hell, I even told him about going to physical therapy—although I didn't mention the part about my obsession with my beautiful therapist.

As heated as I'd gotten with Z about Rose's address, I haven't gone to see her. That's probably why I'm fixated on Serena. Avoidance or some shit.

"Jesus, you're gonna scare every girl away with that mean mug you're wearing," Steer says as he plops a can of Coke on the table in front of me.

I snarl at him in response. He laughs and unfortunately doesn't go away.

Music—at least I think it's music, there are no discernible instruments or lyrics, just a lot of noise and repeated phrases—throbs through the clubhouse.

The party's supposed to be in my honor, but no one consulted me on the activities or the soundtrack. Otherwise, things would be a lot quieter.

Earlier, I scared Sparky out of the corner seat of the couch and stationed myself there, with the intention of having a prime view of everyone coming and going.

"You all right, Gray?" Rock asks, dropping down next to me. He pulls Hope into his lap, locking his arms around her waist.

"I'm fine," I answer without taking my eyes off the front door.

"He's trying to scare all the females away," Steer says.

I scowl at him but don't bother with a response.

Wrath motions for Steer to move over so he can plop down next to me. He leans in. "I'll take you over to Sully's place Monday if that works for you?"

"Who?" Slowly, I turn and stare at him. "Oh, right. The job. Yeah, that'd be good." I roll my shoulder. "I'm hoping therapy works, so I can be of some use."

"Don't worry about that," Wrath assures me. "Go easy. Don't overdo it at PT."

I blast him with the full force of my *fuck off* frown. "Who the fuck you think you're talking to, son? I ain't dead yet. You think I was busy taking sewing classes in prison? Stretches and—"

"Easy." Wrath raises his hands but doesn't back down. "I know how it is to want to get back to normal." He pats his thigh. "I've been there."

Now I feel shitty for snapping at him. "Thanks."

A flash of pale gold hair pulls my attention to the left. It's not her. It can't be. There must be thirty blondes in the clubhouse tonight. I'm seeing things.

I pick out Rooster's big frame over by the bar. He shifts and my gaze lands on two girls.

I sit up straighter.

One of the girls moves to the side, giving me a glimpse of her friend.

*Serena.*

"Grinder?" Wrath's voice is distant noise.

Jigsaw leans down and wraps his arms around Serena.

Another brother's touching *my* woman.

I jump off the couch.

What's she doing here, of all places? Is that really her? Or has she been on my mind so much, I'm imagining her? Picturing her somewhere she has no business visiting.

Like a freight train, I barrel through the room, headed straight for Serena. Her hand's on Jigsaw's arm. A smile curves her dark red lips.

They seem awfully friendly.

I like Jigsaw. Too bad I'm gonna have to dismember him tonight.

For whatever reason, she's here. In my clubhouse.

That means she's *mine*.

"You two know each other?" Jigsaw asks me.

Wait a second. Is she *his* woman?

*Tough shit.*

"Yeah, we know each other." I slip my arm around her shoulders and do a good impression of a lion warning the other males away from his mate. "She's with me."

Rooster and Jigsaw share a raised-eyebrow, what-the-fuck look. But then Jiggy backs away, hands raised in surrender. A smug little smirk stretches across his face. *Punk.*

"All right then." He dips his chin. "Glad I got to see you, Serena."

"You too."

"Jiggy, wait." The girl Serena was standing with grabs onto his sleeve and follows him down the hall.

I pull Serena closer. "What are you doing here?"

The clubhouse is in the middle of nowhere. There's no way she wound up here by accident.

Her wide, confused eyes stare up at me. "I, uh." Her lips part, her gaze trailing after her friend. "Amanda…"

Serena's a physical therapist. A professional. She's got no business hanging around with bikers.

Who cares? I've been aching to see her for days, and like fucking magic, she's *here*. Why question the reason? It doesn't matter.

"You need something to drink?" I turn toward the bar.

"I'm okay." Her body trembles against mine.

Now that we're up close and personal, I take her in. Heavy makeup tonight. A whole perfect airbrushed face full. Dramatic eyes. Like a model headed to a photo shoot. Stunning.

I won't say how much better I thought she looked barefaced at the clinic. Even *I* know that would be rude as fuck to say to a woman who put so much effort into her appearance.

My gaze travels lower. A sweater. One corner of my mouth hitches up. She has to be the only girl in the clubhouse wearing a *sweater*. With a loose, floppy neck that almost touches her chin, no less. The tight knit clings to her curves and provides me with a much better roadmap of her body than her baggy work outfit. Painted on jeans. Boots up to her knees. Easily the most beautiful woman in the room.

*Shit, she has to be half my age.*

How come, in all my fantasizing about her, the cosmic age-gap never occurred to me?

"You look nice," I finally say.

"Thank you." She tugs at the sweater. Her eyes dart everywhere but can't seem to meet mine.

"Come. Sit with me." I jerk my chin toward the back corner. "Somewhere quieter so we can talk."

"Okay."

I curl my hand around hers and tug her into the crowd, making sure she stays close so every man in this room knows she's with me and not to be touched or spoken to without my permission.

"Serena!" Hope jumps out of Rock's lap when we approach. She briefly glances at our linked hands, but gives Serena a welcoming smile.

"Hi, Hope." Serena ducks her head.

I drop her hand. Is she embarrassed to be seen with me? Maybe she came here to see someone else—not get manhandled by the ex-con twice her age. What the fuck am I doing? Hell, she could be related to one of the brothers for all I know.

And here I've claimed her like a psycho caveman in front of everyone without even knowing her story.

# CHAPTER EIGHT

## Serena

WHAT THE HELL JUST HAPPENED?

One minute, I was talking to Jigsaw.

The next, Grayson—*Grinder*—had his arm wrapped around me like a python.

*She's with me*, he'd told Jigsaw in no uncertain terms. Not "she's mine for the night" or "you can have her when I'm done." He didn't drag me into a bedroom either.

No, he led me to a quieter corner of the room to hang out with the president of this club, his wife, and the SAA.

Should I warn Grinder about my history here? Will he be pissed? Embarrassed if he finds out I used to be a club girl?

At least no one outs me. Tawny would've called me a whore within two seconds of seeing my face and given Grinder a detailed list of every brother she suspected I'd ever slept with. Hope actually seems *happy* to see me. Or she's just gracious to everyone. Rock nods at me. Even Wrath acknowledges my presence with a quick chin lift.

Grinder pulls me down next to him. Like he's afraid I'll disappear in a puff of smoke if he doesn't hold on tight.

I fold my coat and tuck it beside me. Should've left it in the damn car. The couch cushions are wide, built for men with big frames to comfortably lounge. I sink into the seat but can't rest my back against anything without folding my legs underneath me. Grinder stretches his arm across my shoulders, encouraging me to lean into him. I settle so we're pressed tight from hips to knees.

He doesn't need to tell anyone I'm with him. His posture says it loud and clear.

A thrill runs through me. This is crazy. I'd hoped to maybe talk to him. I never expected that if I ran into him, he'd act like *this*.

Maybe he's just worried about me. Or thinks I'm out of my depth. That I've never been to an MC party before.

If he only knew.

He leans down. His lips brush my ear and my eyes close. A pleasurable shiver slides along my spine. "You never told me why you're here."

"I came with my friend," I answer.

"Are you with someone in the club?" His penetrating gaze searches my face. "Related to one of my brothers?" He taps the Lost Kings MC patch on his cut.

"No." I turn to explain myself, but he's *right there*. Our noses brush. Our lips are a breath apart, like he's planning to kiss me. Up close, he's even more brutal and beautiful.

My heart pounds an erratic, happy beat.

The kiss never comes.

Instead, he brushes his knuckles over my cheek. "I've been thinking about you since the other day."

"Really?" My voice is a high-pitched squeak. I did more than think about him. I broke all the promises I made to myself to *never* go to another MC party again. Just to see him tonight. "I thought about you too," I admit. "How did you feel after our session? I wasn't too hard on you, was I?"

He frowns and draws back. Damn, I didn't mean to sound clinical. But besides my inappropriate crush, I *have* worried about him. I couldn't help wondering how he was adjusting to life, if I'd assessed his injury correctly, and if the exercises I'd given him were helping at all.

"Fine," he answers.

That's a lie. I felt him flinch earlier. I rest my hand against his leg, recapturing his attention. "I can...I can get in trouble. Seeing you outside of work. Like *this*."

He laughs. Deep, rumbling laughter. Crinkles at the corners of his eyes soften his hard expression. "Sweetheart, what happens here, stays *here*."

My lips pull into a shaky smile. I've certainly heard that before.

He shifts as if he's having second thoughts and wants to take his arm off my shoulders. "Unless you don't want—"

"No." I wrap my hand around his, keeping him in place. Yes, I could get in trouble for dating a client. But we're not *dating*. And I know the Lost Kings well enough. What Grayson said is true. No one talks to outsiders about what goes on inside their clubhouse.

He strokes his fingers over my cheek and rests his fingertips against my chin. "You're so beautiful. I wanted to tell you that the other day."

"Thanks."

Being pretty has never gotten me anywhere.

Beauty brought me the attention of men when I was way too young to understand what they wanted.

My pretty face angered my mother.

Teachers always assumed I was stupid.

From Grayson, it sounds so sincere and kind, that I enjoy the compliment.

He's still studying my expression. Stroking my cheek. "I remembered to do the stretches you gave me." He rolls his shoulder. "They help."

Now *that* makes me happy. I'd gone over his case with my supervisor and she'd made some suggestions that I'm eager to try out with him at our next appointment. "Good. We'll have you riding by springtime."

"Serena?"

I glance up.

Trinity smiles down at me. Wrath has his big hands clamped

around her hips, pulling her into his lap, but her attention's focused on me. "I thought that was you."

"It's me." My tone's cautious, as I try to figure out her intentions.

"How've you been?" She settles into her husband's lap, resting her hands on Wrath's massive arms wrapped around her waist.

"Good." I clear my throat and sit straighter. "I finished school." My voice falters, and I glance at Grayson. I'm torn between wanting to let Trinity know I've moved past my club girl days and not wanting Grayson to know how new I am to my job.

"That's good. Congratulations." Her gaze skips from Grayson to me, questions clearly brewing in her light brown eyes. Wrath nuzzles against her neck, running his beard over her bare shoulder until she laughs and redirects her attention to him.

"Is this weird for you?" He gestures toward a group of guys closer to my age. A smile teases at the corners of his mouth. "Would you rather be hanging out with them, instead of Grandpa over here?"

I chuckle at the question. He's far from any grandfather I've ever seen. "You *are* a whole college graduate older than me," I point out.

"It's not fair you know so much about me and I know squat about you." He cocks his head and stares at my face. "How old are you?"

Heat creeps over my cheeks. "Twenty-eight."

"Fuck," he mutters. He blows out a long, slow breath. "I feel like I never moved past the age I was when I went inside. So, really, I'm only about seven years older than you." His lips pull into a quick smirk, but I sense pain behind his words. What a sad sentiment to share with someone he barely knows.

But he's not after my pity.

"I'm sure you've changed and grown in a lot of ways," I say.

He nods slowly. "Changed. Sure. Sometimes I still feel thirty-five." He scowls at the party going on in front of us. "Other times, I feel like I aged a hundred years."

"I can understand that." It makes perfect sense to me. At twenty-one I knew nothing about the world, even though I'd already survived a round-trip through hell.

"Why physical therapy?" Grayson asks.

A lifetime of looking after people who didn't give a damn about me? Might as well get paid for my habit of trying to fix wounded birds? That sounds too cynical or revealing. "I like helping people heal but didn't think I could handle medical school."

Something flashes in his eyes.

"You don't like doctors, do you?"

"It's not that." He rubs his thumb over my hand. "Go on."

"What else is there to say? It's a job. I'm happy I have it." I blush and meet his intense stare. "It took me a while to settle on the right path."

"You chose well." His gaze never strays from my face. "Don't ever doubt yourself."

His low-voiced encouragement sinks in slowly. If only it were that simple.

For the next hour or so, brothers stop by to pay their respects to Grinder. Wishing him well. Congratulating him. Welcoming him home. He smiles and shows his brothers respect and affection. But I'm close enough to feel the tension rippling through his body with every interaction.

I'm having my own tense moments, waiting for someone to drop the bomb. I turn my body toward Grayson, resting my head on his chest. His body provides a protective barrier.

"We're heading home," Rock says when there's a lull in activity around us. "You all right, Gray?"

Grayson's mouth twitches in annoyance. But he nods. "I'm fine."

Rock doesn't seem bothered by the clipped answer.

Hope reaches over and squeezes my hand. "Good to see you again, Serena."

"Thanks," I whisper.

Grayson watches them leave before turning my way. "Will you come upstairs with me?"

My stomach flutters. It's been a while since I've been with a guy. I promised myself I wouldn't do this tonight but I can't seem to form the word *no*. And it's not out of fear. It's desire holding my tongue hostage.

Grayson asked, and he's waiting for an answer before making a move.

I drop my gaze to where his strong hand is clamped around my thigh. Boldly claiming. I can't stop imagining what it would feel like without my jeans in the way. Or the squeeze of his hands at my hips.

Leaning closer, I press my lips against his jaw. Stubble both tickles and scratches my skin. I kiss my way to his ear and whisper, "Yes, take me upstairs."

My gaze darts everywhere as I follow him to the staircase. Is anyone watching us? Will one of his brothers stop and tell him who I am?

Grinder pauses on the first landing. My eyes land on a photo of two young bikers with big smiles standing next to two Harleys.

"Is this you?" I ask.

He stares at the picture. "Yeah." His hand sweeps in front of him, gesturing toward the other photos along the wall. "Time moved on for everyone but me."

There's no bitterness in his tone. Only regret. Longing.

"You'll make up for it." What a dumb thing to say. You can't recapture lost time. There's no rewinding the clock to make different choices. All we can do is learn from our mistakes.

"I'm going to try." He shifts his gaze from the photos to me and back again. "But some things can't be fixed. No matter how much you might want to."

It's as if he read my mind. "That's a hard lesson to learn."

He squeezes my hand and continues up the stairs.

I stare at familiar pictures along the wall as we ascend. Family. That's what drew me to the club in the first place. Family by choice. Even club girls are treated like family of a sort. More so at the upstate clubhouse. I'm happy this is the charter where Grinder seems to be affiliated.

We reach the top floor. The hallway might as well be haunted with all the unease it stirs in my belly. The urge to flee wars with my desire to be with Grayson. He turns right and keeps walking.

Since he was just released from prison, I expect him to be staying in one of the guest rooms near the staircase. But he continues past all of them. Many of the rooms are occupied anyway. I have no interest in peeking but the sounds can't be ignored as easily. Grayson doesn't slow or peer into any of the rooms either.

We reach the end of the hallway where the officers of the club reside. Well, used to. They've all moved out. I refuse to turn my head to the left where Murphy's room used to be.

Thankfully, Grayson stops at the last room on the right. What was once Wrath's room, I think. I'm not sure what Grayson's role in the club was before he was sent to prison, but obviously everyone has a lot of respect for him.

Inside, my anxiety shoots off the charts again. I'm not ready for this.

Grayson distances himself from me. He hangs my coat on a hook on the back of the door, flicks switches on several lamps, and slips off his cut, draping it over a chair. But he won't meet my eyes.

He seems as conflicted as I feel. That should reassure me. Instead, doubt creeps in. Downstairs, he seemed attracted to me. Did I do something wrong? Ask too many questions? Say something stupid?

Old Serena rises from the dead. The easygoing, do-anything-to-please, flirty girl. She's on autopilot. In a few steps, I cross the room and lean into him, resting my hands at his waist. The top of my head barely reaches his chin. Reaching up on my toes, I attempt to kiss him but only brush against the hard line of his bristly chin.

Nothing.

I know what'll capture his interest. The same thing that revs every man's engine. My hands slide to his belt buckle.

His body tightens. He clamps his hands over mine. "Don't," he warns.

I draw back. Heat blasts over my cheeks.

*Calm down. Deep breath.* Lots of guys—and pretty much every biker I've ever known—prefer to be in charge. Don't be so forward. Let him lead.

"Tell me what you want." I slick my tongue over my bottom lip.

"Stay here." He shakes his head. "Give me a minute."

He turns away and pulls a few items out of his top dresser drawer. "You want a shirt or something to sleep in?"

"Am I staying over?" I ask.

His body stills, but he doesn't look at me. "I'd like you to."

"I don't need anything."

He either doesn't get what I'm implying or he isn't interested. He tosses a T-shirt on the bed.

I'm stunned. My gaze follows him as he walks into the bathroom and closes the door behind him.

A few seconds later, water patters against glass and tiles.

He didn't even ask me to join him in the shower?

I slump onto the edge of the bed, watching the door. I'm not used to bikers giving me the brush-off. Men always want to get down to business.

He just got out of prison. He should *want* to fuck, right?

My gaze strays to the door. I can't even count the number of promises I broke to myself by coming here tonight. Only to be rejected.

Maybe I should find Amanda and leave.

Feeling insecure and unwanted is nothing new. It's been a while since it hurt this much, though. The uncomfortable feelings crawling over my skin fill me with shame. I thought I was beyond the sting of rejection.

I might not be the smartest, but I finished school. Without parents who gave a damn or anyone else to support me, I found a way and did it on my own. I landed a decent job. I work hard. I care about my patients. My past may be a series of bad choices, but I'm trying to do better.

I don't need the approval of a man to feel good about myself. Not anymore. My body, my looks—they're not the only things I have going for me. I'm worth more than how fuckable a man thinks I am.

But the damage I carry inside never completely dies. No matter how many pep talks I recite to myself.

I unlace my boots and yank them off, setting them aside. As conflicted as I am, I refuse to leave. I peel my sweater up and over my head, draping it over the back of a chair. Underneath, I'm wearing an olive-green tank top.

The bathroom door opens with a soft click. Grayson steps out, steam billowing around him. He's already dressed in a black sleeveless shirt and shorts.

I study him, impressed. He's on the leaner side but it's obvious whatever free time he had in prison was spent working out.

"Do you want me to go?" I ask quietly.

Sadness softens his hard edges and the idea that he doesn't want me to leave finally boosts my fragile ego.

"I want you to stay." He nods to the bed. "If you don't mind."

"I don't mind."

Still in my jeans, I slide past him into the bathroom, and shut the door behind me.

I lean against the sink and stare into the mirror. "Why are you doing this?" I whisper.

The girl in the mirror doesn't have any answers. She never does.

Sighing, I wash my face. Without any makeup remover, I do the best I can with a bar of soap to scrub all the eye shadow, heavy liner, and foundation off my skin.

Except for the moonlight spilling in from the uncovered window, it's dark when I return to the bedroom.

"Grayson?" I whisper.

He throws the covers back in answer.

I slide my jeans down my legs and kick them to the side before slipping into the soft, fresh sheets. Unsure of what he expects, I curl up on my side.

The mattress shifts. His warm, soapy scent drifts my way.

"Serena?" he rasps.

Awareness prickles over my skin.

I turn and he's closer than I expected. Dark, glittering eyes find mine in the moonlight.

"It's not you." His voice is thick and raspy, curling around me.

"Oh," I whisper.

He stretches his arm out, filling the space between us. "Come closer. I'd like to hold you."

My pulse hammers as I ease into his space. He curls his arm around my body and buries his face in the crook of my neck, simply breathing me in. He drags his nose along my throat, ghosts his lips over my shoulder. He's tightly coiled, fighting a battle against himself.

He wants me. We're so close. Not even the darkness and the covers can conceal his erection. I could try again. Be bold and wrap my hand around his cock. The shorts will be easier to breach than his jeans. He won't have time to stop me. Once I touch him, he'll change his mind, right?

It's too risky. The rejection will scald. And it feels too much like the dirty tricks that have been played on me in the past. I want him to *want* me, not give in.

He rests one hand on my hip but doesn't slide it under my shirt or explore beyond that spot. His touch both soothes and confuses me as I accept the small doses of affection he's willing to give.

I end up with my head on his chest, one arm tucked under my chin and the other resting over his heart.

The steady thump soothes my inner worries.

He lets out a long, contented breath. "You feel nice."

"So do you."

"It's nice to be...with you."

The loneliness and pain ringing in his words pierce my soul. I hug him a little tighter, wanting to offer whatever comfort he needs.

And maybe take a little comfort for myself.

# CHAPTER NINE

## Grinder

Something sweet and floral tickles my nose, pulling me out of sleep. Or maybe it's the sun streaming through the curtains I couldn't bear to close last night.

God, it feels good not to wake up alone.

The warm, soft weight of Serena rests against my side. Curled into a tiny ball, she looks way too young and fragile to be in my bed.

What the fuck was I thinking? Using her as some sort of comfort object. Not explaining what I expected because I didn't know myself.

I reach out and trace my finger over her shoulder. How many men would kill to have her in their bed? I don't deserve to wake up next to her.

Not when my ex-wife is heavily on my mind.

Careful not to disturb Serena, I roll out of bed, cursing at the aches reminding me that I'm too damn old for her. I stretch for a minute before padding into the bathroom.

She's still sound asleep when I return.

For some reason, I'm torn.

Any man in his right mind would've taken what she was offering last night. Christ, the way she licked her lips and went straight for my belt had me ready to explode like a teenager.

I slip into a pair of jeans and throw on another plain T-shirt. Appreciate more than ever the guys and their wives going to so much trouble to leave me with a closet full of clothes. No hand-me-downs from my brothers. All new. Expensive stuff chosen with care. I rip the tags off a soft green plaid flannel shirt and toss them in the trash. One look out the window says even if I could, I wouldn't be riding. Not with the fresh coating of snow on the ground. I lace up my boots and grab a stiff Carhartt jacket.

At the door, I pause and stare at Serena.

I can't put my finger on why I hate leaving her so much. It feels wrong. But I need closure before we can move forward. Searching the desk, I finally find a small pad of notepaper and pen.

*Serena,*

*I need to take care of some things.*

*I'd like to see you later.*

*G.*

I don't know her well enough to know if she'll be here when I return or if she'll be offended and never come near me again.

Depending on how the next few hours go, that might be for the best anyway.

---

While I appreciate the lesson Murphy tried to give me on using the GPS the other day, it's not necessary. As soon as I hit the highway, I know exactly where I'm headed.

*Finally.*

Only took a few days to gather my balls and make this trip.

I'd hated like hell asking Z for this favor but now I'm grateful that he did it without giving me too much shit.

Rosie doesn't live far from our old place, so once I scanned a map, she wasn't hard to find. For years, all I had was a P.O. Box.

I roll to a stop at the curb in front of a small white colonial-style house with black shutters.

Sparkling, star-shaped Christmas lights dangle over the front porch. Rosie loved to decorate for the holidays. Hated to take the decorations down. She'd leave them up for months if I let her. For some reason, it drove me nuts. Guess no one's around to complain about them now.

Along with the address, Z had given me the make, model, and license plate for Rosie's car. I double-check the paper in my hand with the car in the driveway. Same one. Hopefully that means she's home.

Slush blankets the yard but the sidewalk to the front door is clear. I slowly make my way up, taking a deep breath before setting foot on the first step.

I jab my finger against the doorbell to the left and wait. A few seconds later, I rap my knuckles against the wood.

"I got it!" someone yells inside. The door's thrown wide open. If it weren't for the fact that this girl's the spittin' image of Rosie, I'd assume I stopped at the wrong house.

The happy grin slides off the girl's face as she studies me. "Can I help you?"

Hope beats a steady rhythm in my chest. The girl looks about fourteen…maybe fifteen years old. Could it be? Is it…possible?

*Do I have a kid after all?*

Rose would've told me. Wouldn't she?

Maybe not. What was she going to do? Bring a baby to visit me in prison? Watched plenty of guys with that situation inside. It was torture for them. But it also provided hope.

I clear my throat and attempt a non-threatening smile. "Is your mother home?" I ask.

Curious eyes sweep over me again. "Uh, yeah."

"Grayson?" The soft voice I've longed to hear for years slides over me. I lift my gaze from the girl.

*Rosie.*

Shit, time's barely touched her. Her hair's shorter. Neater and not as wild as I remember. There's an air of seriousness and maturity around her.

"Rachel, go upstairs," she says to her daughter.

*Our daughter?*

The girl's gaze darts between the two of us. "Are you sure?"

"Go on," Rosie urges without answering the question.

I watch the girl jog up the stairs, a thousand questions burning in my mind.

"Grayson, you're out." Rosie doesn't open the door any wider or invite me inside.

I shove my hands in my pockets. "Tried writing to let you know."

Her jaw tightens. "Why are you here?"

"To see you." I lift my gaze to the staircase inside. "Is she—?"

"No." She cuts me off before I even spit out the question.

All traces of hope unfurling inside me die. "How old is she?" I ask in a harsher tone.

"None of your business," she hisses.

"If she's my kid, it's my business."

Rosie closes her eyes and a defeated sigh eases out of her. Without looking at me, she grabs a coat and steps outside, closing the door behind her. The kind of protective mother I always knew Rose would be.

I take a few steps back to make room, keeping my hands in my pockets so I don't do something stupid like hug her. Doesn't take a genius to recognize that my touch isn't welcome.

"Rachel isn't yours," she says in a low voice. Without meeting my eyes, she flashes her left hand at me. How'd I miss that sparkling wedding set? "She just turned fourteen."

No second chances for us. No do-overs for me.

*Fourteen.*

I don't need to do the calculations. Rosie obviously moved on a *long, long* time ago. Pretty much right around when I went to prison. And here I am, showing up like the ghost of nightmares past on her doorstep.

Fury bubbles up inside me. "Kept cashing those checks Rock sent, though, didn't you?"

"It's the *least* the club could do after everything we went through," she shoots back.

Technically, if she wasn't still my old lady, she wasn't entitled to shit from the club. But it was me who'd asked Rock to keep sending her money long after our divorce was finalized. Probably out of guilt. Rock was honoring my wishes. Got no one to blame but myself.

"Kept sending me those short, shallow letters, too." I always assumed her letters had the bare minimum of information because she knew the guards would read them. Now, I have a clearer picture. She didn't want me knowing anything about her new life. Her new *family*.

"I didn't want you to give up hope," she says.

"So you let me keep on thinking we might have a chance…" I shake my head. I can't decide if it's the kindest thing she could've done or the cruelest.

Without that tiny sliver of hope hanging over my head, who knows what I might have done inside. Or where I would've directed my rage. I committed so many evil deeds just to stay alive. But I might have done worse if she'd snuffed out every last thing I held onto. If I'd thought I had nothing to live for.

Gently, almost tentatively, she places her hand on my arm. "After Rob and I married…I took the money, yes. But I deposited it in a separate account. For you. When you got out. In case the club…wasn't there for you." Her expression turns bitter. "They owe you for everything you lost."

"No one owes me shit, Rosie."

"The money's yours. Just tell me where to send it."

"Keep it." I glance at the house—everything Rosie always wanted and I never had a chance to give her. "Rachel will be going to college soon, right? Use it for that."

I sure as shit won't need to worry about sending any kids to college.

If I still had a heart, I'd say that painful sensation was it shattering into a thousand pieces. "Are you happy?"

"Yes," she whispers.

My throat's so damn tight. "Good," I choke out. That's all I ever wanted for her.

Just once I want to touch her. One final time. I dreamed about touching her so many nights while I was inside. How many mornings did I wake, thinking she was next to me only to have the harsh reality around me shatter the dream as soon as I opened my eyes?

Now I know she was never thinking about me.

I reach out and stoke my knuckles over her cheek. Still as soft as I remember. Instead of flinching or pulling away like I expected, she closes her eyes.

"Is he good to you?" I ask.

"Yes." A tear slips down her cheek. "He's a good husband and father."

That's what she deserves. What *I* planned to be for her. Until my whole life got fucked to hell and back.

To keep myself sane, I'd dreamed of a life with Rosie outside the prison walls. It was foolish. I'd suspected she'd moved on, but still, I'd allowed myself to fantasize about the life we'd have together once I was free. That even if she'd found someone, she'd drop him the second she laid eyes on me again.

Stupid. Childish, even. Prison has a way of reducing every man to using the most rudimentary coping mechanisms.

Those foolish dreams are dead now. Invisible ash crumbling to the ground at our feet.

"Did you ever go back to med school?" I ask.

"No." She shakes her head. "I couldn't."

One of many things I ruined for her. Serves me right. Long ago, I crushed her dreams. Now, it's time for karma to return the favor. I deserve nothing less.

"Take care, Rosie."

"You too, Grayson." She squeezes my hand gently. "I'm happy you're free. Please take care of yourself. Stay on the outside."

Too spent for words, I grunt and shuffle to the truck.

I glance back once, and it's like falling through time.

Rosie standing in the doorway with tears in her eyes, watching me walk away.

Only now, I'm not being shoved into the back of a police car, wearing handcuffs.

I may be free, but the one thing I convinced myself I wanted more than anything is dead.

Time killed everything. Stole every dream I've ever had.

And yet somehow, I'm still breathing.

# CHAPTER TEN

## Serena

*Serena,*
*I need to take care of some things.*
*I'd like to see you later.*
*G.*

Is he serious?

I stare at the note but it doesn't change. A few impersonal words. No apology for running off.

Well, at least I didn't spread my legs for him. I can scurry out of here with most of my dignity.

I yank out my phone. The battery indicator blinks a sad shade of red. But I have enough juice to send Amanda a quick text.

*Me: Leaving in ten. Meet me out front.*

She answers predictably and immediately.

*Amanda: Rav said he'll bring me home.*

Of course. Perfect.

Angry at myself for breaking my own damn rules, and not even getting an orgasm for my troubles, I jerk my sweater off the chair and pull it on. My keys jingle as I scoop my jeans from the floor. I lace up my boots and I'm ready to go.

The upstairs hallway is quiet at this hour. Thank God. Hopefully, I can escape without running into anyone.

*Poor Serena, getting the boot after servicing another brother.*

I growl in frustration and hurry down the stairs as quietly as possible.

A bunch of bodies are passed out in the living room, draped over couches or cushions on the floor. A porn movie flickers over the big-screen television. Thankfully, the sound is muted. No one seems to be awake to even watch it.

I make it outside without encountering a single functioning soul. Thank God.

"Morning, Serena." Hope's soft voice carries through the quiet morning.

My eyes squeeze shut for a second before I force a smile and face her.

She's carrying a beautiful little girl with reddish-gold hair, dazzling eyes, chubby pink cheeks, and a big smile. All wrapped up in some sort of neon-pink fuzzy winter snowsuit. I'd forgotten she and Rock have a daughter.

I choke and blink. A kick to the gut would hurt less.

"Morning," I croak. I can't stop staring at the baby. "I'm not sure you want to go in there with her."

Hope's nose wrinkles. "That bad, huh?"

"Well, there's porn on the television in the living room." I force another smile.

"No," she coos and kisses her daughter's cheek. "We don't need that."

"She's so precious," I murmur.

"Grace, do you want to say hi to Serena?"

Grace waves at me, and my heart melts. "Hi, Grace," I whisper.

"You're not staying for breakfast?" Hope asks.

Old Serena would've stayed and helped out in the kitchen. Anything to prove my loyalty and help the club. "I can't." I gesture toward the driveway but don't offer a reason. "You, uh, didn't see Grinder leave this morning, did you?"

"No, I didn't." Her green eyes flash with sympathy. "I'm sorry."

I don't want her pity. Jesus. Ice-cold embarrassment washes over me. Every time this woman's met me, I've been with a different brother. All right, that's probably an exaggeration, but still.

I shiver and cross my arms over my chest. "We didn't…it's not…"

She shakes her head. "You don't owe me any explanations."

This is why I've liked her since the first time we met. She's always been kind and talked to me like I'm a normal person, not a she-wolf out to devour her man.

She tilts her head toward one of the garages. "Rock and Z are in the garage and you know how that goes." She rolls her eyes but it's said with affection.

"They could be in there 'fixing stuff' all morning," I tease.

She laughs. "Tell me about it."

A throaty engine rumbles out of the garage and rolls to a stop next to us. The driver's side door of a shiny, black SUV swings open and Rock steps out. He kisses his wife's forehead, then scoops the baby out of her arms, holding her close.

"Morning, Serena."

I stand tall and try not to flinch under his intense stare. "Morning."

Hope tips her head back. "Did you see Grinder leave earlier?"

Rock's gaze shifts between Hope and me. "Briefly. He was in a hurry."

In a hurry to get as far away from me as possible? Great.

The disappointment must show on my face. Hope reaches out and touches my arm. A light reassuring touch—nothing more.

The baby fusses and Rock takes her over to the SUV and ducks inside the back seat.

"Well, I should get going." I gesture toward the driveway again.

"Oh. Yes. I didn't mean to hold you up."

"No. No. You didn't." God, the last thing I want to do is be rude to the president's wife. Not that I ever plan to show my face here again.

She gives me a quick hug that almost knocks me off my feet, then jogs over to the truck. Rock grabs her around the waist and carries her to the passenger side. My heart thumps. They're so affectionate with each other, I have to turn away. I follow the driveway around the side of the clubhouse and find my car where I left it last night.

The awkward feelings follow me all the way into Empire, to my tiny apartment.

I don't care how much Amanda begs next time. Or if I think I've made a "connection" with a patient.

I won't break another promise to myself.

# CHAPTER ELEVEN

## Grinder

I'M PRACTICALLY THROWING MYSELF A PITY PARTY AS I FIND MY WAY back to the clubhouse.

Somewhere between Rose's house and the clubhouse, my self-pity turns into anger.

But also a sense of relief.

Rose and I are *done*. That chapter of my story is finished. The ending might have been messy and awkward, but at least it's an *end*.

Finally, after all these years, I have closure.

I'm free to turn the page and draft a new future for myself without years of guilt weighing me down.

The more miles I put between Rose and me, the more peace settles over my mind. I didn't ruin her life. She's fine. Been fine for a long time. Strung me along…

Okay, a few shards of anger remain.

*Focus on the road ahead.*

I don't have to bother with the GPS. The few landmarks easily jump out at me as I return to the clubhouse. Eagerness stirs in my stomach. Desire to see Serena as a completely free man. Free in body *and* heart.

The place isn't as big of a mess as it was when I left. Brothers wave and greet me as I pass them in the living room. I acknowledge each one with a quick hello and keep moving. It's noisier upstairs now. People getting up and moving around. Lotta fucking, too, from the sound of things.

I open my door.

The room's empty.

My shoulders slump.

*Damn.*

Did I just miss her?

I run my fingers over the sheets where I'd left Serena sleeping. Cold. She's been gone a while.

I'm sure my note left a lot to be desired. Jotting "Thanks for warming my bed, I'm off to see my ex-wife now" seemed a bit too personal, so I'd kept my words brief and vague. If I'd waited until she woke to explain, there's a good chance I never would have let her leave the bedroom.

I find the slip of paper wadded up in the trash.

Seems like a sign Serena was hurt or offended. Or maybe straight-up pissed. Wouldn't blame her.

I rake my hands through my hair and turn in a circle. There's no way to get in touch with her. I never asked for her number. Can't even stalk her properly, since I have no idea where she lives.

Lots of people around here seem to know her, though.

*No.* Like fuck am I asking anyone for her number. I can wait patiently until our next appointment on Tuesday. I'll smooth things over with her. Explain myself. Well, maybe not the part about visiting Rose.

Fuck waiting patiently. I'll move my appointment up.

I grab my phone and dial the clinic.

*"You have reached Empire Physical Therapy. The office is currently closed..."*

Of course they're closed on the weekends.

Even though it's considerably nicer, pacing my room reminds me too much of being in a prison cell.

Outside. I'll think better once I get some fresh air.

As I reach for the doorknob, a heap of navy blue wool hanging on the back of my door stops me cold.

Serena's coat.

Jesus Christ, it freezing outside. Was she in such a hurry to leave that she forgot it? Or was she planning to return?

Feeling like a pervert, I grab it off the hook. Smells like her. Soft, flowery, and clean.

Examining her coat without her here feels too intimate. But I do it anyway. It's shabby and worn. A hole in one sleeve. Another hole in the right pocket. A few dimes and nickels rattle around in the other pocket. I shove my hand in and pull out the change, a tube of lip balm, and a card for a hair appointment three months ago. The salon's actually out in Johnsonville near the apartment the club rented for me. Maybe she lives out that way?

For fuck's sake, what's my end game? Stalking her at her hair salon? *Fucking pathetic.*

I jam the stuff back in her pocket and drop the coat on the hook again. I'll bring it with me to our next appointment.

Downstairs is empty now, except for Rock. Sitting back and relaxed like a fucking emperor observing his empire.

Whether he happened to be here or he's waiting around for me, I'm not sure. I can take a guess, though. For some reason, his presence pisses me off. My irritation over my visit to Rose returns with a vengeance.

"Did you know?" I ask, thundering down the last few steps.

He cocks his head and answers slowly. "Know what?"

"That Rosie moved on years ago. Married. Had a kid."

He drops his head and mutters, "Fuck."

"So you knew?"

"I *suspected*." He drills me with a narrow-eyed glare. "She made it clear she didn't want me coming around, Gray. Threatened to call the cops if I did."

"Shit, really?" Rosie was pretty pissed back then. Wouldn't put it past her.

"Yeah, and I didn't need the hassle while *I* was on parole." He spreads his hands in front of him. "If you remember, I had enough club business to deal with. You were adamant that I keep sending her money, so I did. She cashed the checks; I never looked any deeper than that."

He's right. It wasn't his job to spy on my wife. He did what I asked. Some MC presidents would've made warming their bed a condition of sending any money. I knew Rock would never do that.

It's my own fault. The minute those divorce papers went through, I should've told him to stop paying her. Guilt wouldn't allow me to make that call.

I drop down on the couch next to him so we're facing each other at an angle. "Sorry."

"Don't apologize." The grief in his eyes rakes over me like jagged stones.

"Stop giving me pity eyes, you little fuck," I growl.

A slight smirk curls his lips. "It's not pity, ya old fuck."

Now we're back on familiar ground.

"And there's nothing *little* about me," he adds.

"You'll always be little to me, Rock. Sorry."

He shakes his head, laughing. "Missed you, Gray. Felt it every day. Hated leaving you behind."

"I know," I say quietly. "You did good, though. Proud of you."

"I'm so damn glad you're here to see it. I used to—" He snaps his mouth shut and it doesn't take a genius to know what he was about to say.

"Worry I wouldn't make it out alive?"

"Sometimes, yeah."

"I'm here. No plans on going back."

"I won't let you go back," he says solemnly. "Sorry I didn't visit more."

"You came when you could. Did everything I asked. I know what a pain in the balls it was to get cleared to see me." I fake a smile. "Since we were partners in crime and all."

Truth was, sometimes his visits made everything worse. Only reminded me of what I couldn't have. But I don't want to lay any more guilt on his shoulders. He carries a heavy enough load.

"She got married?" Rock winces. "Has a family?"

"Yeah, and dumb fuck that I am, I actually thought the kid might be mine."

He frowns.

"She's a teenager."

His jaw tightens. "I should've told you what you wanted to hear but stopped sending her money."

"I'll repay the club."

"That's not what I meant."

"Fifteen years is a long damn time to expect a woman to wait." Now that the fantasy's been shattered, the pain isn't as sharp as I expected. "I'm disappointed, but I don't blame her for moving on."

He's not ready to let it go. "She could've told you."

I shrug. "The divorce was a pretty big fucking hint."

"Glad you managed to keep your sense of humor." He stands and motions for me to follow him into the war room.

No one else is in there. I step up to the chair at the head of the table, running my hand over the carved wood. "I still can't believe you kept this thing."

He stares at it for a few beats. "It reminds me to never become like him."

"Figured that's why you still had it." So he could mentally flog himself every time he looks at it. I slap the back of the chair. "That's exactly why you're the one who should be sitting at the head of the table."

He grunts a noise of agreement. Yeah, he wasn't asking for my opinion on the matter. Still thought he needed to hear it.

He pulls an envelope out of a drawer. My hackles rise. "I ain't taking any more cash from you."

"It's not from *me*. It's club earnings. And you'll take your share." He points upstairs. "Or you can hand over your cut right now."

"Christ, you're a pushy prick," I grumble, taking the envelope and stuffing it in my pocket. "Does this mean the other brothers are taking a smaller share of earnings? I don't want to cause any hardships."

"Gray, everyone understands the hardship *you've* been through. The sacrifices you've made for all of us. If someone has a complaint, they can take it up with me."

"Yeah, 'cause you seem so calm and reasonable."

"I have my moments." He pulls out two glasses and a bottle of scotch.

"None for me." I hold up one hand. "Don't know what to expect next time I check in with my P.O."

He doesn't call me a pussy or try to convince me. Just nods and pours one for himself before gesturing toward the table.

Someone knocks on the door and both of us turn. Z pushes his way inside without waiting for an answer or invitation. "Hey, G. I was hoping you'd be around."

"Yeah? Why's that?"

He has the nerve to pat my cheek like a baby's rump. "I've missed this gruff face and luxurious beard. Wanna soak it all in while I'm here."

I snarl and slap his hand away. "Knock it off, you cocky fuck."

"Still a ray of sunshine, I see." Z shakes his head and grins at Rock.

Always the serious one of their comedy show, Rock doesn't crack a smile. Just gives Z the ol' stare and blink.

When we're all seated, Rock sits forward, lacing his fingers together and resting his arms on the table. "Tell me if there's anything I can do for you."

"Same," Z says, all traces of playfulness wiped from his expression. "We want to help. Anything you need, brother."

"I owe you an apology." I nod at Z. "Went to see Rose this morning. You were right. I shouldn't have bothered."

While Z always enjoyed being a comedian, whenever shit got real, he was the first one there to support a brother. That hasn't changed. "Ah, shit. I'm sorry to hear that, brother."

I shrug as if it hadn't left a mark. "I shouldn't have been surprised."

"Well, you're free to go to Crystal Ball with the rest of the guys tonight." Z grins.

"Yeah," I answer slowly. "That's the last fucking form of entertainment I need."

Rock ducks his head and laughs.

I turn my glare his way. "What's so funny, chuckles?"

"Nothing. Anyone else woulda been side-stage at the first opportunity."

"Yeah, is that where *you* went last time you got out?"

"Nah." Z flicks his hand toward the rest of the clubhouse. "He marched up those stairs and fucked the curl out of his wife's hair."

Rock slowly turns and stares at Z. "The fuck is wrong with you?"

Z spreads his hands in front of him, the picture of innocence. "What? You think Grinder's surprised or something?"

"Or something," I mutter.

"What I meant was, now that Rose is out of the picture"—Z again gestures toward the clubhouse—"find a bunny and make sure everything still works before you try settling down with someone new."

"Thanks for the sage advice, dickwad," I grumble. "The girls you got hanging around here ain't gonna be interested in someone old enough to be their grandpa. For fuck's sake, you do your recruitin' at the high schools now?"

"Please." Z dismisses that with an eye roll. "You're a biker." He sweeps his gaze over me. "According to Lilly, you're what the ladies call a 'silver fox.'"

"Seriously?" Rock mutters.

"I'm just saying," Z continues. "Muffler bunnies wanna fuck bikers. Period. Your forecast is full of panties dropping with a high chance of blow jobs."

"That's precious," I grumble.

"Do you have some sort of problem you need to discuss with us?" Rock asks Z.

Z reaches under the table—to do fuck only knows what—and squeezes his eyes shut. "Lilly's almost ovulating or whatever, and she asked me to conserve...well, you know. I'm a bit wound up."

That's probably the last thing I expected to ever come out of Z's mouth. And I would've been perfectly fine if it never had.

"I'm sorry I asked." Rock shakes his head. "If you're done handing out dick-wetting suggestions..." Rock raises an eyebrow at Z, who wisely remains silent, before turning to me. "Don't hesitate to let us know if you need something—besides a trip to Crystal Ball. You can arrange *that* with Dex." He jerks his head toward Z. "Or clogged drain over here."

I bite out a laugh. "I'm more than taken care of." I hesitate. Rock might not like this next part, but I refuse to hide things from my brothers. "Although, there are a few guys inside I'll probably send some cash to." I pat my pocket, indicating the money he gave me earlier.

Rock and Z freeze. The tension in the room turns thick enough to suffocate.

Rock narrows his eyes. "Anyone you're close to?"

I don't blame either of them for questioning where my loyalties might have wandered. Lost Kings have no other incarcerated brothers. They know damn well that to protect myself, I would've had to make some shady alliances. "It's not *debts* I owe. No one who's gettin' out anytime soon or looking for me. No deals I'm supposed to broker on the outside for any other organization." I'd been careful to extract myself from any ongoing obligations and ensure things were in good hands before I left the joint. It was a delicate dance between the two worlds but I'd never put my club in danger.

Rock's severe expression doesn't change at my explanation. Z shifts his gaze to Rock, then back to me, as if waiting for more details.

"Just some brothers who helped me survive," I add. "Who don't have anyone on the outside, the way I did, to take care of them."

"Sure." Rock blows out a breath, finally satisfied. "You're a good man. Most would forget and move on."

"I can't do that."

He nods. "I know."

We're quiet for a few beats. My mind returns to Serena. Holding her. Waking up with her. Leaving the note and ducking out on her was a cowardly move. I need to fix that. Move forward with my life.

Most of all, I need to silence the ghosts that followed me out of prison.

"There *is* one thing maybe you guys can help me with," I say quietly.

"Anything," Z says.

"Club still got someone who does their ink?"

"Bronze," Rock answers. "Remember him? He set up a shop around here a couple years ago."

"No shit?" I trace the collar of my shirt, tugging at it, unsure. "Inside, I got a few pieces added to my collection I'd really like to get rid of, have covered up, or something…"

"Ah, fuck," Rock sighs. "I'm sorry, Gray."

"It is what it is." I shrug. "I just want 'em off my body."

"How many?" Z asks.

"Just the two. I moved up quick enough. No one got around to inking my fucking face." I finally tug the collar of my shirt down to show off the crude prison ink.

"Fuck," Z breathes out.

"Yeah, prison was tons of fun. I don't recommend it."

"Sorry, brother."

I turn to Rock. "Can Bronze be trusted? Lotta artists don't like working with ex-cons. Or he might be hooked up with some guys on the inside…"

Rock's expression hardens to steel. "Like fuck are any of those scumbags threatening you," he spits out. His hands curl into fists. "We might not have been able to protect you inside, but—"

"We will fucking *slaughter* any motherfucker who tries to come after you," Z finishes.

I swallow hard, grateful to be back in the company of my true brothers.

Their thoughts seem to have run off in a murderous direction. I tap the table in front of them to recapture their attention. "You *did* protect me inside. The money helped. Your connections made my time when I returned to the Pine facility a lot smoother. Don't act like you tossed me to the lions and walked away."

"It feels like it," Rock says.

I slap my hand over the tattoo. "Just help me get this gone." Another thought smacks me upside the head. "I wanna get Rosie's name off me too." I press my hand over my heart. No need to carry memories of her on my body now. She'll stay in the past where she belongs.

Z sits forward and motions for me to pull my shirt to the side again. "What do you want to do?" he asks, squinting at the pieces. "Remove them or cover with something else?"

"Probably cover." I gesture to the Lost Kings emblems on my chest and arm. "Want to get these touched up where they're fading. A few other things."

Z runs one hand over his own colorful arm. "Bronze is solid. I trust him. Hundred percent. He's been working on covering some scars for Lilly and he's been great with her." He glances at Rock.

Rock's narrow-eyed glare suggests he's still hellbent on a killing spree but he snaps out of it when he notices we're both focused on him.

"I've got a kid working for me at the shop. Carter. Teller's soon-to-be brother-in-law. He's a talented artist. Got him helping with the paint jobs Bricks can't keep up with," he explains. "He had an interest in tattooing. Started an apprenticeship with Bronze." He rolls up his sleeve and points out what looks like a recently inked owl on his inner bicep. "I let him experiment on me for his first piece."

"Damn." I lean closer to get a better look. The design is both realistic and artistic. Vibrant and colorful. "Some experiment." I huff out a wry laugh and run my fingers over my throat. "Funny, that's what you picked. I kind of had an owl throat piece in mind."

"Perfect for our wise old owl," Z quips.

"Watch it." I shoot a glare at him. "I *will* gut you, pretty boy."

Z chuckles at the threat. "Carter's a cool dude. Plus, he's terrified of Rock, so you'll be in good hands with him. Or I can take you to Bronze's studio. See if he has any openings."

"All right. I'd like to see your bike shop, too, Rock."

"Any time." Rock nods. "Honestly, I could use another welder if you have any plans to go back to that."

"Jesus, I wouldn't even know…" It's not like I had the opportunity to keep my skills sharp at the Supermax.

"No hurry. No pressure." Rock waves his hands in front of him. "Just know it's an option."

"Thanks, brother."

A soft tap at the slightly ajar war room door draws our attention and halts our conversation.

Rock's tense expression relaxes into a smile. "Hey, baby doll. You can come in."

Hope sweeps into the room, her adoring eyes skipping from Rock to me. "How are you, Grinder?"

"Any day on the outside is better than the best day inside."

She winces, then gives me a soft smile. "I can't imagine." She lifts her chin. "Hey, Z."

"We were talking about you earlier." He grins at her.

"I'm sure you were." Her lips twitch as if she's fighting off a smile. They seem to have an easy, affectionate friendship. Nothing like the animosity Rock's first wife displayed toward the brothers every time she got near the clubhouse.

Rock shoots a glare at Z, then pulls Hope into his lap. She leans over, resting her hand over mine. "If you need anything, please let me know."

"Thanks, sweetheart." I lift my chin. "I was telling these two, I have a few people on the inside I'd like to send money. Keep their accounts flush like Rock always did for me. But I'm not sure if an ex-con's allowed to do that."

Her pretty face screws into a thoughtful pout. "I don't know a lot about post-release, but I can certainly look into it for you." She turns, studying Rock's face. When he doesn't offer any objection, she returns her attention to me. "If not, we'll figure a way to get the money where you want it to go. Between Charlotte and me, we'll devise a plan."

She may *seem* soft, but the woman's confident and determined. Already searching for ways to break the rules. Got some grit under that sweet exterior. Bet she keeps Rock on his toes. "Thank you."

Rock's busy running his hands up and down her back. Not even sure he's still paying attention to the conversation.

"Well…" Z stands and thumps his hand against the table. "I gotta go. Let me know what you want to do about that thing." He taps his chest. "We'll get you set up one way or another."

"Thanks." I shake his outstretched hand, and he pats my back on his way out.

"Where's the little one?" I ask Hope.

"With Heidi." Her lips curve up. "She owes us oodles of babysitting time."

"Damn." I sit back and shake my head. "I think she's the one who drove home how much time has passed the most."

"I bet," Hope says. "I've only known her since she was fifteen and can't believe how much she's changed and grown up." She clears her throat and turns toward Rock again. I can't see the face she makes at him, but Rock's shoulders lift slightly.

"Serena asked about you this morning." Hope's bright green eyes settle on me again. "I ran into her when she was leaving."

I swallow hard. "You did, huh? Was she upset?"

*Do I even want the answer to that question?*

"Not really." She tilts her head, as if she's trying to remember every moment of the interaction to give me an accurate report. "Flustered, maybe."

Murphy pushes the door open and Hope's mouth snaps shut. He hesitates, his gaze shifting between the three of us. "Am I allowed to join the family meeting?"

Rock snorts. "Get in here. Where's knucklehead?"

He jerks his thumb over his shoulder. "Garage."

I study Murphy carefully for a few seconds. "Never mind Heidi.

This one, right here, has aged me the worst," I say to Hope. "You know he barely had some scraggly chin pubes when I went inside. Now, he looks like a lumberjack who got lost in the woods for a few months."

Murphy rumbles with laughter as he makes his way around the table. He slaps my arm before dropping into the chair on my left. "I'd call bullshit, but you're probably right."

"I know I'm right."

There's another brief knock at the door and Teller nudges it open.

"He still can't grow a beard." Murphy gestures to his best friend.

Teller flips him off. Good to see things haven't changed too much between them.

"What's up?" Teller drops into a chair on the other side of the table.

"You see Wrath out there?" Rock asks.

"You're like a shepherd searching for all his sheep, ain't ya?" I ask.

Rock smirks. "Feels like herding turtles half the time."

"He ain't looking *that* hard," Teller says. "Too busy groping his wife."

Hope reaches over and playfully swats at him. He grins at her, and I get the sense it's a common shared joke.

"Stop picking on Mom and Dad," Murphy teases.

Oh, Rock must *love* them calling him *Dad*.

Serves him right. Little shit used to razz my ass by calling *me* Dad. Got Wrath and Z callin' me that too. Karma sure is a wonderful bitch.

The playful grin slides off Teller's face. "How's it going, Grinder?"

"Fine. Stop looking at me like the Reaper's gonna show up on my doorstep any day."

"Great, you're as cheery as he is." He tilts his head toward Rock.

"Where'd you think he learned the art of being a sarcastic bastard, son?"

Rock busts up laughing.

"My husband certainly has a gift for wry humor," Hope says with a teasing smile.

"No patience for bullshit," Murphy adds. "Ours, or anyone else's."

Rock glances at Murphy. "And yet, you two test my patience every day."

"What'd I do now?" Murphy asks.

I rumble with laughter until I'm wheezing.

Rock's eyes narrow. "What's so funny?"

"Nothing at all, brother." I glance around the room, a warmth growing in my chest. "It's good to be back."

## CHAPTER TWELVE
### Serena

"Serena!" Lucy calls.

Damn, I wanted to make it to my office without anyone seeing me. I'm not technically late since I don't have any appointments until ten. But I should've been here about twenty minutes ago.

Still shivering since, in my quest to do as many stupid things as possible over the weekend, I left my damn coat at the clubhouse, I unwrap my scarf and tuck it in my bag. "Morning." I beam a pleasant smile at our receptionist and try to act casual.

She stands and leans over her desk. "One of your patients is here." She glances down at a file. "Grayson Lock? He called, and I told him you didn't have any openings, but he was very insistent that he had to see you." She jerks her head discreetly to the right and I turn, following her line of sight.

Grayson.

Perfect posture. Elbows casually leaning on the arms of the chair.

The full force of his dark gaze focused on me.

How did I miss him when I walked inside?

"Gr—Mr. Lock. What are you doing here?" I almost stumble over my sneakers. This is too weird—my weekend life and my work life colliding.

*He was your patient first.*

He clutches his shoulder. "Been giving me trouble." His expression is calm, unreadable.

"I—uh, okay. Follow me." I stop to grab his file from Lucy and march to my office to drop off my things. The thin carpet mutes our steps, but I'm keenly aware of Grayson's large body so close behind me.

"In here," I say, gesturing to my office so he doesn't crash into me when I stop. I push my door open and he's hot on my tail, following me inside. As if he didn't want me to leave him waiting in the hallway.

I scurry behind my desk and stash my purse in the bottom drawer. Standing up straight, I unzip my hooded sweatshirt and drape it over the back of my chair.

"You forgot this." Grayson holds out a white plastic shopping bag.

My eyes widen as I reach for it. "My coat." I lift my gaze, meeting his eyes. "Thank you."

I shake it out of the bag and move past him to hang it on the back of my door.

"It's got holes in it," he says.

Embarrassment heats my face. My shoulders jerk. "Spring will be here soon enough. I'll buy a new one next season." Feeling bold and maybe a little annoyed, I finally meet his eyes. "Thanks for your concern about my wardrobe, though."

His mouth tilts to one side. "Why'd you leave the other morning?"

I push the door closed and face him. "I told you, I could lose my job." My gaze darts to the door as if my boss has her ear pressed up against the thin particle board.

He steps closer. Too close. I'm forced to back up until my shoulder blades press into the wall. It's not a threatening move, though. More cozy or intimate. "Yeah, you mentioned that. Then you slept in my bed anyway."

My cheeks are absolutely roasting now. "Shh, please."

"Can I take you out?"

"Out? Where?"

He sighs and steps away, jamming his hands in his pockets. "It wasn't my intention to ambush you at your job, Serena. I didn't know how else to get in touch with you, though."

Unsure of what to say, I lift my shoulders again.

"That's it?" He mimics my shrug. "That's all you got?"

"What do you want me to say? You ducked out of your own room so you didn't have to wake up with me. Do you have any idea how awkward I—" I raise my hands in front of me. "You know what? It doesn't matter. I made a mistake. Let's start over and keep this professional. Otherwise, you'll need to find a new therapist."

"Serena." He sighs my name like a prayer. "I wanted to wake up with you. But I had something I needed to take care of."

"Club business?" Lord knows I've heard that excuse many, many times.

"No. Something personal."

"Please tell me you're not married." Not again. What is it with bikers who cheat on their wives? Thank God I didn't screw him.

"I'm not married. Anymore." He runs his hand over his chin and down his throat. "She divorced me while I was incarcerated."

"Oh," I whisper. It clearly bothers him to share such a painful detail. That he does it anyway melts some of my hesitation.

"Look, it's been a while. I'm bad at this." He steps closer. "I don't know what I'm doing." He strokes his knuckles over my cheek. "But I like you. And I want to know you better."

"Why?"

"You need a reason why I like you?"

"You don't even know me."

The corner of his mouth hitches again. "Yeah, that's where that whole 'I want to know you better' comes into play."

"There seemed to be plenty of girls at the clubhouse the other night who wanted to know *you* better."

"Maybe. But they weren't you."

My gaze lands on the clock behind him. "Shoot. I have another patient coming in half an hour."

His fists clench at his sides, but he seems more angry with himself than me. "I didn't mean to fuck up your whole day."

"You didn't."

"What time are you finished?"

"Not until seven. It's my late night."

He scowls as if my schedule bothers him and gestures toward the window. "You're running around in that parking lot out there by yourself after dark?"

I snort-laugh. "Well, I don't fly home."

He doesn't crack a smile.

"There's a security guard." I don't want to explain that I live in a seedy part of Empire. Walking through the parking lot is a breeze compared to the sprint to my apartment door.

"I'd like to take you to dinner."

My lips curl up. "Are you asking me to dinner or just stating a fact?"

"Are you always this difficult?"

I almost blurt out, *"You already know I'm easy."* Thank God, I catch myself.

"Will you have dinner with me tonight?" he asks.

"Sure. Where?"

He blows out a frustrated breath and rubs his hand over his cheek. "Unfortunately, I don't know what's around anymore. What's your favorite place?"

I'm too embarrassed to reveal I don't go out to dinner often. And if I do, it's somewhere cheap and quick. "Taco Bell?"

He scowls. "Somewhere nicer than *that*."

I fight off a smile. How can he be so gruff and kind at the same time? "Uh, the Stonewall Cafe is supposed to be nice. I haven't been there in a while though."

"That sounds good."

"It's not too far from here." But it *is* someplace I know none of my co-workers would usually go.

"I'll follow you, if you don't want to leave your car here."

"Okay. I, uh, have to work tomorrow."

"I'll have you home before midnight." He steps closer, again raising his hand to gently cup my cheek. I'm already getting addicted to his touch. "That sound good?"

"Yes," I whisper.

"I promise to do my homework and find a nice place next time."

"Next time?" I raise my eyebrows. "What if I'm a terrible dinner date?"

"I doubt that. I'm the one who should be worried." A slight frown creases his forehead. "I haven't quite adjusted…yet." The first note of doubt seems to chip at his confident exterior. It only makes my heart flutter faster.

"Seven, then?" he asks.

"Probably like seven-ten."

His mouth pulls into a full grin. "Seven-ten it is."

His gaze drops to my lips, lingering like a gentle caress. For the briefest second, I think he might kiss me. At his sides, his hands ball into fists, then he reaches for the door.

"Oh, I'm sorry." My brain returns to normal function. "We didn't even get to—"

"It's not a problem."

"Are you okay, though?"

A cocksure smile spreads over his face. "Better than okay, now."

"Did you…did you…*lie* to Lucy just to see me?"

"*Lie* is such a strong word, Serena."

He went to a lot of trouble to bring me my coat and ask me to dinner. Maybe he had a good reason for ditching me the other morning and genuinely wants to make it up to me.

Or maybe I'm an idiot for believing anything that comes out of a biker's mouth.

## CHAPTER THIRTEEN
### Grinder

"Stand by the wall and take your shirt off."

The powers that be will probably frown on me for stabbing my parole officer.

"Excuse me?"

"You get any new ink?" My parole officer lifts his hand in the air several times, as if that'll encourage me to strip faster. I unbutton my shirt slowly as I step toward the plain white wall.

Prison already snatched my freedom and dignity away. Why should parole be any different?

"Yeah," I answer slowly. Was I supposed to send him an announcement or something? He didn't mention it the other day when he lazily went over the conditions of my parole. And I'm not about to volunteer information unless asked.

What changed between the last visit and today?

"They're not gang-related, are they?" he asks.

"Never been part of a gang," I answer, swallowing my irritation, "so no."

"Yeah. Right. Lost Kings are a *club*, I forgot." His voice drips with surly sarcasm.

As I slide the shirt off, my gaze lands on a fist-sized dent in the drywall. Did someone aim for Hank's head? The mental image curves my lips. Fucker sure deserves it. He give everyone this attitude, or am I special?

"T-shirt too," he orders.

*Jesus Christ. Give me a minute.*

Twenty years ago, younger me would've cracked a joke about buying me dinner first. Or cracked him in the jaw. Depending on my mood.

I lift the shirt over my head and scan my immediate area for a place to hang the two pieces. Nothing. I lean over and toss 'em on the chair with my coat.

"Need to document the new pieces." His voice grows closer. Every muscle in my body tightens, preparing to defend myself.

I point at one on my bicep. Bronze had done a decent job covering up the crude prison mark. I still wanted to add more to the design but at least I didn't feel like a walking advertisement for the dregs of society. "This one."

He stares at me too long for my comfort, then walks back to his desk and studies my file. "You cover something up?"

"Yeah."

I watch him from the corner of my eye as he picks up the file and his camera, slowly returning to my side.

He glances at the photos inside the folder and again at my arm. A slow smirk curls his upper lip. "What's the matter? Didn't want your biker buddies knowing you made other friends inside?"

I grind my teeth to keep my mouth shut.

"Turn for me."

Hating every second of following his orders, I shuffle around until I'm facing him. Chin up. Blank stare, straight ahead.

"That it?" he asks. "Do I need you to drop your pants next?"

I tap one by my neck and he gets way too close to snap a picture. "That's it."

"Plans for more?" His cheek twitches as he studies my chest and arms.

I touch the *"Rosie"* scrawled in black ink over my heart. "Planning to cover this later in the week."

"Aww." He pulls a taunting sad face. "What's wrong? Wifey didn't welcome you home with open arms?"

Done with this bullshit, I rest my hands on my hips and cock my head. "Tell me something, Grillo. If I get my ol' lady's name inked on my dick, you gonna stroke me off so you can get a nice, clear picture for your photo album?"

"Put your shirt on, Lock. We're done."

Thank fuck.

"Take a seat." He points to the chair as if I'm too senile to locate it.

So much for being done.

I dress quickly and perch my ass on the edge of the uncomfortable metal-framed chair. Swear to fuck it sways under my weight. Must be one of Grillo's mind tricks to keep his parolees off balance—literally and figuratively.

"Where'd you get the money for the ink?" he asks.

Seriously? That's what he's worried about? "Guy who did 'em likes to help ex-cons cover their prison ink. Does it at a reduced rate."

"Got a name?"

I rattle off the name of Bronze's shop—which *does* actually offer free ink to ex-cons. Doubtful Bronze will open up about his clients to anyone asking questions; I'm not worried about Grillo verifying my story.

"How's the job?"

"Headed there right after we finish." *So, if we could speed this up, that'd be great.* Not sure how the fuck I'm supposed to remain "*gainfully employed*" when I gotta take time off to deal with this bullshit.

"Keeping curfew?"

"Yeah. Not exactly lots to do in Johnsonville."

"No socializing with other criminals?"

"No." I don't think of *my family* as criminals, so this isn't a lie.

"No contact with anyone inside?"

"Why the fuck would I do that?"

He shrugs. "I take it that's a no."

"Got no reason to talk to anyone inside. I just want to move forward with my life."

He stares at me for a few beats too long for my liking. "All right. Go on. See you in a few days."

"Can't wait." I grab my coat and get the hell out of his office.

As I pull into the parking lot behind Strike Back Studio, my gaze lands on Wrath's royal blue GMC Denali 2500 with the star emblem in the center of its heavy-duty, matte black front grille.

Shit, he's got his own business to run and he's stuck sitting around here waiting on me.

By the time I gather my stuff, he's standing outside my door.

"Thanks for waiting for me." I step out of the truck and slam the door. "Meeting took longer than I expected."

"Not a problem." He pulls me in for a quick one-armed hug. "I'll wait as long as you need me to, brother."

"Thanks," I mumble.

"Everything go all right?"

Not in the mood to whine about my parole officer being mean to me, I just nod.

Wrath swings the simple metal and glass door open wide and motions for me to go inside ahead of him.

The short hallway consists of light, shiny hardwood floors, leading to a larger area with a reception desk.

Classy place for a gym. Guess that's why it's called a *studio* instead.

Blue floor mats cover the rest of the area. Full length mirrors take up three walls. Beyond the reception area, I glimpse another room that seems to have more traditional weights and machines.

I peer up at Wrath. "Nice place."

"He's worked hard to build it up. You'll like Sully." He lifts his chin at the short woman behind the counter. "And his girl."

"Hey, pixie." Wrath's lips curl up as he approaches her.

She lifts her head and grins, hurrying out from behind the counter.

"Hey, Wrath." Her gaze lands on me and she smiles even wider. "Welcome."

"Grayson Lock, this is Aubrey Dorado. Sully would be lost without her. Aubrey, this is a good friend of mine, Grayson."

Tiny woman. Big smile. Warm eyes. She holds out her hand for me to shake. "So happy to meet you."

"Thank you." I shake her hand quickly. Careful not to crush it.

"I know Sully's looking forward to meeting you." She turns and motions for us to follow her. We don't get far before she stops and knocks on one of the closed doors to our right. She pushes it open without waiting for an answer.

The office is less glamorous than the rest of the place. Seems like the guy puts all his effort into the business and doesn't waste money on frivolous bullshit for himself. I respect that.

The broad-shouldered, dark-haired guy behind the desk stands. All serious. No warm, sunny smiles, like his girlfriend. He nods to her. "Thanks, Aubrey."

She touches my arm lightly. "See you in a bit," she whispers, before ducking out and closing the door behind her.

"Wrath." The guy walks around the side of his desk and nods. He holds his hand out to me and I shake it.

"Sullivan Wallace," he introduces himself.

Wrath runs through the introductions again, making sure to work in that I'm a friend. As opposed to some random ex-con he plucked off the street, I guess.

Sullivan nods to the two chairs in front of his desk.

I glance at Wrath and then the door. But the fucker can't or won't take a hint. He ignores me and plops his bulky frame into the farthest chair. Apparently he's committed to this whole dropping-grandpa-off-at-his-first-day-of-work thing we're doing.

Sullivan focuses on me. "Wrath says you need a job?"

I thought this was a done deal.

Wrath sits forward.

"Yes. It's a condition of my parole. That gonna be all right with you?" Might as well be direct.

"That's not a problem." His gaze strays to Wrath for a second. "We could use some help around here. Cleaning up. Keeping things neat. Towels replenished, stuff like that. A couple days a week."

Wrath opens his mouth and I stop him with a hand on his arm.

"Sounds good," I answer. "I can do all of that, no problem."

Sullivan blows out a breath and his shoulders crawl away from his ears. "Great." He stands and holds out his hand again. "Welcome to the Strike Back team. I'll have Aubrey get you a shirt and we can talk about what hours work for you."

"Thank you." I grip his hand. "Appreciate it."

The relief of having a purpose, a job to do, no matter how small, is immense and not something I take for granted.

# CHAPTER FOURTEEN

## Serena

*Your past is behind you. Your future is uncertain. All you have is the now.*

I save the Insta quote to reread later. Maybe I'll print it out and post it on my mirror.

Even though I try to concentrate on work for the rest of the day, Grayson slips into my mind frequently.

My stomach flutters with excitement each time I realize I'll see him tonight.

Seven can't come soon enough.

It's not until about six-thirty, when I'm finishing up paperwork, that it dawns on me that I have nothing to change into. Stonewall Cafe isn't fancy. From what I remember, it's a place where a lot of young professionals stop on their way home from work.

All I keep stored here are some gym clothes for nights I use the workout room. At least I have makeup in my purse.

After finishing my work for the day, I spend a few minutes in the bathroom fixing my face, and brushing my hair smooth from its ponytail prison.

My dorky work polo shirt sort of ruins the look but I can't do much about it now.

Grayson's waiting outside on the sidewalk when I emerge from the building. My greedy eyes gobble every inch of him as I hurry my steps. Rugged and handsome. *He* had time to go home and change into a crisp flannel shirt. He's still casual, though, so we won't look too odd together.

"Hi." I glance over my shoulder, praying no one sees me meeting one of my patients after work.

"I would've come in to meet you, but..." He raises an eyebrow.

"Yeah, that wouldn't have been good." I quickly scan the parking lot. But, yeah, I have no idea what his vehicle looks like.

"I'm over here." He gestures toward the corner of the parking lot farthest from my building.

"My car's right by that lamp post. Let me drop this off." I point to my car and hold up my tote bag.

He's quiet while I open the back door and toss the bag inside.

"Do you want to take separate cars?" he asks.

"No. As long as you don't mind dropping me off here later."

His warm smile makes me feel like I made the right choice. "Not at all."

More silence on the way to his truck. Is he as nervous as I am? Or worried someone will see us? Regretting asking me out? He's a completely closed book to me.

We stop at a black Ford pickup truck, many years newer than my car. Recently paroled or not, Grayson seems to be doing okay for himself.

He opens my door and offers his hand to help me step into the truck. Heat crackles over my skin when our fingers connect. I stare at him but his face is shadowy from the weak, yellow parking lot lights.

"Thank you." I hoist myself into the seat and he closes my door.

*Deep breath. Why am I so nervous?*

His door swings open, bringing a swirl of cold air inside the cab of the truck. He presses the unlock button and opens the back door. Curious, I peer into the back. He pulls a large white box off the seat and slams the door shut.

"This is for you," he says, sliding into the driver's side and holding out the box to me.

"For me?" I grasp the bulky package and set it in my lap.

"It's not gonna bite you," he says, staring at my hands.

I carefully pry the lid off. Grayson reaches for the interior light and flicks it on so I can see better.

A bright, sapphire-blue ski jacket's nestled inside the box under layers of tissue paper.

I gasp and run my fingers over the material.

"You bought me...a *coat*?" My throat's so tight, I barely get the words out. No one's ever done something this *nice* for me. My own mother didn't care if I had warm clothes to go to school in. Growing up, I spent many, many mornings freezing my butt off at the bus stop.

I barely know Grayson. And yet, he did this sweet thing for me.

He clears his throat and shifts in his seat. "If you don't like it, I can..."

"No. I love it. Really." I unfold it from the box and squeeze it to my chest. It's a brand name I'd never be able to afford. Tags dangle from the sleeve, but someone blacked the price out with a marker.

Grayson reaches over and digs through the tissue paper in the box. "The girl put a gift receipt in there somewhere—"

"I'm not returning it, Grayson."

"It's the same size as your other coat, so I hope it fits."

"I think it will." I'm eager to try it on so he won't worry. I open my door and hop out. Quickly, I shimmy out of my ratty wool coat and toss it on the passenger seat. I unzip the new jacket, noting the double layers of insulation and water-resistant outer shell. I slip it on, and it fits perfectly. No more getting wet and cold this winter.

Grayson's boots crunch over the pavement as he walks around the truck and meets me at the open door. "I hope you like the color. Your other one was blue, so..."

"I love it." I trace my fingers over the sporty hot pink reflective stripe running along the sleeve. "It's really pretty."

The first true smile of the night softens his face.

"Thank you so much, Grayson. You didn't have to do this, though. It had to be expensive."

He shrugs as if the cost doesn't matter. "I wanted to do something to make up for leaving the other morning."

My throat tightens, choking off a response. "You didn't have to," I whisper.

He rests his hand on my shoulder. "Wear it in good health, Serena."

It's such a formal thing to say, and it turns my mouth up. "I will."

"You must be hungry after working all day. Let's go eat."

My grin stretches even wider. "Okay. But let me pay for dinner. You've—"

His harsh bark of laughter cuts me off. "Fuck no."

I think I insulted him. But I try again. "It's only fair…"

"It's not happening," he says in a gruffer tone. "Get in the truck."

I scoot into the truck.

He slams my door shut and walks around the front.

Worried he's mad at me now, I twist my fingers together in my lap.

But he's calm and relaxed as he fires up the engine and backs out of the spot. At the exit for the parking lot, he reaches over and rests his hand on my leg. "Which way, sweetheart?"

"Oh, turn right." I breathe out a sigh of relief and relax. "Another right at the third stoplight."

"How was your day?" His mouth quirks. "After I ambushed you."

His teasing tone further relaxes me and my own lips curve. "Not bad. Yours?"

"Started my new job." He laughs softly. "Sort of. Got the smackdown from my parole officer."

"What do you mean? Why?"

"Nothing much. Just the stay out of trouble, no robbing banks or running wild after curfew lecture." He flashes a tight smile.

The reminder that he's on parole sobers me up. I appreciate his honesty, though. "How long will you have to deal with that?"

"About a year. If they don't toss me back inside for some reason."

"Oh." I'm not sure how else to respond. "That must be very stressful."

He shrugs, almost like he wishes he hadn't brought it up. "Sucks, because I'm not supposed to be around the club." His hands tighten on the steering wheel. "Parole doesn't care that they're the only family I have."

"I'd never...I wouldn't tell anyone."

He glances over. "I didn't think you would."

"That seems like a silly rule, anyway. Don't you need a lot of... support once you get out? You know, to avoid going back *in*?"

He chuckles. "You would think so. But the revolving door keeps the money coming, you know?"

"Sure. So, where is your job?"

"Strike Back Studio. It's a gym out near—"

"Johnsonville. I know the place. The owner offers self-defense classes at a reduced rate."

He lifts an eyebrow. "Someone bothering you?"

I stare out the window. "A girl living on her own can never be too careful."

He grunts in acknowledgment but doesn't say anything. He flips on the blinker and guides the truck onto the narrow, one-way street.

I point out the windshield. "It's ahead on the right. They have a parking lot but it's tiny."

"Got it."

We're lucky and someone's pulling out of a spot a few doors down from the cafe so there's no need to venture into the parking lot.

After shutting off the truck, he turns to me. "Wait there."

A few seconds later, he opens my door and holds out his hand. "Watch the ice," he says.

My heart's melting into a puddle at his concern. The sidewalk's slippery and he grips my hand securely, navigating the icy pavement ahead of me. At the restaurant, he holds the door open and motions for me to go ahead.

The hostess shows us to a small table right inside the door.

"Do you have anything in the back?" Grayson asks, gesturing to a corner table.

"Sure," she answers, whirling around and marching away. We

follow and Grayson pulls out one of the chairs for me and takes the seat tucked in the corner where he has a full view of the room.

The tables are packed with men and women in business suits. Loud laughter and conversation rings out over the clatter of pots and pans coming from the swinging kitchen doors. Every few seconds, Grayson stops studying the menu and scans the other tables.

"Sorry, I didn't think it'd be so noisy on a weeknight," I say, hating that he seems so uncomfortable.

"The noise doesn't bother me," he answers in a gruffer tone than usual.

His hot-and-cold attitude leaves me fidgety and unsure. One minute, he's gently guiding me over the icy sidewalk; the next, he looks ready to run.

I study my menu, seeing but not comprehending the words on the page. *Deep breath. Focus.*

"I haven't seen this much avocado on a menu since the Eighties," Grayson mutters.

I chuckle. "I think it's made a big comeback."

His mouth quirks.

"Now that you said it, I kind of want to try the avocado fries."

This time I get a chuckle out of him. "Order whatever you want."

"What can I get you to drink?" our waitress asks, startling me out of my review of the menu.

"Sparkling water with a slice of lemon," I answer.

Grayson asks for the same. Interesting. I thought for sure he'd order beer.

"We're ready to order too," he says, raising an eyebrow at me to confirm, and I nod as the waitress turns to me.

"Ah…" I scan the menu again quickly. "The avocado fries and the Muther Clucker Chicken Sandwich."

"The Kentucky Bourbon Burger." Grayson hands our menus to our waitress. "Thank you."

When we're alone again, he slides his hands over the table and rests them on my side. Warm and rough, his big hands completely engulf mine. "Are you sure you didn't want anything to drink? Wine or something, I mean."

"I'm not much of a drinker."

He nods. I can't tell if he has any thoughts or feelings on the subject or if it's just another piece of information about me he's collecting.

"Are you still planning to tell me why you took off the other morning?" I ask quietly. Old Serena never would've dared ask that question. She would've accepted what little crumbs of attention were given to her. I squirm in my seat, uncomfortable that I asked, but needing to know.

He lets out a long, slow breath and stares at our intertwined hands.

"I like you a lot, Serena." He lifts his gaze, meeting my eyes.

"I like you too. Otherwise, I wouldn't be risking my job to see you outside of work."

His upper lip curls as if that's an inconvenient fact he'd forgotten. "Now that I've had time to think it over, it was stupid."

I wait quietly for him to continue. What was stupid? Asking me out? Leaving me the other morning? Or something that has nothing to do with me?

"Inside, hanging onto your sanity is a challenge sometimes," he begins in a distant tone. "Long hours. Day in. Day out. It never ends. Nothing to look forward to."

Unsure of what to say, I squeeze his hands, hoping he'll continue.

He sighs. "You let your mind wander but not too much or you might not get it back." He flashes a pained smile. "But when you're not busy trying to survive, you try to focus on the future. Reflect on your mistakes. Think about how to become a better person when you get out."

"Sure. That makes sense."

"I was married when I was sentenced."

*Shit, shit, shit.* His words land on me like a pile of bricks.

I withdraw my hands, resting them under the table in my lap. He doesn't react to my withdrawal.

"We're divorced, Serena. I wouldn't lie about that." He taps the side of his head. "But one of those things I held onto while I was planning my future was getting back together with her."

"And?"

"I met you."

*Huh?* I lean in and tilt my head. "I feel like you skipped some key pieces of information."

He shifts his jaw from side to side. "I didn't go see her right away. But having you show up to the clubhouse the other night, when all I'd been doing was thinking about you, lit a fire under my ass."

"To go see…your ex-*wife?*" I say slowly.

He plows through my sarcasm. "I wanted to be sure…before I started anything with you."

I can't decide if what he did was honorable. I appreciate his honesty but the feeling that I'm some sort of consolation prize creeps into my mind. "And?" I prompt.

"Nothing. She's remarried. Has a kid. A nice house in the suburbs." He waves his hand dismissively but I sense the hurt underneath his words.

"Here's your avocado fries!" Our waitress appears at the side of our table and plops a plate piled high with Parmesan-crusted avocado pieces and chipotle dipping sauce in the middle of the table, then sets down our drinks. "The rest of your order will be out in a few minutes."

Ignoring or not noticing the tension at our table, she stands there beaming at us, waiting for further instructions.

"Thank you," Grayson says without taking his eyes off me.

She spins on her heel, her high ponytail swishing as she bounces away.

I take a second to collect my thoughts.

"So, if she hadn't been married, you wouldn't be here with me right now?" I've been second to last my whole life. Never anyone's priority. Why does it still surprise me? "Is that what you're trying to explain?"

"She forgot me a long time ago."

"That's not what I asked." *Dammit.* I might have made a heap of mistakes, but I'm trying to learn from at least some of them. "I don't want to be a rebound or a transition in someone's life."

"Is that what you think this is?" He doesn't say it like a challenge—more like he's genuinely questioning it himself.

"You tell me." I dip one of the fries into the creamy sauce and take a big bite. That'll stop me from saying anything else.

He sighs and glances down at his plate. "I don't know. I probably have no business with you. You're too damn young. You have a career. I'm still trying to adjust and figure my shit out. I'm an ex-con with not a lot to offer you."

I swallow and take a long sip of my water. "But?"

A confident, bordering on cocky smile curls his lips. "Obviously, I'm *very* bad at doing the right thing."

I snort and almost choke on my water. "I'm familiar with the concept."

"I can't picture you doing anything wrong."

"You need a better imagination, then." I push the plate of fries closer to him. "Try one?"

He studies them for a long time before picking one up, dipping it in the sauce, and taking a bite.

"Here ya go!" Our waitress returns and sets our dinners in front of each of us.

I slide the fries to the side to make room and ask for another water before she skips off again.

"I couldn't stop thinking about you after our first appointment, Serena." Grayson seems eager to return to our conversation.

"Was I the first woman you encountered after…getting out?"

He scowls at the question. "No. Plenty of females hang around the club."

I barely hold back my eye roll at the word *females*.

"You showing up at the clubhouse seemed like a sign that it was time for me to close the door on my past and move forward with my future."

Is he trying to say he sees *me* as his future? I take a deep breath. Admitting this could open a Pandora's box of questions I won't be comfortable answering. "I came to the clubhouse hoping to run into you."

"How'd you know I'd be there?"

I reach over and push up his sleeve, tracing my finger over the Lost Kings tattoo on his arm.

His mouth curves up. "So you felt something too?"

"I did." He's either too polite to ask the natural follow-up question or he doesn't want the answer. Unattached women don't normally hang out at MC clubhouses unless they're there to fuck the members. I would've had to have been to the clubhouse before or known someone to be invited. Recently paroled or not, he has to know that.

Yet, he doesn't ask about my relationship to the club. Or how I found my way to one of their parties so easily.

Over dinner doesn't seem like the right place to bring it up.

So, I don't.

The future may be uncertain, but even *I* know that, eventually, the truth will take a big bite out of my ass.

# CHAPTER FIFTEEN
## Grinder

D<small>AMN</small>, I <small>NEVER THOUGHT</small> I'<small>D LIKE A WOMAN TELLING ME EXACTLY</small> what's on her mind so much.

Serena doesn't hold back. Challenges me to give her answers I haven't even thought about. Confront some harsh truths.

And she felt this attraction from the beginning too.

By the end of our meal, I'm jonesing to get out of this joint. It's loud and crowded. Lots of annoying people jammed into an unfamiliar space. Too many frou-frou items on the menu. Things with weird ingredients that don't belong in bar food.

I've never felt more alien. Out of place. Old as *fuck*.

Serena doesn't seem to notice that I stick out like a polar bear at a tea party. And I'm not about to draw attention to or complain about my unease. I'll suck it up. Adjusting to life outside is its own special hell. Tonight is tolerable only because of her presence.

We split a slice of chocolate cake for dessert. Watching Serena lick the thick frosting off her fork lights a fire in me that takes considerable effort to control.

She pauses, sips her water, and lets out a delicate yawn, covering her mouth.

"You have an early day tomorrow?" I ask.

"I do."

I'm one hell of an inconsiderate prick. Poor girl didn't have time to go home, change, and do all the stuff women like doing before a date. And now I'm keeping her out late. "I sprung this on you last minute, didn't I?" I can't bring myself to apologize. Not when I'm enjoying her company so much.

"That's okay."

By the time we're ready to leave, the place has quieted down. Serena eyes the check when the waitress drops it off.

"Don't even think about it," I warn her, snatching it up and pulling out my wallet. It'd be a cold day in hell before I let my woman pay for dinner.

"I don't mind splitting—"

I growl at the suggestion. "What did I say?"

"Okay."

Fuck, I probably offended her. She works, has her own money, I guess. Girls her age expect to pay their own way, don't they?

Nah, I can't do it.

Outside, she curls her fingers around mine. "Thank you."

"You're welcome."

I'm not ready to say good night to her, and I find myself driving slower than normal on the way back to her car.

A few scattered vehicles remain in the lot. I pull into a spot next to her car and put the truck in park but leave it running. I pull out my phone. "Think I can get your number?" I jerk my chin toward her office. "So I don't have to ambush you again?"

"Sure." She pulls the phone out of my hand and in a blur of speedy little thumbs, she programs her number into my phone, and calls it so she has my number. Thank fuck. It would've probably taken me the next fifteen minutes to figure all that out.

I set the phone on the console and reach for her. My shoulder protests the movement and I hiss out a pained breath.

"Are you okay?" she asks softly.

"I'm fine. Just probably overdid it today."

She unbuckles her seat belt with a soft click. "You can tell me the truth."

"It's no worse than it's been."

She reaches over and kneads her thumb against a tight spot I didn't even realize I had. My body tenses from the pain but slowly relaxes as she continues, following a line of tension from my shoulder to the base of my skull.

"Everything's connected," she whispers.

"Come closer." I reach down to adjust the seat but it's already pushed to its limit to accommodate my long frame.

Her hand remains on my shoulder, but she's stopped rubbing. "Come closer, where? Your lap?"

I pat my thigh. "Sure."

A hint of a smile flickers over her lips. She crawls to my side, her head carefully tilted to the side to avoid bumping it, and awkwardly hovers over me for a few seconds.

My heart hammers hard enough to fill the cab.

I clamp my hands over her hips and pull her into my lap. The weight of her feels so right against me.

"There. That's better." I've been aching to have her close all night.

She rests her hands at my shoulders, her thumbs moving in circles against my neck. A pleasurable sensation, bordering on ticklish. I can't ask her to stop though. Love the way she touches me.

My entire body enjoys having her heat soaking into me. A little *too* much. I shift, trying to relieve the gathering pressure in my groin.

She gasps and pushes her hips forward, pressing right into my growing erection.

"Easy," I groan. Fifteen years of pent-up frustration. She does that again, I might explode all over the truck.

I run my hands over her thighs and hips.

"Grayson?" She rests her palms on my cheeks. I lift my gaze to her questioning eyes. "Why won't you kiss me?"

*Because I'm afraid I won't stop.*

Instead of answering, I cup the back of her head and drag her closer. Her soft lips yield perfectly. The first taste of my sweet girl unchains my soul. Craving more, I thrust my tongue between her lips and gently stroke, overdosing on her taste.

Drugs have never been an issue for me, but I could easily get addicted to the rush of kissing Serena.

Her whole body melts into mine. Her hands slide to my chest, her fingers twisting in my shirt like she's holding on for dear life.

All my senses vibrate with the need for more. I wrap my arms around her completely, molding our bodies together.

She moans into my mouth and wiggles closer. I squeeze her tighter and deepen the kiss.

Jesus, I haven't made out in a car with a girl since I was in high school. But my body hasn't forgotten how. If I concentrate on her and shut out everything else, I can almost recapture the same thrill and forget the lifetime of baggage weighing me down.

Her hands drop to my waist and tug at my belt.

I reach down and pry her fingers loose. "Not here. Not in the truck."

She pushes her lips into the sweetest pout. "Do you want to come home with me?"

*More than anything.* But if I get up in her personal space, I might not leave. I cup her cheek and rub my thumb against her bottom lip. "Not tonight, buttercup."

Through the dim lighting, I catch pink spreading over her cheeks. Shit, this is the second time I've turned her down. No wonder she had so many questions.

"Sorry," she mumbles, pushing away from me.

"Stop," I order.

She freezes.

"It's not that I don't *want* to." Fuck, I want so much from her. But I'm also enjoying discovering her and rediscovering myself. Our first frantic kisses. First touches. I want to savor every memory and sensation. Burn them into my soul. My curiosity and desire to know her—*really* know her—rages harder than my lust.

"Then why?" Her voice is so fragile—scared even.

"Because when I finally have you, you're going to need a few days to recover."

She chuckles.

"I'm not kidding."

For whatever reason, that seems to reassure her instead of scare her away. She falls against me, wrapping her body around mine the best she can in the tight space. I stroke my fingers through her hair. So soft, silky, and thick. I want to bury my face in it and shut out the rest of the world.

"Grayson?" she mumbles against my shoulder. "What do you want me to call you? Would you rather I use your road name?"

It's nice to be called by more than a number, or my personal favorite, "inmate," again. "I like the way you say my name. Gray is fine too."

"Okay."

"Anything but 'sir,'" I add. "I already feel too damn old around you."

She laughs softly. "Yes, sir."

"Smart aleck." I slide my hands down and squeeze her ass. Such a perfect handful.

When she doesn't release me, I pat her behind again. "Come on, buttercup. It's almost turn-into-a-pumpkin o'clock."

She pulls away and tilts her head to the side. "Why buttercup?"

I trace my finger along her jawline. "Those little yellow flowers are one of the first signs of spring. And that's how you make me feel. Like my heart and body are thawing after a long, bleak winter."

Her lips part but she sits there staring at me without saying a word.

I shift my gaze to the window. Maybe that was too much information to share too soon. Normally, I believe in economy of words. Speaking freely is a good way to wind up in trouble.

"You should've been a poet, Gray."

"Maybe in another lifetime."

Carefully, she extracts herself from my lap and climbs into her seat.

She leans over and presses her lips to my cheek. Fast and hard. "I had a really nice time tonight," she whispers.

"Same here." I twist a lock of her hair around my finger and tug gently. "I like when your hair's down."

"Thanks. I do too." She slides out of the truck and smiles up at me before slamming the door shut.

I press the button to open the passenger side window.

"Serena," I call after her.

She stops and turns, her hand on her car door handle.

"It's late. I'm going to follow you home. To make sure you get inside safely. Promise I'm not stalking you."

Her lips part and her eyes widen. She doesn't say anything, though. What the hell kind of men has she had in her life? That I want to make sure she's safe shouldn't shock her so much.

Or maybe she's worried I'm a creep, and she doesn't want me to know where she lives.

Fuck, why is all of this so damn complicated?

# CHAPTER SIXTEEN

## Serena

I DODGE PEOPLE ON THE SIDEWALK AND HURRY INTO THE STARBUCKS across from Empire Med. I glance at my phone for the time and find a *Where are you?* text from Emily.

I scan the crowded room then spot her at a table near the back, waving frantically. My lips curve as I take in her bright red polka dot dress paired with a black cardigan and wide, shiny black belt. She looks like a mashup of a 50s pin-up girl and Minnie Mouse.

"Girl, I was just about to leave." She jumps up and hugs me. "I haven't seen you since before Christmas. How are you?"

"Good." Breathless, I fall into the chair across from her. "Shoot. I should go order. It's busy."

"I ordered two coffees. I hope that's okay."

"You didn't have to do that, but thank you." I gesture toward the counter. "Do you want me to grab muffins or something?"

She shakes her head, her sleek red bob gently shimmering with the movement. "No carbs for me."

"Em-er-ee!" one of the baristas shouts. "Two coffees for Emery!"

"Good grief," Emily moans. "Every time." She jumps up and hurries to the counter.

While I'm alone, I slip off my coat and tuck it into the chair next to me. I can't shake the paranoia that someone in the crowded cafe will spill coffee on it, ruining the nicest gift I've ever received.

Emily returns, setting two steaming cups in the middle of the table. "I poured cream in both." She tosses a variety of sweeteners on the table. "Couldn't remember what you use, though."

I sift through, searching for monk fruit, and grin when I find it. "Thank you."

The rich, caramelized, nutty scent fills my nose as I lift the cup for my first tentative sip.

"Perfect." I wrap my hands around my cup to warm them.

"So, what's been going on?" Her gaze slides sideways. "I like the new jacket."

I reach over and pet it like it's my security blanket. "Thanks."

She leans in, peering at me closely. "What's that face?"

"Nothing."

"Something's up. Spill."

We haven't been friends for years like Amanda and I have been. But Emily knows me way too well.

My life's been too chaotic to maintain many friendships. I have exactly two besties and they move in separate orbits. Amanda's the friend of my past club girl days. We've done a lot together. Used to want the same things—or so I thought. Sometimes I think we're still friends only out of familiarity and obligation.

Emily's my role model friend. She's who I'd like to see future me become. I'm sort of stuck in between—who I used to be and who I want to be.

The stubborn part of me, here in the present, doesn't want to share any information about Grayson with Emily. She won't approve, and I want to keep him all to myself. But I also want to talk it through with someone who knows some of what I've been through.

"I think I've met someone I really like," I say into my coffee cup.

"Really?" Her voice rises. "Tell me more."

Where to begin? "Well, he's a new patient of mine."

She waves that off. "He can find another therapist. True love shouldn't be stopped by petty rules."

"They're not petty," I protest, even though I keep breaking them myself. *Hypocrite, thy name is Serena.*

"He's a bit older," I confess.

Her eyes narrow. "Define 'a bit.'"

I blurt out a ballpark number. Her eyes widen for a second, then she settles into a Cheshire cat grin. "*Hello,* Daddy."

"Eww, no."

She twists in her chair to pat her own ass. "Spank me, Daddy. I've been a *very, very* bad girl."

"Jesus, will you knock it off?" I scold in a hushed tone, casting a furtive glance around the cafe. Maybe I need to search for a new role model. "People are looking at you."

She drops the sex kitten act and shrugs. "So what?"

"Anyway." I drum my nails against the table. "He's sort of part of the same organization my last ex was part of." *Can I even call Shadow an ex?*

"Oh, shit, Serena, seriously?"

I've never mentioned *motorcycle club* or the Lost Kings MC to her specifically, but she understands the broad strokes.

"I thought you were done being used by bad boys?"

"Well, he's definitely *not* a boy. Besides, it's not like that. I met him as my patient first. It's coincidence." *Or divine, cosmic interference.*

"How'd you never meet him before?"

"Uh, well, that's probably the most complicated part. He was just released from prison."

She stares.

I squirm.

It sounds so bad when I say it out loud.

"Serena, I say this with love, but you deserve better."

"You don't even know him. He's very…kind."

"He's such a nice guy that he was sent to *prison*?"

"Yes."

"All right." She touches her fingertips to her temples. "Open mind. Tell me all of it."

I give her bits and pieces, including that he was once married, and end with our dinner date and the coat.

"He bought you a coat?" Emily stares at my jacket in disbelief. "How strangely romantic."

I run my hand over the sleeve. "No one's ever done anything so sweet for me before."

"And he *didn't* expect you to hop into bed with him?"

My cheeks heat and I stare at my coffee cup. "No. Actually, he's turned me down twice now."

"Serena." She sighs. "I thought we made a pact. No dick jumping until—"

"I know. I know. Six months." An evil grin twitches at the corners of my mouth. "I couldn't help it. He's really hot."

"For an old guy?"

"For *any* man."

"Don't get mad." She holds out her hands like a traffic cop, looks both ways, then leans in. "What if he's put you off because of *erectile dysfunction?*"

My cheeks burn. "I don't think *that's* the problem."

"How can you tell, if he won't…"

"Because I was in his lap and could feel—"

"Oh, my." She slaps her hand over her mouth. "Scandalous."

"Will you be serious for one second?"

"Yes, yes. Sorry." She raises her eyebrows several times. "Tell me more."

"If I didn't have his medical info, I would've thought he was in his forties." I squeeze my bicep. "He's pretty built."

Her eyelids flutter shut. "God, I love a man with nicely defined arms."

"His arms are more than *nice*. Everything about him is fine as hell."

"What about the forearms? There is nothing sexier than a man rolling up his sleeves and showing off that wrist to elbow area." She drags her fingers along her own arm. "A manly man with arms that look strong enough to easily build me some bookshelves or toss me over his shoulder."

I burst out laughing. "Okay. That's random."

She shrugs. "What? I like *functional* masculinity. Plus big arms equal better protector."

"I *do* feel safe around him," I say quietly.

"Well, that's a start." Her voice softens. "He's nice to you? No red flags?"

"Not yet."

"Heavy drinking?" she asks.

"I haven't seen him drink *any* alcohol yet." I wait patiently. She's going to list an entire checklist of red flags we've come up with for our future dating prospects.

"He's not pressuring you for sex." She taps her finger against her chin. "None of that negging bullshit?"

"No, he compliments me often. He's kind." I can't fight another smile. "Gentle, even."

"A gentle ex-con," she muses. "Well, he's not one of those macho pigs who's too manly to let a female medical professional treat him. That alone speaks well of him."

"That's true. I sure get plenty of so-called upstanding men who are rude and dismissive."

"Oh God, did you get rid of the one who mansplained physical therapy to you every time?"

"Yes, thank God."

"Continue."

"Nothing—you're right. He listened and followed my directions. Took me seriously." My lips curve. "Although, he definitely didn't want to let on how much pain he was in—"

She wrinkles her nose and waves that off with a flick of her wrist. "But that's most guys."

"Right."

"He was honest with you about his wife," she continues. "That shows good character. Wanting to wrap things up with *her* before seeing where things might go with *you*."

"Once I'd had time to think about it, I thought so too." I pick up the empty sweetener packets and shred them into confetti. "Not like you-know-who, when I didn't even find out he was married until—"

"Don't go there." She waves her hand in front of me like a magic wand. "That's in the past. You've learned, and you're moving on."

*With another biker when I swore I'd never go near one again.*

"Anyway," she sighs. "It's still too early to tell. Just keep your eyes open."

"I am."

"You don't sound so sure."

"I'm worried *I'm* not healthy enough to be in a relationship yet."

"Then it's good that you're taking things slow." A sly smile spreads over her face. "Now, I have a favor to ask."

Wary but amused, I wait with a raised eyebrow.

"Libby's school play is coming up and I promised to help her sell some tickets."

My grin widens, and I laugh as I pick up my coffee cup. Libby's even more dramatic than her big sister. "Is this the one she has a lead role in?"

"Yup." She presses her hands together in prayer. "Please come."

"Of course I will."

"I swear, these kids are *so* good. You won't think they're high school performers."

I laugh even harder. "You can stop with the hard sell. I already said I'll go."

She squeezes her hands together and squees like she's closer to her sister's age than mine. "I'll buy the tickets. I just need bodies in the seats."

"You've got it."

"Maybe," she sing-songs with a wicked glint in her eyes, "you can bring your boyfriend so I can check him out."

"Oh my God." I drop my forehead to the table. "I can't ask him to do that."

"Why not? It's a fun date," she says with a hint of snark in her voice. "You can tell stories for years to come about how you fell in love during Johnsonville High's stirring performance of *Peter and the Star Catcher.*"

"What's it about?"

"A boy who won't grow up."

"Great," I groan.

My phone buzzes, and I flip it over and catch the time. Shoot, it's almost time to go back to work. A text pops up.

*Grayson: Thinking of you. Hope you're having a good day.*

"Is it him?" Emily cranes her neck to peer at my phone.

"Yes." I spin it around before she breaks something and let her read the note.

"Aw. He's direct but sweet."

"That's how I'd describe him."

She jumps out of her chair and skirts the table, leaning in to wrap me up in a fierce hug. "Remember, fear imprisons us. Maybe not behind bars. But it cripples."

I sigh and hug her back. "I know all about that."

"I know you do, sweetie." She pulls away and returns to her chair. "Be smart, go into this with your eyes open, but don't let fear rule your life."

## CHAPTER SEVENTEEN
### Grinder

"A SCHOOL PLAY?" I'M TOO SHOCKED AND AMUSED TO THINK OF another response.

On the other end of the phone, Serena sighs. "You don't have to. I'm sorry—"

"No, no." Anything sounds good, as long as I'm not rotting away in a cell. Sitting next to Serena all night sounds damn near close to heaven. "I'll go with you."

"Really?"

"Just tell me where and when."

🔒

I HADN'T BEEN THRILLED THE NIGHT I FOLLOWED HER HOME AND FOUND out she lives in one of the shittiest areas of Empire. Not the cutesy rundown look of the historic brownstones near the capitol building. No, these are the seriously rundown brownstones on the outskirts of the city. Hers is the nicest building on the block but it's kinda like saying the fifth circle of hell is cooler than the seventh. You're still in hell.

I park in front of her building and send her a text to let her know I'm coming up.

*Serena: Second floor.*

Well, I guess that's better than the first, where anyone could crawl in the street-level window.

Front door's busted and hanging ajar. *Great security.* Looks like there's an intercom. Doubt it's worked since the Seventies. At least there are no names on the mailboxes to advertise to the world she's a woman living alone.

I push my way inside and stare at the long, dark wooden staircase, then the rest of the area. Looks like two apartments down here. The lighting is so dim Serena wouldn't have a chance of seeing someone waiting for her until it was too late.

This ain't right.

At least the stairs are sturdy and in good shape. The ancient tiles on the second-floor landing have seen better days. So dirty it's hard to tell if they're supposed to be white or brown. There's only one door on this floor.

I knock.

"Hang on!" she shouts from inside.

A click and slide later, she opens the door wide.

Fuck, that smile.

To see me.

*All mine.*

"Hi!" She smiles wide and waves me inside with one hand while fussing with an earring with the other.

I scoop her into my arms and press my lips to hers. She lets out a soft sound of surprise, but recovers fast. Wrapping her arms around me, she clings tight while I kick the door closed.

"I missed you, buttercup. Been a rough week," I say, then take another taste. Haven't even seen what she's wearing yet. Feels like a dress. I turn and pin her to the door, hiking the fabric up her legs, skimming my fingers over the thin netting covering her thighs.

Using me for leverage, she raises her legs, wrapping them around my waist, drawing me close to her center.

"That's right," I whisper against her lips.

"Gray." Her voice is raw and desperate. "Please."

"What?" My hands reach her hips under her dress. Pantyhose? Whatever's in my way feels thin and easy to rip. I pull away, staring at her flushed cheeks and smeared lipstick. I swipe a hand across my mouth and come away with red-stained fingers.

"Oh no." She laughs softly. "Sorry. I should've waited until *after* you got here to finish my lipstick." She gets her feet under her and takes my hand. "I have something that will take that off."

Despite the shabby exterior of the building, her apartment's nice. Painted a soft gray with pink and pale blue accents, it suits Serena. There are lots of lamps glowing with a warm, low light. Worn hardwood floors that have seen better days. A beat up sectional couch breaks up the living room space. There's no television, but an entertainment center piled with books and small cardboard boxes.

She leads me down a short hallway and into a room. Hundreds of white, twinkly lights cascade down the entire wall to my left. Pink, gauzy curtains are attached to the wall and held back to resemble a window, I guess. To the right, she has a long white table with a bunch of drawers along the wall. Little clear plastic drawers and containers brimming with stuff are scattered over every surface. A white square mirror with dozens of light bulbs surrounding it is secured to the wall. A laptop, tiny tripod, and camera are set up on the table.

"You, uh, making home movies here?" Jesus, according to Ravage, girls make their own porn at home these days. I can't picture Serena doing that, though.

"Oh." Flustered, she rushes over to the table and picks up a large, clear bottle of liquid. "Sort of. I do some beauty vlogging when I'm not working."

"Beauty what?"

"Video blogging?"

I'm still lost.

She uncaps the bottle and squirts some of the liquid onto a white, cotton square. As she advances toward me, I realize whatever she's got is meant for me.

"Uh, what're you doing?" I wrap my hand around her wrist, holding her at bay.

"Wiping this off you." She shakes loose of my hold. "Unless you'd like to go out with unicorn blood smeared over your chin?"

"Pardon me?"

Laughing softly, she dabs and swipes the cool, cotton pad over my bottom lip and chin. "Got it." She shows me the pad, then tosses it in the wastebasket by her desk.

Finally, I'm able to take her in. And, fuck is she a knockout. Tall black boots that lace up the front hug her calves. I was right—black pantyhose with some sort of pattern cover her legs. A plaid, wool jumper-dress flares out and stops mid-thigh. A black turtleneck underneath sets off her fair complexion.

"God, you're beautiful," I breathe out.

Her red-stained lips twist into a mischievous smirk. "Since we're going back to high school, I pulled out my schoolgirl dress." She grabs the edges of the skirt and dips forward.

I groan. "No schoolgirl jokes. I feel old enough around you."

She runs her hands over her hair. "I almost wore pigtails."

This time, I growl. "No pigtails, please."

More laughter. Like fucking music, and I never want to change the channel.

She points at her feet. "I went with Doc Martens instead of Mary Janes."

"Good." I tug her close again and cast a look around the room. "Where do you sleep?"

She points toward the wall with all the lights. "My bedroom."

"You have a two-bedroom apartment by yourself?"

Her jaw clenches. "I lived with roommates for years and couldn't stand it anymore." She flaps her hands toward the desk. "I wanted a separate space for my makeup stuff."

"You need all that for your *makeup*?" I've noticed she wears a lot when she's not at work, but a whole room for it?

She rolls her eyes. "For my vlog. It's my side hustle."

"Like a part-time job?"

"Sort of." She pulls away from me. "I'm trying to dig my way out of debt and it brings in extra money."

I don't understand the connection. "But you're a professional. In a medical job."

"Yes," she says slowly, clearly irritated. "And it cost money to get my degree. Lots and lots that I now have to pay back. Plus, I had a few years where I was dumb and lived on credit cards, then defaulted on them, so I've been working hard to clear that up. I'd like to be able to buy my own house someday."

She lifts her chin, daring me to criticize her. "If I keep going, I should be debt-free by my thirtieth birthday," she adds, obviously proud.

Can't fault her for working hard. "Where's your family?" I ask gently. It's about time I got to know more about her than the way she makes *me* feel.

Her gaze darts to the side. "I don't have any, really. I went to live with my grandmother when I was fourteen. She died when I was seventeen." She coughs and drops her gaze to the carpet. "I couldn't live with my uncle or go back to my mom's, so I've been on my own since then."

"Hey, come here." I reach for her but her feet stay planted where they are. "You've been alone since you were seventeen?"

She lifts her shoulders slightly. "I'm used to it," she answers stiffly.

"Yeah, I see that." I understand it better than she probably thinks.

I curl my arms around her but her posture's still rigid. "Will you finish the tour for me?" I gesture toward her laptop and camera. "You'll have to explain the *vlogging* thing to me later. When you've got a few spare hours."

She giggles and leans her forehead against my chest. "It's not that complicated." She curls her fingers around mine and leads me into the hallway.

Her bedroom's similar to the rest of the place. Soft gray, pink, blue, and mint-green hues. Lots of fluffy, candy-colored pillows scattered over her bed. Feminine. Soft. Pretty. Like her.

A curious sort of jealousy rakes over me. Has she had any other men in that bed? "So, you've never had any roommates here?"

Her brow wrinkles. "Here? No. I mean, my friend Amanda crashes here sometimes—" She stops and tilts her head. "What are you asking?"

"Nothing. It doesn't seem like a safe building, that's all."

Indignation flares in her eyes and she opens her mouth, probably to protest.

"Downstairs door was open. Looks like it's broken," I say before she has a chance to argue.

Her shoulders relax and she nods. "Yeah, it's been that way for a while."

I follow her back to the living room. Two-bedroom or not, it's actually a small space. The kitchen's off to the side, only distinguished by a strip of cheap metal to transition between the hardwood floor of the living room and the aging linoleum in the kitchen.

"I should've asked, do you want something to drink?" she calls out.

"No, thanks." I wander into the kitchen. Small fridge, one counter, stove, and a double sink, although one side's taken up by a rack with one plate, one glass, a coffee cup, and one set of utensils. A small square table with two chairs takes up the extra space. One of the chairs is piled high with laundry she hasn't folded yet. Not only does she live alone, but it looks like she wants to *keep* it that way.

For some reason, she's decided to let me in. Bit by bit.

And I intend to stay.

## Serena

I love my apartment.

Sure, it's in a seedy part of the city. It's small and outdated. But it's mine. No roommates to annoy and endanger me. No one to haggle with over the bills.

With the windows shut, some aromatherapy candles burning, and a few fans running for white noise, it turns into my peaceful little sanctuary.

Now, anxiety simmers inside me. Having Grayson examine my home twists my stomach into knots. It almost feels too intimate and familiar. But at the same time, it's nice to let someone in who genuinely seems to care.

At the door to my apartment, he studies the locks. "Would you be offended if I reinforced these?" He pulls at the doorknob, jiggles it around, and studies the slot for the deadbolt.

"I...I'd have to get my landlord's permission, I think."

"Seriously? Ain't too concerned about that front door. Doubt he'll notice a few new locks."

"A few, huh?"

He knocks his knuckles against the area around the doorknob. "Like to reinforce this, too, if not change the whole door out."

I stare at him, completely baffled. "My. Whole. Door?"

"All the locks in the world won't do much good if a ten-year-old can kick it open by hitting a weak spot."

"I'm going to have nightmares now."

His hard expression softens, and he reaches for me. "Sorry. I'm not trying to scare you." He hesitates and glances away. "Don't forget, I just spent fifteen years socializing with the worst of society. I know all too well how they think. How they choose the people they prey upon. That's all."

I'm overcome with the urge to hug him. I slide my arms around his waist and squeeze. His clean, crisp scent wraps around me, adding another layer of affection to all the things I already feel for him. He returns the embrace and kisses the top of my head.

"What's this for, buttercup?" he murmurs.

"I hate thinking of you surrounded by so many bad people."

He hugs me a little tighter. "I never said *I* was a good guy."

That's true. He didn't. I've never even asked what he went to prison for. Honestly, I don't want to know. The only thing that matters is how he treats me *today*, not who he was fifteen years ago.

"I think you're a good man," I whisper.

"That's all I care about." He pulls away slowly. "We're going to be late if we don't leave soon."

Damn. I can't let Emily down. I nod to the door. "You can examine it later."

"Later, huh?" His lips curve into a teasing smile.

"Yes, later." I laugh and slip my arm through his.

"Thought we'd stop by my place after the play. It's not far. If that's all right with you?" he asks.

"Sure."

He leads the way down the stairs, shielding my body as if he's worried snipers might be hidden in the shadowy foyer and beyond.

Outside, he stands on the stoop. His head turns left and right, slowly studying the area before he continues to the car. The neighborhood's not great, but it's not a war zone. Still, I'm charmed by his concern.

"Are you sure you're okay with this tonight?" I ask as he holds open the passenger side door. I keep the skirt of my dress pressed to my legs as I step up into the truck.

"Yes." He waits until I'm belted in before closing my door and jogging around to the other side.

"I know a high school play isn't the sexiest date," I continue once we're on the road.

He turns and quickly sweeps his gaze over me, his eyes lingering on my legs. "I beg to differ."

"You know what I mean. I *have* to go. Emily's a good friend. Her sister's adorable. She's so talented too. Honest, the shows the school puts on are *so* good. At least, the few I've been to." He's a biker. Probably interested in getting back to the wild clubhouse parties, not attending children's theater. What was I thinking?

"Serena, you don't have to keep selling me on it. Or apologizing. I'm happy just being with you."

Why do those words tighten my throat to the point of pain? I stare out the window and focus on breathing. "I like being with you too," I finally whisper.

"Besides, I just got out of prison. You need to ease me in slow to becoming a refined citizen and stuff."

"What?" I laugh.

"Tonight, high school play. Maybe next month, a Broadway musical. Baby steps."

Uncontrollable laughter bursts out of me. "I can't picture a biker on Broadway."

He shrugs and shoots me a quick grin. "I was never good at conforming to stereotypes."

I pick at a few stray balls of lint on my dress. "I lived in New York City for a while. I did some modeling. Thought I'd try acting eventually."

"I'm not surprised." He glances over again. "You're beautiful."

Heat settles over my skin as his rough-voiced compliment sinks into my brain. "I wasn't tall enough."

"You must be, what, five eight, five nine? That's tall for a woman."

"Five eight. But they wanted you to be five eleven and up." I rest my hands on my hips and squeeze, remembering weigh-ins and long lectures every time I gained an ounce. "I was too 'curvy' for runway work."

"That's absurd. You're a knockout."

His outraged tone and genuine compliment take the chill off hurtful memories. "Anyway, it got too expensive to live down there. I had like a dozen roommates at one point and hated it. No privacy. Lots of sketchy characters. I didn't want to get hooked on drugs to keep my weight down or be up all night. Watched my mom do enough of that," I mutter.

*Whoa. Slow down.* That was a lot to reveal. I snap my mouth shut. Why'd I blurt out all that crap?

"You made a good choice," he says.

"Oh, no." A bitter laugh escapes me. "I made *lots* of bad choices. Bad decisions were my addiction."

"We all do dumb things when we're young." The weight of experience seems to drag his voice down. "Don't beat yourself up forever."

"It's hard sometimes."

"I know," he says quietly.

We're silent until the exit for Johnson County.

"I think I know the way." He points ahead and crooks his index finger. "Left after the toll booth?"

"I don't think it's a toll booth anymore." I point to the sky. "They have the scanners out here now too."

"The fuck?" He peers out the windshield.

I reach forward and tap the E-ZPass glued to his windshield behind the mirror. "It'll scan this and come off your tab."

He chuckles. "Guess I owe Murphy some money."

So, *that's* where he got the truck. Seems like everyone in the club has done a lot for Gray since he was paroled.

"Yes, it's a left," I confirm his earlier question. "Then right on Route 30 for ten miles or so."

"Haven't been out here in years," he mutters.

"Is this…this is still Lost Kings' territory right?"

He peers over at me with a curious expression.

"Am I allowed to ask that?"

"Yes. We're fine," he says, which doesn't exactly answer my question, but as long as he's not worried, I guess we're fine. He's not wearing his cut and from what I always understood, it was wearing your three-piece patch in another club's territory without permission that was the greatest sin in the MC world.

I slip out my phone and text Emily to let her know we're almost there.

*Emily: I'll meet you inside the doors to the auditorium.*
*Me: Okay.*

"Pretty out here." I peer out the windshield at the black expanse of sky. The highway lights are few and far between on this expanse of country highway, providing a dazzling view as we climb some of the steeper hills.

"Sure is." He stares up for a second. "That's what I missed most about being locked up."

"Does your place have skylights?" I ask.

His lips quirk. "No, but it's on the top floor, so maybe I'll ask management to install some."

"Good idea."

The large high school looms up ahead, the parking lot lit up like it's game night.

"They get this kind of turnout for a *play*? Or is there a basketball game or something going on?"

I chuckle at his confusion. I'd asked the same question the first time Emily asked me to attend a performance.

"What? Am I showing my age?" he asks.

"Not at all. I thought the same thing. But it's a big deal. The school puts on elaborate productions. A lot of work goes into all of it."

He slides the truck into a spot in the back row of the parking lot. I send one more quick text to Emily, then silence my phone and shove it in my purse.

Grayson opens my door and offers me his hand. After shutting the door, he stares at me and adjusts my jacket. "Warm enough?"

"Oh, yes." I pull the zipper to my chin.

He slips his hand around mine and we head for the entrance.

As promised, Emily's waiting right inside the door. She squeals and races over to hug me. Caught off-balance, I stumble into her and we both laugh.

"Easy," I tease. "I just saw you the other day."

She squeezes me one last time before letting go and raking her gaze over Grayson.

My body tenses. Emily's observant. She's also ruthless and sharp-tongued at times. I just hope *now* won't be one of those times.

I take Grayson's hand again. "Grayson, this is one of my best friends, Emily. Em, this is Grayson." I speak each word slowly so she catches my warning not to start trouble.

After a long perusal, she blinks up at him and actually smiles. "Serena had such nice things to say about you. I'm glad we could meet. And thanks for coming." She gestures toward the theater. "I know it's probably not everyone's first choice of entertainment."

"I'm intrigued after the bits of information Serena's given me," Grayson answers smoothly.

On the way to our seats, Emily hooks her arm through mine and tugs me toward her. "Guuuurl, you weren't lying," she whispers in my ear. "Your man is fine. Hot enough to make me reconsider my hard *no* to age gaps."

I snort-chuckle. "Well, find your own. This one's mine."

She smiles even wider.

Maybe this won't be so bad after all.

# CHAPTER EIGHTEEN

## Grinder

THERE'S SO MUCH CREATIVE ENERGY FROM THE KIDS ON STAGE. It leaves me hopeful but also stirs up old regrets. Sitting so close to Serena helps. The frequent funny lines and light-hearted musical numbers keep me entertained and help me forget I'm in a crowded room full of strangers.

The tiny seats weren't meant to accommodate a man my size. Serena's friend went out of her way to find an aisle seat for me so I can at least occasionally stretch one leg.

Serena silently slips her hand into mine and squeezes. We stay connected in some way until the curtain drops for the final time.

"Did you like it?" A worried note colors Serena's question.

"I did." It gave me two and a half hours to take my mind off the constant dread of screwing up and going back to prison and all the other thoughts that constantly haunt the inside of my skull. Almost made me feel *normal*.

Emily scoots out of the aisle behind us and flanks Serena's other side. "There's a concession stand in the cafeteria. Drinks and some baked goods. To raise money for the theater program."

Serena glances up at me. "I want to congratulate Libby and give her something. Maybe buy a muffin to show my support."

"I'm fine." We follow the herd of people into the cafeteria where the noise volume and chatter rises to an intolerable level.

I assume no one's gonna try and shiv me here, but I've been wrong before. Got the scars to prove it.

I don't want to ruin Serena's smile as she searches the horde of teenagers and their families for her friend, so I keep my discomfort to myself and maneuver my big body into a spot where I can keep my back to the wall and my eyes on Serena.

Emily pushes a paper cup full of red liquid into my hand and smiles up at me. "There's no alcohol in it, unfortunately." She leans in and loudly whispers, "But I bet we'd find some vodka if we raided the teacher's lounge."

"This'll do fine." I take a sip of the ultra-sweet juice. "Thank you."

She watches me for a moment. What'd Serena tell her friend about us? Did she warn Emily she was dating an ex-con old enough to be her dad? Emily hadn't recoiled when we met but now, her gaze drops to the ink on my hands and travels up. Like she's trying to figure out if I'm good enough for her friend.

"There's Libby-beans!" Serena squeals, dragging Emily's attention away from me.

The girl I'd call the star of the show runs over and tackle-hugs Serena. "You came! What'd you think?"

"You slayed it, girl."

"Straight fire," Emily adds.

Libby slowly rolls her eyes at her big sister. "Stop being so cringey, Em."

"What? Serena can steal your slang, and I can't?" Emily teases.

"Ugh. I dropped an entire line in the last scene." Libby glances over her shoulder. "I don't know how. I memorized every word."

"I couldn't tell," Serena says.

"Really? You're sure?"

"Deadass serious, Libby." Serena holds her hand up like she's about to swear on a stack of Bibles. "In fact..." She pulls the program and a marker out of her purse. "Can I have your autograph?"

"You *should* get it now before I'm famous." Libby dramatically throws her long, red hair over her shoulder and uncaps the marker with her teeth. She scrawls *Libby* with huge swirling letters next to her name on the first page. "There ya go."

"I'll treasure it," Serena says with a playful grin.

Libby opens her mouth but her gaze lands on me and she frowns.

"Oh." Serena hooks her arm through mine. "This is my friend, Grayson."

"Great show, Libby." What the fuck else am I going to say?

She tilts her head and stares at me, then shifts her eyes to Serena, clearly wanting to ask some questions. But finally, she nods at me. "Thanks for coming to the show."

"Before I forget." Serena rummages through her purse and pulls out a black envelope with silver stars drawn all over it.

"There better not be glitter in there," Emily warns.

"*Psh*." Serena waves her off.

"Oooh! What is it?" Libby grabs the envelope and tears into it. From what I can see, it's a card with what looks like a credit card tucked inside.

"Fifty bucks at Pretty Cheeks!" She hugs Serena again. "Thank you."

"It should be enough for that lipstain you like and some bright liners."

"I *sooo* want that electric blue one."

Serena brushes the girl's hair back and studies her face. "That would look amazing on you."

"Can we please not clown paint my little sister's face?" Emily begs.

"Ugh." Libby wrinkles her nose and sticks her tongue out at her sister.

Serena just laughs, so this must be the norm for the three of them.

A bunch of other kids from the play call for Libby.

"Go on," Emily says.

"Thank you, Serena." She waves at me. "Nice to meet you, sir."

The girls laugh as Libby runs off.

"She's such a firecracker," Serena says, giving Emily a light shove.

"You want her? You can have her. She likes you better, anyway."

"That's because *you're* the authoritarian parental unit."

Emily pulls a wide-eyed sad face. "That's the meanest thing you've ever said to me." More seriously, and in a lower voice, she adds, "You didn't have to give her so much. That's a lot of money."

Serena shrugs. "The company gives me gift cards sometimes. It's okay."

"Don't you need to buy stuff to review with that money, though?"

"Nah, I've got plenty of product. Let her have fun with it."

Emily's eyes soften and she squeezes Serena's arm. "Thank you."

Serena glances up at me. "We can go now."

"Whenever you're ready." Listening to them reminds me that I'm old as fuck, but also gives me something to focus on besides how crowded it is in here.

The girls hug again.

I glance at the concession stand. "You want something to go?" I ask Serena.

"Oh, yes. A blueberry muffin." She reaches in her purse.

"I got it." I tap her bag as she pulls out her wallet. "Put that away."

I pick up a muffin the size of a softball and hand the kid behind the counter a twenty. When he passes me the change, I stuff it in the can on the counter labeled "Theater Camp."

"Let's roll." I hand her the muffin, take her hand, and we get the hell out of the crowded room.

At the exit, I help her slip into her coat.

"Was that okay?" she asks softly as we cross the parking lot. "I didn't realize the play was so long."

"It was fine."

Her teeth chatter as I open her door, and I hurry to start the truck and crank up the heat.

"She's a cute kid," I say, easing us out of the parking spot. "Hell of a voice."

"I know, right?"

"It's just the two of them? On their own?"

"Yeah." She sighs. "Their parents died, and Em's been raising her since she was nineteen."

"Damn, that's tough. How'd you meet?"

She turns toward the window. "Ah, Emily and I met at this support group thing. We were both trying to make big changes in our lives. Our goals and what we wanted to accomplish lined up. We just *clicked*."

It's clear she doesn't want to share specifics, so I don't probe for more information. Hell knows, I've got plenty of my own details I want to keep to myself.

"So, your place?" Serena asks. "I'll finally get to see it?"

"To be honest, I haven't spent a lot of time there myself yet." I glance over. "You're my first guest."

She reaches over and rests her hand on my thigh. "I like that."

I curl my fingers around hers, and we stay like that until I pull into the lot behind my apartment.

"This is a nice place," she says, staring up at the new brick building.

"It sure beats my last housing situation."

She doesn't laugh at the joke. Probably because it wasn't all that funny.

"You weren't kidding about being all the way upstairs," she says once we're three flights up.

I've been too busy staring at her legs as she climbed ahead of me. The skirt of her dress swishes and teases the hell out of me with every movement. I don't dare raise my gaze to her ass.

I'm so focused on controlling my hands so they don't *accidentally* flip her skirt up, I don't notice when she stops at the top of the stairs. I plow into her, almost knocking her over, and have to grip her arms to keep her upright.

"Mr. Lock," a deep voice says. "There you are."

*This cocksucker had to show up tonight.*

My parole officer warned me that he might make home visits to make sure I wasn't out creating havoc after ten p.m. At the time, I hadn't taken him seriously, since the club said he would go easy on me. I should've known better.

"Evening," I growl.

He dips his chin at Serena. "Are you going to introduce me to your *friend?*" The way he says friend sounds more like *hooker,* and I don't like it one bit.

"Serena, this is my parole officer, Hank Grillo."

She doesn't offer to shake his hand, just nods hello.

He does a slow twist of his wrist and checks the time. Asshole could've been in the show we just saw, he's so fucking dramatic. "It's after ten, Mr. Lock."

*Look at you, telling time like a big boy.*

"It is," I answer.

"One of your conditions of parole is to be home by ten." His gaze lands on Serena again. "And where did you two meet?"

Again, he seems to be assuming Serena's some random woman I picked up for the night, and it's pissing me off.

Serena's nervous eyes meet mine. *Fuck.* She's not going to want to tell this prick she's my physical therapist. She could lose her damn job if he decides to verify our story.

"Where've you been tonight, Grayson?" he asks when she remains silent. "You're not supposed to be at bars and—"

"We were at Johnsonville High for my friend's play," Serena cuts him off with an easy answer.

He scoffs. "Seriously? I'm supposed to believe the King of Cell Block A was at a kid's show?" He rakes a scornful gaze over her. "Where'd he pick you up, honey?"

"My name isn't honey," Serena says through clenched teeth. She opens her purse and pulls out the program. Thrusting it into his hands, she explains, "My friend's sister is in the play. That's where we just came from. Look." She flips the page and taps Libby's autograph. "She signed it for me."

I raise my eyes to the ceiling. *Thank you, Libby.*

He stares at it and clearly wants to dismiss what's right in front of him. But the date's on the program in black and white.

"It ran longer than I thought it would," Serena says. "I didn't realize Gray needed to be home at a certain time or we would've skipped the reception afterward."

His eyes ping-pong between us for a few seconds, finally landing on me.

I shrug. "It was dark; I didn't notice the time. We came straight home after."

"Do you live here, Serena?" A hint of a smug smirk plays over his face.

*Fuck.*

"No," she answers. "I live in Empire."

Hank's upper lip curls, like he thinks he finally caught me. "Did you drive yourself tonight?"

Again, Serena's eyes flick my way. "No."

"How are you planning to get home, then, if Mr. Lock can't drive you?"

*This just keeps getting worse.*

It wasn't my intention to trap Serena tonight. I never thought the curfew was going to be this much of a headache.

If Serena's mad, it doesn't show. She slides her arms around my waist and leans into me. "Not that it's your business, but I *wasn't* planning to go home tonight."

"I'm allowed overnight guests, aren't I?" I ask.

Hank's eyes narrow, but after a few seconds of rolling his options around in his big, bald head, he seems to relent.

"All right." He hands Serena the program and slips on a knit cap. "High school play's a pretty wholesome night for an ex-con, so I'll let it slide. But try and watch the time from now on."

*Wholesome.* I like that.

Too bad none of the feelings I'm having for Serena right now are anywhere near wholesome. I'm harder than a telephone pole after watching her stick up for me and go toe-to-toe with Hank.

He moves past us and I pull out my keys.

"Sure thing. I'll keep my eyes on my wristwatch from now on," I say. No one's gonna be handing me an award for *my* acting abilities any time soon.

He eyes Serena again. "Can I have your last name?"

"No," she answers.

I choke back a laugh.

Hank doesn't know what to do with her refusal.

"Monday morning, Grayson. Don't be late," he snaps, then scurries down the stairs like a rat after some cheese.

I unlock the door and push inside without another word.

"I'm so sorry, Gray. You did mention a curfew. I forgot. I didn't mean to keep you out—"

I cut off her apology with a kiss. Wrapping my arms around her, I lift and pin her to the door. She gasps and curls her arms around my neck, dragging me closer and returning the kiss.

"Hey." I draw back, studying her face. "I wasn't trying to trick you into staying over. I really—"

She presses her finger to my lips. "I want to stay."

"Good." I set her down. "I am sorry, though. You shouldn't have had to put up with that because of me."

"I can handle some snarky comments." She curls her fingers around my arm. "Get back here and kiss me again."

### Serena

"Thank you," he whispers, dropping a kiss on my cheek.

"For?"

"Not getting rattled." He presses another kiss to my jaw, closer to my neck, and I shiver. "Sticking up for me."

"I was worried you'd be mad."

"Nah. A good ol' lady always sticks up for her man." He tugs my turtleneck aside and kisses my throat. "But also knows when to back down and not make the situation worse."

A shudder of fear rolls over me. What if his parole officer hadn't believed us and took him to jail tonight?

*Record scratch.*

Did he refer to me as his *ol' lady*? Feeling brave, I lift my chin. "What did you just call me?"

He blows out a breath. "I know you're not *old*. It's how the club—"

"I know," I say quickly. No one's *ever* called me that before.

His lips press against mine again. The pleasure of that endearment blends with the shivery sensation of his lips trailing across my jaw.

"May I?" He teases one finger under the thick strap of my dress.

Dear God, how can those two words be so hot?

I nod quickly.

"No, Serena. Say it. I want to hear the word."

"Okay."

He pulls away.

"What are you doing?"

He shrugs. A smile plays over his lips. "*Okay* didn't sound very enthusiastic."

"Do you want me to do cartwheels?"

He eases his big body closer, pressing one palm against the door next to the side of my face, and then the other, caging me in. I'm forced to tip my head to stare up at him.

Oh God. Smoldering eyes, staring down, devouring me. "No cartwheels, buttercup." He returns to playing with the strap. "Yes or no?"

No one's ever cared so much about what *I* wanted before. I'm way past turned on. I'm on *fire* for him.

I rest my palm against his cheek, forcing him to meet me eye-to-eye. "Yes, Gray."

He rumbles, a happy sound of approval. "Turn around."

Shivering, I turn and press my hands to the door.

His fingers brush my back, grasping the zipper and giving it a gentle tug. Why am I wearing so many damn layers tonight?

He doesn't even slide the zipper halfway down before he mutters, "Fuck it," and grabs me around the waist. He yanks me closer, and scoops me up.

"Gray!" I yelp. "Your shoulder. You can't carry me."

"The fuck I can't," he growls, pushing his way through another door.

Moonlight spills through the windows, illuminating the sparsely furnished bedroom. He gently sets me on the king-sized bed and steps back to stare at me.

Slowly, he slides his fingers under the straps of my dress and guides them all the way off my shoulders. The top of the dress pools at my waist, leaving me in my turtleneck, tights, and boots.

*I cannot believe I wore a turtleneck on a date with the man I've been dying to jump.*

Curling my fingers in the soft elastic band around the edge, I attempt to strip off the sweater, but Grayson stops me with a low, admonishing hum. "Easy. I want to do that."

I hold my hands up over my head. One corner of my mouth quirks while I hold his gaze.

"I love your fire, Serena."

Me, fiery? I like that he sees me that way. I haven't always had the courage to speak up when I should.

He leans in and teases his fingers under the edge of my sweater. Heat flickers over my skin as he drags the sweater up, up, up, his knuckles grazing my sides. The sensation's shivery, hot, and a little ticklish.

The sweater's tight around my head, and for a moment, I can't see a damn thing. Fear stirs in my stomach, then dissolves.

Light. I can see again. He tosses the sweater on the nightstand.

"Now what are you going to do with me?" I ask.

He reaches toward the nightstand and clicks on a soft light. "Stare. Absorb every inch of your beauty."

My heart flutters so fast I'm scared it will fly right into his hands.

I wasn't sure we'd end up here, but I was hopeful. I'm wearing a pretty black lace bra with extra-thin straps arching over the tops of my breasts, showing them off. I pull my shoulders back and peek up at him through my lashes.

His hot, hungry eyes slide over every inch of me but he seems frozen.

I'm burning. Hot all over. "Kiss me, Grayson."

The next kiss, when it comes, starts slow and tender. Soft nibbling, exploring, then exploding into deeper searching, our tongues sliding together. My hands reach for him, curling into his shirt and tugging.

Closer—I need his body so much closer. On the bed with me. Over me, caging me in so I feel safe and protected.

His thumb brushes the side of my breast, and I reach behind me to unhook my bra.

He draws back, watching intently. I slow my movements. Undoing the clasp, then taking my time sliding the straps off my shoulders.

He lifts his gaze to my eyes, as if he's peering into my soul. It leaves me more exposed than sitting here almost topless.

"Go on," he whispers.

I drop the bra to the side.

There's a sharp intake of air and he drops to his knees in front of me, resting his hands on my legs. I inch them apart, making room for him to move closer. Holding my gaze, he dips in to kiss one nipple.

I sigh and tilt my head back, exposing my neck and offering myself. His hands slide over the outsides of my thighs, under my dress, seeking, searching for the top of my tights. He hooks his fingers into the waistband and tugs. My underwear peels away with the tights and I lift myself enough for him to roll them past my hips. He leans in and presses a kiss to my inner thigh.

"I had a hard time not doing this all night," he whispers, kissing my other thigh. His beard tickles and scrapes against my sensitive skin. I brace my palms against the mattress to steady myself.

He gently unlaces my boots and tugs everything off the rest of the way, stopping to kiss certain spots. Behind my knee, my calf, my ankle. He appreciates and admires every part of me.

"Lie back for me."

Another pulse of heat rushes over me. I stretch out, raise my arms above my head, and stare at the ceiling for a second.

Firm hands wrap around my ankles, lifting and placing my feet on the bed. I let my knees fall together and press my skirt down, suddenly shy.

Gray doesn't seem to mind. He kisses one knee, then the other, gently stroking my legs. He's the most patient man I've ever known.

My knees part. Rough fingers stroke my inner thighs. I open wider and he growls. "That's beautiful."

I reach for him, my fingertips grazing his cheek.

He dips to kiss my inner wrist, then curls his fingers around mine.

Our hands linked together deepens everything, grounds and connects me to him in a way I didn't expect.

With his free hand, he strokes between my legs, slowly running his thumb over my lips. My body jolts, arches into his touch.

"Gray, please?" I whisper urgently.

"Serena, it's been an eternity." He runs his hand down my leg again. "Please let me take my time and feast on you."

Oh my God. I'm not sure I can handle this.

He stares at my body for several heartbeats. Like maybe this is a tease or a test, and he's afraid I'll disappear any second.

"Gray?" I roll my hips, bumping his hand. "Touch me again, please? Take your time. But don't stop touching me."

My whispered plea seems to snap him out of his trance.

He grips my hips and yanks me to the edge of the bed, admiring, kissing, appreciating every inch of skin he comes into contact with.

Finally, he pushes my skirt up around my hips. Why didn't I take this off? I twist and wrestle with the wool. I wasn't kidding about it being from my school days, and it's a bit tight in the middle.

"Leave it," he orders.

His rough demand sends a shiver of desire down my spine.

My eyes snap to his.

The corner of his mouth lifts. "I like it on you."

His gaze slowly travels up my body, drinking me in like he's discovered a treasure he's been seeking his entire life. "You're sure, Serena?"

Like a treasure he doesn't think he deserves.

"God, yes."

In answer, he uses his big fingers to gently peel back my lips, leaving me throbbing and exposed. Arrows of pleasure shoot straight to my center just from the anticipation of his mouth on me.

He licks once. My entire body shudders. He licks again. I arch my back. He sucks my clit into his mouth, and I gasp.

*Dear God, he got there fast.*

My toes curl into the comforter.

More shivers race to my core.

His head bobs, his beard scratching my inner thighs. He slides his hands under my ass, pulling me closer.

He wasn't kidding about wanting to feast.

Grayson's not shy. As he said, it's been a long time. He's a man who knows exactly what he wants, and he's *ravenous*. He licks, groans, and savors my flesh until he's panting hard.

*Talk about enthusiastic.*

I bite my fist so I don't scream. Nothing has ever, ever been *this* amazing.

He pushes a finger inside me. I was wrong—*this* is the most amazing feeling. I squirm, almost afraid of the intense pleasure barreling down on me.

"Easy," he murmurs against my skin.

Desperate to watch what he's doing, I lean up on my elbows.

He flicks his gaze to mine and sucks harder, presses two fingers deeper inside, rubbing against a spot that sends stars sizzling in front of my eyes. I fall back against the bed, completely boneless as he continues.

All my muscles clench tight. Pleasure burns up my legs to my center. I spear my fingers through my hair and tug, desperate to ground myself.

"Gray," I chant over and over.

My hips jerk; my muscles clench around him. I'm completely helpless as my release slams into me. I bow off the bed and scream.

He holds my hips and presses me to the mattress. More bliss than I think I can handle rolls over me.

Slowly, he brings me back to earth. Still tasting and kissing, but slower, longer licks and nibbles.

The mattress dips as he presses his palms on either side of my legs and stands. Leaning over me, he kisses my stomach, brushing his beard over my belly button. My body jerks and laughter bursts out of me. He kisses his way over my ribs, stops to suck on one nipple, then the other. His beard gleams with my juices, and a flush of pride warms me. He kisses my collarbone, my neck, along my jaw, finally stopping to stare into my eyes.

"Thank you," he whispers.

"Thank *you*." I raise one shaky hand between us. "I'm still quivering."

Instead of laughing, he turns and kisses my palm, then pushes away, standing before me. I sit but lean back on my palms and watch as he slowly unbuttons his shirt.

He raises an eyebrow.

"I'm dying to see you, Grayson. But the last two times, you stopped me, so…"

"Fair enough," he rumbles.

He unbuttons one cuff, and I sink my teeth into my bottom lip. The man just ate me into oblivion but the sight of his arms ignites a new ache inside me.

My dress is still twisted around my waist. It's scratchy against my skin and I struggle to turn it around to unzip it. I glance up at him. "It's starting to itch."

"Can't have that." He motions for me to kneel and helps me pry the zipper free and pull it off over my head. "Jesus, Serena," he breathes out. "You're beautiful. So beautiful all over."

He's so achingly sincere, tears prickle my eyes. I sit back on my heels and continue watching him slide each button of his shirt free.

Unable to be patient any longer, I reach for him, spreading the shirt open to reveal his broad chest. My gaze lands on shiny plastic film covering what looks like a fresh tattoo over his heart and one in the middle of his chest. In the low light, I can't make out either one.

"Do they hurt?"

He glances down and shrugs. "Not really. I'm supposed to keep them covered a little longer though."

"I'll be gentle," I tease. My gaze is drawn to the light sprinkle of hair on his chest, then travels lower. "I'll try, anyway."

I rest my palms against his abs, the muscles flexing and rolling under my touch. "You take good care of yourself."

"Only have one body. Best to take care of it."

My gaze is glued to the V at his hips. "Indeed."

He laughs softly and tugs at his belt, undoing the buckle, then unbuttoning his pants and pushing them to the floor.

Our hungry gazes collide. He remains still. Waiting. I tease my fingers around the waistband of his boxer briefs and ease them down thick, strong thighs all the way to the floor.

*Worth the wait.*

*So worth the wait.*

I reach between us and grip his cock with one hand.

He groans and shudders from that small touch.

I grip him with my other hand, lazily sliding up and down, getting acquainted with his topography. Gaining confidence, I use firmer strokes. His breathing turns choppy. I roll my thumb over the glistening head of his cock and lean in to swipe my tongue against him, spreading the slickness.

He groans louder and his legs shake. Gathering my hair, he grips, holding my head back, stopping my exploration. "Wait."

I've never known a man with this much self-control.

He leans toward the nightstand, grasping at the top drawer until it slides open. My pussy throbs, eager to have him inside me, praying he's going for a condom.

Finally, he grabs one and releases my hair to slide it on. "Get in the middle of the bed."

I can't scamper backwards fast enough. He climbs onto the bed, meeting me in the middle, and rests one hand on my hip. I nuzzle against him, kissing his neck and cheek. "Grayson, I want you inside me so much."

He growls but still seems conflicted. "I don't know where to start."

I cup his cheeks, staring into his eyes. "Kiss me, and we'll go from there."

He leans in and roughly takes my mouth, driving his fingers through my hair to hold me the way he wants. I grasp his shoulders, desperate to hold onto something as he devours my mouth. He pulls me down to the bed, our legs tangling, mouths still fused together—wild and all-consuming.

I arch my body against him, needing to feel more of his skin on mine. The crisp hairs on his chest, tickling my breasts. His hands digging into my hips. I spread my legs and lift, inviting him in.

With a restraint I didn't think he'd be capable of, he presses into me inch by inch. My eyes roll back in my head. *Finally, finally.*

I never want this to end.

"Fuck." He drops his forehead to mine and squeezes his eyes shut. "You feel so good, buttercup."

I tease my lips against his. "You too." I squeeze my inner muscles and he groans. "You fit me just right."

At first, he fucks slowly, teasingly. Gray still wants to savor every moment. Never rushing.

He studies my reactions. As if pleasing me feels better than fucking me. I've never been with someone so tuned in to what brings me pleasure. The intimacy overwhelms and scares me in equal measure. His soulful eyes study me until I have to look away.

"No, stay with me, Serena." He stops thrusting and slowly grinds himself against my clit, setting off sparks.

"I'm here." I curl my hands around his neck. He cups my cheek and holds my gaze, reinforcing our connection.

A swell of lust rises inside me, building into a storm of sensation and emotion. He hammers his hips into me harder, sending me spiraling into a screaming orgasm.

"That's it. Scream as loud as you want." He dips down and sucks at my neck, dragging his teeth over my pulse. My heart thunders, blood roaring through my ears. His thrusts turn savage, dragging out my release or triggering a new one. I can't tell. Tiny pulses of pleasure fire between my legs, flowing outward.

"Gray, ahhh, oh my God, I'm coming again."

"Goddamn." He sucks in a harsh breath. His whole body shakes, on the edge of release. He pumps into me erratically and groans, dropping his head onto my shoulder. A look of utter peace and satisfaction melts over his expression. Tension drains from his body.

He kisses my cheeks and my forehead. I drag my fingers over his shoulders and along his spine. He lifts himself off me, stretching along my side so we're still glued together.

"Did I hurt you?"

I swing my lust-drunk puppy eyes his way. "Not at all." Laughing, I rock my hips. "I didn't think I could come that many times in a row."

A feral grin spreads across his face. "That right?"

"Yes." I roll closer and rest my cheek against the curve of his bicep.

Warm and content, I snuggle into the protection of his arms and one thought throbs through my mind—I've never felt so cherished in my life.

# CHAPTER NINETEEN
## Serena

Sunlight stabs my eyes.

I turn over and burrow under the pillows to get away from the brightness.

*Wait, why is it so bright in here?*

Soft, crisp sheets. Clean scent. Different from my lavender-scented bedding.

I blink my eyes open. Grayson's bedroom. A smile curves my lips as images from last night warm my body. At some point, he'd given me a sleeveless tank top to sleep in. It's a few sizes too big; my breasts are now spilling out of the sides. I shift, readjusting myself, and open my eyes wider.

I'm alone.

Did he leave me alone in his bed *again*?

After such a beautiful night, he had to get away from me first thing in the morning.

What is it about me that repels him so much once the sun comes up?

Hurt and furious, I fling the sheets away and stalk out of the bedroom.

The rich scent of freshly brewing coffee hits my nose.

*He's here.*

Light spills out of the kitchen. The bang of a frying pan. A sizzle and pop. The scrape of metal.

*Is he...making breakfast?*

The bathroom's across the living room to my right, the kitchen to my left. I need a moment to arrange myself, so I scurry to the right, quietly closing the door behind me.

There's a new-in-box toothbrush on the counter.

Did he leave that there for me?

Hoping that it is indeed mine, I rip it open and scrub the sleep from my mouth. Staring into the mirror isn't as bad as I'd feared. I fix a few stray smudges of leftover eyeliner and finger comb my hair into something a little less stuck-my-finger-in-a-light-socket looking.

As presentable as I'm going to get wearing no pants, I quietly walk to the kitchen.

Grayson's at the stove. Back toward me. A plain black T-shirt stretches tight against his broad back and biceps. Jeans. Bare feet.

"Morning," he says over his shoulder.

"Hey."

He turns. "Can't sneak up on me, buttercup."

"I wasn't trying to." I slide onto one of the stools on the other side of the counter where I can watch him work but not be in the way.

He sets a mug of coffee in front of me. I close my eyes and dip closer to inhale the nutty, fresh scent. "Mmm."

"I realized I didn't have anything here, so I got up early and ran to the store." He rests his elbows on the counter and leans over, pressing a soft kiss to my cheek. "Bacon, eggs, and toast okay with you?"

"That sounds good. You should've woken me up. I would've gone to the store with you." To cover the sharpness of my words, I take a sip of coffee.

Concern darkens his eyes, and he cups my hands in his. "Thought you needed some rest after last night."

"You did quite a bit of activity yourself." I raise an eyebrow as I take another tentative sip of my coffee. "I wanted to wake up *with* you."

"I'm always up early. No matter what." The easiness from our banter ebbs away. "Don't think that'll change any time soon."

My nose wrinkles at the bitter coffee. "Sweetener?"

"Uh." He turns, searching the items laid out on the counter near the refrigerator. "I've got sugar here somewhere."

"Oh! I might have some in my purse." I slide off the stool and search the living room. My gaze lands on a small coatrack near the door, and I find my purse dangling from a hook next to my coat. I shove my hand inside, fishing around the bottom until my fingers encounter a few wrinkled packets. "Aha!"

I yank the little orange rectangles out victoriously and return to the counter.

Grayson studies the packets without comment. I stir my coffee and take a sip. Much better.

"I'm fussy about certain things," I explain.

He holds up his hands. "Coffee's something you don't want to mess with." He sets a container of half-and-half on the counter. "I'm thrilled to have access to the real thing again."

My sweetener preferences seem a little silly now. "Sorry."

"Don't be." He lowers his gaze. "Have I mentioned how good you look in that?"

I peer down and realize my right boob is trying to make a run for it again. Laughing, I readjust the shirt. "I don't have anything else to wear."

"We can fix that." One corner of his mouth lifts again. "But I like how this looks on you."

I slide out of my chair and round the corner, stepping into the kitchen.

His eyes slowly travel down my legs. "Yes. Definitely like how that looks. Turn around for me."

I turn slowly and peer at him over my shoulder.

"Fuck," he mutters.

Something pops and snaps on the stove, and I duck for cover. Grayson twists the knob to turn down the heat under the frying pan. "Still haven't gotten the hang of this yet," he mutters.

"Do you want me to—"

"No." He jerks his head to the side. "Go sit down. It's almost ready."

His harshness stings but I see how important it is to do it on his own, so I return to my seat.

A few minutes later, he sets a plate of extra crispy bacon on the counter followed by eggs, toast, and butter. "Bacon's a bit overdone." He gestures to the stove behind him. "I can make more."

I grab a slice and pop a piece in my mouth. "I like it this way. Less fat."

He runs his gaze over me. "That's not something you need to worry about."

We eat without talking. Instead of sitting on the stool next to me, he stands on the other side of the counter. An undercurrent of tension or unease simmers below the surface. Is he mad we slept together? Ready for me to go home?

"Not hungry?" he asks, staring at my plate.

"Oh." I pick up my toast and take a bite. I'm too lost in my own head, worrying last night was a mistake. Or that he thinks it was a mistake.

*Be direct.*

I open my mouth to ask what's wrong but he leans toward the end of the counter and slides a newspaper my way. "I thought we'd go look at a few apartments today."

I choke on my toast and quickly sip some coffee. "Apartments?" I sputter. "Why?"

Have I been reading this wrong all morning? Is he suggesting what I think he's suggesting? I glance at the newspaper. My stomach twists.

He rests his hand over mine. "It's too soon for *us* to live together," he says gently, killing that thought before I even express it. "But I gotta be honest—the place you live in isn't safe and I don't feel right about it."

I blink and sit back.

"I don't like my woman living somewhere she's not safe." He points to the paper. "This place is five minutes from your job. Nice neighborhood."

Still too flabbergasted to speak, I stare at the listing.

"You know, you can just look these up online now. You didn't have to go *buy* the paper."

"Just look at it," he growls. "No need to remind me I'm old as fuck."

"That wasn't what I meant," I mumble, scanning the first listing he's circled. My eyes bug when I read how high the rent is.

"I can't afford this place." I push the paper toward him.

He runs his hand over his freshly inked chest, absently scratching. I lean over the counter, gently prying his hand away. "Stop. Let it heal."

"Oh. Damn." He glances down and almost seems embarrassed. "Forgot." He captures my fingers and dips his head to kiss my knuckles. "Thank you."

I'm about to swoon right out of my chair if he keeps that up.

"I'll pay for the apartment," he says.

"Huh?" He's still holding my hand, rubbing it between his palms. I squirm in my seat. Whoever heard of getting turned on by holding hands?

"Oh. Right. Apartment." I take another glance at the listing. It's a two-bedroom. He actually *listened* when I explained about my side hustle. Sure, he had no idea what I was talking about, but it didn't matter. He understood it was important to me.

*Damn.*

"You'll still have the space you need," he adds.

"It's not that." I duck my head. "I can't have you pay for my apartment like I'm some…kept mistress or something. I can't."

"Serena," he pleads.

His touch is too distracting. I pull my hand away. "What if we… don't work out?" I ask. "Then I'll be homeless and need a place to live. I can't go through so much upheaval." *I've had enough in my life.*

"I won't…I wouldn't *kick you out on the street*, Serena." His voice has a hard edge, like he's deeply offended. "That's not the kind of man I am."

"Still, it would be awkward."

"Why?" Frustration roughens his tone. "You can take the money you're spending on rent now and save it, if you're worried. Or, you said you're still trying to pay down some debt? Use the money toward that. I'll take care of the move and everything. To avoid too much upheaval," he says, using my own words. "Fuck knows, I understand the need for peace in life."

It's a tempting offer.

But I've had many tempting offers presented to me by different men in my life.

They were all illusions.

Violently ripped to shreds at some point.

"I'll think about it."

My answer clearly frustrates him. But it's all I can give.

His jaw clenches.

The urge to *run* thrums through my veins. I curl my hands around the edge of the counter, prepared to flee.

He exhales slowly. The tension flows away with his breath. "Okay," he says. "If you want to look at it, let me know. We'll go together."

Calm and reasonable. No yelling or threats. My heart's still wildly thumping but I loosen my grip on the counter and relax.

"Will you at least let me fix your door?" he asks.

"Okay."

"Good. Thank you."

I chuckle. "I can't believe you're thanking me."

"You're stubborn."

"Me?" No one's ever called me that before. Pushover, maybe.

"Is it so terrible that I want to take care of you?" he asks.

There goes my stupid heart, fluttering all over the place. "You barely know me."

He raises an eyebrow and shoots a look toward his bedroom. "I think I know you pretty well."

Heat bursts over my cheeks. "That's sex."

His jaw drops like I sucker punched him.

How is every word out of my mouth making this worse?

"Right," he says. "Understood."

"I just meant...we haven't been *together* that long. Are we together?"

"I don't use the term *old lady* lightly, Serena." He holds out a hand. "But I realize you don't understand the significance."

I open my mouth to explain that I *do* understand.

Then stop myself.

## Grinder

I search her face. "I sense a *but*."

She drops her gaze to the floor. "Can we talk about how to handle your therapy appointments?"

"What do you mean? I'll keep going. Keep our relationship on the down low."

"How? If we tell anyone how we met...it will look really bad, especially if I'm still treating you. If your parole officer wants to make trouble for you...or me, all he'd have to do is call my supervisor."

She's really stressed about this. I come around to her side of the counter and take her hands. "I won't let that happen."

My gaze drops briefly. *Her legs.* Those long, toned, sleek legs. I'd kissed every inch of her last night, and it still wasn't enough.

"Grayson," she says in a sharper tone clearly meant to grab my attention. "I really can't keep you as my patient if we're...if this is..."

"Sweetheart, it's not like I'm going to complain to anyone."

"That's not the point." Her tone sharpens as her patience with me slips. "If my job found out, I'd probably get fired, if not worse."

"Serena—" I stop myself. Isn't me being a pushy bastard what forced Rose to give up on med school?

Here, Serena's already done all the hard work, and I'm going to ruin it for her because I can't stay away? After all the reflection I did in prison and promises I made myself, I'm already repeating old patterns and fucking up.

"What should we do, then?" I ask.

"I can refer you to someone else. I know a great guy at—"

"No fucking way am I having some dude put his hands all over me." Nope. Dealt with a male therapist inside, and he was lazy as shit.

"Well, I don't want another *woman* putting her hands on you," she snaps back.

I might be an asshole for liking that so damn much. "Guess we're at an impasse."

She blows out an annoyed breath and glares at me. It'll probably piss her off if I tell her how beautiful she is when she's mad, won't it?

At the strangest times, her beauty sneaks up on me. At first glance, she's pretty, sure. That's obvious to any man with eyes and a dick. But up close, her midnight-blue eyes flash with determination. Her skin glows. I haven't felt this way in so damn long.

She takes my breath away. When she looks at me, it's like she sees who I should've been. Who I can still be if I stay on the right path. I have no business steering her off of *her* chosen path just because I'm a stubborn old goat.

"All right," I say quieter than before. "Refer me to your friend."

As much as I hate it, it's the best solution. Sometimes the best way to win a battle is not to engage at all. I can't be the reason she loses everything she's worked for. And breaking things off with her isn't an option. Not for me. Not now.

"Thank you."

"Or," I say without thinking it through, "you could treat me yourself. Outside of work."

"You want me to work all day and then come home and work some more?" she asks slowly.

Well, shit, that does sound bad. "Give me the referral."

"I'll do it." She waves her hand in the air. "I don't trust anyone else to take care of you the way I will."

Hell, that's a sweet thing to say. It's my job to take care of *her* but damn if I don't like how that sounds.

## CHAPTER TWENTY
### Grinder

"All fixed." I hand Serena the keys to the new door.

She stares at the key ring. "It's going to take me forever to get in my front door now."

"It's *one* extra lock. That actually works," I remind her. "Those are extras."

"Oh!" She holds up the keys and studies them, then slides two off the ring and hands them to me.

"What's this?"

She does this adorable head-tilt, shoulder-shrug.

"You don't have to give me a key to your place, Serena." I've been thinking more and more about having her move in with me, except it's a long drive for her to go to work.

"I want you to have it. Just let me know if you're stopping by." She hesitates. "You don't have to give me—"

"No. I want you to have mine too. I don't have a spare with me right now."

She still seems antsy, with her nervous blue eyes skipping all over. And it doesn't seem to be about the keys. "Everything okay?" I ask.

Frustration twists the corners of her mouth, like she's debating her words. "I have some stuff I'm supposed to catch up on." She waves her hands toward the hallway.

"I can go."

"I don't want you to go…I need to do some filming for my channel. It's boring, though. I mean, you'll be bored. But I'm a little behind and need to catch up."

I can't help being curious. Since I've been out, I've been too overwhelmed to explore a lot of the ways the world's changed. I've also been consumed with getting to know Serena. But asking if I can stick around and watch sounds creepy as fuck. I also don't want to force Serena to be my life coach, helping me readjust to society. That's just fucking pathetic.

"You can stay and watch if you want…You don't have to." Nervous laughter bubbles out of her. "It's about makeup, so you'll be bored to tears."

"I've never heard of…whatever you called it. But I'm curious since it sounds important to you."

Her eyes widen as if she never expected that answer. I shift and glance at the door. Maybe this is too much.

"Okay." She motions for me to follow her. Along the way, she stops and collects a few boxes from the entertainment center. "I'm going to film a few clips at once so I'll be set with content for the next couple of weeks."

She drops off the boxes in the spare room, points me to a seat, and disappears into the hallway. A few minutes later, she returns with a handful of clothes on hangers and neatly hangs everything on a rolling rack in the corner.

I watch quietly as she sets up two mini-tripods. One for her cell phone and one for a small camera. She places several poles with lights on top in strategic places around the desk and mirror, carefully checking each one.

"I'm going to review these makeup remover cloths a company sent me." She holds up one of the boxes she brought in from the living room. "But first, I'm going to do a full-face tutorial. A two birds, one stone situation." She grins at me.

"Sounds good." As if I even know what she's talking about. But hell if I'm not charmed by every single thing she does.

She leaves again, and I hear water running from down the hall. A few minutes later, she returns dressed in a silky robe, her hair held back by a wide headband, with a squeaky clean face.

"Blank canvas," she says.

"Beautiful." Damn, she's perfect.

She flashes a quick smile and flicks on the curtain of lights on the wall behind her. After sitting in front of the mirror and cameras, she checks a few more things, sets out a bunch of index cards, lays out assorted items I couldn't name with a gun held to my head, then flicks the cameras on.

"Hello, Sparklers!" She waves cheerfully into the lens. "A lot of you have been asking, so today I'm going to show you how to do one of my favorite glam makeup looks."

She holds up and names several items before picking up a sponge and dotting what she calls *foundation* all over her face. I'm biased as fuck, but all her movements are graceful, her chatter to the camera so charismatic, I can't help thinking whoever discouraged her from modeling was a fucking fool who missed out big time.

"Are you bored yet?" she asks, turning my way.

"Are you still recording?"

"I paused everything." She gestures toward the cameras.

"I never knew it took so long to do all that. I'm fascinated."

Her smile fades. Shit, she probably thinks I'm being sarcastic, when the truth is I'm utterly bewitched by her.

"I'm being serious, Serena. You're mesmerizing."

"Thank you." She turns back to the mirror and flips through her index cards. When she continues recording, she carefully applies a set of false eyelashes, talking into the camera the whole time like it's the most natural thing in the world.

When she's completed "the look" she takes several pictures, films another short spiel about it, then shuts everything off.

"I'm going to change my top for the next one."

I sit back and cross my arms over my chest. "Fine by me."

She laughs and unties the robe, slowly letting it fall down her arms and pool at her feet. Pity she's wearing a tank top and tiny shorts underneath. She slips a shoulder-baring T-shirt over her head and sits at the table again.

"Hello, Sparklers!" She films another introduction asking anyone who's watching to "like and subscribe," same as she did earlier.

"Today, I have a special product we're going to try. Moon Pod Glow Cloths." She waves a package in front of the camera. "I'll leave a link and discount code below in the comments."

She has a whole script written out but reads everything in a natural, friendly way. The makeup comes off and she deems the pod-thingies worthy of five sparkles. By the time she's finished, she's as fresh-scrubbed as when she started...four hours ago.

Shit, I didn't even realize that much time had passed. I stand and stretch as quietly as possible. A few seconds later, she turns everything off.

"Are you done?" I ask.

"Sorry that took so long."

"I'm fine. Really. Stop apologizing."

"I'll probably go through and edit everything tomorrow. But..." She grabs her phone and taps on the screen for several minutes. "I *will* post a teaser now."

She pulls up a page on her laptop of colorful squares and pretty pictures in saturated colors. "That's my Instagram."

"Uh, okay." I peer over her shoulder. "*Tranquil Sparkle?*"

She shrugs. "It was a play on my name. Serena, but serenity seemed too close. Tranquility was a pretty word but my messaging is all about makeup and making yourself—*sparkle.*" She pauses and tilts her head. "I picked the name years ago without thinking and it's my brand. If I were going to do it again, I'd probably choose *Tranquil Glow* because it fits my vibe better now."

My brain short-circuits as I try to follow her explanation, but eventually the smoke clears. "Makes sense. I guess."

*I've never felt so fucking old.*

But she's sweet and patient with all the explanations. Never points out that I'm basically a defrosted caveman lurching into the twenty-first century.

"Anyway." She points to the screen. "There's the teaser I posted so my followers know what's coming."

While we watch, little hearts pop up in the corner of the screen. "That's people liking the post," she explains.

Comments start popping up under the photo.

*Cutehiccups2019: omg ure so pretttty!*

*DustyCarrots: Wow! Can't wait!*

*Dreamingofhamburgers17: Love your hair.*

*Feathergirl515: your voice is so soothing!*

*FlockingFabulous1921: Great look! Gold is so pretty on you!*

She taps a few responses to the comments.

"They seem to like it," I say, watching the number at the bottom climb into double, then triple digits.

She grins at me. "My followers are really sweet."

*ThorMant08: Whore face.*

I lean in closer, glaring at the screen "What the fuck?"

"Ugh." She waves off the fact that someone just called her a *whore*. "Some weirdo troll always stops by to give his unwelcome opinion." She clicks a few times and the comment disappears. "I never engage with them. Just delete and block."

*Animkaz: ur lips would look better around my cock.*

"Who the hell is that?" I growl.

"Another creep." A few clicks later, the comment disappears. She shrugs and closes the screen. "It's a wild world out there."

I rest my hands on her shoulders, and she tips her head back and smiles up at me. "I don't like people talking to you like that," I say.

Her lips curve into a soft smile and she rests her palm against my cheek. "There's not a lot I can do about it, so I don't waste time worrying."

"Is that safe, though? Having your face out there like that? With those creeps saying shit like that to you?"

She squints at me. "Everyone does it."

I grunt an unconvinced noise.

She hooks her arms around my neck and drags me closer. "Thank you."

"For?"

"Watching and not complaining. Or making fun of me."

"Why the fuck would I make fun of you?"

She lifts one shoulder. "And worrying about me."

"Of course I worry about you." I gesture to the screen. "If someone said that shit to your face, I'd yank their spine out through their throat." Christ, my blood's boiling again.

"How graphic," she teases and leans up to kiss me.

"I'm serious," I say against her lips. I urge her up into my arms. She pulls away and stares into my eyes. "Grayson, would you like to see my bedroom?"

"Very, very much." My heart pounds as she leads me into the hallway and to her bedroom. It's shadowy and dark, with heavy drapes covering the windows. She flicks a switch and thousands of tiny lights blink on, covering one wall and the ceiling. "That's pretty."

"They make me happy."

I swallow a bitter ghost of regret, remembering how much Rose had loved Christmas lights. Back then I was an asshole who told her it was stupid to leave them up all year long. Such a simple thing brought her joy but I complained and made her miserable until she took them down.

"Grayson?" Serena's concerned voice sounds a mile away.

The ghosts of my past recede, like Serena's voice is a magical potion to transform them into dust. "Right here, buttercup."

"Is your shoulder okay?" She reaches up to touch me.

I jerk away. "I'm fine."

"Will you let me massage it a little?"

"It's fine." *Why am I saying no to a massage?*

"Please?" She teases her hands under my shirt, her fingers tickling my skin.

"What if I want to rub *you* down?"

"How about this? If I do a good job, you can massage me when I'm done."

"Deal."

She nods to the bed. "Strip down and stretch out. I'll be right back."

"Strip down? You ask all your patients to do that?"

"Only the hot ones." She prances out of the room.

Laughing, I take off everything and stretch my big body in the middle of her bed, resting my head on my arms, facing the door.

My breath catches when she returns wearing nothing but her bra and underwear.

"Mmm. Very nice, Grayson." The bed dips as she rests her knee at the edge and climbs on.

I reach one arm toward her, sliding my hand along her smooth thigh.

"Not yet," she whispers. She straddles my body, hugging her legs to my sides. A few seconds later, soft, slippery hands stroke along either side of my spine. I let out a long, contented groan.

"That's it," she whispers. "Relax for me."

Relax, nothing. My dick's so hard it hurts.

She continues the long, soft, gentle strokes, increasing the pressure with each pass. Slowly, she shifts the focus of her touches to my right shoulder, kneading and rubbing almost to the point of pain.

When I think I won't be able to stand another second, she switches to my other shoulder, evening out the sensations.

She scoots down and focuses on my lower back and hips. "You're tight here," she whispers, following lines of pain and tension I didn't even know I had. "Relax. Breathe in for me. One, two, three. Breathe out."

It's like my lungs operate under her orders or something. My body follows along with her soft instructions.

"That's it." She slides lower, digging her fingers into my ass and thighs. "I've never been so turned on by a man's legs before," she murmurs.

"Oh yeah?" I lift on one arm and turn to watch her.

"Eyes forward, Grayson," she scolds playfully.

Laughing, I rest my head again, almost falling asleep as she continues the full-body rub.

"Turn over, please?" Her weight lifts off my lower body and she settles next to me.

Groggy, almost in a dreamlike state, I turn onto my back and stretch my arms over my head.

She gasps. "Oh."

Soft, slippery fingers wrap around my cock and squeeze.

I open one eye. "Couldn't help it."

"I'm not complaining." She holds my gaze while slowly stroking her hand up and down.

My eye closes again. Everything she does feels so fucking amazing. I reach for her, resting my hand on her knee, rubbing my thumb over her satin skin.

She shifts. The warm, wet heat of her mouth closes around my cock.

"Ahh, fuck," I groan and stretch again, my whole body shuddering with pleasure.

"Mm-hmm," she hums, the vibration singing through my veins.

"Serena."

Without taking her mouth off me, she crawls between my thighs. One of her hands follows the path of her mouth, slicking her saliva all over my shaft.

"Fuck." Opening my eyes is a mistake. One look at her flicking her tongue over me then sucking deep has my body coiled tight, ready to blow. So warm, wet, and perfect.

"Serena," I urge, running my fingers over her arm. "Get on top of me."

She pulls off with a pop but keeps rubbing her hand up and down.

"Come on." I'm panting and wave toward the floor. "Condom. In my jeans."

Keeping one hand on my dick, she leans over the side of the bed and snags my pants.

"I'm not gonna go soft," I say. "You can let go."

She laughs softly and rips into the condom. Carefully she slides it on, and fuck, she even makes that a sensual experience.

I push my hand between her legs, finding the thin strip of her underwear. "Fuck, you're wet." I slide the material to the side and slip two fingers inside her.

She gasps and stops moving, squeezing her eyes shut. My thumb strays to her clit, and she bites her lip. Her hand squeezes my cock.

"Ladies first." I work my fingers faster. "Come for me like this and I'll let you have my dick."

"Oh, God." She gasps and rocks her hips into my hand. Hard, quick movements.

"That's it." Christ, I want her wrapped around me so fucking bad. A few seconds later, she shudders against my hand, pulsing and squeezing my fingers.

She's still whimpering as I guide her over me. "That's it." I hold her panties to the side and flex my hips, filling her with one hard thrust.

"Gray." Her eyes open.

"Right here." I rest my hands on her shoulders, pushing her down while thrusting up.

"Oh my God." Her body quivers.

"Get that bra off." I tug at the straps.

Laughing, she reaches behind her to undo the clasp and tosses it aside.

"That's better." I cup her breasts, playing with her nipples, tugging, watching her face to see what she likes better. "Ride my cock, buttercup."

My entire world narrows to the sight of her moving on top of me. Raising and lowering herself. Rocking back and forth. Testing every variation of what feels good. Juices coating my thighs. So hot and slick.

"Gray." She reaches for me and I take her hands, holding her as she rocks faster, bucking her hips, completely wild.

"So beautiful, Serena. Come again for me."

"Oh." She squeezes her eyes shut and slips one of her hands free, pressing it to her chest. Pink circles her neck and climbs all the way to her cheeks. "I'm going to. I am."

"Good." I grip her hips, feeling how hard she's chasing release. Finally, she clenches around me and moans, working hard to maintain a steady rhythm. I clench my teeth, impossibly close to blowing.

"I'm coming," she chants.

Molten lava races down my spine, and I can't hold out. My vision fades. Sounds narrow to only our breaths as I explode.

I'm floating for a few seconds, completely lost. "Fuck."

She falls against my body, and I wrap my arms around her. Our sweaty skin slides together. My brain blinks into functioning mode again, and I turn to kiss her forehead. "I couldn't hold out anymore, woman."

She giggles softly, and scrapes her teeth against my nipple. "The timing was splendid."

I've never been so content. "That's the first and best massage I've ever had."

"How do you know it's the best if it's the first?" she teases, lifting her head to smile at me.

I groan, reaching to grab the condom. "Lift up, baby." I kiss her cheek as I slide free.

She rolls to the side and stares up at the ceiling.

"I'll be right back," I promise.

*Can I even walk straight?*

I stumble into her bathroom and dispose of the condom.

When I return, she's facing the door, lifted on one elbow. I scoop my arms under her and pull her close. Flushed cheeks, soft eyes, and wild hair. She's so much more beautiful than I have any right to be with. I kiss her cheek, her eyelids, and her forehead.

Her hair tickles my arms as she rests against my chest. She twines her legs with mine. I take her hand, and she rubs her thumb over my knuckles. She sits and studies the scars on my hand. Proof of my struggles to survive.

"Got no business being with you, Serena. Too old and too worn down."

She rubs her lips against my knuckles and peers up at me "It's better to grow old—even if not gracefully—than the alternative, don't you think?"

"What alternative?"

"Not growing old at *all*."

My chest squeezes and warms at the same time. "You're good for me. I'm not so sure I'm good for you."

"Well, I'm a big girl. Why don't you let me decide that for myself?"

Cupping her cheek, I pull her closer and answer with a kiss.

I never expected to feel this strongly about anyone.

Little by little, she's owning my soul.

And there isn't a damn thing I can do to stop it.

# CHAPTER TWENTY-ONE

## Serena

I'VE NEVER CUDDLED WITH SOMEONE THIS MUCH. GRAYSON AND I ARE like magnetic Velcro. Neither of us strays far from the other. While I'm in his arms, all the possible problems seem far away.

The lighting in my bedroom is low, so I reach over to tap the lamp on my nightstand.

"Fuck, that's bright." Gray squeezes his eyes shut while I stretch and press the button to dim the light.

"Better?"

He cups my breast, rubbing his thumb over my nipple. "Much. Goddamn, woman. You're perfect in every light."

Laughing, I push him back and sit up. "You're not so bad yourself." I tap right below the newly inked skeleton key on his chest. It's a heavy, dark piece. "I like this a lot, by the way. That's why I turned on the light. So I could study your new ink better."

Instead of sharing some tidbit of information about the meaning behind the design, he sighs and absently rubs over the key. "I wanted to cover Rose's name as soon as possible."

*Did he?* Wait. "Is *that* why you didn't want to…sleep with me for so long?"

He stares up at the ceiling for a few heartbeats. "Maybe."

"You didn't have to cover it for me." That had to be expensive and painful. "I would've...understood."

"It was time." His voice turns distant.

An ugly thought snakes into my head. "Grayson?"

He's busy studying my tits again, and I blow out an annoyed breath to regain his attention.

He lifts his eyes. "Have mercy on me. You're gorgeous, and I haven't had much beauty in my life, Serena."

Now I feel even shittier for what I'm about to ask. "I'm not a way for you to get over your ex-wife, am I? A placeholder or substitute?"

His eyes widen in shock and he stares at me.

"No. Fuck no. Jesus." He tugs on my hand. "Get over here."

I shift closer but not close enough for his taste. He grabs my hips and lifts me, guiding me over his legs until I'm straddling his blanket-covered lap. Vulnerability scratches at me like steel wool. I'm not only nude, but I've exposed one of my biggest fears with that question.

He brushes my hair out of my face. "Is that how I make you feel?"

"No." *Cherished* is how I feel with him but that's too big to say out loud. "Were you disappointed that she wasn't waiting for you?"

"*Disappointed* isn't the right word. In the moment, I felt foolish. But now, I'm relieved." He shrugs. "We hadn't seen each other in fifteen years so I should've seen it coming."

"She *never* came to visit you?"

"I didn't want her to see me in there. Or get targeted by anyone inside. I did enough to ruin her life. I didn't need people coming after her when I wasn't there to protect her."

"Then why did you...?"

"We wrote letters." His mouth twists, and he glances away. "Hers were superficial and short."

"And she never mentioned she had a husband and kid?" It seems a bit cliche to criticize his ex, but that's so *cold*.

"No. Not even a hint." He shrugs again. "Who the hell knows. Maybe she thought they'd be safer that way."

A phone buzzes from somewhere on the floor. Mine's still in the other room, so it must be Gray's.

"Someone's looking for you," I whisper, crawling over him.

He groans. "Sorry."

I locate his phone and hand it to him. "I'll give you privacy."

I take a shower, hoping he'll join me, but finally give up.

When I return to the bedroom, Grayson's zipping up his jeans.

"What's wrong?" I try not to pout but can't keep it out of my voice.

"Need to go up to the clubhouse." He buckles his jeans and glances at me. "You can come with me. I'd like you to."

"Are you sure? I don't want to cause…trouble." Every second we spend together without me telling him the truth is dangerous. When we're here, it's so easy to forget and pretend that's not part of my past.

At the clubhouse, it's almost impossible.

"Why would you cause me trouble?" He frowns. "Of course I want you with me."

"Oh." My heart races as he crosses the room in only his jeans.

He stops in front of me and takes my hands. "After Grillo dropping by unannounced, I don't want to chance not being home tonight. So I don't plan to stay long." He strokes his knuckles over my cheek. "Pack a few things to bring with you."

"Are you asking me to spend the night?"

His jaw tightens. "Yeah."

"Okay." I kiss his cheek before darting off to gather my clothes.

"Serena?" his gruff voice rumbles behind me. He presses his body against my back and wraps his arms around my waist, dropping a kiss on my shoulder. "I have a lot of regrets. I don't want to mess this up and have you be one of them."

I lean against him. "I don't want you to regret me either."

That's not quite how I meant it. "Never."

I turn and rest my forehead against his chest.

"Look, I know you saw some things at the clubhouse the other night. It's not always like that."

I swallow hard and look away. I know all too well what goes on in motorcycle clubs.

"Hey." Misunderstanding why I can't look at him, he presses a finger to my cheek. "Everything okay?"

Here's where I should tell him the truth about my history with the club. It's a perfect opportunity. If he's going to leave me because of it, we can break clean now. Before my feelings for him get any bigger.

I should've told him before we slept together. And I definitely should've said something after he bared his soul to me about his ex-wife.

Now, it might be too late.

# CHAPTER TWENTY-TWO

## Grinder

ROOSTER AND HIS GIRL, JIGSAW, TELLER, AND WRATH ARE ALL IN THE living room at the clubhouse when Serena and I arrive.

"The fuck did I run up here for if we're not sittin' down for church?" I ask, hanging my coat in the closet, then Serena's.

Wrath chuckles. "Rock does this to us all the time."

"Hurry up and wait," Teller grumbles. His eyes land on Serena, and he frowns slightly.

She stops and looks back toward the door. I get that the brothers can be intimidating, but she's got nothing to worry about when she's with me.

I curl my hand around hers and drag her forward.

Wrath's staring at his phone. "Trin needs my help." He slaps Teller's arm. "If he gets his ass here anytime soon, tell Rock I'll be right back."

"I'm not your messenger." Teller slaps him back. "I got my own shit to do."

They head off toward the dining room, arguing.

Shaking my head, I drop into a seat near Rooster. "Where's everyone else?"

"Z and Steer are out at Z's construction site, I think," Rooster answers.

"Heidi and Murphy are still at their place," Shelby adds.

"I'm here." Jigsaw spreads his arms wide like he's biker Jesus. "What more do you need?"

Rumbling with laughter, I pat his back. "You're right. My life is complete now."

"Ah, you seem much more chipper, Grinder." Jigsaw grins.

Rooster elbows him.

I lean into Serena and pass her my phone. "Can you pull up that thing you showed me before? With the boxes and the comments?"

"Instagram?" She raises her eyebrows. "Why?"

I grit my teeth. Never dealt with a woman who asked so many questions. "I wanna ask Rooster something."

Her wide, round eyes bounce between Rooster and me. "I, uh…not a lot of people in my real life know about it."

I stare at her, trying to figure that out.

She squirms. "I try to keep my real life and online life separate."

"Good luck with that," Shelby says.

"You manage okay," Jiggy says to Shelby.

"Only because Rooster's managing my social media now."

"You do that stuff?" I ask Rooster. See? I knew he was the one to ask.

"Yeah," he answers slowly. His gaze darts between Serena and me. "Why?"

I wiggle my fingers at Serena in a *hurry up* motion. "Give me the phone."

"Ugh." Serena blows out a frustrated breath and yanks her phone out of her purse instead. She taps at it a few times and brings up a miniature version of what was on her laptop earlier.

"Whatcha got going on, Serena?" Jigsaw asks.

"Not porn," she snaps.

I frown in her direction, surprised at her tone. It seems to roll off Jigsaw, though.

*I never asked how they know each other.*

"What am I looking at?" Rooster asks.

I pass her phone to him. "She gets these creeps leaving disgusting comments. Any way to track them down?"

"Hoo-boy," Shelby mutters. "You get dick pics too?" she asks Serena.

"What?" I thunder loud enough to rattle the windows.

"A few, unfortunately," Serena mutters.

"What a way to ruin a day," Shelby laments. "Shrimpy ol' dick pics. Just, why? Why is that a thing?"

Serena chuckles but doesn't comment.

"You have one of these too, Shelby?" I ask.

She sort of ducks her head and looks at Rooster. "Yeah, I kind of have to. Pretty much everyone our age does."

"She's a singer," Rooster explains.

Shelby passes her phone to me, and Serena peers over my shoulder.

I glance at Rooster, then Shelby. "You have three *million* people following you?"

"Oh!" Serena exclaims. "You're Shelby Morgan. I *knew* you looked familiar." She slides her gaze toward Rooster. "How in the heck did you two meet?"

"It's the most adorable story," Jigsaw says in a high-pitched girls-who-gossip voice.

Shelby swats him. "Don't you be making fun of our story."

"Oh, I'm not, songbird. It makes my shriveled up, black heart pulse with joy every time I tell it."

"Good grief." Shelby rolls her eyes and aims a grin at Serena, who laughs.

*Our girls are going to be trouble together.*

Rooster's quiet, not paying attention to their chatter. He seems to be examining Serena's account closely. "You've got a lot of creeps following you, Serena," he mutters.

"I block and delete the ones I can."

"We can keep an eye on this, brother," Rooster says to me.

"What are you going to do? Watch my 'which blush is right for your skin tone' videos?" Serena asks.

Rooster chuckles. "Beats the shit I'm monitoring for others."

"Hey," Shelby says.

"Not you." Rooster hooks his arm around her shoulders and draws her closer, kissing her temple. She leans in and whispers something in his ear, then stands and holds out a hand to Serena. "Come on. Do you do yoga? You look like a yoga girl. They have a great lil' studio here. Let's check it out."

Serena hesitates before accepting the invitation.

Rooster watches them leave. Once they've cleared the room, he explains, "One of her fans was stalking her. The fucker kidnapped her after one of her shows. I've never felt more helpless or been more terrified."

My worst fucking nightmare. "Jesus Christ, you kidding me? Was she…is she okay?"

"Yeah, she's good now. But I'd rather not talk about it in front of her—that's all."

"Where's the guy?"

"Very dead," Jigsaw answers. "And missing a pinky." He wiggles his own pinky fingers at me.

"Good," I grumble. Sounds like club justice was served.

"Club handled it. But I wish I'd gotten to do it myself," Rooster says.

"Long as he's not around to bother Shelby again—that's all that really matters," I say.

"Amen." He pulls out his phone. "Anyway, I keep a close eye on all of Shelby's social media now. I track a few of the girls who work for our film company too."

"Film? Lost Kings runnin' a Hollywood studio now?"

He smirks. "Porn, brother. It's porn."

"Ah, right." That explains all the porn stars who showed up for my welcome home bash.

"Grade A." Jigsaw kisses his fingertips.

"I expect nothing less."

Rooster continues swiping and clicking on his phone. "And now, I'm following Serena." He studies the screen. "Smart move not using her real name or location. Doesn't matter, though. Hopefully she's got a P.O. Box. Some of these fuckers can track you by the smallest details."

"I got no fuckin' idea about any of this shit." I cough and look away. "Making me feel old as fuck."

"Eh, don't sweat it. I only got dragged into social media out of necessity. Plenty of people opt out of this bullshit." Rooster shakes his phone from side to side. Not sure if it's for technical reasons or to emphasize a point. "It's cool because it connects people together in lots of ways. But it's also making people crazier and more miserable than ever. Double-edged sword or whatever."

I appreciate his effort to make me feel like less of a relic.

"World's changed a lot," Jigsaw says.

"No kidding. I hadn't noticed," I growl. "You have one of these things too, Jiggy? Post pretty pictures of yourself?" I reach over and pat his cheek a few times.

"Fuck no." He laughs and swipes my hand away. "Not for personal stuff. Only to help Rooster do some work."

Rooster scratches his head. "You help me work? Since when?"

"Fucker," Jigsaw laughs.

Ravage strolls up behind Rooster and peers over his shoulder. "Woo, she's hot. Shelby know you're creepin' on other chicks' Instas?"

"Shut the fuck up." Rooster waves at me. "I'm helping Grinder with something."

"Right." Ravage perches on the edge of the couch. "Rooster hooking you up?"

"I don't understand all that shit."

Ravage squeezes his eyes shut. "You are missing out on one of modern life's greatest miracles, Grandpa."

"You're gonna be missing your tongue if you call me Grandpa again."

Ignoring the threat, Rav hops off the arm of the couch and throws himself next to me. He sets his phone on the table and pulls up the same thing Serena uses.

"So *many* hot chicks out there now," Ravage explains in a frenzied rush. "You got no idea what you've been missing. All these hot chicks in need of validation basically post porn for free. It's amazing." He flips through several screens of pretty young women.

"When I was your age, I had to walk my ass down to the gas station and cough up five bucks for a magazine full of pics like that," I say.

"Yeah, now it's free and right at your fingertips. Technology is great." Rav swipes over the screen until he finds more X-rated photos. "You can pay for access to the hardcore stuff too. Like, just regular girls."

Rooster rolls his eyes. "You're a degenerate."

"I'm a healthy, average, red-blooded man."

"At least you admit you're average." Sparky cackles at his own joke.

"Holy shit!" Ravage jolts, throwing his arms in the air. "Look who materialized from the basement. Announce yourself next time, ya sneaky stoner."

"Boss said we had church." Sparky glances around. "Where is everyone?"

"Don't know." Ravage settles into the couch again. "I'm introducing Grinder to Instagram. There's *so* many other places—Oh! Brother, we've got online hookup apps now too. Empire isn't crawling with high-quality tail, but if you're willing to travel a little—"

"For fuck's sake," Rooster growls. "Really?"

"Can we wrap up the porn lessons for ex-cons?" I snarl. "I'd like to finish talking to Rooster about my *actual* concern."

"What's wrong?" Sparky asks.

"It's personal."

"Yikes." Sparky puts his hands in the air and walks away backwards all the way to the hallway leading to the dining room. Rav jumps up and follows him, asking about edibles.

"Eh, I shouldn't snap at Sparky," I grumble.

"He won't remember by the time we sit down for church," Jigsaw assures me.

"So, Serena's got a nice little following. Half a million subscribers is no joke," Rooster says without looking away from his screen. "Lots of engagement with her videos on each platform." He squints and studies the screen. "I fucking hate fucking TikTok," he mutters, casting a furtive glance over his shoulder. "Thank fuck Shelby hasn't had any interest in it, and Greg still doesn't even know what the fuck it is yet."

Jigsaw chortles.

"There's *more* of those fucking…apps?" I ask. "More creeps?"

"It's a sea of creeps." Jigsaw spreads his arms wide. "An ocean of lonely, pathetic creeps, crawling out from under rocks and squinting at the sunshine for the first time."

"Fantastic."

The front door opens and Murphy strolls in, followed by Steer and Z.

Rooster passes Serena's phone to me. "You ever got questions about any of it, just ask me, brother," he says in a low voice.

"Yeah, don't ask Ravage," Jigsaw adds. "Unless you want to learn how to transmit herpes through Bluetooth."

*What. The. Fuck?*

Rooster slaps Jigsaw. "He's kidding. That's not possible."

"If there's a way, Ravage will discover it," Jigsaw assures me.

*What a great time to be alive.*

# CHAPTER TWENTY-THREE

## Grinder

Serena's waiting outside the war room when we emerge from church. "One second, Serena," I say, holding up my hand.

"Okay."

The clubhouse is starting to fill with people. I duck inside the war room to catch Rock and Wrath before they leave.

"What's up, Gray?" Rock asks.

"You need me anymore tonight?"

"No," Rock answers slowly.

"What's wrong?" Wrath asks.

"Nothing. I got hassled by my parole officer for breaking curfew the other night. So I'll probably jet by nine."

"Seriously?" Z asks. "The fuck?" He shoots a glare at Wrath.

"Shit, brother. I thought we had that worked out," Wrath says. "I'm sorry."

"It's fine. I got less than a year left of dealing with that bullshit."

"I'll take care of it," Z says.

"No. Don't. If he's already got it out for me…I don't want to do anything that might make it worse." I've had some time to think it over. "I'll lay low."

"How'd you get out of it?" Wrath asks.

I laugh and run my hand over the back of my neck. Can't believe I'm going to admit this in front of my brothers. "I was out with Serena. She explained we were at a play to him."

At the mention of Serena's name, Murphy's head snaps up.

Wrath stares at me. "At. A. *Play?*"

"A musical or whatever. A friend of hers was in it." I wave it off. "That's not the point."

The corners of Rock's mouth twitch. "Sounds like a good night."

"It was. Until that jackass showed up."

"You sure you don't want me to try and handle it?" Z asks.

"Nah, let it ride."

"All right, but if it gets worse, let us know," Rock says.

"I will," I promise.

I leave them to their officers-only pep rally and search for my girl. Hope smiles and waves at me from the couch in the corner. I approach her slowly, scanning the room for Serena.

"She and Shelby went upstairs for a minute," Hope explains before I even ask.

"I'm gonna run down to the dining room and grab some coffee." I jerk my thumb over my shoulder.

"I'll let her know."

I push through people to get to the hallway. Even the dining room is crowded. Steer's sitting on top of the bar with a bottle of Jack Daniels.

"They done?" he asks me.

"No idea." I pour a cup of coffee from the full, fresh pot at the end of the bar. The girl fixing drinks back there can barely see over the bar. "Swan, right? Is there any cream?"

"Sure thing. Hang on a second." She glides over to a small refrigerator and returns with a carton.

"Thanks, sweetheart."

"Hey, Grinder." Lilly settles her hand on my shoulder. "How's it going?"

"Not bad." Jesus, she's a stunning woman. No wonder Z's so hooked on her.

"Are you and Serena sticking around?" she asks.

Guess word travels fast. "Planning to for a little bit."

"Good."

Steer slowly turns and stares at us.

"The fuck you lookin' at, son?" I ask.

"Me? Nothin'."

Lilly's gaze darts between us. "Trinity and I are baking." She gestures toward the kitchen behind us. "Let Serena know she's welcome to join us if she wants…"

Is it that obvious how serious I already am about Serena? Or is Lilly this nice to everyone? "Thank you, darlin', I will."

Armed with my coffee, I turn to leave.

"Hey, Grinder, right?" a pint-sized brunette asks.

"Yeah?" I answer warily.

"Shari." She holds out her hand and flashes a dazzling smile.

Ignoring the hand, I nod at her. "Good to know."

Steer walks up and slings his arm over my shoulder. "Shari's a doll, aren't ya, hon?"

She bats her big eyes at him. "I do my best."

I shrug Steer off. "Great, I'll leave you two to it. I got someone waitin' for me."

Steer follows me out of the dining room.

"Grinder, did Lilly say you're here with *Serena*? Did I hear that right?"

I stop dead. "The fuck you know about her?"

"Uh, I know you don't need to saddle yourself with a whore who's been with a bunch of brothers downstate and probably half the ones upstate."

The coffee falls from my hand, splashing my boots and jeans. The mug shatters at my feet.

Cobra-fast, I wrap my hand around his neck and slam him against the wall. "Say that again, motherfucker."

I don't give a fuck if it's the whiskey talking. No one talks trash about Serena.

He's a big guy, but old or not, I'm no slouch. He wears the SAA patch now. But I had one stitched onto my cut by the time this fool had discovered hand lotion and his dad's *Playboy* magazines.

His eyes go saucer-wide. "What?"

"About my girl."

If it's even possible, his eyes expand to dinner plate-size. "Serena? Your girl?" He chokes out each word. "You're serious?"

I snap him closer and then slam him into the wall again. He grunts and struggles to get free. "The fuck you know about her?"

"Easy, brother," Murphy says in a low voice behind me. "What's going on?"

"Grinder," Z says a tad louder from my other side. "What's wrong, bro?"

I don't take my eyes off Steer or loosen my grip. "Our boy here needs to watch his fucking mouth."

Steer holds his hands up. "Sorry, brother," he sputters. "I didn't mean..." His gaze shoots to Murphy and Z. "It's my fault. I shouldn't have said anything."

"Grayson?" Serena calls out.

Ah, fuck, if her sweet voice doesn't settle the beast inside of me right the fuck down.

I release Steer. He doubles over and wheezes in a few breaths before holding out his hand. "Sorry, brother. No disrespect."

No disrespect my ass.

Protocol, brotherhood—everything says I should shake his hand and let it go. That a woman shouldn't come before brotherhood.

I can't do it, though.

"Give us a second, hon," Z calls down the hallway to Serena.

Right like that, my blood pressure hits the red zone again. I spin around and jab my finger in Z's chest. "Watch who you're calling *hon*, brother."

"Grinder," Z says, using the patient, president voice he's adopted. Before, it made me proud. Now I just want to punch him. "What's gotten into you?" He stares at where I'm still poking him in the chest and raises an eyebrow.

"Nothing." I shoot a glare Steer's way, but he's already pushing his way back into the dining room. "He started talking shit about my girl."

"Serena?" Z asks.

"Yeah."

Z closes his eyes briefly. "Good. All right."

Not what I expected from him.

"You made it clear she's with you?" Murphy asks.

I flex my hand. "I think I made my point."

"I meant with *her*."

Guess Murphy's looking for an ass-kicking too. "What's that supposed to mean?"

"Nothing." Murphy holds up his hands.

All those questions I should've asked sooner fire off in my head. "How do you know her?"

Z side-eyes Murphy like he wants to staple his mouth shut. "Serena used to hang around Downstate," he explains carefully, seeming to measure each word.

My world rocks sideways. Single women don't just "hang around" motorcycle clubs. "What are you talking about?"

The two of them exchange more anxious glances.

"If she's with you, that's good," Murphy says, which doesn't answer my question.

"Serena's a good girl. She wasn't treated very nice by the last Downstate VP. That's all," Z explains. "No one had seen her in a while. It's all good." He thumps my back before hurrying into the dining room.

I curl my fist in Murphy's T-shirt and yank him closer. "I ain't buying that happy horse shit. What else did you want to tell me?"

"Nothing." He glances down at my hand.

I release him but keep staring him down until he rolls his eyes.

"Nothing bad. Z's right. Shadow—the old Downstate VP—was a real piece of shit." He pauses and looks away.

"You trying to tell me she was a club girl?" Not my Serena. She seemed so awkward and uncomfortable here that first night.

"Just be nice to her."

"Of course I am." I narrow my eyes, studying his expression. Looks a lot like when he was a kid and I'd catch him in the garage sittin' on one of the brother's bikes. "Why? You got a thing for her?"

"Christ, brother. You know I'm fucking married now." He gestures in Heidi's direction.

Didn't miss the word *now*. "*Had* a thing for her?"

Murphy's always had too much respect for his elders, otherwise he would've punched me for asking that question. "*Before* Heidi, yes. We had a thing. And I probably strung her along more than was right. Then, Shadow treated her shitty but"—an evil gleam enters his eyes—"Z handled *that* motherfucker. He got what was coming to him." His expression shifts. "Honestly, I'm surprised she'd even come back here. She was always a nice girl. Loyal to the club. So, treat her well—that's all I'm saying."

If I wasn't so torqued up, I'd be proud of Murphy's concern. Rock's influence has obviously soaked into the younger members. "Who else?"

He cocks his head. "Who else, *what?*"

"Don't be dumb, Murphy. Hasn't worked for you since you were a kid."

His gaze darts around the room. Deciding if he should warn some brothers or not seeing anyone who fits the bill?

"I honestly don't know. No one else Upstate, I'm pretty sure." He crosses his arms over his chest. "I've been a little busy to stay pen pals."

"Don't get cute with me."

"Brother, the second Heidi moved home, I kept my distance from *all* the club girls. So, I'm sorry, but I don't have a lot of information for you." He stares at me until what he's trying to say sinks in.

"Heidi got a problem with her?" Shit. So far, all the old ladies have been nice to Serena.

Murphy glares hard enough to set a lesser man on fire. "I don't think so. They were around each other when I was helping Z run things Downstate and I didn't see any issues. But it's not like Heidi and I sit around chatting about our exes."

"I'm sorry I'm putting you on the spot. But I need to know. So I don't get blindsided." *Again.*

"She *never* mentioned it?" Disbelief drips through his words.

"Don't worry about our conversations. Who else is gonna smart off like Steer did?"

He blows out an annoyed breath. "I don't know. Besides Shadow and his fuckery, Tawny was always shitty to her."

"She's always been hostile to any woman associated with the club," I say. "I remember that much. It was just a matter of if she was nasty to their face or if she stabbed 'em in the back."

"Got that right," he mutters. "Anyway, after all that shit went down with Shadow, Serena vanished. As far as I know, she stayed away from the club."

*Until I dragged her back.*

That flicker of fear on her face when we met makes sense now. She wasn't reacting to my ink in general. She reacted to the Lost Kings emblem *specifically*.

*That's* how she knows Jigsaw and Rooster. That's how Hope knew her.

*Holy fuck.* I've been so damn dazzled by her, I never asked a bunch of obvious questions.

My club treated her poorly. Yet, she's here. Because of me.

"Ask Rooster or Jiggy. They'd know more and won't talk trash like Steer."

I finally nod at Murphy. "Yeah, okay."

"We good?" he asks.

I nod at his question, but my gaze lands on Serena in the distance to my left.

More specifically, on Serena grabbing her coat and heading for the front door.

Too many people stand between her and me. I pound down the hallway and burst through the dining room and into the kitchen, where I slam my way outside.

My boots crunch over the ground as I circle to the front of the clubhouse, eating up the distance between us.

She can't outrun me.

I grunt and lunge, crashing into her.

She yelps.

My arms lock around her waist and I lift her in the air, slamming her back against my chest. "Where do you think you're going?" I whisper against her ear.

"I tried to warn you I'd cause trouble."

"*You* didn't cause trouble." Steer did with his big fucking mouth. But I handled it. I trust it's done and won't happen again.

When she finally goes limp in my arms, I set her down.

She turns and faces me. "I can't do this again, Grayson."

"Do what?"

Serena tilts her head, and fuck, she's more than I deserve. Is it too much that after so many years of ugliness I want to wake up to beauty and grace every morning? I want to take care of her. Have her look after me. Every day. Why doesn't that seem to be in the cards?

"I can only imagine what Steer said to you," she whispers.

"Trust me, he won't say it again."

She shakes her head. "What'd Murphy tell you?" A slight sneer curls her lip.

"That you're a good girl, and I should be nice to you."

Her expression softens. "That asshole." She huffs a sad laugh. "He always made it hard to hate him."

"He said my club didn't treat you well. And I'm sorry."

Her blue eyes widen. "Why? You weren't even here."

"Doesn't matter."

"All the really bad things happened Downstate, anyway." She glances over her shoulder. "They might as well have been two different clubs the way Sway ran things."

I growl at the mention of Sway. There's one motherfucker I'd like to choke.

"You saw my ink. You knew this was my club," I say. "Why'd you come here that first night?"

Her body trembles, and she wraps her arms around herself. "To see you," she whispers.

"Why?"

She shrugs.

"Tell me."

"I've told you." A note of exasperation colors her explanation. "I wanted to see you outside of work. I could get in trouble for dating a patient. But I knew *no one* would ever talk about what went on at the clubhouse."

"Why risk it, though?" My heart's racing. I just tried to choke out one of my brothers for disrespecting her. I need her to say it.

She narrows her eyes. "I *liked* you."

"Why? You got a daddy fetish?"

She lifts her chin, tilting her head to the side. "Yeah. *That's* probably it."

Damn, Serena's defiant streak runs deep and I fucking love it.

I snort and she laughs, then pokes me in the chest. "It's not funny." She drops her head. "I like you, Grayson. A lot."

*Like.* It's been years, but what I think I'm starting to feel for this woman goes way beyond like.

I'll do anything to protect her. Even go after one of my brothers.

I might not have been looking for a relationship so soon after obtaining my freedom, but I think I've found exactly what I need. Everything about us feels so right.

I just hope it doesn't end wrong.

# CHAPTER TWENTY-FOUR

## Serena

THE CAT'S FINALLY ESCAPED THE BAG.

Grinder knows my past. Maybe not the specifics. That I allowed myself to be used and discarded by his brothers for far too long before I came to my senses.

After Z took over Downstate, Shadow paid me one last visit to vent his frustration. It took him almost killing me to finally get it through my head that bikers are bad news.

Grayson has never been anything but gentle with me.

Shadow was nice in the beginning, too, but never gentle. There were so many red flags I missed completely or straight-up ignored.

What Gray and I have is different. *Real.* Instinctively, I know they're nothing alike. I've always known it.

He reaches out and touches my cheek. "I like you too, Serena. Obviously." One corner of his mouth hitches to the side. "Never gone after a brother before."

"You're not mad at me?" I whisper.

"Mad? At you? No. Why?"

"That I didn't tell you myself."

He tilts his head and lifts one shoulder in a playful way. "A heads-up mighta been nice." His expression turns serious. "But I'm *not* mad."

Can he really mean that? "It doesn't…*bother* you?"

He stares long and hard at the clubhouse, then at my face. "No, buttercup. Whatever happened before isn't my business."

Maybe that's his way of telling me to never ask about *his* past.

No one's ever chased after me before. Bullied and threatened, sure. Chased out of fear of losing me? Never.

It means a lot to me that Grinder did, even if I didn't make it farther than the parking lot.

"Are you mine now?" he asks.

"Yes." But I can't stop worrying about how much of the conversation between Steer and Grinder everyone overheard. "You're not worried your brothers will think you're settling for a club whore?"

Anger flashes through his eyes. "Don't ever talk about my woman like that again." He takes a few breaths. "You said you were mine. Were you lying?"

"You're sure you want me to be?"

"That's not the question." He gently grips my chin and forces me to look at him. His rough thumb brushes over my cheek. "Don't be difficult."

"Yes."

"Yes, what?" he insists.

Why is it so hard to say? Bikers always claim their women. Not the other way around. "I'm yours."

He bows his head, pressing his mouth to mine. "That's right," he whispers against my lips. Still watching me, he draws away. "I'm the ex-con—the one who has no business being with *you*. I don't want to drag you down—"

I open my mouth to protest, but he silences me with a finger against my lips. "I wasn't finished."

When I nod to indicate I'll wait my turn, he leans down and presses his lips to mine again. He trails his fingers through my hair, tipping my head back even more. I'm up on tiptoes, curling my arms around his neck, returning his demanding kisses, forgetting where we're standing and that I was about to leave.

I'm absolutely breathless and drunk on him when he finally pulls away. "Let's go," he says.

"Go where?"

"To my apartment."

My stomach clenches tight. After all this? "You don't want to be seen with me now?"

"No. Fuck no, Serena." He cups my cheek, forcing me to look at him. "That's not it at all. I thought you'd be uncomfortable here after that scene." He waves his hand at the clubhouse. "It's noisy too. We can be alone and it would be quieter there—that's it."

My gaze shifts to the clubhouse and back to Grayson. "I don't want to look weak in front of your brothers. They already think I'm a whore—"

"Don't fucking say that."

"It's the truth."

"No. It's. Not," he growls. "And if any of them ever even *hint* at that, you tell me right away."

"You want me to rat out your brothers? That won't make them like me."

"It's not *ratting* them out. It's your man protecting you." He brushes his knuckles over my cheek. "I don't give a fuck if they like you. But they will show you respect." He throws a possessive arm around my shoulders, much like the way he did that first night.

"Why'd you do that the first time I came up here?" I ask.

He steers us toward the front door and boldly steps inside. In front of everyone, he leans down and plants a kiss on my forehead. "Because I wanted everyone to know you were mine."

"And now?"

"They need to know that I'll choke anyone who disrespects you."

I scan the room, but thankfully, no one's paying attention to us. "I can't believe you lifted Steer off the ground. He's built like a bull."

Gray's body coils tight, and I realize what he's thinking. I dig my elbow into his ribs. "I've never slept with him." I point two fingers at my face. "I have eyes."

"I didn't say anything."

I turn toward him. "Are you going to wonder if I've slept with someone every time I mention a name? Do you need a list?"

His jaw clenches. "No."

"Yo, Grinder," Wrath calls from the war room door. "You got a minute?"

"Son of a bitch," he mutters. "You all right?"

My gaze skitters around the party.

"Promise you won't leave?"

"I won't get far," I mumble.

"Hey." He presses a finger to my chin and tips my head back. "Lilly said she and Trinity were baking stuff in the kitchen. She specifically invited you to join them."

My lips curve. "I like Lilly. She's a sweetheart."

"Good." He stares down the hallway as if he's calculating how many obstacles I might encounter on my way to the kitchen.

"I'll be fine," I assure him, casting a glance Wrath's way. "I wouldn't keep Wrath waiting."

## Grinder

I watch Serena until she disappears into the dining room, then join Wrath.

He shuts the war room door closed behind us. Neither of us sit.

"You planning to stand there and stare at me all day or did you actually need something?" I ask.

"Heard you were about to throw down with Steer." He arches a blond eyebrow, but his usual smirk isn't anywhere to be found.

"He had it coming. I don't care what he thinks he knows. I'm not allowing anyone to disrespect my woman. *Especially* a brother."

"Oh, I get it, Grinder. Trust me." Wrath's more serious than I've seen him in a while. "I agree. If you're planning to claim her, make it crystal clear. If anyone disrespects her, put an end to it fast."

"Well, that's what I did."

"Good."

I pull back and stare at him. "Are *you* advocating putting a woman before the brotherhood?"

He stares right back. "No. I'm saying protect your woman *for the good of the brotherhood*. There's a difference. Anyone who disrespects her after you've spelled it out is disrespecting the entire brotherhood. Every one of us."

"Did you know?"

He crosses his arms over his massive chest. "Know what?"

"Don't be cute, you big fucker. Did you know she used to hang around the club?"

"I've had my own shit to deal with, Grinder, so I don't exactly keep a journal of every—"

"Don't you fucking dare call her a—"

"Easy." He holds up one hand. "Yes, I recognized her. But what was I supposed to say? I didn't know you two were *that* tight." His fierce blue eyes drill into me. "For fuck's sake, you just got out of prison. How was I supposed to know you'd get this twisted over the first woman you stumbled over?"

"You think I'm too old to kick your ass?"

"Brother, please." He cocks his head, almost daring me to throw the first punch. "You like her?"

"I know it sounds ridiculous. We just met and—"

"You're old enough to be her dad," he points out.

I glare at him. "Thanks, I hadn't noticed."

There's that cocky fucking smirk I expected earlier. "Does she make you happy? Well, as happy as a grumpy old goat like you is gonna get."

"Yes, asshole."

"She must, if you're tagging along to high school musicals with her." He snickers.

"You're an even bigger dick than I remember."

"Thank you." His grin slides off his face and he flips to serious again. "You make *her* happy?"

"I want to. I think so."

"Then fuck what anyone else thinks." He lifts his gaze to the ceiling for a moment. "No one finds their way here by accident, Grinder. The brothers, the bunnies, the prospects, the hangarounds—they're all missing something in their life. All been betrayed or neglected by someone. The ones who stay find what they needed all along."

Damn, that sounds eerily similar to something I said to Wrath a lifetime ago. "Gee, I wonder who shared that brilliant piece of wisdom with you?"

"*You.*"

"Glad it stuck." I consider what he said again. "Sounds like she had a fucked up family from stuff she's said."

"Didn't we all?"

I run through the stories that I know of my brothers. Can't say I know anything about their women. Although, I can guess Trinity didn't have it easy.

"What happened to Trinity after Bishop died?" I ask.

His expression turns to steel.

"I remember seeing her at the Demons' compound a couple times when she was little," I explain, combing my memories for lost nuggets of information. "When Saints and Demons were on the outs, and Bishop went to prison. I lost track of her."

"Seems like everyone who could've done something lost track of her," he growls.

"Glad you two found each other."

"Yeah." His voice and expression turn distant. "Don't fuck it up, Grinder. Time's a bitch to get back."

"Don't I know it."

### Serena

Baking isn't an adequate word to describe what Trinity and Lilly are doing in the kitchen.

They have trays of brownie kiss cupcakes, mini apple cakes shaped like flowers, cinnamon rolls, bacon popovers, chocolate-dipped cherry cookies, fudgy mocha cream brownies, and a few cakes spread on every surface of the industrial-sized kitchen.

Sparky seems to have appointed himself the official tester of all the treats. He's perched on a chair at the kitchen table, nibbling on one of the cherry cookies with his eyes closed. "These are my fave, Trin," he says in a blissed-out voice.

"I thought the brownie kisses were your favorite," Lilly says, elbowing Trinity.

The two of them share a laugh.

Without opening his eyes, Sparky holds out his hands. "Let me have another brownie."

I set my knife down, careful not to smear cream cheese frosting all over the counter. "I got it."

"Careful," Trinity warns. "There won't be any left for anyone else."

I drop a brownie in Sparky's hands.

"Thank you, Serena."

"You're welcome."

His blissful smile widens. "You smell like carrot cake."

Laughing, I turn toward Trinity. "I'm done with mine."

She glances over and nods. "Thank you."

The back door flies open. Heidi and her daughter stomp into the kitchen, shaking snow off their coats. "I hope we're not too late."

I knew I'd eventually run into Heidi but I wasn't exactly looking forward to it. I don't have a problem with her, but I can't say she feels the same about me. Maybe if I stay still, I'll blend into the wallpaper.

"Aunties!" Alexa races over and throws herself at Lilly's legs.

"Hey, lil' monster." Lilly scoops her up and kisses her rosy-red cheeks.

"Where's my kisses?" Trinity asks.

While they're joking around, Heidi hangs up their coats and sets their boots on a tray inside the door. I pick up my knife and mess with the carrot cake some more.

"Oh. Serena, hey," Heidi says.

I glance at her and force a smile. "Hi."

We stare at each other for a few awkward beats.

"I roped her into frosting duty," Trinity explains breezily. "Serena's got a steadier hand than Mr. Munchies over there."

Sparky grins. "I'm your taste tester."

"Parky!" Alexa runs over to him.

Heidi glances at all the treats. "Sorry. I thought I'd make it over earlier."

"No worries. You feeling okay?" Lilly asks.

Heidi clutches her stomach. "No." She wrinkles her nose. "Is something burning? My nose is so screwy lately."

"Oh, shit!" Trinity yelps and races to the wall oven.

"Told you we were doing too much at once," Lilly mutters, popping a square of chocolate in her mouth.

"Eh." She pokes at a cast-iron skillet. "The bottom of the chocolate skillet cookie's a little black. But the rest is still edible."

"Bring it here." Sparky holds out his hands. "I'll hide the evidence, Trin."

I need to get away from this cozy little scene. "I'm going to run to the bathroom."

I sprint out of the kitchen before anyone answers. A tremor of fear runs through me as I snake my way through the dining room. Without Grayson by my side, I'm not sure who might stop me. But it seems ridiculous to ask one of the girls to be my bathroom buddy.

I hurry out of the dining room and down the long, wide hallway to the ladies' room. It's the size of a locker room—and even has a row of lockers to the left for club girls to leave their stuff. One row even houses a bunch of girly products for everyone to use. At one time, I thought that was such a thoughtful thing to do.

As soon as I step out, I run smack into a brick wall.

Nope, back up. I crane my neck. The brick wall is *Wrath*.

I can't think of any reason *he* shouldn't like me, but he's still scary as hell. "I—uh, sorry. I didn't mean to..."

"It's all right. Where you rushing off to?"

I gesture toward the dining room. "Kitchen. Your wife has me frosting cakes."

"Gray just went down there looking for you." His crinkled brow softens. "How's it going with you two?"

I blink, unsure of his intention. He can't possibly want to stand here and dish about my love life. "Good, I think."

"He tried to choke out a brother. Has to be more than *good*."

Heat singes my cheeks. Damn it. He's so damn big, taking up so much space, and I can't easily get away. "I like him a lot."

"Like, huh?" he mutters. "I think he's feelin' more than *like* for you."

"Well, that's really between me and Grayson," I snap, tired of overgrown men pushing me around.

He chuckles. "That's good. Keep that energy."

"What?"

"If you're gonna be his old lady, you can't take shit from any of us."

Is he out of his mind? "Women don't mouth off to bikers."

"They don't *mouth off*. They *stand up* for themselves." He cocks his head. "Trin always said you were loyal to the club but mousy."

*Trinity mentioned me to her husband? When? Why?*

"That won't fly being Grinder's ol' lady," he continues. "Find your spine. Reinforce it with some steel." He glances away, and it's a relief not to be under his burning stare for a second. "Hope'll probably take you under her wing. Guys are scared of her anyway."

"They're scared of *Hope*?"

"They're scared of Rock murdering them if they disrespect her," he clarifies.

"Oh." I'm so nervous, I'm trying to remember everything he says to examine later when I'm not half a second away from peeing my pants. "You really care about Gray, don't you?"

"Fuck yeah, I do."

"You go way back?"

"All the way to when I was a lowly hangaround."

"Wow, here I always imagined you were born wearing that cut." I nod to his SAA patch.

His mouth quirks. Glad I could amuse him.

Feeling a little braver, I cross my arms over my chest, mirroring his stance. "You don't have any *opinions*, like Steer did?"

"Nope. Not my business. As long as my brother's happy, that's all I'm worried about. He's been through a lot."

Who knew the brutal enforcer had so much love and concern in his heart?

"He did time for his club, Serena. No one takes that sacrifice lightly. All of us want to do what we can to make up for all he's lost."

I swallow hard and nod.

"I'm pissed his P.O. is giving him a hard time. That shoulda been handled," he mutters. "I know Gray ain't gonna tell us if he gets hassled again. So if *you* hear anything, let me know."

This feels like a test I'm woefully under-prepared for. "I can't go behind Gray's back," I finally say. The club doesn't respect snitches, right? Which choice is Wrath hoping I'll make here? Stay loyal to Grayson and not spill his secrets? Or be loyal to the club who's looking out for Gray's interests?

All of the above?

Or none?

## CHAPTER TWENTY-FIVE
### Serena

Sunlight stabs me in the eyes way too early.

But I finally have my wish—I'm waking next to Grayson.

He's a big man. Takes up a lot of space. I wiggle closer, luxuriating in his warmth. The hard lines of his face are softened by sleep. He almost looks vulnerable—my own lost king, who can only be woken by *my* kiss. My heart squeezes as his chest rises and falls, steady and constant—almost hypnotizing.

Sometime later, I wake again.

Grayson's rough hands roam over my body in lazy, exploratory circles. I don't think he stopped touching me the entire trip home from the clubhouse, then all night long. Gentle, reverent caresses. Soft kisses and tickles of his beard whispering over my skin.

In a way, the truth set us free.

At the moment, he seems fascinated with the small of my back. I stretch out on my stomach next to him and hum while he skims his palm over my rear end, then traces his fingers along my spine and pushes my hair aside to kiss my shoulder.

"Mmmm," I mumble without opening my eyes.

"How are you so perfect?" He clutches my hip, my butt, then down to my thighs. "Like you were made just for me."

Those words strike something deep in me. I've never felt good enough for anyone. Emotion burns my eyes and squeezes my throat.

"Serena? What's wrong?"

"Nothing," I whisper.

"Look at me."

I blink my eyes open and lift my head. His expression is so full of concern.

"What's wrong?" he asks, gruffer this time.

"Nothing. I love the way you touch me."

He lifts an eyebrow and leans in to kiss my forehead, my cheek, and finally, my lips. "That's good. Because I'm having trouble keeping my hands to myself."

To demonstrate, he skims his fingers over my shoulder and down my arm. I shift closer to his big, warm body.

"Good thing we left early last night," he says, continuing to stroke his fingers over my back.

We'd come home to Grayson's parole officer waiting at the front door again. "He's going to give you grief all year long, isn't he?"

"Probably. As long as he doesn't throw me back inside, I'll jump through his hoops."

I roll over what Wrath said last night. Am I supposed to call him and tell him what happened? Tell Grayson that he should let Wrath know?

"You're so perfect," he whispers. "Ain't doing a damn thing to get taken away from you."

"You better not." I sit up and trace my fingers over his chest.

I'm really not looking forward to the lonely week ahead.

# CHAPTER TWENTY-SIX

## Grinder

Shaking off the wet and cold, I trudge up the stairs to my apartment. At the landing before the last set of stairs, my gaze lands on a stranger sittin' on the top step. His arms dangle over his legs in a casual, yet somehow arrogant, pose.

I stop and stare. Something about him rings my goon radar. Don't recognize him as one of my neighbors, although the gal across from me seems to have a lot of people in and out of her place.

The tall, lanky guy unfolds himself from the concrete, adjusts his ball cap, then lazily skips down the steps.

Sensing danger, I casually slip my hand in my pocket and curl my fingers around the handle of the knife I carry. Won't do me much good if he's planning to shoot me, but if it's my time, I'm going out stabbing.

"Can I help you?" I ask in my least helpful voice.

He shoves his hands in his pockets and hunches his shoulders. "You Grinder?"

"Who's asking?"

He looks me up and down. Irritating, cocky little fuck. I might stab him just for pissing me off tonight.

"You look good for someone who just got out of the pen."

"Thanks. I don't swing that way."

That wipes the annoying smirk off his face. He swipes his hand over his chin, and my gaze lands on the lion inked onto the back of his hand. I've seen it before. Gang tat, I'm almost positive. Just what I fucking need if my P.O. decides to drop in.

"You validated, motherfucker?" I'm not going back to prison because this gangster clown showed up on my doorstep.

"Nah, I ain't been inside for more than a minute."

"Great. You mind statin' your business? I ain't in the mood for a social call."

"Yeah," he says in a lethargic, grating way that he no doubt borrowed from some low-budget gangster film. "I got a message from Big Chief for you."

My body goes rock-still but my face remains expressionless. Fuck, this is bad. "Our business concluded when I walked out of prison."

He steps closer. One more inch and I'm burying this knife in his belly and sawing my way to his chest cavity. "You think his reach don't extend out here? Naw, man. That ain't how it works."

There's no way Big Chief would trust anything important to this punk. More likely, now that he's taken over running the prison, he wants to see how far he can push me.

My gaze drops to the lion tat on the back of his hand. "You're a pay-for-a-day messenger. Your crew know you're taking on side gigs for Big Chief?"

He quickly jams his hand in his pocket as if that'll wipe my memory clean. This kid's either really dumb or he hasn't been in the game long. *Sloppy little pissant.*

"Don't worry about me, Gramps. Worry about yourself." He thrusts a piece of paper at me.

"I don't want it," I say, refusing to accept whatever the fuck it is.

"I did my job." He throws the note down, then holds his hands in the air and skirts around me. "Big Chief don't want your club involved, so I'd keep this to yourself," he says before running down the rest of the stairs.

I consider following him. But even if I catch his license plate, I doubt it'll help.

*Fuck.*

More annoyed than rattled by the visit, I bend over and pick up the slip of paper. It's tempting to see what it says right now but I trudge into my apartment and slam the door behind me, first.

Inside, I set the note on the kitchen counter and pull a bottle of water from the fridge. I take a deep swallow before shrugging off my coat and hanging it on my coatrack.

"Fuck." I need to make sure Serena doesn't come by my place any time soon. Still not used to sending texts and wanting to hear her voice, I dial her number.

"Hi, Grayson," she answers. Hell, the simple sound of her voice soothes me immediately.

"How are you?" I flick the television on, leaving the sound off.

"Not bad. I'm on my way home from work now. Unless…"

"Tonight's not good." I glance at the TV. "Snow's supposed to come down hard until morning."

"Ugh, I hate driving in the snow. I'm so ready for winter to be over with."

"I know, buttercup." Bet that little car of hers doesn't handle rough roads well. "What're you planning to do tonight?"

"Probably edit some videos and plan out my next few projects."

"Send me a picture later?"

She hesitates for a moment. "Sure."

As soon as we hang up, I check my watch. I've got a few hours to get up to the clubhouse, sit down with everyone, and get back here before officer time clock could be on the prowl.

Finally, I grab the note from Big Chief and flip it open. It's nothing more than what I assume is a date, time, and set of GPS coordinates.

"The fuck?" I mutter. Whatever's happening is going down about a week from now. What's Big Chief thinking? I'll show up for kicks? Do his bidding?

Stupid motherfucker.

As much as I hate doing it, I gotta call Rock and let him know what happened. To protect me, yeah. But also to protect the club.

I locate the safe number Rock had given me to use for an emergency like this.

I'm dumped into voicemail.

"It's me. I have a problem. You might want to call a few people to the table to sit down for this one."

After I hang up, I stare out at the darkness beyond my windows. Woods. I can barely make out the tops of some trees and a hint of velvety black sky.

No matter how happy I was to finally get out, in my heart, I knew it was only a matter of time before the ghosts of prison past chased me down.

## CHAPTER TWENTY-SEVEN

### Grinder

When I arrive at the clubhouse almost an hour later, Teller and Murphy are sitting at the bar by the front door.

"What's wrong?" Teller asks as soon as his eyes land on me.

Rock steps out of the war room. "You're here. Good."

Murphy slides off his stool. "Everything all right, brother?"

Christ. Way too many people in my face at once. "I'm fine," I snap, gesturing for Teller and Murphy to keep moving. Don't need all of 'em crowding around me like I'm a dancing circus bear. "I'll tell everyone at the same time."

Dex and Wrath are already inside the war room. Murphy closes the door behind us and everyone else takes their seats. I stand, pacing behind Wrath's chair.

"Gray," Rock says. "Have a seat."

Wrath pulls out the chair next to him. It's starting to be my regular spot.

"P.O. hassle you again?" Wrath asks.

"Yes, but that's not what this is about." I take a deep breath. Tension wraps around my chest, squeezing from all angles. "You know better than anyone how hard I worked to secure our position on the inside."

"Of course," Rock says.

"After you got out," I nod to Rock, "I was the only Lost King on the inside, except for a few short stays here and there. But no one ever made it to where I was at the Supermax."

"Right." Rock sits forward. "Go on."

"I had our connections through the Demons and DeLova's crew that helped keep me safe."

"We've always maintained that relationship with the Demons." Wrath turns toward Rock. "DeLova not as much."

"Didn't matter," I say. "It's a different world in there. Once I had the pressure from the outside lifted—when you got Ruger off my back," I nod at Rock, "things were easier for me. But in some ways, it was also harder. Green Street Crew and Little Reds were at each others' throats. Keeping out of it was impossible. GSC and I came around to an agreement first."

"Good to know kissing Loco's ass all these years wasn't a waste," Rock grumbles.

"He still alive?" I ask. "He had his cousin gunnin' for him not that long ago."

"Yeah, the cousin didn't make it." Murphy angles a finger gun toward the carpet and pulls the trigger. "Pow."

"Loco wasn't in a forgiving mood," Wrath explains. "Not even for family."

"Good. Kidd was a weasel." I really couldn't give a shit about GSC's petty business. "Moving drugs through the prisons is big business," I continue. "That's not news to anyone at this table. And even though you may have extracted the club from dirtier criminal enterprises out here—"

"I get it, Grinder. You don't have to explain yourself to us," Rock says.

"I'm not explaining shit. I did what I had to do to keep power and survive."

"We get it," Rock assures me.

"Eventually, I brought the two main factions to a truce. Anyone not affiliated with either of them, fell in with me. Ain't saying we sat around a campfire holding hands and making s'mores together but we kept the peace. Guards appreciated it—gave 'em more time for naps and shit. And it gave us more leeway."

"That couldn't have been easy," Dex mutters.

"It wasn't. But by the time I returned to Pine for the rest of my sentence, I'd crafted a delicate balance inside. Kept myself at the top of the food chain." This last part's important. I wait a beat before delivering this reminder. "And I kept the club out of it."

"You know we would've done anything to help," Wrath says.

"There wasn't much you could do from the outside. And you didn't want to get tangled up with inside business. It's a tricky web in and out. Some gangs work together on the inside, but they're sworn enemies outside."

Rock intertwines his fingers on the table in front of him and sits forward but doesn't say a word.

"That peaceful coexistence you brokered went out the window when Broadbent Crew's shot caller got sentenced, right?" Dex asks.

"It did." Dex and I had spoken about this—as much as we could—when it happened.

"Those assholes," Murphy grumbles. "Had no business stepping foot in New York."

"Big Chief shouldn't have been able to get near you," Rock says.

Should've known Rock pays attention to everything.

"He couldn't." I roll my shoulder. "But he started upsetting the balance. Since I knew the club didn't want any of the action, I made plans to hand it off once I got out."

I've got everyone's full attention now.

"It should've been split between GSC and Little Reds. They have better distribution. Minute Squad came into play and had some small responsibilities."

"This who you wanted to send the money to? The ones you turned it over to?" Rock asks. His tone's completely neutral, so devoid of emotion, I'd be concerned—if I still feared death.

"No. Those guys are both unaffiliated. Not cut out for the life. Money will keep 'em out of the crosshairs." I slap my hands together in front of me to drive home the point I want to make. "I walked out completely separated from any business going on inside. GSC and Reds knew I was out. They knew better than to fuck with us on the outside."

"I should hope so," Murphy mutters.

I continue without answering his comment. "If they wanted to bring anyone else to the table, that was on them."

Wrath turns toward Rock. "How involved you think Loco is in this?"

Rock shrugs. "He's never brought it up. So either he stays out of prison business like we do, or he didn't have any issues with how it was being handled. Fuck knows he's got no problem annoying me when he needs something."

"He's been a good friend to the club," Teller reminds him.

Rock turns slowly, settling his frosty stare on Teller. "Did I say otherwise?"

"Just stating a fact." Teller holds his hands in the air even as a smirk tugs at the corner of his mouth.

"Cool story, kids. Can I go on?" I ask, not bothering to hide my irritation.

Ignoring me, Rock glances at Wrath. "I'm thinking we should give Z a call."

"Not yet." Wrath shakes his head.

Apparently satisfied with his enforcer's answer, Rock sits back. "Continue."

"When I got home tonight, I had a surprise visitor. Not someone I recognized." I slap the piece of paper the kid had given me on the table. "Big Chief apparently thinks I work for him on the outside."

"Fuck." Rock closes his eyes. "They had a shakeup as soon as you left."

"Sounds like it."

"A few more of his crew were sentenced right before Grinder got out," Dex says.

Rock casts a sideways glance at Murphy. "Seems like something my VP should've been aware of."

Murphy's ginger eyebrows crawl up his forehead. "Am I supposed to monitor the courts for every criminal going into the system?"

"Set up a Google alert," Wrath suggests with a smirk.

"Google this, dick." Murphy flips him off.

"Simmer down." Rock unfolds the paper and scans the few lines. "What is this? A drop?"

"Don't know. Little punk didn't provide much information."

Wrath plucks the paper out of Rock's hands. "Shit. This is Demon territory. We can't be anywhere near whatever it is."

"I can't be near it no matter what," I remind him.

"Easy." Rock's let's-coddle-Grandpa tone doesn't do much to calm me. "Most important thing right now, is that you need protection—"

"I can't have any of you at my apartment in case my P.O. shows up. And I can't stay here overnight."

"Fuck," Wrath groans. "This motherfuckin' P.O. wasn't supposed to be so much of a pain in the ass."

"You can't be left unprotected," Rock insists. "We don't know who they'll send next."

"I think we know a few people out that way who could assist us," Dex suggests.

"Ah, yes." Wrath shoots a smug grin across the table at Murphy. "Sounds like a job for our support club."

"Fuck yeah." Murphy sits up, eager and bright-eyed, apparently thrilled at the chance to redeem himself. "They're not officially affiliated with anyone. No ink connecting them to us. Juvie records are sealed. They already live close to Grinder, so it's not weird if they're at his apartment—"

"Uh, I don't know them, so it might be weird," I point out.

Ignoring me, Murphy continues selling the idea to Rock. "Griff and Remy already work out at Sully's place, so they won't raise any red flags. Eraser will be down to help. Vapor too, if anyone can track his ass down."

"Since when do we have a support club?" I ask.

"We don't. Yet," Teller answers.

"We're reeling them in slow," Dex adds.

"Slower than molasses in January," Rock grumbles.

Teller raises an eyebrow. "You're not even a hundred percent on board with them as support. Haven't come out with us to vet them once."

Damn, Teller must be itching to have his ass kicked tonight.

Rock slowly tilts his head in Teller's direction. "What are you, my activities coordinator now?"

"I'm just—"

"Because I don't recall asking for your opinion—"

Wrath raises his hand to cut Rock off. "I vetted Remy and Griff plenty when we were in Virginia." He lifts his chin at Murphy. "Murphy, Dex, Rooster, Jiggy, Ice—"

"I don't think Ice is gonna offer up a glowing recommendation for Remy," Murphy says.

Wrath blows out a whatever breath. "Because of Anya?"

Murphy tips his head down and snort-laughs. "You didn't witness it."

Rock knocks on the table. "Stay on track. You trust them or not?"

"You know I trust Vapor, full stop," Dex says.

"Yeah, he's solid," Rock agrees.

"Jake will help out too." Wrath lifts his chin at me. "Sully's brother."

"I met him." At least Jake would look the part of a bodyguard. Who knows about these other guys. I trust my brothers' judgment though. "You realize it's gonna look weird that a bunch of younger guys are rotating in and out of my apartment, right?"

Teller smirks. "No one's judging in that building."

"Just say you're mentoring them on the dangers of a criminal lifestyle," Rock suggests with his own smirk.

"Fucker." I rumble with laughter.

As much as I hate dragging my club toward trouble, at least I'm not dealing with this alone.

# CHAPTER TWENTY-EIGHT

## Grinder

"You tell Serena to steer clear of your place?" Wrath asks.

"Weather did it for me." And hadn't that hurt like hell. Telling her not to come over because of the fuckin' snow. As if I wouldn't have driven to Empire and taken her home with me the second she said she wanted to come over. Until I have a handle on this situation, I need her to stay away.

"Sorry, brother."

"Ready?" Dex claps my back. He insisted on following me home.

"Yeah, let's go. Don't wanna miss officer punch card if he shows up."

Wrath scowls. "You sure you don't want us to—"

"No. I don't wanna do anything to draw more attention to me. Hopefully he'll get bored and bother someone else."

His bottom lip twists as if he's not convinced.

"I mean it, Wrath. I know you want to help but don't disrespect me by going behind my back."

He nods once. "All right, brother. But keep me up-to-date."

"Will do," I promise, convinced he'll keep his word.

The drive to my apartment feels longer than usual. Maybe I'm being too cautious. When I was younger, I would've said 'fuck it' and stayed at the clubhouse and thumbed my nose at parole.

Now, I understand how much is at stake.

Freedom shouldn't be taken for granted. Learned that lesson the painful way. And I don't plan to repeat it.

I'm hyperaware of the entire landscape as I pull into the parking lot behind my building. I scan each vehicle. Nothing seems out of place or unusual. Dex backs his truck into a space on the other side of the parking lot and shuts off his headlights. Pretending not to notice him, I go inside.

No one's waiting outside my apartment and nothing seems amiss. I step inside and send Dex a message. A few minutes later, he knocks on my door.

"Did you search the place?" he asks.

"For what?" I frown at him. "No one's been in here."

He cocks his head, a disapproving scowl pinching his face.

"Go ahead." I sweep my hand toward the living room. "Not much to search."

While he prowls through the place, I put on a pot of coffee, smiling when my gaze lands on the sweetener I'd picked up for Serena. My phone buzzes and I pull it out.

*Serena: Home safe. Miss you.*

*Me: Just thinking about you.*

There's another knock at the door. I set my phone on the counter.

"I got it," Dex says, hurrying to greet our guest.

"You know I can handle myself, right?" I ask.

Ignoring me, Dex opens the door and invites whoever it is inside.

"Hey, Griff." Dex shakes his hand. "Wasn't sure if it was you or Remy coming tonight."

"He won't leave Molly alone overnight. But he'll be here in the morning."

Dex slaps the kid's back and pushes him toward me. "Griff, this is Grinder. Grinder, Griff's a good friend of the club."

"Evening, sir." He dips his chin at me.

"Thanks for coming over."

"Not a problem."

"Coffee?" I offer.

"Sure."

Griff eases his large frame onto one of the stools at the counter and remains silent.

I like this kid already.

Dex also takes a seat at the counter.

I slide mugs to each of them. When the coffee's finished, I bring the pot over and fill both cups.

My attention's drawn to Griff's scarred knuckles. He's either a brawler or a damn hard worker.

"What do you do, Griff?" I ask. "Besides babysitting grandpas for the local MC?"

"Here we go," Dex mutters.

Griff huffs a quick laugh. "I work at a garage. Hoping to buy the owner out eventually. We restore old cars, trucks, and bikes." He glances at his coffee. "Remy and I run a small amateur fighting ring too."

"By amateur, you mean illegal?" I guess.

"Eh." He lifts one shoulder. "You know how it is. A few friends get together to knock the shit out of each other a couple times a week. Maybe a little money gets tossed around to show our support." A smirk plays at the corners of his mouth.

Dex chuckles. "He's being modest. They run a tight operation."

"You from around here, Grinder?" Griff asks.

"Before I went inside, yeah. Been a little out of touch the last few years, though."

He doesn't laugh at my attempted joke. "You remember the detention center the State ran out here?"

"The kiddie jail? Yeah, I remember it." I glance at Dex. "Teller spent a couple months there not long after I first went inside, right?"

Dex smirks. "Probably."

"We got a whole alumni association going, don't we?" Griff chuckles. "Anyway, the State closed the facility a few years back. They auctioned it off after it sat around for a bit. Remy and I bought it."

"Big purchase." Illegal fighting must pay more than it did when I was Griff's age.

"Haven't had the funds to renovate much." He scoffs. "Or decide what the fuck we're gonna do with the place long-term."

"That where you learned to fight?" I ask. "Inside?"

He stares at his hands for a few seconds. "Yeah. They didn't really give us much of a choice."

I curl my hands into fists. "I did some prison boxing. In and out of a ring."

"We got all styles. If you're ever looking for a match…"

"Thanks, I think I'm good."

Dex chuckles and slaps his hand on the counter. "I'm heading out." He catches my eye. "Let me know if you need anything."

"Thanks."

I lock the door after Dex leaves. Griff's still at the counter, sipping his coffee.

"You really don't need to stay."

Griff shrugs. "It's no big deal. Dex said they're worried about some guy who showed up on your doorstep making threats?"

Shit, the kid doesn't even have the full picture of what he's getting into and he's still here? "Yeah, guy has ties to one of the prison gangs. Apparently we don't see eye-to-eye on the terms of my retirement."

His expression doesn't change. He's either dumb or brave.

"I'm sure it's not easy to untangle yourself, even if you're on the outside," he says.

Not dumb.

"Some people need things explained more than once."

He lifts one fist in the air, then the other. "I'll help you drive the message home."

The club should be looking to patch this kid, not as a support club but a full-patch. "You're not even a prospect, Griff. Why're you here?"

"We owe Murphy." The corners of his mouth twitch. "Heidi too."

"Heidi, huh?"

He nods once. "Your club's helped us out. I want to return the favor. Besides, this is my home. Don't like some outsider rolling in and threatening my neighbors, you know?"

"You got family around here?"

He shakes his head. "My mom's up north. Wouldn't really call her 'family,' though." He lets out a wry laugh. "Remy and Molly. Eraser, Ella, Vapor, and Juliet. They're the only ones I count as family."

I understand all too well what he means.

### Serena

H*AVE COURAGE OR ACCOMPLISH NOTHING.*

Tonight, I decided to try something new on my YouTube channel, so that quote feels appropriate.

As I click off my camera, a muted bump and shuffling sound draws my attention.

Since I'm working in my little home studio, I left the lights in the rest of the apartment off. Enough light spills from my office to make out most of the shapes in my living room as I tiptoe to the front door.

All the locks are in place. I should thank Grayson for replacing the door and adding the extra security. I've felt safer ever since.

Another thud from the hallway.

I freeze in place, as if whoever's out there has x-ray vision to see through my door and spy me standing in my darkened living room.

Light as a feather, I tiptoe to the door and peer through the peephole.

Distorted hallway. Dark and shadowy as usual. A shape near the stairway moves and takes on the form of a person.

Shouldn't be the couple who lives upstairs. Neither of them ever linger on my floor.

Unless they need help with something.

I curl my hand around the knob, then freeze.

If they needed help, they'd knock on the door and ask.

Could it be Grayson trying to surprise me?

"Grayson?" I call out.

The shape stills.

That was stupid. Gray wouldn't be out after ten and risk getting tangled up with his parole officer. I should've kept my mouth shut. Now whoever it is, knows I'm here.

I reach into my pocket, then remember my cell phone's in the other room.

Damn.

*What am I going to do? Call the cops? I'm sure they'll speed right over.*

Whoever's out there starts walking. They've got their hood up so I can't see much more than a blurry, baggy outline. Maybe they dropped something. From the size and shape, I think it's a man, who slouches by and lopes up the stairs two at a time. Friend of my upstairs neighbors, I guess.

Unsettled, I back away from the door and roam around my apartment, checking that the windows are locked up tight. Not that anyone should be able to climb up to the second floor, but it makes me feel better.

Alarm set. Teeth brushed. Face washed and moisturized. There's nothing left to do except turn back the covers and slide into bed.

Without Gray next to me, it takes a long, long time to fall asleep.

# CHAPTER TWENTY-NINE
## Grinder

Sunlight bounces off the blankets of snow outside, waking me early the next morning.

Griff's still sprawled out on my couch, legs hanging off the end. Better feed him since the kid wasted a whole night here.

I'm almost finished frying up some bacon when he drops into one of the chairs at the counter. I pass him a mug of coffee.

"Thank you." He yawns and scrubs his hands over his face.

"Sorry about the couch."

"I've slept in worse places."

There's a knock at the door and both of us turn. Griff pulls out his phone and checks the screen. "It's Remy."

He strides over and checks the peephole before opening it.

"Morning, brotha!" the newcomer's voice booms from the hallway.

"Easy. It's early," Griff warns.

The kid who strolls in is even larger than Griff. I glance at the refrigerator. Gonna need to make another trip to the grocery store if I'm feeding these two all week.

"Grinder, this clown is Remy. Remy, this is Grinder."

Remy extends his hand and I give it a quick shake. "Morning. Thanks for coming over."

"No problem."

The two of them wolf down breakfast. I brew another pot of coffee.

"I gotta get to work." Griff stands and stretches. "You got my number, Grinder. Give me a call if you need anything."

"No one needs you." Remy reaches out, lightly punching his friend in the gut. "I'll be here."

Griff smirks and lifts his chin at me. "Like I said, let me know if you need something."

"What's on the agenda?" Remy asks after his friend leaves.

"Need to go into Empire." I glance at the clock. "And I need to leave soon."

He claps his big hands together. Kid seems to have trouble sitting still for long. "Let's do it." He turns serious. "We'll take my truck to make sure no one's tailing you."

Good to know he's got a brain and some common sense under his cocky exterior. "Thanks."

I grab the stuff I need and we trudge downstairs and into the foul weather. "Need to stop somewhere and buy a shovel," I warn him.

"I got two in the back." Remy says over his shoulder as he leads me to an old Ford Bronco with a beat-up plow on the front end.

"This truck has to be older than you are." The interior's worn but clean. "Looks good, though."

"Yeah. Griff and I took it on as a weekend project for a few years, restoring it to its former glory." He chuckles and pats the steering wheel affectionately. "I mostly use it for plowing in the winter." As he pulls onto the main road, he asks, "Where we headed?"

"Southside of Empire."

"Okay."

"You missing out on making money this morning?" I wave at the windshield and the snow on the road.

"From?"

"Plowing?"

"Oh. No, I don't do it for cash. Just our driveway and a few of the neighbors'. Already did my rounds this morning. I'll hit 'em again later."

"Just doing it out of the kindness of your heart?" Maybe the entire world hasn't gone to shit while I was inside.

He scowls but doesn't take his eyes off the road. "I live in my grandparents' house. A few of their friends are still around but can't do the shoveling or whatever." He shrugs. "Takes me an extra couple minutes."

Not what I expected from such a cocky kid. But I trust my club's judgment a lot more.

"So, why aren't you staying at the club if some dude's hassling you?" Remy asks.

It burns my ass to talk about this with another stranger but since he's giving up his day to drive me around, I might as well. "I'm on parole. Not supposed to be around the club."

One corner of his mouth slides up. "For real? I thought big, bad outlaws would tell the cops to fuck off."

Is he tryin' to test me? "This ain't a TV show, son. This is real life. I just got *out* of prison. Not interested in going back."

"I hear you."

"I should hope so. You're on the young side to need a hearing aid already."

His lips twist into a smirk.

"What do *you* do? Besides play chauffeur for the local MC."

He taps his chest. "I prefer *bodyguard*." The smug smile slides off his face. "My grandparents ran a bar and grill. They left it to my sister and me. I'm trying to keep it going. You know, keep their memory alive."

"Think you'd have more respect for your elders then," I mutter. Dick thing to say, sure. But how will he respond?

"Nah, my grandpa taught me respect was earned not blindly given."

"Smart man."

"Yeah." Remy stares straight ahead. "He was."

"Griff mentioned you take care of your little sister?"

His mouth twists into a smirk. "I'm sure he did."

"How old is she?"

"Molly is seventeen going on thirty-five." He laughs.

"He mentioned you run a fight ring, too."

"Griff was a chatty boy, huh?" he grumbles.

"Dex might've mentioned it first."

"Ah, the mysterious Mr. Dex." He chuckles. "Yeah, we have a good thing going. You should come check it out one night."

"I think I'm a little old to dance around the ring."

"We got a cage." He glances over. "You look like you could still put a hurtin' on someone."

I grunt in response. Damn right. I can kill a man with a fucking toothbrush in eight seconds flat. Prison didn't leave me with many options.

Once we're off the highway, I direct him to Serena's neighborhood. He slows to a crawl, careful of the narrow, poorly plowed city streets with cars parked on both sides.

"What a mess," he mutters. "City living makes me twitch."

"They don't exactly kill themselves cleaning this up." I point to an open spot a few doors down from Serena's place. "There."

We bounce over a heap of snow and ice to slide into the space.

Serena's car's still buried under the white, icy mess. I check the time. Good thing I was itching to see her. She's gonna be late and hasn't even started her car yet.

"Would you mind giving me a hand cleaning that off?" I nod to her little hatchback.

"Yeah, sure." He claps his hands together and rubs like he's eager to get to work.

Serena appears on the front steps of the brownstone. So fuckin' pretty as she stares at the snow-covered sidewalk and wrinkles her nose.

"There she is." I grab the cup of coffee I'd brought with me.

"Oh, is that your daughter?" Remy asks with a straight face.

Great. I'd prefer it if he was just fucking with me, but I think he's serious. "No," I growl, flinging the door open and stomping onto the sidewalk. "You wanna make use of one of those shovels or are you planning to sit there and look pretty all morning?"

"Yeah, yeah." He shuts off the truck and steps out. "Respect, man."

"Serena," I call.

Like a cornered kitten, her shoulders hunch, her fingers tighten around the handrail, and her eyes nervously scan the area. Shit, I hadn't meant to startle her.

Her posture relaxes and her lips curve when her gaze lands on me. "Grayson?"

### Serena

In a few months, I'll be grousing about the summer heat. But right now, I'm questioning why I've never moved to Florida.

I hate the snow. *I hate it so much.*

Actually, I just hate driving to work in the snow. And being cold. If I could stay bundled up in my fuzzy jammies and socks, and sip hot chocolate by a crackling fireplace, I'd probably love winter in all its icy glory.

Stepping outside, I take a deep breath. And promptly burst into a coughing fit. Stupid cold, dry air. It should be spring by now.

I tug my hat over my ears.

"Serena?"

I jump and grip the handrail, preparing to run back inside the safety of my apartment building.

Then my eyes land on Grayson walking toward me.

And my heart pounds for different reasons.

"What are you doing here?" I navigate each stone step slowly, careful not to slip on the ice.

He meets me at the bottom of the stairs and holds out his hand for me to grab onto. "No one cleans this?"

"There's a maintenance guy. He'll stop by eventually to shovel and salt the steps and sidewalk."

He grunts and hands me a stainless steel travel mug.

My eyes light up. "You brought me coffee?"

I accept the warm metal into my chilly hands and cautiously take a sip. Someone paid attention to how I like my coffee. Full of cream and a dash of sweetener. "Thank you."

"Thought you might need it."

"You drove all this way in shitty weather just to bring me coffee?" I may be freezing my ears off but I'm ready to melt into a puddle at his feet.

"Well, I also wanted to do this." He leans down and curls his arms around me, drawing me into the warmth of his body. He presses his lips to mine. A gentle morning greeting that quickly slides into something hot and demanding. The air around us sizzles and the noise of the waking city fades. I sigh into his mouth and his hands slide to my waist.

He groans and pulls away, dropping his forehead to mine. "Missed you, buttercup."

My gaze remains fixed on his chest, wishing we didn't have so many layers of winter clothing between us. "Me too."

He rests his knuckles against my chin and tips my head back. "You all right?"

"Just upset I'm running late. I'd rather spend time with you." Why do I have to sound so damn needy?

The corners of his mouth lift. "I'd love to spend more time with you too, but I knew I'd only be able to see you for a few minutes. Thought I could help." He nods toward the street where my car's buried under a pile of snow at the curb. A younger guy's currently shoveling around my tires. "Well, I thought Remy could help."

He brought someone with him to shovel the snow away from my car? "I usually just ram through the snowbank. If I clean out a spot, it won't be here when I return."

Grayson frowns. "Good way to bust up your front end."

I shrug. "I'm usually running late and I hate getting wet and cold before work."

"We need to find you a better place," he mutters.

Oh no. I don't want to revisit the apartment discussion. I'm still so chilled from my heat not working last night, I might cave and say yes this time.

"Uh, Grinder." Remy jams the shovel into a pile of snow, leaving it sticking upright, and waves us over. "She can't drive in the snow with these. They might as well be racing slicks."

Despite the cold, heat spreads over my nose and cheeks. I was hoping to make it through the winter without buying new tires.

Gray takes my hand and tugs me closer. "Serena, this is Remy. He's helping me out with a few errands today. Remy, this is my girl Serena."

Remy smirks at the explanation. I study his handsome face and mischievous blue eyes for a second. He seems familiar but I can't remember where we might have met. Probably through the club, even though I don't think he's a full-patch. The idea that he might recognize *me* ties my stomach in knots.

Gray squats next to one of the rear tires, running his thumb over the tread. I squirm where I'm standing. My gaze darts everywhere to avoid making eye contact with Remy.

Finally, Gray stands and leans in to confer with Remy. I only make out a few words here and there of the conversation.

Remy nods and hands over a set of keys. "I know a place."

They go back and forth for a few more seconds. When they've reached some sort of agreement, Gray steps back and holds out his hand to me. "Can I have your keys?"

Without thinking, I pull them from my pocket. "Why?"

"It's going to take a minute to dig out your car," Remy explains.

"Sorry," I mutter, thoroughly embarrassed this stranger got roped into shoveling my car out of its snowy grave.

Remy flexes his arms and winks at me. "Not a problem, darlin'."

"Watch it, kid," Gray orders.

Chuckling at Gray's quick warning, I lean up on tiptoes and kiss his cheek. "Seeing you this morning is the best present," I whisper against his ear.

He smiles and turns; our foreheads touch, our cold noses rub together for a moment. "Yeah?"

"Definitely."

"I'll drop you off at work." Grayson reaches for my tote bag, unburdening my hands. "You can trust Remy with your car."

"Oh, I do." No one in their right mind would try to steal it. "Thank you."

"No problem." Remy nods at me and returns to shoveling.

Gray leads me over to an older Ford Bronco with big, meaty tires and a plow on the front. "Guess you have no problem ripping through the snow in those." I nod to the treads.

"We did all right." Gray opens the passenger door and helps me inside.

"Is Remy a prospect?" I ask when Gray puts the truck into drive. "Did we just steal a prospect's vehicle?"

Gray smirks. "No on both counts."

"Is he your nephew or something?"

"Don't have any family besides the club, Serena."

"Oh."

His gloved hands tighten on the steering wheel briefly. "Why are you so worried about him?"

"I'm not. I'm worried about *you*."

"What about me?"

"Well," I answer slowly, "you told me parole won't allow you to socialize with the club. But you're out and about with someone who—"

"Ahh." He blows out a relieved breath. "It's okay. He's not affiliated with the club in any official capacity."

"All right."

He glances over and smiles at me, then rests his hand on my leg, gently squeezing. "Got worried for a second."

"About?"

"He's a good looking kid. Closer to your age…"

"Pfft." I snort-giggle. "He must be a few years *younger* than me. And all that swagger announces to the world that he's a pure player. Not my type. Although, I do appreciate him helping me out," I hurry to add, not wanting to sound ungrateful. I glance over at him. "Do you honestly think I notice *anyone* else when you're around?"

"How about when I'm *not* around?" His tone's neutral, calm even. Not accusatory.

I understand that our age difference bothers him so I answer seriously. "No, Grayson. You're the only man occupying my mind no matter where I am."

"Same, Serena. I want you to know that."

I swallow hard and nod. He's focused on the streets out of my neighborhood, so I doubt he notices.

The pavement is thick with snow. Gray takes his time, carefully commanding the unfamiliar vehicle. With him handling the driving, I'm able to sit back and relax, mentally preparing myself for the challenges ahead.

"Do you have a busy day?" he asks.

"My schedule is full but I bet I'll have a few cancellations." I gesture toward the windshield. "Because of the snow."

"Your place doesn't close down?"

"Maybe if there's a state of emergency or something but otherwise, no. This is my first winter working here, though." I stare at the few fat snowflakes still lazily drifting from the sky.

As we get closer to the hospital, the roads improve. Plows have clearly passed more than once and salted the streets. The pavement's shiny and wet but easier to navigate.

Too soon, he's flipping on his blinker and making the right into my parking lot. He pulls up to the curb and stops. "Door-to-door service, buttercup."

I lean over and press a kiss to his cheek. "Thank you for making my morning so much better."

"You don't have to thank me." He nods to a row of empty parking spots. "I'll drop your car off so you're not stranded."

*Don't pout.* "I won't see you later?" I hope that didn't sound too whiny.

"I'll try but I have a few things to take care of today."

"Well, I'm glad I got to see you first thing."

"Me too." He presses a quick kiss to my lips. "Have a good day."

I gather my stuff and slide out of the truck, careful to avoid the piles of snow on either side of the walkway.

---

A FEW HOURS LATER, LUCY CALLS ME TO THE WAITING ROOM.

I recognize one of the security guards leaning over her desk, chatting with her. He smiles when he sees me. "Your friend wants me to give these to you." He holds out my car keys.

"Oh. Thank you." I stare at them for a few seconds before stuffing them in my pocket.

The guard returns to chatting up Lucy and I walk back to my office. Why didn't Gray text me? I would've met him outside.

*Well, you did make a big deal about not being seen together or you'd lose your job.*

He was probably trying to be respectful. Maybe he left a note in my car. Checking the time, I hurry into my coat and let Lucy know I'll be right back.

Outside, it's snowing again. My car's sitting under the closest lamp post sparkling clean, except for a few slushy splatters around the wheel wells. My lips curve. Of course that's where he left it. As I approach, my attention's drawn to the tires. The shiny, black, nubby-treaded tires. I squat down next to the rear tire on the driver's side and press my thumb into the tread. Definitely not the nearly bald tires I'd had this morning. Slowly, I walk around the vehicle.

Four brand-new snow tires. They probably cost more than the value of the car.

I open the door and slide into my seat. It's pushed all the way back and a smile tugs at the corners of my mouth, thinking of Gray needing to adjust it to fit his long legs. I pull open the glove box and flip down my visor. No note.

Underneath his rough and gruff exterior, Gray is incredibly sweet. He doesn't make typical romantic gestures. No flowers or love notes. But if he sees that I need something, he wastes no time fixing it.

My comfort and safety have never been anyone's priority before.

I wish he was here so I could thank him in person.

Pulling out my phone, I dial his number.

"Hey, buttercup," he answers, his warm, rich tone filling me with happiness.

"Thank you."

"For?" A light note of teasing colors his question.

"Well, I happened to notice four brand-new winter tires on my car."

"Huh." He chuckles. "Wonder how that happened?"

"You didn't have to do that," I say softly.

"I wanted to."

"I wish I'd been able to see you when you dropped it off. Say hello…" *Damn, why do I have to sound so clingy when he did such a nice thing?*

He sighs. "Serena, I didn't think it was a good idea to pop into your office."

"No, you're right," I answer quickly. "Sorry."

"Don't be sorry. About killed me to be so close and not see you."

"I can come over tonight after work," I offer.

He's silent on the other end.

"Grayson?"

"That's not a good idea. New tires or not, the roads won't be great."

He's right but the explanation feels wrong.

"Is everything okay?" I ask.

"Just busy."

"I'll let you go."

"Serena, wait. It's supposed to snow this weekend. Let's try to get together. We can be snowed in together."

"I'd like that." I glance up and notice someone who looks a lot like my next patient crossing the parking lot. "I have to go."

"Call me when you get home."

"I will." I want to say so much more but I'm not even sure where to begin.

And I'm out of time.

## CHAPTER THIRTY

### Grinder

"Everything all right?" Wrath asks. "Your kids behaving?"

I groan. The guys have been making "kids" jokes at me all week for having Remy and Griff as my shadows.

No more visits from shady gangsters, thank fuck. Big Chief hasn't reached out in any other way. While it's a relief, I'm also left feeling like an ass for worrying over nothing and causing so many people to go out of their way for me.

"They've been good, except neither of them will take any money from me." Griff had accepted cash for the tires I asked him to install on Serena's car. And I've fed both of 'em all week. But it still doesn't feel like enough. The little shits won't let me pay them for all the time they're wasting hanging out at my place.

"We'll take care of them." Wrath's expression turns more business-oriented. "How's Serena?"

"All right." Ain't gonna admit to Wrath that I'm missing her like someone carved out my heart. I need whatever's going on to end so I can see my girl.

"Z coming up?" I ask.

"Probably not today. This weekend, though, most of Downstate will be up here."

"You might have 'em all weekend. Supposed to snow again."

"Yeah, I saw. It's fine. Got the room." He waves his hand toward the stairs. "Trin and Swan placed a large order this morning, so we'll have plenty of food and supplies." His mouth twists. "Hate that you can't just stay up here and hang with everyone. Even if you wanted to bunk at our house to avoid the noise." He cocks his head. "Your P.O. been by again?"

"Yup. Pretty sure he thinks I swing both ways since Griff was there this time."

He snorts. "Fuck. How'd you explain that?"

"Griff shared a moving story about how I was a friend of his dearly departed grandpa. And on ol' grandpa's deathbed, Griff swore he'd look out for me if I ever got out of prison. Kid belongs in Hollywood. It was quite a performance."

Wrath doubles over laughing. "That's priceless. Wish I'd seen it."

"It was smart. No one around to call bullshit on the story if Grillo tries to verify it." I'd been impressed with Griff's quick thinking.

"Good." He slaps my arm. "It's gonna be a few minutes."

"I'm gonna go down to the dining room. See if I can find some coffee."

"Trin's down there. She'll help you out."

"Thanks." Club's quiet as I make my way to the dining room. I poke my head in an open door. Lights are off but I can make out the mirrors on the wall, cushions on the floor. Guess that's the yoga room Shelby mentioned.

Hope's in the dining room with Grace in her lap and a spread of food on the table in front of them. I grab my coffee and glance around the empty space before approaching.

"Morning, Hope. You got a minute?"

"Of course." She pats the chair next to her. "I think Rock's in the war room if you need him."

"Nah, I'll talk to him in a minute." I drop into the chair and automatically reach for one of Grace's little blue booties.

Hope shines a warm smile my way and extends her arms. "Do you want to hold her?"

More than anything. But it's not like I've handled a lot of little ones in my life. She looks so damn *breakable*. I flex my hands. "Probably shouldn't."

Hope scoots her chair closer to me. I reach for Grace and she wraps one tiny hand around my finger. "Strong grip, little one."

She blinks up at me and giggles.

"You're a sweet one. Gonna ride your own hog with that grip one day? Are you?"

More laughter. She bobs her head as if she's agreeing with me.

"She get you up early?" I ask Hope.

"All the time." She tilts her head toward the kitchen. "Trinity's in there with Swan."

We won't have much time alone then. Better ask my questions quickly. "How well do you know Serena?"

Hope's serious eyes study me for a moment. Bet she heard all about what went down with Steer running his mouth.

"Not that well. I ran into her a few times Downstate. She used to hang out up here…sometimes." She's careful with each word, probably trying not to alert me to any other brothers Serena's spent time with.

Instead of finding that annoying, I like that she's discreet. Almost like she wants to protect Serena instead of toss her under the bus like a lot of ol' ladies might do.

"She was always kind. A little shy." Her mouth twists. "From what I could tell, Tawny was mean to her."

I'm guessing there's no love lost between Hope and Tawny.

*I knew Hope was a smart gal.*

My lip curls. "Besides Tawny, you think the other old ladies will accept her?"

Hope raises an eyebrow. "I don't see why not. Lilly likes her a lot. She was upset when Serena…stopped hanging out Downstate."

"I don't mean that I need their approval. I just don't want…"

"Anyone putting her down?" Hope finishes for me.

"Yes." My jaw clenches. "I won't have it. Don't give a shit what happened or who she was with before we met. I won't tolerate anyone disrespecting her."

She reaches over and squeezes my forearm. "I think, and this is ancient history, Heidi was a little prickly because...well, you don't need me to explain it. But she's grown up a lot. I'm pretty sure she's over it by now."

I snort. Poor Heidi. Can't imagine the shit she was exposed to while I was inside.

"You think I'm a disgusting old pervert, trying to settle down with the first young thing I see?" I blurt.

She sits back and blinks. Can't blame her. Not many men would ask that question or care about her answer.

"I don't think that at all," she finally says. "I've always had the impression Serena hasn't had an easy life. That can certainly age a person beyond their years."

I let out a grunt.

"You seem to be asking for my advice?" she ventures.

I lift one shoulder. *Is* that what I'm doing? I don't need her approval, but I'm interested in her opinion.

"The age difference isn't what I'd be concerned about the most." Now that she has my attention, Hope steamrolls ahead. "I'd be cautious because you're going through a big shift in your own life. Readjusting to things." She stops and clears her throat. "On the outside."

"Don't use her to get myself adjusted and then discard her? Is that what you're trying to say?"

"Not exactly."

"I went to visit my...ex." The word rolls off my tongue unnaturally. "Stupid of me." I clench my fists in my lap and stare at them for a few seconds. "I really thought...maybe...then this girl...this *teenager*...opened the door and I had a brief, stupid burst of hope that she was my kid. Didn't even care if it meant Rosie hid my kid all these years..." I realize I'm not making sense and don't even understand why I'm blathering all this nonsense to a woman I barely know.

"And?" Hope prompts in a soft tone.

"The girl wasn't mine." I glance down at little Grace. "Rosie found someone else a long, long time ago."

"I'm sorry."

"Nah." I tap my chest. "I probably knew all along but didn't want to admit it to myself."

"You needed something to hold on to so you could survive."

Damn, for such a soft, clean woman, she sure seems to understand the darkest thoughts.

"Exactly." I glance over my shoulder quickly. "I know most people would think it's crazy to settle down with the first woman who gives me the time of day—"

"Grinder, that's not true." Her lips curl into a teasing smile. "I saw the girls all over you at your welcome home parties."

Slightly embarrassed, I dip my chin. "That was only out of obligation to the club or wannabe pity fucks."

She snorts out a laugh. Good to know she doesn't offend easily.

Her laughter cuts off abruptly. "Wait, you said settling down? Are you already thinking about that?"

I dip my chin and flash a sheepish smile. "Yeah. This is just between us, right?"

She raises her right hand. "Lawyer oath. I won't tell a soul."

Grace giggles and reaches up to slap at her mom's open palm.

"How about you, Grace?" I ask.

She whips her head around and beams at me. I press my finger to my lips. "This is a secret between the three of us, okay?"

Grace bobs her head up and down.

With that settled, I return to Hope's original question. "I want to get my situation straight first, but yeah, we have something good. I don't need to go fuck around to figure out I wanna be with her."

"That's good."

"I need to be able to offer her more than a ten p.m. curfew, surprise visits from parole, and living in an apartment, though."

Her lips curve up. "She's a physical therapist now, right? They usually do pretty well."

"She's just starting out. Still has a bunch of bills and stuff from school."

"Oh, I know *that* story very well. My law school loans were crippling." She swallows hard and looks away. "Rooster mentioned she has a YouTube channel too. Sounds like it's pretty successful."

"Yeah, I don't understand a damn thing about that." I laugh. "But she seems really into it. She's got a whole separate room all set up where she films her videos. I was thinking I'd like to find a house with a big space for her to use. Build her some shelves for all her stuff. Get her proper lighting and everything."

"Grinder." Hope presses her hand to her chest. "That's so sweet."

Maybe I'm getting carried away. "I don't know. It seems to make her happy." I can't interpret the look on Hope's face. Disbelief? Joy? "You think I'm nuts or getting ahead of myself, don't you?"

"No. I really don't." She reaches over and touches my hand again. "Honestly, if I was still practicing law and you were a client I was counseling, I'd probably advise you to take things slow. Not to rush into anything."

"But?"

"Love doesn't care about what's rational or practical. It takes over and consumes you whether you're ready for it or not."

"Shit, woman." That's exactly how I feel even if I haven't said the *love* part out loud yet. "I spent a lot of time inside going over all the places I went wrong in my life."

"Rock's always given me the impression the two of you were set up."

I suppose that's her polite way of asking if I was innocent. "We were." I walk my fingers on the table in front of me. "Doesn't mean I didn't make a lot of missteps along the way that put me in a place where I *could* be set up."

She nods. "Fate's a powerful force."

"Ain't that the truth. Anyway, I fucked up a lot with Rose. And I made all sorts of promises to myself inside, that I'd do better."

"Why do you think you're fucking up with Serena?"

She's kidding, right? "Look at me. I'm an ex-con. She has a great career. She's so good at what she does, Hope. And I could've ruined that for her."

"Because she's not supposed to date patients?"

"Right."

She bites her lip. "I might not be the best person to comment on *that*."

"Is that how you met? You were Rock's lawyer?"

"I was assigned to him against my will." She flashes a wicked smile. "But it worked out."

I touch Grace's toes again. "Yes, it did."

"Honestly, Gray, I think it sounds like you're taking all the right steps. Getting to know each other, spending time with each other. Keep doing what you're doing."

"Yeah. I don't want to do anything official until I'm off parole."

The dining room door swings open, and Wrath pokes his head in. "Rock's lookin' for you, Grinder."

I press my palms against the table and stand. "Thanks, Hope."

"Not a problem."

Wrath slaps me on the back as he passes, already making noises at Grace who responds with baby giggles.

---

Rock wasn't just looking for me. Teller and Murphy are at the table too. Wrath joins us a few minutes later.

Wary about the reasons for this meeting, I sit back and wait.

"How'd it go this week?" Rock asks.

"With?"

"Everything."

"Been a pain in the balls looking over my shoulder every second. Thought I'd get a break from that once I got out. Otherwise, it's fine. Been doing my thing. Keeping my head down."

"How'd it go with Remy and Griff helping you out?" Murphy asks.

A grin twists my mouth up. "Remy's a cocky asshole." I shift my gaze to Rock. "Reminds me a little of *you* at that age."

Teller and Murphy burst into laughter that they can't hide no matter how hard they try, pressing their fists to their lips.

"But," I add, "he seems smart. Understands the value of loyalty. Not afraid to work hard. Same with the other one, Griff. Don't understand why you're trying to set up a support club instead of making them patch-in with us."

Rock turns toward Murphy and Teller and raises an eyebrow.

They both stop laughing and sit up straighter.

"They've got a lot of business ventures," Murphy explains. "They aren't gonna drop all that and be at our beck and call twenty-four-seven."

"It makes sense." Rock shrugs. "Allows us to extend the territory we control without stretching ourselves any thinner."

Once they explain, I understand better and I can see they've given it a lot of thought. "Sorry, wasn't trying to question—"

"You can question anything at any time, brother," Rock says.

Teller coughs.

Rock's eyes narrow. "Something you want to say?"

"Nope." Teller thumps his hand against his chest. "Not me."

"You can bring any *intelligent* questions to the table any time," Rock says. "That's how this works."

Wrath shoots a glare at Teller. "If you're just being a whiny little bitch and questioning the prez's orders because your feelings got stepped on, then keep it to yourself."

"The fuck?" Murphy says, scowling at Wrath.

Always ready to jump in and defend Teller no matter what. Just like when they were kids.

Wrath grins and shrugs. "What? Just spittin' facts, little brother."

Despite the tension, I bust up laughing. "Christ, Z must have had his hands full playing mediator between your two teams." I gesture between Rock and Teller. "And I'm guessing Dex isn't quite ready to tangle with all the dynamics here."

"What are you rambling about, old man?" Wrath asks.

"Oh, I need to spell it out for ya, big guy?" I point to Rock, then Wrath. "You two been tighter than ticks since Rock dragged your hostile, overgrown ass home."

"I'm about to show you hostile," Wrath grouches.

I point to Murphy. "Same here. Except, Teller adopted you a little sooner than Rock adopted Wrath. And I suppose being married to his sister makes you two even closer. True family, now. So you'll have each other's backs even when you're pissy with each other."

Teller shoots a look at Rock, then back to Murphy. "Sure."

"It's good. You need each other to balance out all these strong personalities. Dex has Z's sensitivity—"

Wrath snorts. "Z's sensitive?"

"Once Dex figures out the right path," I continue, ignoring Wrath's interruption, "it'll all be good." I glance at Murphy. "You've got it too but you still see Rock as a father figure. You're not quite ready to challenge him when he needs it. I have faith in you. You'll get there."

"He's got no problem opening his mouth," Rock says.

"Murphy's as sensitive as an ox," Teller adds.

"No, that'd be *you*." Murphy shoves Teller's arm off the table.

I shrug. "Just calling it like I see it, kids."

"Thank you, Gray," Rock says, not sounding one bit thankful for my observations.

I grin at him. "You're welcome, Prez."

# CHAPTER THIRTY-ONE

## Grinder

The following Friday, I'm fixing up the mess my parole officer made of my apartment, when someone *else* knocks on my door.

If it's motherfuckin' Grillo again, I swear to fuck, I'm gonna choke him and just deal with the consequences. Fucker's been here three times this week.

Since the date of the drop came and went without another message from Big Chief, I've been able to relax. Once he got no reaction from me, he probably lost interest. Found someone else to do his bidding on the outside.

I peer out the peephole and catch a mass of blond hair.

"Serena." I throw the door open. "What are you doing here?"

My tone's harsher than I intended.

Her jaw drops and she shifts the bags in her hands.

I grip her arm and yank her inside. Jesus. I don't need any of Big Chief's people to see her. Don't want anyone on the inside even knowing she exists.

She blinks. Her mouth opens and closes, but no words come out.

"I'm sorry." I take what looks like groceries out of her hands. "You surprised me, that's all."

"We said we were going to spend the weekend together. Snowed in, remember?" Hurt still dances in her nervous eyes.

Shit, I had suggested that, hadn't I?

I should've warned her about what was going on, so this situation right here didn't happen.

"I'm also agitated because Grillo showed up again. You just missed him."

"Oh, no. I ran into him in the parking lot. It was kind of embarrassing because I have a trunk full of boxes of makeup I picked up at my P.O. Box on the way over." She rolls her eyes. "He made some snarky comment about how I was too pretty for all that gook on my face. Like, dude, no one asked you."

"Shit," I growl, fucking pissed he was anywhere near her when I wasn't around.

"He helped me with my bags and held the door for me. Offered to help me carry them up but I didn't want to—"

"You should've called. I would've come down and met you."

"I was excited to see you." That anxious expression flows over her face again, tugging at the corners of her mouth. "We canceled our afternoon appointments and closed early." She follows me to the kitchen. "I stopped at the store. So we wouldn't have to go out. I can go home, though, if you changed your mind."

Like fuck is she leaving. I set the bags on the counter with a thump and go to her, taking her hands and pulling her closer. "Come here."

I wrap her up in my arms. She's stiff at first, taking a few seconds to hug me back. I burrow my nose against her neck, inhaling the crisp winter wind mixed in her hair. A warm vanilla scent hits my nose as I inch closer to her skin.

"Missed you, buttercup." My lips find the soft spot below her ear.

She shivers and melts into me. "Are you sure?"

I pull back. Boy, I really fucked up good here. Need to fix it fast. "Yeah, I'm sure." I reach up and unzip her coat.

"Oh." She glances at her wet boots on the tan carpet. "Sorry."

"Don't care." I squat down in front of her and start unlacing the left one.

"I feel like a reverse Cinderella." She holds up her foot so I can tug the boot off. I chuck it toward the door and start working on the other one. I toss it near the first. It hits the wall with a thump, leaving a faint black mark.

"You're never going to get your security deposit back."

"Ain't worried about it." I stand and pull a bulky backpack off her shoulders and tug off her coat, this time hanging it on the rack "Now. Let me greet you the right way," I say as I approach her slowly.

Suddenly shy or nervous, or maybe annoyed with my grumpy ass, she twists her hands together in front of her. "I should've called first." Her gaze drops to the floor. "It's rude to just show up. What if you had someone over?"

"You're my girl." I clamp my hands around her hips. "You can show up whenever you want. Only people who've been over here are Dex, Remy, and another kid." My face screws into a frown. "And fucking Grillo, but he wasn't invited. Just seems determined to annoy the piss out of me."

"I was going to call but I didn't want to mess with my phone while I was driving." She's still using that hurt, apologetic tone that wraps around my conscience and squeezes.

"Good. Don't want you distracted." I graze my knuckles against her chin and tip her head up. "I'm happy you're here."

Finally, she seems to relax and accept my words. Underneath her fire, Serena's got a vulnerability I need to protect. Need to watch my damn mouth. Can't snap at her like I would a brother.

She's soft and eager as I pull her into my arms this time. I could stand here all night with her pressed up against me like this and be perfectly content.

"What's in the bags, buttercup?"

She steps back and shyly ducks her head again. "You seem like a steak and potatoes man. So that's what I thought I'd cook tonight. Tomorrow maybe we could roast a chicken or we can do it Sunday? A few other things." She shrugs. "I'm not trying to take over your kitchen or anything."

"Take over anything of mine you want. But you didn't have to spend so much money."

"You put *tires* on my car. I think the least I can do is prepare a few meals."

I grunt a non-answer. "It's my job to provide for *you*."

"And what's my job?" She rests her hands on her hips and tilts her head to the side—all challenge.

"To let me do it."

Her lips twitch and a laugh spills out.

## Serena

I need to get myself under control. Once again, I'm too giddy. Too eager. Rushing things. Showing up on Gray's doorstep with bags of groceries and a backpack full of clothes without checking to make sure he even wanted me here all weekend.

Another promise to myself broken.

Sure, he seems to feel bad for his less-than-enthusiastic greeting and spends time reassuring me that I'm wanted. Probably because now that I'm here, he might as well fuck me.

That's not what happens, though. He's affectionate. And if I move *just* right it's easy to tell he's *definitely* interested in going to bed. But it seems more important to him to apologize and talk first.

Once he says it's his job to provide for *me*, I'm swept under.

It's been nothing but me against the world my whole life.

"What else can I do?" I pause for a dramatic beat. "Besides let you provide for me?"

He curls his hands around mine. "Be patient with me. I've had a lot on my mind this week but I'm happy you're here."

"Are you hungry?" I ask.

He pats his stomach. "Actually, yeah. But you shouldn't be cooking for me after you just got done working all day."

"I've had cereal for dinner almost every night this week. I've been looking forward to this." Why'd I have to say that out loud? It sounds so pathetic. "That's my polite way of saying *don't get used to it*," I add to dial back the desperation.

I tug him toward the kitchen and together, we empty the bags.

"I don't know if I have enough room in the fridge for all of this," he teases, folding one of the paper bags and tucking it into a drawer. "Were you planning to throw a dinner party?"

"No." I glance at the counter full of food. Maybe I did get carried away. It's been a while since I've had anyone in my life I wanted to cook for. "Your kitchen's a lot nicer than mine. I thought I could make a few things…"

"I'm kidding, Serena. I can pack away the food, don't worry. And I was a little light on groceries, anyway. Remy and Griff about ate me out of house and home this week."

Curious why he's been hanging around with them but not wanting to ask in case it falls under 'club business,' I nod. "Maybe we should ask Remy over for dinner. I still need to thank him for digging out my car."

"I took care of it." He slips in behind me, gently touching my side, then my hip. "Besides, I want you all to myself."

The note of possession in his voice turns my knees to jelly. "Okay."

He curls his arm around my waist, while I reach to turn on the oven.

"What are you doing?" he asks.

"Preheating the oven. For the potatoes. Is that okay?"

"Sounds good." He rests his chin on my shoulder. While he doesn't ask any more questions, he does release me so I can wash the potatoes, season them and set them in the oven. But he doesn't go far, watching my every move, allowing me to bump into him from time to time.

"How long will those take?" He nods to the oven while I finish seasoning the steaks with garlic and rosemary.

"Maybe an hour. You don't happen to have a cast iron pan, do you?" I bend over, searching one of the lower cabinets.

"Actually, yes." He opens a different cabinet. "Trinity sent me home with one. She said it was 'seasoned' already." He sets it on the stove with a clank. "Careful, it's a heavy sucker."

"Grayson." I can't hide the scolding in my voice. "You shouldn't be lifting that with your shoulder."

He side-eyes me. "The day I can't lift a *pan* is the day I'm throwing in the towel."

Such a perfectly Grayson answer. "Have you been doing the exercises?" I bite my lip. "I hate that I haven't seen you all week. And I'm guessing you never went to see Jason?"

He rolls the shoulder. No signs of pain twist his handsome face. "Yeah, I've been doing them like you asked. Honestly, it's felt better. I haven't thought about it a lot."

I breathe a sigh of relief. "Good. At least I'm not a totally terrible therapist."

"Serena." He clutches my upper arms, forcing me to meet his intense face. "You're great at what you do."

"*Pfft.* You barely had any appointments with me."

"Yeah, and I'm already improving." He strokes his knuckles over my cheek. "The second you touched me, I felt better."

I tilt my head and stare at him. *Really?*

"Okay. Maybe not the *first* touch. You have shockingly strong fingers for a woman your size."

I burst into laughter.

"But your manner, and the way you treated me—you have a gift."

"I gave you the same treatment I give all my patients."

"No, I mean, I didn't feel like a faceless number on your to-do list. You saw in my file that I'd been in prison but you didn't judge me for it."

"Oh," I whisper.

"You acted like I mattered and we were going to figure things out together like a team."

"You *do* matter."

"Even though you didn't know me."

"Everyone matters."

"That's what makes you special and so good at your job."

"Thank you."

His words touch the lonely girl inside who spent years feeling like her existence mattered to no one. I never want anyone else to feel that way.

Overwhelmed, I flip the water on and scrub my hands. Grayson moves in behind me again. Caging me in with his hands braced against the sink. His lips graze a slice of skin between my neck and shoulder left exposed by my shirt.

"Serena." His voice is a low, raspy rumble.

My pulse races.

He curls one arm around my waist and uses his other hand to push my hair to the side, pressing his lips against my neck. His beard tickles my skin, enhancing the pleasurable sensation.

I sigh and lean into him. He doesn't budge. His strong arms and body easily support me.

"How much time do we have?" he asks, moving the collar of my shirt to kiss my shoulder.

"All...all weekend." My brain can't seem to form coherent thoughts.

He gently turns me in his arms, without letting go. I'm swallowed whole by the adoring way he stares down at me.

He leans down and brushes his lips over mine. His arms band tight around my waist, tethering me to his hard body. I loop my arms around his neck and consider climbing him. Anything to get closer. As if he has the same thought, he slides his hands over my ass and lifts, urging me to wrap my legs around him.

Breathless, I pull away. "Do you mind if I take a shower first?"

"First?" He raises an eyebrow.

My cheeks heat. Why am I always rushing things?

"I'm teasing, buttercup. Anything you want." He kisses the tip of my nose and carries me toward the bathroom.

He sets me down on the counter and turns the shower on full-blast.

"You need any items from your bag out there?" he asks.

"Actually, yes. There's a small, flowered pouch in the top—I can go grab it."

"It's fine." He gestures toward the shower. "Go on."

I hurry to undress and step under the warm spray, washing off the stress of my afternoon.

There's a soft click outside the shower. The whir of a fan starts up. The shower door slides open and my pouch appears.

"Thank you." I pull out a small assortment of little bottles, lining them up on the empty shelf built into the wall.

"Mind if I join you?" Grayson asks.

"No." I open the door and pass the empty pouch to him. "Mind if I watch?" I wiggle my eyebrows at him while he unbuckles his belt.

"Haven't had much privacy in the last fifteen years, so watch away."

His words are more gruff than playful, killing the light, teasing atmosphere.

"Sorry," I mumble, sticking my head back inside the shower and sliding the door closed.

A few seconds later, the door slides open. Cool air swirls around me, quickly replaced by Grayson's warm body. He curls his arm around my waist. "Nothing to be sorry about, buttercup. I like your eyes on me."

"Sometimes, I forget…I didn't mean to…"

"Shh." He turns me around to face him, his hands settling at my waist. "Some days, I feel like I got a neon sign over my head blinking 'ex-con.' So, I'm glad *you're* able to forget." He flashes a pained smile. "Means I'm doing a good job assimilating back into civilized society. Maybe I'm not as feral as I feel."

My breath catches. It's such a deep, intimate thing for him to share. And I'm honored he trusts me so much. I slide my arms around his neck, pressing my slick, wet body against his. "You're only feral in the good, sexy way."

He playfully growls and nips at my neck. "Oh yeah?"

"Yes."

"Turn around. What are we doing here?" He runs his hands over my wet hair.

"Washing it. But you don't have to—"

"Which one of these many little bottles?"

I pick up the shampoo and hand it to him. "Sorry, I'll take them all with me when I'm done."

There's the soft click of the cap opening and his slick hands rubbing together a second or two before scrubbing into my scalp. "Serena, leave whatever you want here. Maybe bring bigger bottles, though."

What a sweet way to casually remind me our relationship is more than a few sleepovers to him.

After a thorough and generous scalp massage, he uses his big hands to capture the water and rinse my hair free of suds. "Next?"

I pass the conditioner over my shoulder, and step back from the spray. Something hard bumps into my back.

"Can't help it," he murmurs. "Got a sinfully beautiful woman, wet and naked in front of me."

Reaching behind me, I wrap my hands around his cock at the same time his fingers work the conditioner into my hair.

He hisses in a breath and stops moving for a second. "Let me finish."

"Oh, I will."

This time he turns me so my back's toward the water and rinses my hair clean. I pick up the small bottle of shower gel and squeeze some into my hands. "Your turn." I lather it into a foamy mass and slide my soapy fingers over his shoulders, to his chest.

Our eyes lock and there's an undeniable hunger simmering in his. "I wasn't finished with you."

His low, raspy words double my heartbeat. I can't tear my gaze away. Blindly reaching for the soap, I hand it to him, then continue my exploration.

He groans when I step closer, pressing my breasts into him. He wraps his arms around me, letting his hands run up and down the length of my spine. I dig my fingers into the muscles of his back down to his firm ass.

"You're done." He leans down and kisses my cheek. "Get out and let me finish."

"Rude." I pout at him.

He slides the door open and steps aside.

Slightly confused, I grab one of the towels he set out for me and wrap my hair, then use the other one to dry off. Securing the towel around me, I step out of the bathroom and find my backpack. My gaze darts around the living room.

Bedroom. Get dressed. Finish making dinner. Worry about whatever happened in there later.

I grab my clothes and take them with me. In the bedroom, I unhook the towel and finish drying off.

I'm about to step into my flannel pants when Grayson nudges the door open. "What're you doing?"

"Getting dressed so I can finish dinner." I infuse a teasing lilt into my voice. "I don't *like* to cook naked."

He closes the door behind him. My gaze narrows on the towel wrapped around his hips. Drops of water zigzag down his chest. The urge to trace every single one burns my tongue.

He curls his fingers into my pants and yanks, tearing them out of my hands.

I stare at him with wide eyes. "What's wrong?"

"I asked you to leave because I don't have any condoms in the bathroom and I was dangerously close to pinning you against the shower wall."

Well, that's direct.

# CHAPTER THIRTY-TWO

## Grinder

Serena's pretty blue eyes blink rapidly at my explanation. It's weak but true.

"Why didn't you just *say* that?" She tiptoes closer.

I cup the back of her head and drag her against me. "I don't like feeling out of control."

"I make you feel that way?"

"Yes," I whisper against her lips.

Her sneaky little fingers slip under my towel, tugging it away. "You can always tell me anything, Gray." She climbs into the middle of the bed and sits back on her heels. "I'd rather know, than think I did something wrong."

My gaze slides over her clean, glowing skin. Her damp hair clings to her shoulders and chest. Hard nipples play peek-a-boo through the wet strands.

*What the fuck is this goddess of a woman doing with me?*

I stretch out next to her, my not-quite-dry-yet skin sticking to the comforter. "Come closer."

She snuggles along my side and I curl my arm around her. Feels so good having all her soft warm skin sliding against mine.

I stare up at the ceiling. Maybe I'll get an answer to the questions

I'm about to ask if I'm not looking right at her. "Why are you always worried about doing something wrong? Or making me mad? I'm a cranky old fuck. Ain't got nothing to do with you."

She's quiet but with her face pressed against my chest, I feel her jaw working like she's trying to form an answer.

"My life's been dark, I guess," she finally whispers.

Figured that was the case.

I turn my head and stare at this beautiful woman who brightens up my world whenever she's near. Being with her makes me happier than I thought possible. The desire to murder and maim anyone who's been cruel to her beats against my chest.

"Mine ain't exactly been sunshine and rainbows, sweetheart. I just spent fifteen years in prison."

She winces and I regret my harsh tone. As much as I hate using it with her, I don't know any other way. She deserves someone gentle and kind. Things I've never been and can probably never be. But for her I want to try. "You're my light, Serena. The first brightness in my life in a long damn time."

"I don't know if I can be that, Grayson. For anyone."

"Then we'll be each other's light." I reach over and rub my thumb over her cheek.

"You are," she whispers. "You mean...you mean a lot to me, Grayson."

"Good. You mean a lot to me too." *The world.* Another feeling burns hot in my chest, but I push it aside for now. "If I seem grumpy or mad about something, it's not you, Serena. I'm frustrated. With myself. With the world. With everything. But never with you."

"It seemed like you were avoiding me all week." She hesitates and slides her tongue over her lips. "I thought you might be trying to brush me off."

"No. Fuck no." I cup her cheek and tilt her head to stare in her eyes.

Should I tell her what happened? It's clear she thinks she did something wrong and that's why I kept my distance. I used to always think it was better to leave women *out* of club business.

A wry smile twists my mouth. Technically, this was prison business, not club-related. Does that make it better or worse to share with her?

Keeping secrets from Rose never did me any favors. Serena's a much different woman. Made of tougher stuff. But we're so fucking new together. I hate to keep reminding her of my past and all the things I want to forget.

### Serena

"Serena," he rasps. "I'd never brush you off. In fact, you're going to have a hard time getting rid of me."

"I don't *want* to get rid of you."

"Good."

He stares at me for so long my heart thuds. *What's going on in his head?*

"I can't…give you everything I want right now."

Fear stabs into my stomach. I reach for the blanket to cover myself. If he's about to break up with me, he's not going to do it while enjoying the sight of my tits.

He frowns. "Are you cold?"

"No. Finish what you were about to say."

He works his jaw. "I hate that all I have to offer you is this tiny apartment. I can't take you away for the weekend because I have to be here in case parole shows up." His voice takes on a bitter edge. "I'm a grown man with a curfew, for fuck's sake."

Each admission frees one of the scared butterflies fluttering in my chest.

"I'm falling for you and I can't even do it right."

Falling for *me?*

"Is there a *right* way to do it?" I whisper, ignoring the fact that we're both skipping over any mention of the L word.

He sits forward and reaches for me. "Yeah. Slow, easy, putting smiles on your face, making sure you know how important you are. I hate that I make you doubt yourself."

"It's not you. It's me. I can't help feeling that way sometimes," I admit.

"Why? Who made you so skittish?"

Where do I even start? My parents? My stepfather? My uncle? Every man who came after, until Grayson?

I cross my arms over my chest, cupping my shoulders. The dirt of my past clings to me, tarnishing the way I see the world. I may not have jumped in the mud willingly the first few times, but the filth followed me anyway, soiling all my future actions and decisions.

"Some habits are hard to slay. No matter how hard you try to learn and do better." I shrug. "Sometimes the dirt that molded you seems impossible to shatter."

"Nothing about you is dirty." His tone leaves no room for argument. "But I think I understand what you mean." He pushes my hair out of my eyes. "Feeling like the dirt follows wherever you go."

"How can *you* say that?"

"From prison. Everyone looks at you differently. Treats you a little distantly. Even my brothers. I know they mean well. It's not scorn or judgment from them. It's pity and guilt. And I think sometimes, that makes the filth even harder to shake."

Oh, how his words punch me right in the stomach. Pity and guilt. Two of the many reasons I've ruthlessly whittled my circle of people down to almost nothing over the years.

"They love you, though," I say. "It's easy to see that."

"I know. That's why I haven't fucking clocked any of 'em. Yet."

"You *choked* Steer."

He snorts but the corners of his mouth curl up ever-so-slightly. My heart kicks. I like that I have the power to make him smile, even as we're baring our souls.

He reaches for me, brushing his knuckles against my cheek. "Serena?"

I meet his serious gaze again.

"I might not understand everything you've been through. But I admire you. You've accomplished so much on your own." He shakes his head. "It's inspiring. I know it's probably not my place to say that, but—"

"Thank you." I capture his hand and rub my thumb over his knuckles. "Emily's the only person who's ever said she's proud of me. Amanda doesn't understand why I bothered finishing school."

"I knew I liked Emily," he says without taking a dig at Amanda. "You realize how much courage it takes to make the leaps you have, all by yourself?"

I shrug, knocking the sheet loose from around my shoulders. "I've screwed up a *lot*."

"You're so young and already have things back on the right track. Be proud of that."

It's dangerous, but I want to soak up every ounce of his attention, luxuriate in his touches, drown in his affection until it fills all the tiny cracks and chases every last shadow lingering in my soul.

He holds out his arms. "Come here."

I eagerly slide into his embrace, resting my head on his chest and my leg over his. "You're very cuddly for someone who thinks he's so grumpy."

His laughter rumbles against my ear. "I could hold you like this for the rest of my life and die a content man."

"Don't talk about dying." I slide my fingers over his chest, up toward his face. He jerks as my touch skates over his neck.

"Ticklish little fingers," he teases, turning to kiss my wrist.

"Gray?"

"Hmm?"

"Will you please kiss me?"

He answers by cupping my cheek and pressing his lips to mine. I part my lips and stroke my tongue against his. He groans and shifts his body closer, running his hand over my ribs, down to my thigh and back.

Breathless, we pull away, staring at each other.

He cups my breast, his warm, rough hand sending tingles over my skin. My gaze is drawn to his thumb gently flicking over my nipple.

I gasp and focus on his face as he watches the tip harden to a stiff peak. He captures it between his thumb and index finger, rubbing in maddeningly slow tugs. Each movement shoots sparks to my core.

"You like that," he murmurs, leaning in to suck the hard tip into his mouth.

I run my fingers through his hair, twisting to hold him in place. "Yes."

He shakes free of my hold and captures my other nipple. "Perfect," he murmurs, taking his time lavishing attention on each breast.

I squirm, the throb between my thighs growing more incessant by the second. "Gray?" I whisper urgently.

He slides his hand over my belly and nudges my legs open. A low, growly sound of approval rumbles against my chest as he slides his fingers over my slick flesh.

"I love how wet you are." He kisses my throat. "Every time I touch you."

I'm breathless and panting, even though he's barely grazed my center.

"You...you do that to me," I whisper. "I've never..." My words die as he pushes one thick finger inside me.

"Never what?" He drags his finger toward my clit but doesn't quite make contact before pushing inside me again. "Tell me."

My thoughts scatter as my awareness narrows to that same teasing path he continues tracing.

Slick sounds fill the silence. He kisses my cheek. "Hear that? Fuck," he groans.

I've never been this excited, this *turned-on* by anyone in my life. His wild appreciation only increases my need.

He kisses his way down my body, sliding lower and lower. "I need to taste you."

I'm halfway to exploding when he buries his face between my legs, using his big hands to spread me as wide as he wants. He pushes his tongue inside me, licking and exploring. My hips buck wildly, begging him for more.

He stops and kisses my inner thigh. "God damn you taste good."

I whimper a plea for him to continue.

"Yeah?" He drags his tongue through my slit. "You want more?"

"Yes. Yes." I wiggle my hips. "Please make me come."

Finally, he stops teasing me. Velvet-soft, his tongue flicks against my clit. My body jerks. "Yes, God, thank you."

He rumbles but doesn't take his tongue off me. Now that he's finally where I need him, he alternates between gentle suction and soft licks from every angle until he finds the one that makes me gasp and draw tight.

"*Ohmygod*, right there," I chant over and over. The orgasm hits me, violently shuddering through me. My back bows, limbs shake. Tears leak from the corners of my eyes, rolling into my hair.

And he's not finished. He pushes two fingers in me, curling and stroking, drawing my climax out longer and longer until I'm not sure if it's the same one or a new one.

Fire licks over my skin. The excruciating pleasure leaves me gasping for air and begging for a reprieve.

Tickling kisses drag over my thighs, then up my belly.

"What did you do to me?" I whisper, wiping damp trails from the corners of my eyes. "I've never *cried* from an orgasm before." Not happy tears, anyway.

He swipes his thumb over my cheeks. "You're bright red."

"I think my soul left my body." I point to the ceiling. "She's up there watching and saying, 'get it, girl.'"

He rumbles with laughter and teases one of my nipples between his fingers.

I turn my head and grin at him. "Thank you. For a second I was worried you forgot where my clit was."

He roars with laughter and pulls me up against him. "I love teasing you, buttercup. Keeping you close to the edge, so when you finally go off, it's like an earthquake." He strokes his hand against my side. "Can't get enough of your body and the way you react to me."

I gently curl my fingers around his damp beard. "You've discovered pleasure zones I didn't know I had."

"Good. Let's discover some more." He stretches his body toward the nightstand.

"Gray?" I rub myself against him, lifting my thigh over his.

"Hmm?"

I drape my arms over his shoulders and kiss his cheek. "Before I started my job, I had to have a physical," I whisper in his ear.

He rumbles an interested sound. "I had one too. Before I got released. Then before I came to see you."

"I haven't slept with anyone since then." I drag my fingers through his thick hair and rock my hips. "And I'm on the pill."

He rests his hands on my shoulders and pushes me back. "You're the only woman I've been with since I got out, Serena. Told you that before and I wasn't lying."

"I trust you."

He drags his fingers over the curve of my shoulder. Back and forth. Like he's contemplating life and death.

I lift myself, hovering over his lap and rest my forehead against his, staring into his eyes. "I'd really like you bare inside me." I reach down and wrap my hands around his cock, squeezing and stroking to emphasize how much.

He sucks in a deep breath, his whole body shuddering from my touch. "That what you want?"

"Mmhmm." I roll my hips.

"How bad?" The shock seems to have worn off. Danger glints in his eyes. A hint of savagery in the twitch of his lips.

He clamps one hand on my hip to stop my movements and pries my hand off his cock. "Lean back."

"Why?"

"Because I told you to."

My core throbs from the power of his demanding tone. I arch my back, resting my hands on his shins. "Like this?"

"Yes," he whispers slowly, placing his palm between my breasts and sliding it down my body. "How bad do you want me inside you? Hmm?" His body shifts under me. His teeth graze my nipple and my hips jerk. He slips his hand between my legs, gently cupping, and groans. "Think you're ready for me?"

"God yes." I tip my head up so I can see him. A shiver of anticipation rolls along my spine. "Touch me."

He slides a finger inside me and slowly grinds the heel of his hand against my clit. Still sensitive, I jump at the contact.

"Easy," he whispers, clutching my hip and pulling me toward him.

I position myself, sliding myself against his cock. "You're going to feel so good inside me, Gray."

"Fuck," he groans. "You don't play fair."

He thrusts up as I slide down. The shock of him impaling me doesn't register at first.

"*Fuuuck.*" He groans and lifts his chin, squeezing his eyes shut.

Taking my time, I rock my hips until he's fully inside. "You're so hot, Grayson."

"Yes," he says through clenched teeth.

I stop moving. "Are you okay?"

He opens one eye. "I'm trying to hold out."

Laughing, I loop my arms around him and kiss his cheek.

"Ah, Jesus." He tucks his hands against my waist. "Stop fucking around and ride me. I wanna watch you come on my bare dick before I fill you up."

His dirty words send fire streaking down my spine. I swoop in and kiss him quick on the lips. "I love all the sweet things you say."

"I got plenty more." He thrusts up.

I lean back, resting my hands on his legs and work my hips faster.

"Fuck. Like that." His greedy gaze consumes every inch of me. He licks the pad of his thumb and slides it around my clit.

Sensation jolts me out of my rhythm. "Oh!"

He lets out a dirty chuckle and continues rubbing a firm, steady circle.

"That's it," I whisper, moving against him faster and faster until the heavy tension snaps. White light bursts behind my eyelids. Bliss rocks through my blood.

My world tumbles backwards.

Keeping us connected, Gray rolls me onto my back, throwing one of my legs over his shoulder. He stares into my eyes while his hips snap into me.

"I'm still coming," I whisper.

He groans and smashes his mouth against mine. All my thoughts scatter away. I'm only aware of rolling waves of pleasure, our mingling breaths, and my pounding heart.

"Serena," he whispers. His body stills. His hips jerk—once, twice. He meets my eyes, branding me with an intensity that burns into my soul.

As if I'm the only thing he's ever wanted.

# CHAPTER THIRTY-THREE

## Grinder

"You might kill me yet, woman." I roll to the side so I don't crush her.

My heart's pounding and the words I swallowed down earlier threaten to break loose.

"If I'd known I'd find you when I got out, the last fifteen years wouldn't have been so hard." I've had this thought several times but never planned to say it to her.

She slides her hand over mine. "I'm glad we found each other now."

"Same, buttercup." I sit on the edge of the bed and she crawls behind me, digging her fingers into the knots in my shoulders and neck. "Jesus, how do you do that?"

"What?"

"Find all the sore spots I didn't know I had."

She stops rubbing. Her skin brushes against mine as she crawls across the bed on hands and knees, reaching for something on the nightstand.

I cup my hand over her ass and squeeze. "Need to fuck you like this."

She peers at me over her shoulder. "We have all weekend."

My cock stirs, apparently seeing that as a challenge.

Her body's lean and long. Graceful like a lioness. I can't stop staring. Admiring every inch.

"Watching the way you move is a gift." I run my hand over her leg again. "You're so graceful and flexible."

She laughs softly as she returns to her spot behind me. This time, her fingers are slick and lightly scented with something clean and herbal. "One of the go-to phrases at the clinic is 'motion is the lotion.'"

"Meaning?"

She slides her body against my back, the oil creating a silken, slippery sensation. "Moving your body lubricates the joints to keep everything healthy."

Christ, now I can't stop thinking about wrapping her legs around my *neck*. "Well, then, you're *very* healthy."

"We only have one body, right?"

I chuckle the playful way she tosses my own words at me. "Yes, and yours is exquisite."

"Exquisite, huh?" Her warm breath skates over the back of my neck, leaving goosebumps. "I like that."

I sigh and drop my head as she trails her thumb along painful paths from my shoulder to the base of my skull.

"Shouldn't I be giving *you* the rubdown?" I ask, reaching behind me to touch her bare leg.

"You can do anything you want to me when I'm finished." She adjusts my arm and continues kneading my flesh.

"Anything, huh?"

"God, your back is so sexy," she whispers as she traces lines on either side of my spine, sending a pleasurable shivery sensation over my skin.

"Mmm, say more things that help me not feel like one of your patients."

She rests her chin on my shoulder. Her arms wrap around my chest, hugging me to her. "Trust me, I've never given any of my patients a naked massage before."

"I didn't mean it like that."

She kisses my shoulder and neck. "I like touching you, Grayson. I don't think you're weak and I'm not trying to treat you like a patient."

Well, God damn if she doesn't have me figured out better than I do.

Her fingers skate over a horizontal line above my right hip, another along my side. "What happened here?" she whispers as she traces one of my larger scars.

"Establishing the pecking order on the inside is a ruthless business."

She gasps. "I thought it was from an accident or surgery or something."

I glance over my shoulder. "Yeah, another inmate tried to *surgically* remove my spine with a shiv he fashioned out of a ballpoint pen." I touch or point to different battle scars. "Razor, knife, pointy end of a broomstick—that one hurt like a bitch."

"Gray," she whispers, hugging me again.

"Don't ever plan on going back, buttercup."

"Good." She squeezes more oil into her hands and continues rubbing my back in silence. My body vibrates as if I can feel the waves of affection she infuses into every touch.

Her movements stop.

She sniffs. "Shit!" The mattress wobbles as she leaps off the bed, reaching for the pants I'd yanked out of her hands earlier. "The potatoes. I never set a timer."

*Potatoes.* All I'm thinking about is the sweet jiggle of her breasts as she tries to hop into her pants and yank them up her legs.

"If you run, it'll just make me want to chase you," I warn.

"Oh, really?" She draws out the word to a teasing pitch. "That might be fun." She gives up on the pants, tossing them at my face and sprinting for the door.

Naked.

And I'm on the hunt.

Too bad for her, the apartment's small. I catch her with my arm around her waist as she's about to pass the couch. Our bodies collide with a thump and slip.

I spin her to face the couch and bend her over the back of it until her toes barely graze the floor. She grunts and tries to wriggle away.

I slide my hand into her hair, grab a fistful and tug. Her body goes still. My other hand grips her hip, holding her tight.

She arches her back and presses her ass into my thighs.

Bending over her body, I kiss her shoulder and lightly bite her neck. "You like being hunted down, huh?" I whisper against her ear, giving her hair another gentle tug.

"By you," she whispers.

I take that as a yes. "Watching you run flips my need-to-chase switch. Sorry if you thought your old man wouldn't be able to get it up again so soon." I slide my erection against the seam of her ass to prove my point.

She groans and squirms some more.

"Every time I think about how good it feels sliding into your hot cunt with nothing between us, *this* is what's going to happen."

"Oh God." Her entire body shudders under me. "Yes. Please."

Love how eager she is. I wedge my thigh between her legs. "Open up. Gonna fuck you hard and fast now."

It's an unfair request since I have her pinned under me but she wiggles and tips her ass up until I get the right angle and slide right in. "Buttercup," I groan. "You're still so slick from before. Still got my cum running down your thighs."

She lets out a desperate little groan.

"Am I hurting you?" I ease my grip on her hair.

"No," she pants. "Say that again."

"What? That I like you all wet and messy for me?"

"Mmhmm. Fuck me harder."

*Fuck.* I squeeze my eyes shut and try not to laugh *or* come. She's searing hot against me and crazy about all the filthy stuff I whisper in her ear. Feels so fucking good bare inside her. "Brace yourself."

She pushes her hands against the couch cushions. "That's good right there. Gray, please."

"I got you. Don't worry, buttercup." I slam into her and a scream tears out of her throat. I grip her hair again, tugging her head back, and slide my other hand between her legs, running two fingers along her clit.

Her body trembles. I pound into her, one long savage stroke after another. A relentless pace. We're both beyond words. Just a lot of animalistic grunting and screaming that the whole building can probably hear.

*Let 'em listen.*

I grit my teeth and barely hang on as she tightens around me. Her arms give out. She folds like a rag doll against the cushions. I grab her hips and drive into her again and again. My release hits fast—a blinding rush of pleasure.

My hands shoot out, bracing myself against the couch frame so I don't crush her body. She slides her hand over mine, joining our fingers together. I kiss her shoulder. "You okay?"

She rubs her thighs together. "I need another shower."

Laughing, I push myself upright. She turns and faces me, standing on wobbly legs.

"Ah, shit." I trace a red line across her upper thighs where I must've pounded her into the sofa frame.

She glances down. "I think it's fabric burn."

"Why didn't you say something?"

"I didn't notice in the moment." She brushes my hand away. "I'll be fine. Better my legs than my nipples."

"Come here." I pull her closer and lean down, pressing my lips against hers.

She cups my cheek. "I woke a predator, huh?"

"Yeah, you did."

She flicks her gaze around the living room. One corner of her mouth teases up. "It's not fair. I need more room or a bigger head start next time."

I hug her closer. "Doesn't matter how fast or far you run, buttercup. I'll *always* catch you."

# CHAPTER THIRTY-FOUR

## Serena

After our wild start to the weekend, we finally sit down to dinner. The potatoes are salvageable, but more cement-like than light and fluffy.

Grayson doesn't seem to care. "How'd you get the skin like this? Tastes like what I used to only find in a restaurant."

"It's a Cargill secret." I wink at him.

"Cargill." He seems to roll my name around in his mouth. "I don't think I've ever met another one. Where are your people from?"

"My *people*?"

He shrugs, then moans around a bite of steak. "Good God, Serena."

"The steak came out okay?"

"Better than okay." He takes a sip of water. "A popular game inside was listing all the meals you planned to have when you got out. Steak and baked potato was always at the top of my list."

"I'm glad my instincts were correct."

He reaches over and covers my hand with his. "I didn't expect you to go to so much trouble for me. But I really do appreciate it."

Between his compliments and all the orgasms tonight, I should be glowing like a light bulb any second.

"Your family?" he prompts, reminding me of his earlier question.

"Well, my *people* were from Pennsylvania. But my mom moved around a lot."

"You said you went to live with your grandmother when you were a teenager?"

No one has ever paid attention to the things that come out of my mouth the way Grayson does.

Uncomfortable talking about that part of my life, I nod and stuff another piece of steak in my mouth.

"What about your father?"

I shrug.

"Not around?" he persists.

I set my fork down. "Why are you asking? I'm not attracted to you because I need a daddy figure, Grayson."

His eyes widen and he sits back, staring at me. I hold his gaze for a second, then stab my fork into my over-done potato.

"I was joking when I said that, Serena."

"Jokes always have an element of truth underneath."

"That's…fair, I guess." He drums his fingers against the table. "But I'm direct when I need to be."

"I've noticed." I spear a piece of broccoli and twirl it on my fork. "There's not much to tell about my sperm donor. He was married with kids when my mom got pregnant with me. For a while, he was in and out of my life. His wife and kids weren't exactly eager to accept me into the family." I shrug like the rejection doesn't matter. As an adult, I understand why it was so painfully awkward for everyone. But as an innocent kid, who had no control over the situation, it crushed my soul. "Eventually, he was out for good."

"That's terrible, Serena."

"Yeah, it sucked." I shrug and force a smile. "I don't care anymore."

He grumbles something that sounds like disagreement.

We finish our dinner in silence.

The tension is almost too much to stand. Why'd I have to reveal so much? I hate talking about my family. People either feel sorry for me, look down on me, or want to use it against me somehow.

Grayson slides his hand to my side of the table and runs a finger over my knuckles. "What's next?" He jerks his head toward the window where the snow's falling at a steady rate. "Too cold to build a snowman."

I chuckle, appreciating the light tone after talking about too much darkness. "I bought an apple crumble for dessert. And maybe we could watch a movie? I brought my laptop to hook up to your TV just in case."

"I'm a little out of touch, so you'll have to pick the movie. Our entertainment options were limited to local channels and basic cable inside. Movies were usually old and strictly PG."

"Hmm." My mind's already spinning with all the possibilities.

"No crime or gangster films, though. You don't wanna give me any ideas." He winks at me. "No prisoner redemption stories, either. Hits too close to home."

"Gray," I groan.

"I'm too old for cartoons."

"You're narrowing our choices to 'annoying teenagers picked off by a serial killer' or 'superheroes who save the world' movies."

"No cheesy movies with men running around in their underwear and a cape."

I slap my hand over my mouth and giggle. "Oh, Grayson. It'll be my pleasure to introduce you to *Captain Marvel*."

He frowns. "Which one is he?"

Grinning wide, I stand and start collecting the dishes. He jumps up and jostles the plates out of my hands. "You cooked. I'll clean this up."

"I'll heat the crumble and make some coffee."

"Sounds good, buttercup." He stops and kisses my cheek on his way to the kitchen.

# CHAPTER THIRTY-FIVE

## Serena

T<small>HOSE WHO KNOW THE STORM, DREAD THE CALM BEFORE IT</small>. -C<small>HINESE</small> *Proverb*

Y<small>IKES, THAT'S MORE OMINOUS THAN</small> I <small>WAS EXPECTING THIS AFTERNOON</small>.

I click out of Instagram and slip my phone in my jacket pocket. My gaze searches the cafe for a glimpse of Emily.

Nope, not yet.

For once, I'm here before her.

"Se-LEAN-AH!" someone yells.

*That can't be.*

"Two hot Ventis, room for cream for Selena!"

Yup, that's me.

I trot up to the counter and grab the coffees, stopping to pour cream in both and grab a handful of sugar packets for Emily, then hurry back to the table I claimed.

Even though my jacket is prominently draped over one of the chairs, a guy's sitting on the opposite side when I return.

A wide grin spreads over his face as I approach, like he's been waiting for me.

"Oh, excuse me. My friend and I are sitting here."

He slides his gaze over me in a distinctly creepy way. I scan the cafe for an unoccupied table to relocate to.

Nothing. The place is packed. He pulls his long, muscled frame out of the chair and sweeps his arms toward the table as if he's granting me some sort of gift. "Just wanted to say hello, pretty girl."

I'm *so* not in the mood to be hit on by some random clown today. "Uh, thanks."

*Don't entertain him. Stare him straight in the eyes so he knows not to fuck with you.*

Easier to say than do. My face flames hot, but I pull my shoulders back and drill him with my *not interested* stare. "Anything else?" I infuse as much boredom into my tone as possible and cross my arms over my chest.

A smirk tugs at the corner of his mouth. "Nah, that's it." I take in his black track suit, close-cropped black hair, and inked hands. He could've walked off the set of a low-budget gangster movie.

Over his shoulder, I catch sight of Emily and wave to her.

My unwanted visitor swaggers away and out the door, empty-handed.

"Who was that?" Emily asks, turning to watch him through the plateglass windows.

"Some creep who thought his empty compliment would be the highlight of my day."

She trills with laughter and throws herself into the chair across from me. "Creeps gonna creep."

"Isn't that the truth."

"Gimmie." She grabs the coffee and takes a deep sip. "Thank you for this and thanks for waiting for me too."

"No problem. Coffee's got cream in it, no sugar." I nudge the sugar packets her way.

She rips into several packets at once and dumps them in her cup. "So, how's the silver wolf?"

I sputter on my sip of coffee. "I thought the expression was silver *fox?*"

"Oh no. A man that fine is a *wolf*. He had all those sexy predator vibes going on. Jesus, Serena. The way he kept his eyes on you at Libby's play, I thought my own panties were going to burst into flames."

I snicker.

"I'm serious. You know how some people get second-hand cringe when something so embarrassing happens to someone else you want to melt into the floor? Well, the way that man looked at you gave me second-hand *singe*. So yes, he's a silver wolf."

"Dear…God…" I gasp between fits of laughter.

"Unless silver wolf has some weird porno connotation I'm not aware of." She wrinkles her nose. "Does it? I can't keep track of the kids' lingo these days."

I laugh even harder. "Grayson is fine."

"See, even his name is sexy."

"It is." I can't help grinning. "So is he."

She leans over the table. "Did you…finally?"

The question squelches my laughter. I don't want her to be disappointed in me. "I know it's not the six-month wait time on our list of dating rules, but—"

She holds up her hand to cut me off. "I'm considering amending that rule. Continue."

My cheeks warm and I glance down at my cup, suddenly not eager to share any intimate details. "It was good. Really, really good."

"Ahhh." She wags her finger under my nose. "You don't want to elaborate. That means you *really* like him."

"I do. We got snowed in at his place last weekend and it was nice."

"Snowed in, huh? Is that code for wild sex romp?"

"Yes, but we did other stuff too." I give her a brief rundown of our blissfully domestic weekend of cooking and movie marathons.

"Very sweet. He seems good for you." She waves her fingers in the air between us. "Even though there are some challenges."

"We talked about that a little bit too."

"He can actually communicate?" She raises her eyebrows. "Rare."

"Eh, he needs a little prodding, but yes."

"Okay." She takes a long, dramatic pause and angles her body into a prim pose, signaling there's *nothing* proper about whatever she's about to say. "How are the orgasms? Or I should I ask, *are* there any orgasms?"

Hunching over the table, I snort-chuckle into my coffee, then wiggle a finger to motion her closer. "I literally lost count of how many he gave me in one night."

"Gah! I'm so jealous. The last guy I dated was so off-putting, it left me drier than the surface of Mars."

"That's…weirdly specific. And sounds painful." I wrinkle my nose at her. "Anyway, *that's* not an issue. I'm like a slip-and-slide down there with him."

She giggles uncontrollably, even stamping her feet on the floor. "I will *never* get that image out of my head now."

"Neither will I, Martian pussy."

We both burst into fits of giggles, my body sagging until my forehead hits the table. Something sticky pulls at my skin and I jolt upright.

"Eww." I rub the sticky spot.

"Here." Emily passes me a small package of wet napkins.

"You're so organized." I swipe at the spot until the stickiness is gone. "Thanks."

"So, the orgasms are good. I assume that means there are no… technical difficulties with his late model…hardware."

"Late model…Jeez, Emily. No. Good God, he has more stamina than guys I've been with who were half his age." My whole body shivers at the memory of him hunting and capturing me in the living room.

Her teasing expression fades. "So, you're happy?" she asks.

"I am."

"Good, then I'm happy for you." She discreetly flips her phone over and checks the screen. "I have to jet. We should have a girls' night. Libby really wants to hang with you." She pulls a fake sad face. "I'd be wounded if I didn't love you so much myself."

"Aww, we definitely need to get together. Is she doing okay?"

"Star pupil. I'm so proud of her." We both stand and she gives me a quick hug. "Text me later."

She darts out the front door. I check my phone for the time and still have a few minutes.

A text buzzes through.

*Gray: How was coffee with Emily?*

*Me: Good! She just left. Heading back to work now.*

I suck down the rest of my coffee, clear our table, and duck into the bathroom to quickly brush my teeth.

Outside, slushy remnants of last weekend's snowstorm cling to the sidewalks and curbs. The temperature's warm enough that it's not icy. I keep a brisk pace all the way to my office, enjoying the last bits of fresh air for the afternoon.

Trish is at the front desk, talking to Lucy when I enter. She smiles and my gaze flicks to the clock.

Five minutes to spare. *Phew.*

"How's your surprise patient progressing?" Trish asks. "Grayson…?"

My entire body freezes.

Slowly, I remember to smile and act casual. "Okay. I, uh, actually ended up referring him to Weston PT."

She frowns and rolls her eyes. "Yeah, he seemed like the type who wouldn't like taking direction from a female therapist."

The urge to defend Gray rises up, but I bite the inside of my cheek. I feel lower than a slug lying to Trish when she's been so good to me. "Well, it was a location issue. He was looking for somewhere closer to where he lives. This was a bit of a drive." At least *that* part's true. Downtown Empire is almost an hour away from Gray's apartment.

"Well, we have to do what the patient wants, right? Too bad since he was self-pay."

"Right." I nod weakly, guilt still clinging to me for lying *and* for feeling like I'm getting away with the lie.

# CHAPTER THIRTY-SIX

## Serena

Hours later, I'm tired and ready to leave my day behind. I'm thinking of the video I want to shoot tonight and mentally composing a response to a sponsorship offer I'd received from a cosmetics company as I step outside and breathe in the soggy, evening air. Smells like dirty water and bus fumes.

"Serena Cargill?" a gruff voice calls out my name.

My heart jumps in my throat. My mind quickly flips through all my bills and creditors.

*Did I forget to pay someone?* I've been pretty wrapped up in spending time with Grayson and growing my *Tranquil Sparkle* brand lately, but I haven't let anything slip. Have I?

"Yo, Serena Cargill, that's you, right?"

*Is one of them finally suing me like they're always threatening?*

My attention's drawn to the shadowy space between the building I work in and the parking lot. A man steps into view.

No, he'd come inside the office and serve me with a lawsuit. Not accost me in the parking lot. Right? The one time I'd been served, they knocked on my door and tossed legal papers at my feet.

Too late, I realize I stupidly looked for whoever called my name. But who doesn't respond when they hear their name?

I glance over my shoulder and try to mentally calculate if I have time to sprint back to the safety of my office.

"You Serena, right?" He asks with more impatience coloring his ragged voice. He has an accent. Somewhere downstate. Not the nasal whine and long vowels of Long Island. More like the rapid, *r-less* dialect of one of the boroughs. Bronx? Brooklyn, maybe?

He steps out of the shadows into a pool of light from a nearby security lamp. My car's less than fifteen feet away. But *he's* less than ten.

Tall. Well-built. Arms bulging out of the sleeves of his black T-shirt. Like the cold doesn't have any effect on him. Loose black sweatpants. Expensive-looking black and red sneakers. Bet he spends hours at the gym preening in front of the mirror and has a closet full of barely worn 'kicks.' I feel like I've seen him before.

Despite the muscles, he slouches in that wanna-be casual gangsta pose so many younger guys adapt to look 'cool.'

My cervical spine aches just looking at him.

"Damn." He whistles. His reptilian eyes slide over my body like ice cubes, leaving me frozen with fear. "I gotta say, you even more *sparkly* in person. Nicer than all those over-filtered Instas you always postin'."

Amanda was right. Creepy dudes *are* stalking me online. The longer I stare at him, the more unease crawls over me. It's the same guy from earlier. Did he follow me from the coffee shop and hang out all afternoon waiting for me?

A hysterical laugh threatens to burst out of me, but I force it down. Once I start, I might not be able to stop.

In another life, I might've been flattered by the unwanted attention. Ignored the danger pounding in my gut and fawned over his backhanded 'compliments,' while, deep down, praying he didn't hurt me too much.

Not today. I answer him with nothing but a frosty glare.

He walks closer and mockingly slicks a finger over each eyebrow —which could use a trim—and licks his full bottom lip.

"Loved your little video about how to get the *perfect* arched eyebrow." His voice rises to a girlish pitch.

Typical scrote, insulting my interests. As if his lifting weights and jacking-off-to-porn-all-day hobbies are somehow superior.

"Thanks, it's my highest rated," I say with a whole lot of *fuck off* in my tone.

He squints and circles his finger in the air. "Why ain't you wearing all that face paint when you out and about?"

"Why do you care?" I don't want to take my eyes off him, but someone has to be leaving the building soon, right? I'm scared if I try to run for my car, he'll grab me. Attacker vibes roll off him like clouds of toxic dust.

"You look better without it anyways."

My temper shoots through the fear holding me in place. "Like I give a *fuck* about your opinion," I spit out.

*Where is the security guard when I need him?*

"Spicy. I like that." He nods slowly to himself.

I back away toward my car. Slow and casual. Inch by inch. *Nothing to see here.*

"Why you lookin' so scared, girl? I just wanna talk." He circles closer with each word.

"Well, it's pretty creepy to stalk someone from a coffee shop and sneak up on them hours later in a parking lot."

*Why are you trying to reason with him? He knows he's a creep! He's being creepy on purpose!*

Done toying with me, he closes in, fully cutting me off from the building.

I dash for my car, jamming my thumb against the unlock button on my key fob, praying it doesn't decide to stick, and thanking the heavens I disabled the passenger side from opening at the same time.

Would-be gangster boy laughs. He actually has the nerve to *laugh.* If I make it to my car, I swear, I'm going to run over his stupid, oversized clown feet.

"Why you runnin' girl? What's the hurry?"

My parking lights flash once.

*Now he knows which one is mine.*

But at least my door's unlocked.

I hit the car and yank on the handle so hard, at least two of my nails snap. Pain sears through my fingertips.

My hair's viciously yanked to the side and back, making my ruined manicure the least of my problems.

I shriek and struggle.

It's so unfair. My car's *right there*.

My back slams into the metal door of the car behind me. Air whooshes out of my lungs. I'm too stunned to draw another breath.

Blackness dots my vision.

"I just need to talk to you for a bit." My attacker looms over me. "Why you trippin,' girl?"

Great, he's trying to gaslight me into thinking this is a normal conversation. Too bad for him, I've been manipulated by far worse men in my life and know all their tricks.

I cough and wheeze, trying to draw in oxygen. If I pass out, God only knows what he'll do to me.

Up close, my gaze zeroes in on a tattoo near the corner of his eye. Some sort of red X. His arms sport a lot of ink. What looks like a roaring lion covers his right hand. The lion's wearing a crown, because *of course* it is. All these delusional clowns think they're *kings*.

*Grayson would kick the absolute shit out of this guy. So would any one of his brothers.*

"Damn, dat ol' man of yours must got it goin' *on*." He licks his lip and moans an obscene noise. "When I first looked you up, thought you'd be some ol' biddy. Here you are all young and tight," he murmurs, more to himself than me. "Lucky old bastard."

*Wait. What?*

He's not some wacky fan of my makeup tutorials.

He's here because of *Grayson*?

I'm not sure which is worse.

"What…do…you…want?" I gasp each word, then cough. Sweet air finally fills my lungs.

"I need you to deliver a message."

*Of course you do.*

"Ol' G's pissed off the wrong crowd. He don't get to skip out of prison carefree. He's got obligations."

He grips my chin with iron fingers and jerks my head up, banging my head into the roof of the car.

My vision swims again.

"You listening, Serena?" He's right in my face. Foul breath bathing me in his stink.

An unintelligible noise passes my lips. My head hurts so bad, I couldn't answer even if I wanted to.

"Tell Grinder to fall in line, or shit's gonna be ugly next time. You feelin' me?"

I groan and try to nod, but his grip's too strong.

"Big Chief don't like to be ignored." His hand slips from my chin to my neck, gripping in a tight hold. "You got all that?"

My eyes bulge as I struggle to breathe.

He squeezes harder. "I been to that dank little brownstone you live in." He slaps my cheek lightly and flicks his gaze over my shoulder. "Know where you work. Your car. You gettin' the picture?"

He releases me. I double over, coughing and gasping.

"I got it," I whisper, clutching my knees and staring at the ground.

"Good."

Feeling too vulnerable bent over, I struggle to stand and keep my feet under me. "Who are you?"

"Don't matter. He'll know who the message is from."

"Serena?" a female voice echoes over the parking lot.

My attacker's head snaps up. His gaze shoots to somewhere over my shoulder, then to my face.

"Serena!" Trish's voice has never sounded more angelic. "What's going on? Get away from her!"

Gangster leans in one more time. "Don't forget."

I nod quickly.

"I'll catch you later, Sparkles," he sneers.

*It's been a pleasure, asshole.*

Unable to hold myself up another second, I slump against the side of my car and slide to the ground, landing on the hard, wet asphalt with a jarring thump.

The guy dashes for the line of trees separating our parking lot from Empire Med's complex and disappears into the darkness.

"Serena?" Trish's sneakers squeak over the wet ground. She squats next to me and touches my shoulder. "Are you okay? Who was that?"

I cough and shake my head. "I don't know."

"Oh my God." She yanks out her phone and quickly makes a call.

"No," I groan, weakly. "No cops."

"Serena, I have to. Do you know that man?"

I shake my head.

Pain stabs through my skull.

"You shouldn't walk out alone," she scolds. "911, yes! One of my employees was just attacked in our parking lot."

"No. Don't need 'em." I slap at the phone in her hand. She stands and paces a few steps away to finish the call.

*Shit.* I can't tell the cops anything that will get Grayson in trouble. My head's so fuzzy, I'm afraid I'll say the wrong thing.

*Mugger.* Say the guy tried to rob me. Keep it simple.

I close my eyes and rest against the car. *Mugger. Rob me. Coffee shop. No. No coffee shop. Mugger.*

"Serena?" Trish touches my arm. "Honey, are you okay?"

"I'm here," I mumble.

"Who can I call for you?"

*I need Grayson.*

"My phone's in my pocket." I roll to the side, so she can reach in for it. She pushes it into my hands a few seconds later.

Blinking, I try to focus on the screen in front of me and press the entry for *Grayson*.

"Hey, buttercup." His warm, rich rumble washes over me.

I burst into tears.

"Serena, what's wrong?"

"I need you, Grayson," I sob.

"Where are you?"

"At work."

Sirens pierce the air.

"Baby, what happened?" he shouts into the phone.

"This guy. Attacked me. In the parking lot."

"What guy?"

"I don't know."

"Are you hurt?"

"Yes."

"There's the police and the ambulance!" Trish jumps up and waves her arms in the air.

"Serena, I'm all the way in Johnsonville. Gonna take me at least an hour to get to you."

"No, don't come. The cops are here," I whisper.

"It's okay. I'm gonna ask someone from the club to meet you. I'll be there as soon as I can."

"Miss, are you okay?" someone barks above me.

The phone falls from my hand, clattering faceup on the ground. I glance at the paramedic and weakly shake my head. Trish squats down and scoops up my phone, checking the screen quickly before turning it off.

Our eyes meet.

*Oh, shit.*

There's no time to say anything. Paramedics rush over to check me out.

When I refuse to go to the hospital, Trish has them take me inside the office to tend to my injuries.

Fear hits me from ten different angles.

*Grayson's in danger.* From some wannabe crime lord or prison gang. And he'll also be in trouble with parole. They'll accuse him of associating with other criminals or something. Probably throw him back inside. I can't let that happen to him.

*The club.* Could he get in trouble with his brothers? Will they punish him for working with another gang behind their backs? As much as they seem to respect Gray, their brotherhood always comes first.

*My job.* I'm probably going to get fired, when Trish puts two and two together and comes up with I slept with a patient.

*My life.* I can't go back to my apartment. I can't stay at Grayson's. I can't even go to Emily's house. I'd be putting her and Libby in danger. *Oh my God,* what if he saw Emily earlier today and threatens her next?

My head really, really hurts.

"How'd this happen, Serena?" yet another paramedic asks.

I explain what I remember, leaving out the parts of the conversation that involve Grayson.

He asks me a series of questions. In the back of my mind, I understand he's trying to assess my cognitive function.

A cop shows up to take my statement. He's nice enough but questions me until my temples throb.

"Easy, officer," the paramedic grumbles. "Back away."

As he's finishing testing my reflexes, there's a commotion at the door. Loud voices. A blur of people blocking the entry.

"I'm here for Serena."

I recognize the deep, menacing voice.

"It's okay, Trish," I call out weakly. "He's here for me."

Gray promised to send someone.

And he did.

Teller's big frame slides through the cluster of people, worry and annoyance creasing his brow. His bright blue-green eyes scan everything in his path before landing on me.

His scowl deepens.

*Yeah, well, you're not exactly my first choice, either.*

His irritation seems to transform into concern as he crouches next to me. "What happened, hon?"

"Is he your ride?" the paramedic asks me, stepping away from Teller. "You can't drive."

"Yeah." Teller stands. "I'm here to take her home."

I shake my head. I *can't* go home. But I don't want to say that in front of everyone.

The paramedic explains that I probably have a concussion and since I won't go to the hospital, I need to go home and rest for at least one to two days. "Can you make sure she does that?"

"She'll be taken care of," Teller promises.

*Not exactly reassuring.*

"Work," I protest. "I have—"

"I'll cover your appointments," Trish says. "Just go home and take care of yourself." She touches my arm and spears me with a meaningful look. "We'll talk in a couple days."

Great, something to look forward to. Getting fired.

"Come on." Teller helps me stand. I almost scream as pain slices through my skull. "Are you sure you don't want to go to the hospital?" he asks.

"I hate hospitals." I stuff all the information the paramedics gave me in my purse.

"I hear that," he mutters, opening the door for me. "Let's get out of here."

His truck's parked with two tires up on the curb. "Lot was jammed." He flashes a tight smile.

"Hey, that's what trucks are for, right?"

He chuckles. "Which one's your car?"

I point to my hatchback.

"We'll have someone grab it for you. Bring it up to the clubhouse."

Tears of relief roll over my cheeks. "You're not taking me home?"

"Fuck, no." He holds out his hand to grab onto, boosts me into the truck and slams the door shut.

I rest my head against the seat and close my eyes.

The truck starts with a deep, throaty rumble and I hurry to buckle the seat belt. Bile crawls up my throat as the truck's stiff suspension rocks forward and we bounce off the curb.

"Sorry," Teller mutters. "Trying to take it slow."

"It's okay."

He reaches behind my seat, grasping for something, and a few seconds later pushes a bottle of water into my hands.

"Thanks," I whisper, uncapping it. "Why are you always the one driving me home after I get smacked around?" I take a shallow sip of water.

"I don't mind giving you a lift," Teller sighs. "But I'd rather not have you get smacked around at all. By anyone."

"Me too," I mutter.

"I came because I was in the area and closest to the hospital," he explains.

"Oh." Better Teller than Murphy. This is awkward enough.

"Grinder didn't want you waiting for a ride," he explains. "He's gonna meet us up at the clubhouse."

"He can't be there. What time is it?"

"Don't worry about that." He glances over. "You give the cops an accurate description of the guy who did this?"

"Yeah," I answer carefully. While I glossed over the details of the *why* the guy attacked me, I told them what he looked like. Doubt they'll do much to catch him anyway. Some woman got attacked, who cares?

"Wanna tell me what happened?" he asks.

I study his profile for a second. While he has the good looks of a handsome, carefree athlete—someone you'd find shirtless on a beach tossing a Frisbee during the day and nailing chicks in bikinis all night—if you stare at him too long, the ruthless predator in him shines through. He's a longtime member of the club—the treasurer—and I know damn well he didn't earn that patch by being warm and friendly.

If this *isn't* club-related, and Grinder's in some sort of trouble the club doesn't know about, I don't want to be the one who rats him out to one of the club's officers.

Besides, Rock could've sent him to get me to give up information about Grinder.

"Serena?" he prompts.

Nope, definitely not telling him.

"I'd rather wait and talk to Grinder first." I use the most stubborn tone I can come up with.

"Yeah, okay. Go ahead and close your eyes. Rest. I'll wake you when we get to the clubhouse."

*He gave up awfully fast.* I peer over at him and swear the corner of his mouth twitches, like he's trying not to smile.

The truck rolls to a stop at a red light. Teller sits forward, squints, and peers up at the sky. "Damn it. Looks like another storm's coming."

I close my eyes.

*Those who know the storm, dread the calm before it.*

If tonight was the calm, what the hell's coming next?

# CHAPTER THIRTY-SEVEN

## Grinder

"Where the fuck are they?"

"Calm down, Gray," Rock warns. "They should be here in a few minutes."

"If you tell me to calm down one more motherfucking time," I snap.

"Easy," Wrath adds.

"Fuck off." I pace alongside the clubhouse and return to the front steps. "This *has* to be Big Chief. I *knew* that motherfucker wouldn't quietly slink away."

"We'll handle it," Rock assures me.

"We haven't even been together that long and this shit happens? I can't do this to her. How'd they even know she exists?"

"I don't know, brother." He rests his hand on my shoulder. "We're going to take care of it."

Finally, headlights slice through the darkness. A truck, high off the ground, slowly winds up the driveway. The three of us walk to the front of the clubhouse to meet it.

Teller stops right in front of the porch steps.

I yank the passenger side handle, swinging the door wide. Serena's asleep in the front seat, her head at an awkward angle.

"We need to wake her up," Teller says, jumping down on the other side. He walks around the front of the truck to stand by my side. "Paramedics said she shouldn't sleep for too long. She's probably got a concussion."

I'm going to start murdering people any second now.

Bumping him out of the way, I push into the open space and touch Serena's hand. Two fingers are wrapped in thick white gauze.

"What happened?"

"I don't know." Teller runs his fingers through his hair. His mouth curves to the side. "She said she wanted to talk to *you* first. Wouldn't tell me a damn thing."

My chest squeezes so tight. How can she have something so awful happen and still be worried about protecting *me*?

I lean in and unhook her seat belt. "Hey, buttercup. Time to wake. You're at the clubhouse," I whisper. "You're safe now."

She moans, then gasps. "Gray?"

"I'm here."

She curls her arms around my neck, and I slowly lift her out of the truck.

"You need help, G?" Wrath asks.

"I got her."

Everyone backs off but they follow us into the clubhouse.

I set her down inside. She wobbles on her feet and squints at the bright lights.

Rock flicks a few switches and twists a dial, turning the lights down. "I didn't call everyone to the table yet, since I wasn't sure what we're dealing with. But Z's on his way."

"Rooster's upstairs," Teller says. "You want me to grab him?"

"Not yet." Rock keeps his eyes on me. "I think you, Wrath, Z, and me need to sit down first."

Teller nods and runs his hand over the back of his neck. "I gotta run back to Empire and pick Charlotte up from her office. Take me about an hour."

"That'll give us some time," Rock says.

Teller glances my way. "You want me to have Charlotte drive Serena's car up here?"

"No," Rock cuts in. "I don't want you two separated right now." His gaze lands on Serena. "Not until we understand what's happening. Ask Stash to go with you and drive her car. That all right with you Serena?"

She slowly turns in my arms and pulls her keys out of her pocket. "Sure." She focuses on Teller for a second. "Thank you for coming to get me."

"No problem." He grabs the keys. Rock wraps his arm around Teller's shoulders and speaks to him too quietly for me to hear. After a few minutes, Teller leaves.

"Gray," Serena whispers urgently. "I need to talk to you. Alone. Please."

Holding onto her arms, I pull away and look her over. "What happened? Where are you hurt?" Rage explodes in my chest when I notice the red marks on her face.

She gingerly touches her scalp. "I hit my head when he pushed me." She sways to the side a little.

"Come on, let's sit down." I curl my arm around her and lead her over to one of the couches in the back corner.

I drape her over my lap and secure my arms around her. "Tell me what happened."

She rests her uninjured hand on my shoulder and strokes my cheek with her soft little fingers. "Gray."

"Right here, buttercup. What happened?"

"I thought...I thought he was a stalker from my YouTube channel. He...but he wasn't. He wanted me to give you a message."

Inside, what's left of my soul shrivels.

*I knew it.*

I'm barely in her life five minutes and someone hurt her to get at me.

The prison of my past will never release me. It was stupid to think I'd be able to make a fresh start.

A sigh of defeat eases out of me. "What message?"

She picks her head up and stares over her shoulder at Rock and Wrath, now speaking in low tones near the open war room door.

Rock catches my eye and lifts his chin.

Serena turns to me, eyes wide, and shakes her head. Leaning closer she whispers in my ear, "Please let me tell you this when we're alone."

"You can say anything in front of them. It's okay."

"Grinder," Rock says. "Z's gonna be a while. Take her upstairs. Let her rest for a bit."

She nods eagerly and slides out of my lap.

"All right." We're wasting time not going after this fucker immediately. But my girl needs me right now.

In my room, I help her strip off her ruined clothes and take a quick shower. As I'm drying her off, someone knocks on the door.

"You all right here for a second?" I ask.

"I'm fine." She grabs her toothbrush. "Want to get this awful taste out of my mouth."

Trinity's waiting in the hallway. "Is she okay?" she asks in an anxious voice as soon as I open the door.

"Yeah. I think so."

She holds up an overstuffed tote bag. "We're about the same size. I wasn't sure what she might have here, so I brought over a bunch of stuff."

I swallow hard and accept the bag. "Thank you, Trin."

"No problem." She hesitates for a second. "If she needs anything, call me. No matter what time it is. Even if she doesn't want to be alone…in case you need to step out."

Yeah, growing up in the life taught Trinity that whoever touched Serena will pay in blood.

"I will. Thank you."

I close the door and turn toward the bathroom. Serena's on the threshold. Her bottom lip trembles as I hand her the bag.

"That was sweet," she whispers.

"Trin's a good girl." I nod to the bag. "You need help?"

"No." She dumps the contents on the bed and sorts through everything, setting aside a pair of flannel shorts and a short T-shirt.

After digging through everything, she lays out a pair of long pants, a sweatshirt, and a pair of thick socks. "I'll get dressed when we go talk to everyone."

I sit on the edge of the bed and pull her into my arms. "Tell me what happened. What were you so afraid of anyone else hearing?"

I clamp down on my fury while she walks me through the story.

"So, you know who this was and what it's about?"

There's no anger in her tone. Just concern. She should be pissed at me. Should tell me to get the fuck away and leave her alone.

"Yeah, I know what it's about."

"Does the club know?" she whispers. "Are you going to be in trouble with them?"

My eyes widen. "That's what you're worried about?"

She shrugs helplessly. "I don't know everything you went through inside, Gray. If you had to…work with other people to…"

"I wouldn't betray my club for any reason, Serena. But yeah, there's some stuff I thought was behind me when I left. Club knows all about it. So we're good there."

She blows out a long, slow breath. "Okay."

"It's *not* okay. I'm so sorry. I should've warned you. Shouldn't have let you come anywhere near my place while this was going on. This is my fault."

"No. It's not. I don't know all the ins and outs of how the club operates. But working with another club…or organization…I was so worried they'd be mad at you."

God, I love her for thinking through all of that and wanting to protect me from my own club.

I lean in and kiss her temple. "Club knows everything. I went to them first thing. I didn't do anything wrong, Serena. It's complicated, but I'm not in trouble with anyone here."

"I know it's been a hard adjustment…"

"It's okay." I kiss her again. I don't even have words to express how much her desire to protect *me* means. "Thank you."

Now that she's been assured the club's not waiting to take me out back and shoot me, the weight of sleep seems to fall over her. Her eyelids droop. The bruises on her cheek and forehead seem to have darkened.

"All right." I shift her to the mattress. "You need some rest. Once Z gets here, they're gonna want you to repeat the whole story."

"I know. I'll be fine."

"You're going to rest for a bit," I insist.

She yawns. "They told me to have someone wake me up every few hours."

"I will. Come on." I tuck her under the covers, then duck into the bathroom to clean up and change. When I return, she's out cold. I ease into the bed quietly, trying not to disturb her but she turns and curls up against me.

Sleep's not coming for me.

*This is bad.*

What if they'd done worse? Came at her when she was home alone?

The savage need to protect her claws at my chest. Something else burns in my heart. I pull her closer and kiss the top of her head. "I love you, buttercup."

Saying it when she's asleep seems a hell of a lot safer.

I should let her go. End things now. Before she gets dragged into anything else.

But it's too late.

Way too fucking late.

# CHAPTER THIRTY-EIGHT
## Grinder

I doze with Serena in my arms for maybe an hour. At some point, she yawns and stretches, sliding her leg against mine.

My cock jumps to attention.

*Not now, you sick motherfucker.*

Serena gasps. Her eyes pop open wild and terrified until they land on me.

"Oh, thank God." She lunges, wrapping her arms around me.

"Easy, buttercup. I'm right here."

She quiets down and I think she's fallen asleep when she drags her fingers over my chest and pulls herself up toward the pillows. Her soft lips press against my cheek. She uses her teeth to tug at my earlobe. The gentle pull sends a streak of fire straight to my dick.

"What're you doing, buttercup?"

"Make me feel...make me feel better, Grayson, please."

"What do you need?"

"Touch me."

Is that going to make her feel better or make things worse?

"I think you need more rest."

She rolls to her back and lifts her hips, wriggling her shorts down her legs.

"What are you doing?"

Without answering, she shackles her hand around my wrist and pulls. I slide closer, gathering her in my arms.

"Mmm." She rubs her face against my chest. "I feel so safe when you hold me."

"Good. You're safe here."

She bumps her hips into my hand.

I slip my hand between her legs and slide her underwear to the side. "This where you want me to touch you?"

"Oh," she sighs, her head rolling to the side. "Yes."

Wet. So wet. I slick my fingers through her center, stopping to rub her clit. Her hips jerk.

"Yes, yes," she whispers. Her nails dig into my bicep. I slip my free arm under her, pulling her against my chest. My fingers awkwardly grab and tug at her cutoff T-shirt until her breasts pop free.

I suck the closest nipple into my mouth, lashing my tongue over the hard tip. She moans and arches, spreading her legs wider.

"Please," she whines. "Make me come."

Christ, if those aren't my three favorite words out of her mouth. I swear that sweet little plea follows me in my dreams some nights.

I slide my hand lower, pushing my middle finger inside her, while grinding the heel of my hand into her clit.

"Like that?" I whisper, kissing her cheek.

"Yes," she hisses, rocking against my hand. Her breathing quickens. "Harder."

I add another finger, pushing deep, watching her face for her reaction.

"Oh." Her body shudders violently. Around my fingers, her muscles flutter and tighten.

"That's it," I encourage. "Feel good?"

She moans and nods, her body still quivering. My cock's suffocating to death in my briefs, wanting all that wet, slick heat my fingers are slipping through.

"Uh." Her body jerks away from me and she slams her legs shut.

"Too much?" I tease, pulling my hand free.

She laughs softly and stares up at me, gently tracing her fingers over my cheek. "Thank you." She rubs her thumb over my bottom lip. "I hate to be greedy, but I need more."

"I love when you're greedy. But I don't want to hurt you."

"I know how gentle you can be." She reaches down, tugging at my briefs. My cock springs free and she curls her fingers around me, softly stroking. "Please."

"Ah, fuck." I squeeze my eyes shut.

"Please," she whispers again.

I shove my shorts all the way off, kicking them to the floor.

She watches every move.

"You sure you feel all right?"

Holding my gaze, she hooks her fingers in her underwear and drags them down her legs, gracefully pulling them off and tossing them aside.

As if I'm not already crazed, she pulls her knees up, digs her heels into the mattress and spreads wide. "Come to me. I want to feel you on top of me, Gray."

I reach for one of the pillows, stuffing it under her hips, then gather her in my arms, slowly guiding myself inside her.

She sighs and gasps, lifting her legs to wrap them around my waist. "That's what I wanted." She loops her arms around my neck, dragging me closer.

"Whatever my buttercup wants, she gets." I tease my lips against hers.

"Harder, Gray. You're not going to hurt me."

"Give me a second. I'm enjoying your tight, wet cunt wrapped around my dick right now."

She laughs softly. "That is the *worst* word." She traces her fingers over my lips. "But it's *so* hot when you say it."

I kiss her fingertips. "'Cause you know I'll only say it to you when I'm deep inside your tight little *cunt*."

Her lips curve and she tightens her muscles around me. "Ah, fuck." I stop moving. "Don't do that."

She squeezes again. "Do what?"

"Keep it up, little witch. This isn't gonna last much longer."

Her grin is full of mischief. "Wait, am I your buttercup or a little witch?"

"When you're trying to hex me with your pussy, you're my little witch." I grind my hips into her until her eyes roll back in her head. "How's that, little witch?"

"Urgh." Her nails dig into my ass, urging me on. I hammer into the one particular spot that seems to make her lose it.

Her whole body tightens, snapping my last bit of control. I drive into her harder and faster. White lightning streaks down my spine, as I empty myself inside her.

I groan with satisfaction, loud enough to rattle the damn windows. "Fuck."

She grabs my face and pulls me toward her. Our mouths fuse in a chaotic storm of kissing, nipping, and licking.

When the ride's over, I peel myself off her and roll to the side. "You all right?"

She touches her forehead and winces.

"Hey." I sit up. "Are you okay?"

"Just a bit of a headache at the end."

"Ah, shit." I climb out of the bed. I knew better. Dammit.

"Gray, I'm fine," she calls after me.

I stalk into the bathroom and flip on the water, wetting a washcloth and filling a glass.

"Here." I hand her the water and help her sit on the edge of the bed.

She sucks down the contents of the glass and sighs. "Thanks. It's not from you. They said I might get headaches."

"Yeah, I'm sure being pounded into the mattress didn't help."

She chuckles and pushes the glass at me. "But the orgasms helped a *lot*. Haven't you ever heard of sexual healing?"

"Lie back for me."

With her eyes on my face, she leans on her elbows. "Why?"

I wag the washcloth at her. "I want to clean you up."

"Oh." She closes her eyes and rests her heels on the edge of the bed, opening for me.

*Clean her up.* What a lie. Like a sick fucker, I end up staring and watching my cum spill out of her, then run my fingers through her slit, pushing it back inside.

"Serena?" I rasp.

"Hmm?"

*What would it take to get you off the pill?*

*No, can't say that.*

Not yet.

Need to be able to offer her a hell of a lot more than late night attacks in parking lots, small apartments, and a husband with a curfew.

*Husband.*

I need a ring.

Something big, but classy, with a *lot* of sparkle. I stare at her slender fingers, trying to picture a stack of diamonds wrapped around one—a promise that I'll never let anything bad happen to her again.

She needs a property patch too. Whole world needs to know that fucking with her is a death sentence.

Jesus Christ, I can't even wear my *own* cut in public right now, but I want to give her my patch?

I rest my chin on her knee, watching her face as I keep working my fingers in and out of her.

She gasps. "Are you cleaning me or making a bigger mess?"

"Little of both. Feel good?"

"Oh my God, *yes.*"

I gotta get off parole. Find the right house for us. Give her all the things she deserves before I ask her to have my kids.

I kiss her leg, feeling her tremble against my lips. "Think you can come again?"

Already on the verge, she answers with soft, shuddering breaths.

I splay my big hand over her stomach, aching to see it rounded with my child.

*Time. We've got time.*

Well, *she's* got time.

I sure as fuck ain't gettin' any younger.

# CHAPTER THIRTY-NINE

## Serena

With four oversized bikers looming, I feel like the buttercup Grayson always calls me—surrounded by a ring of redwood trees.

"Back off," Gray warns, as if he understands the claustrophobia threatening to choke off my air.

He's been growly and snarly ever since Z tapped on our door and asked us to join the guys downstairs.

Well, growly with his brothers. Not me. He hasn't strayed more than a few inches from my side.

"Easy, G," Wrath rumbles. "We need to know what happened."

"So we know who to kill," Rock adds.

Finally, I pick up my head.

"Shit, Serena." Z stares at my cheek under the bright fluorescent lights and stretches his arm as if he wants to examine the injury.

His dark blue gaze slips to Gray's murderous expression and he backs off.

"Let's get this over with," Gray rumbles. "We're wasting time not looking for this guy."

"Teller got ahold of the police report," Rock says. "Steer and Murphy went to see Loco. He's got the description. Soon, everyone upstate will know we're looking for him."

"I think he's from the city," I blurt out.

All eyes focus on me.

"His accent." I wiggle my fingers in front of my mouth. "When I lived down there, I heard it all the time. No one in upstate New York talks like that. It sounded like the Bronx, maybe, or Brooklyn. His vowels were too clipped to be Queens."

They continue staring.

"What?" I shrug. "I lived down there while I was modeling. But I wanted to be an actress, so I studied accents and dialects all the time."

"Could be one of twenty different crews working in the city," Z says, glancing at Rock who nods in agreement. "But that's a good start. Thank you, Serena."

"Can you think of anything else?" Wrath asks.

My mind blanks. I feel so helpless and useless.

"Let's start before the attack. What'd you do today?" Rock's tone is smooth and mellow. Like we're old friends chatting about life. He reaches over and slaps Wrath's arm, motioning for him to sit in his chair.

Without everyone hovering over me, I'm able to clear my mind and focus. "Uh, on my lunch break, I had coffee with my friend Emily. He was there. The guy."

"Jesus Christ," Gray mutters. "He was stalking you all day?"

"I think he's been to my apartment too. He said as much when he threatened me. But there was a night a couple weeks ago when I swore someone was skulking around my hallway."

"Why didn't you tell me?"

I shrug, feeling stupid now. "I forgot about it."

"Go on," Rock encourages. "Did he talk to you at the coffee shop?"

"Yes, I went to get my order and when I came back, he was sitting at my table. Gave me some cheesy line about wanting to talk to a pretty girl. I just thought he was a regular creep trying to hit on me."

Grayson growls again.

"It happens all the time," I tell him.

Z shakes his head and flashes a dimpled smile. "Not making it better, Serena."

I appreciate his attempt to make me laugh. Then, a hot poker of fear stabs me. Is Emily in danger now too? "He's not going to go after my friend, is he? She's got a little sister to look after. They live by themselves."

"Aw, fuck," Grayson mutters. "They're sweet girls."

"You know 'em?" Rock asks.

"Yeah. The play I told you I went to was Libby's."

*Grayson told them about going to Libby's play with me?*

"Any chance they'll want to stay here for a few days?" Rock asks me.

"Ah, probably not. Emily's not really the motorcycle club type."

"Give me her address." Wrath slides a piece of paper my way. "We'll have someone watch her house."

Great. How the hell am I going to explain that to Emily?

I write it out and hand it over.

"Okay. Go back to the coffee house," Rock prompts. "Did you see him or anyone else watching you? Anyone follow you to your office?"

"No. I don't think so, but I wasn't really paying attention." Nothing unusual stands out about my walk. "My afternoon was normal. Saw my patients. Left at a decent time. He was waiting for me outside my building."

"How'd he approach you?" Rock asks.

"Uh, he called out my full name." I glance down at my lap. "I got so scared it was someone trying to serve me with a lawsuit or something."

"Why would you think that?" Z asks.

"None of your business," Grayson growls.

"All right. Settle down, G."

I rest my hand on Gray's arm. "It's fine. He made some snarky comments about my YouTube videos. I got scared he was a crazed fan—"

"Hold up," Wrath says. "Your *what?*"

My cheeks must be glowing red by now. "I have a channel where I do makeup tutorials, reviews, and stuff. I have a presence on all the major platforms."

Wrath nods, like he's actually impressed.

"Serena has a big following on that Insta-thing," Grayson says. "Lotta dirtbags say nasty shit to her, too."

*Boy, he's still stewing about that, huh?*

"How the fuck did *you* find your way to Instagram, old man?" Wrath jokes.

Grayson grumbles a bunch of curses in response.

Rock's severe expression doesn't suggest he's amused by the detour in conversation. "How'd you realize he was there because of Gray?"

Grayson flinches as if Rock's question punched him in the side. "Ah, he said Gray was a 'lucky old bastard' and implied that he thought *I'd* be older."

Z snickers and covers it up with a cough behind his hand.

"Laugh it up, you dimple-faced little fucker," Gray grumbles.

"*Then* he said he wanted me to deliver a message." I swallow over the painful lump in my throat and struggle to remember exactly what the guy said. "Gray 'pissed off the wrong crowd.' And, uh, he couldn't leave prison without taking care of his obligations...something like that."

"Someone told him about you," Rock says. "Who else knows about your relationship?"

Gray and I look at each other. He cups my unbruised cheek and rubs his thumb over my skin. "The club. Remy went with me to her apartment. My parole officer."

"Fuck," Wrath mutters.

"My money's on the P.O. He's been a dick from the jump," Z says.

"Do people ever recognize you from your videos, Serena?" Rock asks.

"Not really."

"We need to put a 'no celebrity girlfriends' clause in the by-laws," Wrath jokes. "First Shelby, now Serena. No names that start with 'S,' either."

"Don't be an asshole." Z smacks the back of Wrath's head.

I can't help laughing, which makes my head hurt. "Ow." I touch the lump on the back of my head.

"How bad is it?" Z frowns and comes closer.

Gray carefully moves my hair and shows him the goose egg.

Z hisses out a pained breath. "Damn. Are you all right?"

Tonight's brought back some really awful memories. And Z's question scrapes the scab all the way off. I stare him straight in the eyes. "I've taken much worse hits."

His jaw twitches.

Gray swings his gaze between Z and me. "What are you talking about? From who? When? What's she talking about?"

"Shadow?" Z asks me.

"Who else?"

"Jesus Christ," Rock mutters.

Z blows out a breath. "Motherfucker."

"You said he wasn't *nice* to her," Grayson grits out each word like a slow accusation.

I curl my arms around my middle and lean over, trying to force away those memories. *Not nice* is woefully inadequate. But Z probably never guessed at the details. No one knew. Not Amanda. Not anyone.

After all the club has done for Gray since he was released, I don't want *my* past to be the reason they're at odds.

"He didn't know, Grayson," I whisper.

"The clubs weren't as close when Sway was president," Wrath explains.

"Gray, I swear, the first time I saw him put hands on her, I shut it down," Z says. "That's never what our club was supposed to be about."

"After he got even with me, I heard he paid you back with a knife in the leg later," I say, forcing a smile.

Z brushes it off. "Doesn't matter. Wait, he came after you again? After that night?"

Unable to make my mouth work, I nod quickly.

"I'm so sorry, Serena." Z stops and meets my eyes. "I should've understood how pissed he was. Showing him up in front of the whole club that night was a bad move."

"You saved me from a painful night," I mumble. *Or postponed it.*

Gray wraps his arms around me, as if his body has the power to protect me from the whole world.

"When you didn't show up to the clubhouse again, everyone assumed you were done with us," Z says. "We got updates through your friend here and there. No one wanted to bother you if you'd moved on. If I'd known—"

"I *was* done," I whisper.

Gray squeezes my hand.

"How'd he find you?" Wrath asks.

"We had *unfinished* business." I slick my tongue over my dry lips but it doesn't help.

"What?" Rock asks, sitting forward.

"Nothing to do with the club."

Everyone's quiet. Waiting.

They're going to force me to spill every sordid detail, aren't they?

I catch Grayson's eyes, silently pleading with him to let this go.

"What happened?" he asks quietly.

Rage bubbles up my throat and my jaw tightens.

*Fine.* Except for my therapist, I wasn't able to tell anyone when it happened.

Maybe it'll alleviate some of my heartache to blast them with the truth about what a monster their "brother" truly was.

"He wanted to make sure I'd had the abortion he'd been trying to talk me into," I spit out, stabbing a furious glare at each one of them, even Grayson. "And when I told him *no*, he decided to solve the problem with his *fists*."

All the pain and terror of that afternoon pulses to life, threatening to swallow me whole. "He didn't want his *wife* to find out."

And hadn't discovering he was married been the extra-rotten cherry on top of an already shitty sundae?

"I'm *still* paying off the fucking hospital bills." I want them to understand *what* happened without me having to say the actual words.

"Serena, I'm so sorry…" Rock says.

Wrath's pained eyes meet mine. "We never would have...none of us knew he was *that* bad."

Z's face is a mask of horror, almost worse than Gray's. He kneels in front of me, taking my uninjured hand in both of his. "He will *never* hurt you again, Serena. I can promise you that."

The realization of what Z's actually telling me sinks in.

Maybe he didn't say the exact words—*I killed Shadow*. But the certainty in Z's tone is unmistakable.

Out of guilt or respect for Grayson, Z trusts me with information that could harm the whole club and I don't take that responsibility lightly. "Thank you."

"Did Sway know?" Rock's eyes glitter with deadly interest.

"About the last beating?"

"Any of it."

"I...I don't think so. Shadow always tried to isolate me at the club. And Tawny was...well, I tried to steer clear of Sway as much as possible." A rough sob tears out of my throat. I was *done* with this.

I tucked all that pain and anger away in a box and buried it in my heart with all my other misery to deal with when I felt stronger. A day I assumed I could avoid forever, as I gained distance and changed my life.

Humiliation burns my anger to dust. I can't believe I had to share this story with the man I love in front of three of his club brothers.

I'm not even sad about the loss anymore, so why won't the tears stop flowing?

I quickly brush the back of my hand over my damp cheeks.

Even though I wished for his death many, many times, knowing that Shadow's gone doesn't provide the peace I thought it would.

# CHAPTER FORTY
## Grinder

I stroke my knuckles over Serena's cheek until she collects herself and finally peers up at me. "Will you wait in the living room for me, buttercup?"

"Yup." She jumps up like her ass is on fire, refusing to look at anyone.

The door closes with a click behind her.

Z pulls out his phone and taps out an angry text. His rage is an almost tangible storm cloud.

It's no match for mine.

The fury I've been holding back erupts all over the three brothers I trusted to fix the club when I went inside fifteen long years ago.

"What the *fuck*?" I swing my accusatory glare around the room. Wrath—furious. Rock—seething. Z—about to go nuclear.

"Jesus Christ," Rock mutters. "What the fuck was Sway *doing* down there?"

"We know what he was doing," Wrath growls. "Nothing."

"Where is this Shadow fucker, Z?" I step dangerously close, bumping his chest. "And don't be cute, this time. Spell it out for me."

"Easy, Grinder," Wrath says.

"Don't fucking tell me to go *easy*." I point to the door. "You heard what she said, right? What he did to her. How the fuck did someone like that ever wear our colors?"

"I heard," Wrath says quietly.

"You patched-in a brother who would do that to a friend of the club and no one had a fucking clue?" I rage. "Are you fucking serious?"

"He's six feet under, Grinder," Z says. "I slit his throat myself."

I squeeze my eyes shut and blow out a long slow breath. "Did he suffer?"

"Whole club went at him before I finally ended it."

"Someone else *had* to know," I insist.

Z flicks a look at Rock. "We didn't make the decision to take him out lightly, Grinder. It was a club vote."

"He fucking *stabbed* you. What else did you need?"

"He attacked Lilly too. That's *why* he stabbed me. He was desperate. It was a precarious time." Z glances at Rock and Wrath who both nod. "Priest installed me there without their approval. Shadow was VP. It was…awkward. Shadow betrayed the club in a lot of ways. But almost everyone supported me when I stopped him from going after Serena."

"What do you mean *almost* everyone? Who didn't?"

"Jesus Christ, Grinder. You know how some of these guys are."

"Who?"

"Smoke—he's an older brother. He said he was taking off for Florida after the Shadow incident." Z glances at Rock again. "Rooster ran into him out in Washington, though."

Smoke's a common road name. Could be one of a dozen bikers from back in the day.

"Who else had a problem?"

"Tiny, he's a younger brother. He moved down to Mississippi last I heard."

I grunt, not convinced all the bad apples have been eliminated. But I'm finally starting to get a clearer picture of *why* the New York club split into two different charters after Rock took over here.

"I honestly don't think anyone knew it was *that* bad between them," Z says. "Sway's an asshole, and we had different opinions about a lot of things. But I don't think even *he* would've been okay with *that*."

Someone knocks on the door and it opens.

"You rang?" The grin on Rooster's face freezes, then fades as he scans our faces. "What's going on?"

"Jiggy out there?" Z asks.

"Yeah." Rooster sticks his head out the door. "Hey, chucklefuck, you're wanted in here too."

"I'll chucklefuck you, motherclucker," Jiggy responds. Like Rooster, he drops the carefree attitude when he sees us. "Fuck, what's going on?"

"Close the door." Rock motions them inside.

Rooster seems to perform a mental head count. "Want me to grab Steer and Murphy?"

"They're not back yet," Wrath says.

"What did Myra tell you about Shadow?" Z asks Jigsaw.

He blinks and runs his gaze over us again. "Why you asking about Myra *now*?"

"Just answer the question," I snap.

Jigsaw's eyes widen and his mouth puckers into a smirk. "*Alllrighty* then." He turns toward Z again. "He was a piece of shit. Cheated on her. Not just with club girls, apparently."

"What else?" Z asks.

Jigsaw turns his head toward Rooster and the two of them have some sort of silent exchange that ends with a subtle shrug from Rooster.

"He was violent," Jigsaw said. "She showed me pictures." He swallows hard and glances down at his hands. "It was bad. Real bad. But she said the cops wouldn't help her."

"They didn't want to go after our VP?" Z asks. He glances at Rock. "Think they would've run with that information. Used it for leverage of some sort."

Rock shrugs. "Go on."

"That's all I know." Jigsaw holds up his hands.

"Why you asking?" Rooster directs the question at me, then glances at Z. "Shadow's...long gone."

"Grinder knows," Z says. "We told him."

Rooster nods. Can't get a read on his thoughts on the matter.

"Serena never went to the cops," Wrath says in a low voice.

"Serena? Why are you...oh fuck," Jigsaw mutters.

Ignoring him, Wrath focuses on me. "Did she? Shadow put her in the *hospital*. Someone must've asked her questions. She never pointed *anyone* in the club's direction."

I can't tell if he's stating thoughts as they pop in his head or if he's asking me for answers.

"What the fuck?" Jiggy explodes. His wide eyes turn on Rooster. "Why wouldn't she have said something to *us*?"

Rooster's gaze drops to Jigsaw's cut and he lifts an eyebrow.

"No. Z made it clear that night. We backed him up." Jigsaw shakes his head. "I would've helped her. *Fuck*."

"You two have a thing?" I ask calmly.

"What?" Jigsaw scowls at me. "Bro, she's too young for me."

That they're actually around the same age seems to occur to him and he shakes his head. "Sorry. I just like my ladies...aged a tad longer. Like fine scotch. Or wine."

"Christ," Rooster mutters, rolling his eyes toward the ceiling.

"As entertaining as we all find your circus act," Rock says, "can we focus?" He turns toward Wrath. "Where were you going with that?"

Wrath drills each of us with an intense stare before opening his mouth. "It sounds like she's shown the club more loyalty than we deserve. And we owe her a debt."

# CHAPTER FORTY-ONE

## Serena

Grayson emerges from the war room and jerks his head toward the stairs.

I jump off the couch and rush over. "Is everything okay?"

"Yeah, Rock's calling everyone to the table. But I got a few minutes. Wanna talk to you."

Fear swirls in my belly but I follow him up the stairs. "Gray? You're not *all* going to discuss what I shared with the *entire* club, are you?"

Enough people look down on me here. I don't need the whole club to know I couldn't protect my own baby.

He opens the door to his room and ushers me inside before answering.

"No. The details won't go any further than the four of us."

I'm not sure I quite believe him. The club *always* comes first to the brothers. But the club's secrets also run deep. "Okay."

He touches my shoulder lightly. "Come here."

Stiff and uncertain, I allow him to pull me into his arms. He leads me to the overstuffed chair by the window, sits, and draws me into his lap, wrapping his arms around me securely.

After a few seconds, I relax against him, resting my cheek against his chest. He kisses the top of my head and pulls my legs up over his.

The steady, reassuring thump of his heart slowly chases the ugly shadows away. "I'm so sorry, Serena."

"For?"

"That you got hurt because of me tonight. That someone in my club hurt you before. And that I put you in a position to share all of that in front of my brothers without any warning."

Pain encircles my throat, forcing my words down. My cheek slides over his soft shirt as I nod to acknowledge his apologies.

"I need to ask you something, okay?"

*Haven't I bled enough of my soul tonight?*

Cautious, I pick up my head and stare at him. "What?"

The firm set of his mouth and the crinkle between his eyes warns that I won't like what's coming.

"Did you ever go to the cops?" He swallows hard but doesn't take his eyes off me. "When you were in the hospital, did you tell anyone who…"

"No!" I push away from him but he bands his arms around me tighter. "I would *never* do that."

"Okay, okay. I'm not asking for club reasons. Well, not the reason you're thinking."

"Then why?"

"His wife. He…hurt her too. But she said the cops wouldn't help or do anything."

"Big surprise." I roll my eyes toward the ceiling.

"That why you didn't go? You thought the cops were on the club's payroll and wouldn't help?"

I blink. "Actually, no. *That* never occurred to me. I saw the cops hassle the club over stupid stuff a bunch of times down there. They even dragged me in for questioning once. Just to be dicks."

He raises an eyebrow, silently waiting for me to come up with an explanation.

Fine, I'll give it to him.

"Running to the cops never did me any good in my life." I can't hide the bitterness in my tone. "Going to the cops about my stepfather got me ridiculed and scolded for 'tempting' him. Because, you know, it's the fourteen-year-old girl's fault a grown man can't keep his hands to himself."

His jaw tightens but he doesn't say anything.

"What would I have done? Gotten a restraining order? So they could give him my address and enrage him even more? Give him time to beat me to death, while waiting on hold with 911? No thanks. Cops never helped my mother either. Learned that lesson early. They're the *last* place I would've sought help."

"Everyone finds their way to the club for a reason," he murmurs.

I rub my palms over my leggings and wiggle my aching jaw. "Yeah, well. I was *done*. I wanted to get the hell away from him. He was behaving so erratically by that point, I suspected he had something to do with Sway's shooting—"

"And you didn't tell Z?"

*Is he nuts?* "Hell no. Accuse the VP of shooting the old president? Z was nice to me, but I'm not crazy."

He sighs. "Yeah. I get it. What was your plan?"

"Finish school. Focus on getting healthy." I tap the side of my head and then over my heart. "In mind *and* spirit. I stayed with Emily for a while. She'd been through her own situation. And we have similar goals. She was someone *way* outside of club life. I didn't even tell Amanda where I was. God love her, but she'll sing like a canary if a man pays her enough attention."

I swipe a stray tear off my cheek. "Eventually, I heard about the fight Shadow and Z got into. And that Shadow had 'gone nomad.' *Nomad my ass.* I figured Z had taken him out and I thanked the Lord." I glare at him. "And, no, I'd never express my suspicion to anyone but *you*."

He squeezes me tight. "I know that, buttercup."

"That's it."

He rests his hand over my stomach, rubbing gently. The motion soothes and hurts at the same time. Losing my baby on top of all the other horrible things that happened still haunts me.

"Don't." I rest my hand over his, stopping him.

"Are you okay?" he asks.

I could take that question a thousand different ways. Mentally okay? I thought I was, until tonight.

Physically? Again, I *was* until tonight.

Can I still have children? According to my doctor, yes.

"No. I'm not okay." I release a long breath, freeing some of my anger. "But I will be."

# CHAPTER FORTY-TWO

## Grinder

Armed with more information, I return to the war room. The door's open. Wrath, Z, and Rock are still at the table. Rooster and Jigsaw are lingering in the living room but follow me inside.

"She all right?" Z asks.

"We'll see. When's everyone getting here?"

"On their way," Rooster says.

I shift my chair closer to Wrath. "Got an answer to your question."

He lifts one blond eyebrow.

"She doesn't trust cops. They did her dirty in the past."

He nods slowly. "Not a surprise."

I catch Z's eye. "You said Shadow betrayed the club in a lot of ways. He responsible for shooting Sway?"

Z doesn't look away or get cute with me. "Yeah, he admitted it at the end. He was trying to work out some bullshit deal with Vipers MC that Sway wouldn't agree to."

"Hope you're doing a better job vetting brothers than Sway did," I mutter.

"Easy, Grinder." Rock's quick to defend Z. "Z walked into a pile of shit."

"Z worked hard to fix things," Rooster adds. "Fast. He worked *with* us too. Didn't come in and steamroll over everyone."

"He could've told us to fall in line or else," Jigsaw says. "He had Priest to back him up. But he still worked to earn our respect."

"You're making me blush, guys." Z grins and waves his hands in front of his face.

Rooster lifts his wide shoulders and stares at the ceiling. "He's insufferable, but we love him anyway."

"I've been saying that for years." Wrath nods at Rock. "It's nice to be validated."

The front door slams open and feet stomp over the hardwood floors. Teller appears in the doorway a few seconds later, wet hair plastered to his forehead and a scowl embedded in his face.

Rock watches Teller make his way to the opposite side of the table. "What do you have for me?"

"Mud all over my truck."

"You chose the life." Rock smirks. "You don't like running down leads in bad weather, maybe you should apply to law school or something."

"Hilarious." Teller throws himself into a chair and shakes his head, sending raindrops splattering everywhere. He lifts his chin and focuses on me. "How's Serena doing?"

"All right for now."

"Brave girl." Teller shakes his head again, pushing his hair off his forehead. "Held up under questioning. Never uttered your name." He tosses a wet, wrinkled piece of paper on the table. "Police report makes it sound like a simple mugging attempt."

Rock plucks the paper off the table, smooths it out, and scans the contents.

"I emailed you a copy," Teller says to him.

Over the next hour, all the brothers make their way to the table. Upstate and Downstate.

It's a full house and a bunch of the younger guys cluster together on a leather sectional at the back of the room.

Rock gives everyone a moment to catch up before banging his gavel on the table.

"Tonight's not a social call. We have serious business to discuss. One of our women was attacked earlier."

Murmurs of *what the fuck* and other questions circulate around the table.

"Who?" Dex asks.

I shoot a sharp look at Steer, daring him to open his mouth. "*My* woman. Serena. Someone tried to get to me through her."

More loud murmuring. Guess word hasn't spread that she's with me now.

"Is she okay?" Steer asks.

"No," I growl. "He roughed her up and scared the shit out of her."

"This about you not heeling to Big Chief's order?" Dex asks.

"Yup. Sounds like it."

From the back of the room, Ravage raises his hand. "Not to be rude but—"

"Choose your words wisely," Wrath warns.

Ravage actually stands, so we can all see him better. "It, uh, from the reactions of some of my fellow brothers, it seems not everyone here at this table even knew Serena *was* your ol' lady, Grinder. So, how did an outsider know to get to you through *her*?"

He returns to his seat.

A beat of stunned silence settles over the room.

Teller finally lets out a long, low whistle. "Holy shit. That has to be the smartest observation that's *ever* come out of your mouth."

Ravage stands again.

Rock holds up one hand. "Don't ruin it, Rav."

Rav sits without opening his mouth.

"We were discussing that earlier," Wrath says. "It's a narrow circle of people who could've pointed this guy in her direction." He drills a hard stare into Murphy. "Real narrow."

"Our contestants are," Z announces, standing and counting off on his fingers, "The few of us in the club who did know about Grinder and Serena."

Everyone boos that option.

"Just being upfront," Z continues. "Grinder's parole officer, Remy Holt, and a friend of Serena's who's unaffiliated."

"No way it was Remy," Murphy argues.

"Shit." Dex scrubs his hand over his face. "I've known Remy a while. I can't see him betraying us like that."

"He's not a brother," Wrath points out. "Besides, if someone made casual inquiries he might not have realized he was giving anything up."

"He's not *that* fucking stupid," Murphy snaps.

"I don't believe it was Remy," I say.

Wrath turns and scowls at me. "Why?"

"The guy who went after Serena didn't know she was younger." I hate like fuck admitting this in front of everyone. "When Remy drove me over to her apartment, he thought she was my daughter at first."

Wrath chokes and tries not to laugh.

"Keep your mouth shut," I warn him. "The guy who went after her expected her to be my age."

"That's real fuckin' thin, Grinder," Z says.

I shrug. "I can't see Remy *not* mentioning it. Grillo, on the other hand, has met her a couple different times. He could've followed her home from my place. It'd be easy for him to get her address from—fuck!"

"What?" Rock asks.

"He helped her with her bags one time when she came to visit me. She said she was embarrassed because she had a bunch of boxes of makeup and stuff that had been sent to her and he made some wisecrack. That's how the guy who attacked her could've known about her channel. They told him to look her up so he'd be able to recognize her to deliver the threat. Grillo could've gotten her address from her license plate. He passes that on to Big Chief inside, then…"

"Okay, that actually does sound more reasonable than Remy," Wrath says.

"Thank you," Murphy mutters.

"Uh, makeup?" Bricks waves his hand in the air. "You lost us, G.

"It's not important." Rooster sits forward, leaning over the table to look at me. "It sounds like your parole officer is dirty."

"He's dirty all right," Wrath grumbles.

"And apparently double-dipping," Z adds.

Ignoring them, Rooster continues. "Who's the guy who *actually* attacked her? We need him—"

"LOKI fucking justice!" Ravage hollers.

"Easy, cowboy," Dex says.

"We find him, he'll give up his source." Rooster's gaze slides to Jigsaw. "Jiggy can make him talk."

Behind me, there's an urgent tapping at the closed door. Wrath pushes away from the table and answers.

The familiar lilt of Serena's soft voice hits me and I jump out of my chair, pushing Wrath out of my way. I wrap my arm around her. "What's wrong?"

She blinks, her gaze shifting from Wrath to me. "I, uh, I remembered something else—"

"Let her in and shut the door," Rock orders.

Serena's body shakes against me. Everyone's attention focuses solely on her, which seems to increase her agitation. I wrap my other arm around her and she curls one hand around my wrist, hanging on tight.

"What is it, hon?" Z asks.

After a few shaky breaths, she pulls her shoulders back and lifts her chin. I release her but stay close.

"His ink." She tosses her hair over her shoulder, returning to the confident woman I know in front of my eyes.

"Ah, fuck," Z mutters. "We got sidetracked before and didn't—"

"Sidetracked by what?" Steer asks.

"None of your business." I squeeze Serena's shoulder. "Go on."

She touches the corner of her eye. "He had a red X tattooed here. I couldn't get a good look at everything on his arms but he had this on his hand." She flutters a piece of paper in front of her. "Trinity helped me come up with a rough sketch. It's not exact but it's close." She rubs her forehead. "From what I can remember."

I glance at it quickly. "Looks similar to the one on the guy who visited me. I figured Big Chief hired someone outside his regular circle."

"Ooof, good way to buy a ticket on the Reaper's roller coaster," Jigsaw mutters.

"Let me see it." Rooster stands and reaches over the table for the paper. "Rock," Rooster's gaze sweeps from one end of the table to the other, "Z, we've seen this before." He holds the square of paper up against his throat. "At Chaser's anniversary party?"

"Motherfucker." Wrath sits forward and reaches for the sketch.

"You saying this guy's affiliated with the Devil Demons MC?" I ask. "Since when do they patch-in baby gangsters?"

"No, not the MC," Wrath says. "A whole different beast."

# CHAPTER FORTY-THREE

## Grinder

"It's one of Quill's guys. I guarantee it," Rooster says after Serena leaves.

All the ways the world changed while I was inside just keep on slapping me in the face. "Chaser's got half brothers? From some cartel guy? What'd Stump have to say about that?"

"Don't know," Rock says. "Chaser didn't seem thrilled about the situation himself. Didn't exactly share details of the family reunification, though. He made the introduction and left it at that."

*The fuck?* "Demons have been an important alliance for years. We need to be careful how we rock that boat," I say.

"Fuck. That," Wrath growls. "Anyone who fucks with you, fucks with the whole club."

"Chaser understands how this works," Z adds.

"Your brothers have your back on this, Grinder. It's not even a question," Rock assures me.

After so many years of not being able to trust anyone inside, it feels good to have the support of my brothers.

"We all heard him promise this thing with Quill wasn't going to impact us," Rooster adds. "It's been what, a minute, and one of these fucks went after a brother *and* one of our women?"

"No fucking way," Jigsaw growls, pounding his fist against the table. "We need to hit back hard. Send a message. This won't be tolerated."

Rock drills me with his steady gaze. "I'll make the call to Chaser and set up the meet."

"I need to be there."

"You will," he says. "But you're not going alone."

"Hell fucking no," Wrath adds. "We'll be there."

"Easy," Teller says. "The whole club can't roll up like we're kicking off a war."

"We need to go in hard," Jigsaw argues.

Rock stares down at the table while a few of the guys debate both methods.

"Teller's right." Z holds up his hand to Jigsaw. "I hear what you're saying, brother. If it were any other club, I'd agree."

"Yeah," Rock says slowly. "My gut says we need to play this carefully. Trust me, Jiggy, I'd rather go in guns blazing. But we don't know exactly what we're dealing with."

Jigsaw sits back in his seat with a thump and runs his hand over his chin. "I get it. I don't fuckin' like it, though."

"None of us do," Z says.

Rock stares at each brother for a few seconds before seeming to come to a decision. "I want Z, Wrath, Rooster, and Dex with Grinder and me when we sit down with Chaser."

"Rock," Murphy protests. "Come on."

Rock glares at him and continues speaking. "I want Teller, Jigsaw, *Murphy*, and Steer waiting nearby. Just in case." He glances at Z. "That all right?"

"Fuck yeah." He raises an eyebrow at Jigsaw, then Steer.

"Rooster's got the closest relationship with Chaser right now," Rock explains. "That's why I want him there."

"Yeah," Rooster says slowly, "I don't know if Chaser's gonna see it the same way."

"He needs a reminder that he's got more at stake here than just *territory*," Rock says. "Give him a reason to rein in these brothers of his."

"Jesus," Rooster mutters, shaking his head.

"Unfortunately," Rock crosses his fingers in front of his face, "the two worlds are inextricably linked now, Rooster. For better or worse."

"Yeah, I get it."

"Good."

If I wasn't so fucking pissed off and worried about Serena, I'd be damn proud of how Rock's running things. And Z. The two of them together make a fine team. Taking time to assess everyone's strengths and weaknesses, reassure, educate, but most of all not take any shit. Lot of strong personalities to manage.

"Hold up." Z raises his hands in the air. "I want everyone not riding with us to stay here and look after the girls." He glances at Rock. "Lilly's gonna stay at your place."

"There's room at our house for anyone who doesn't want to bunk upstairs," Wrath offers.

"This isn't party time," Z reminds everyone. "It's *lock it down* time."

"What about Downstate?" Hustler asks. "We need to warn Sway and the girls down there."

"Fuck." Z scans the table. "Hustler, I want you, Suds, and Butcher at our place. Tell the girls they either stay at the compound or they stay out. No coming and going." He smirks. "That goes for Tawny too. She don't like it, she can take it up with me."

"You got it, Prez." Hustler stands and slaps Z's back.

"All right." Rock stands and raises his voice above the rising chatter until the guys settle down. "Everyone has their assignments. Those coming with us, stay at the table, everyone else is free to go."

After the room thins out, Rock takes his seat again. Brothers switch chairs so we're all clustered toward Rock's end of the table.

"This needs to look like a casual chat to inform Chaser he's got a problem, and collect information," Rock says. "Everyone's easy. Friendly. We're not there to throw accusations. No open hostility, unless provoked."

"Then civility's out the window," Z says.

"Fuck yeah." Jigsaw punches his fist in the air.

"Simmer down," Rock snarls, then says to Teller, "You're about to get your wish, knucklehead."

"Oh, yeah?" Teller smirks. "What's that, Prez?"

Rock's gray eyes flick my way. "I think I'm going to suggest we meet Chaser at Remy's place."

"Good choice," Murphy says. "But why now?"

"It's a good halfway point. Semi-neutral territory-wise."

"Not for long." Murphy smirks.

After Rock dismisses everyone else, I close the war room door and return to my seat.

Rock glances at me with a raised eyebrow. "What's on your mind?"

"It's not my business, but what the fuck's going on with you and Teller?" I ask.

His expression flattens and he slowly sits back. Almost trying too hard to seem casual and disinterested in the question. "Why are you asking?"

"He seems to get away with a lot of mouthing off to you."

"Mouthing off is *literally* how he got his road name," Rock says in a bored tone.

"Yeah, I heard." I contemplate my next words carefully, since I'm making a big reach and overstepping. "You're kind of rough on Murphy, though. And he's not the one giving you lip."

Rock's jaw clenches tight.

*Looks like that arrow of truth landed in a soft spot.*

"He's your VP," I continue. "He's gotta be free to disagree with you."

"He does. Plenty."

Time to wrap this up. I said what I wanted to say. Gave Rock something to chew on.

"I respect you, Rock. You've done great things with the club, obviously—"

"Do you remember that girl Tina?" he asks out of nowhere.

"You're gonna need to be more specific."

"The girl who used to 'babysit' me."

A memory surfaces and I groan in disgust. "Jesus. How could I forget that? You thought you were Don fucking Juan when you nailed her. What were you? Eleven? Twelve? She musta been sixteen or seventeen at the time? Good Christ, that was fucked up."

"Somewhere around there," he answers tightly.

"You were an insufferable little bastard after that. Hittin' on every woman who crossed your path." I sit back, laughing my fuckin' ass off.

Rock doesn't join in on the laughter.

The expression on his face is downright scary. Or it would be to someone else. Me, I just continue poking at him.

"Shit, you remember hittin' on Chaser's wife? It's a miracle Chaser didn't cap your ass then and there."

"Yes," he answers slowly. "Mallory shared that charming little story with Hope. It was a real trip."

"I bet." I grin even wider. "Must've been quite a pill for Chaser to swallow with you runnin' your own MC first."

"I doubt he wasted a lot of energy on it." He glances out the window. "I dealt with Stump more than Chaser in the beginning, anyway."

"You must've had to work your ass off to repair all the damage Ruger did to the relationship between our two clubs."

"We...found common ground, eventually."

"I knew you would."

"Stump still ran things long after Chaser came home from Hollywood."

No surprise there. "Ornery old bugger."

"He could be," Rock agrees.

"Eh, I shouldn't talk shit about Stump." I wave my hand in the air. "He did right by me when I was out at the Supermax. I know that had a lot to do with the work you were doing back here, Rock."

He shrugs it off. I may tease him about being cocky, but he's always had a hard time accepting a compliment.

"Why's Rooster so hesitant to be at this meet?" I jerk my thumb toward Rooster's empty chair.

"You think he was?"

Rock's not that blind. "He seemed to feel a certain way."

"Chaser, apparently, still works in the music industry—"

"No shit?"

"Yeah. And Shelby's gotten to be good friends with Chaser's daughter. She helped Shelby write a bunch of songs. So, there's a business relationship that exists now."

"Rooster won't want anything interfering with his girl's career."

"Right." He taps his fingers against the table. "But Chaser's got business outside the club I'm sure he doesn't want messed with either."

"Risky." Christ, Rock turned into one calculating son of a bitch.

"I don't need Rooster to say a word. His presence there will be enough."

While all that stuff's entertaining to a certain degree, and good to know for our meeting, I can't help returning to Rock's earlier question. "What made you ask about your old babysitter? You planning to hire her to watch Grace, because I gotta say, her references are shit."

"Fuck no." He shifts in his seat. "You ever run into her later?"

"Run into her *how*?"

"See her around." Irritation twists through his words. "Talk to her."

"Not that I remember. Thought her family moved. Why?"

"You remember Teller coming to you about his mom? She had a boyfriend with an unhealthy interest in Heidi when she was real little?"

"Fuck yeah, poor kid. He asked Lucky and me to have a chat with his mom and the boyfriend. He was hoping we'd scare that fuckhead away." I loop my finger around my ear a few times. "Mom wasn't all there. Talking to her made my skin crawl."

"Nothing about her rang a bell for you?"

My mind blanks, unsure of what he's getting at. "I didn't talk to her that long. We worked the pervert boyfriend over. Told him if he went near Heidi again, we'd feed him his dick and balls."

Something's not right here. "Where are you going with this, Rock?"

"She didn't look familiar to you at all?"

The questions he's asking skid to a collision in my head. I try reaching that far back in my memory but I've come into contact with a lot of faces since then and can't remember more than a few impressions. "Are you trying to say your old babysitter was Teller's *mother*?"

He nods slowly. "That's what I'm saying."

"They didn't even have the same name. Your girl's name was Tina. His mom had some ugly name, I can't remember now. Irma, Bertha, something like that."

"Right before Grace was born, we had some issues." He drills me with a don't-you-dare-fucking-laugh stare. "Club got hit with a paternity lawsuit."

"The *whole* club?" I bite back every joke trying to worm past my lips. "What's that got to do with Tina and all this other ancient history?"

He rests his arms on the table and hunches closer to me. "You can't share this with anyone." He rolls his eyes toward Teller's empty chair. "Although at this point, more people seem to know than don't."

"Know what?"

"The lab that ran the DNA tests for the lawsuit had some screw up. Teller and I had to go in twice."

I'm so out of touch with things, I have no fucking idea where this is going. "So?"

"Our DNA *matched*. He's *my* son."

"Fuck," I breathe out. "How's that even possible?"

"How do you *think*?"

"Tina, really?" I try again to recall some useful memory from around that time. "Fuck. Weird how you ended up meeting when he was around the same age."

"I've had the same thought. Several times."

"How'd the rest of the club take it?"

"We haven't made it public."

"Seriously? Why not? How the fuck's he keeping a secret like *that* from Murphy of all people?"

He shrugs but guilt's crawling all over his face. "I would've told everyone right away. He wanted to wait until after Heidi's wedding—"

"Wait, *Heidi* doesn't know yet either?" I let out a long, sharp whistle. "That's downright reckless and cruel to hide that truth from her."

"A lot of shit went down before their wedding—"

"They're married now." I point to the door. "Saw the wedding photo on the wall upstairs."

He nods. "Yeah. I know. He wants to retake the test before telling them. I'm trying respect his wishes since it's all so fucking awkward but…"

"You feel guilty."

"Of course I do."

All humor about this situation vanishes. It's too tragic to make fun. Besides, I'm wondering if there's another answer.

I sit back. Is opening this door to the past worth causing him more grief? "I'm no scientist but are you sure the test said you were his *father*. Not his *brother*?"

His eyes widen and he slumps against his chair. I could've kicked him in the stomach and he'd look less stunned.

"Why would you say that?" His eyes narrow as the shock wears off. "You know something I should know?"

"Tina had been coming around your house for *years* before she tickled your barely hairy balls. Your father dipped his quill in every ink pot he—"

"Are you fucking serious? She was a teenager."

"You think that would've stopped him?" I wave my hand in the air. "You *weren't* even a teenager and she still got down to business with *you*."

"Come the fuck on, Grinder," he snarls. "That's different."

"Is it?"

"I can't remember the exact number on the report but it was supposed to be nearly one hundred percent accurate."

"Like I said, I'm not a scientist. But I helped enough felons with their appeals to know those forensic labs get shit wrong sometimes. Knew one guy who spent over a decade inside before he was finally exonerated."

He frowns. "Paternity testing should be straightforward." His eyes turn distant as if he's considering the possibilities. "I honestly don't know if being brothers makes the situation better or worse."

"You're brothers no matter what, Rock." I reach over and thump his arm. "Have been for a long time."

# CHAPTER FORTY-FOUR

## Serena

*Mistakes are the pebbles of your path to success.*

Two days later, the relentless pounding in my head has subsided to a dull roar.

And I'm still staying at the clubhouse.

No one's given me information about the man who attacked me. Gray says they're working on it and I trust him. He leaves around nine every night and returns late morning, so he doesn't risk trouble with his parole officer.

I'm not thrilled about sleeping at the clubhouse alone. But there's a sense of security in it too.

I've been too nervous to spend time outside of Gray's room when he's not here. But this morning, I get dressed and head downstairs early. Maybe I can help Swan with breakfast and at least feel useful.

But no one's in the kitchen when I make it down there. The clubhouse is quiet.

I perch at the kitchen table with a bowl of cereal, staring out at the woods. I didn't even bother bringing my phone downstairs to distract myself. With my face all bruised up, I'm too depressed to bother checking Instagram or any of my social media. Posting a how-to-cover-your-bruises tutorial feels all kinds of wrong.

After washing my dishes, I grab a cup of coffee. Might as well head upstairs and wait for Grayson. Part of me is eager to go to my apartment and make sure all my stuff's okay. Maybe I'll ask if we can do that later.

The swirling music of a Disney movie echoes down the hall as I return to the living room. At the end of the hallway, I stop and stare.

Heidi has a huge blanket spread out on the floor with a bunch of pillows. Her daughter's in her lap and Z's son is curled up next to them.

Should I go back to the kitchen? I'll have to walk right past the television if I try to escape up the stairs.

Heidi glances up and nods at me. "Hey. How are you feeling?"

"Uh, all right. Better." As I approach, my gaze lands on Sparky stretched out on one of the couches. "Hey, Sparky."

"Morning." He flashes a bleary smile and holds out a jumbo bag of cheese puffs toward me.

I hold up my coffee. "I've got my morning fuel. But thanks."

Heidi wrinkles her nose. "Trinity and Lilly are on their way over with real snacks."

"It's gonna be all fruit and healthy crap," Sparky warns.

A bit of nervous laughter bubbles out of me. "That's okay." I shift from foot to foot, not sure if it'll be rude to scurry upstairs or worse if I hang out when I'm not invited.

"Join us. I mean, if you want to," Heidi says. "We're doing *The Lion King*."

Sparky giggles. "You said *doing* the lion king."

Heidi rolls her eyes and ignores him. "Personally, I voted for *Frozen*." She points two fingers at the kids. "But I was outnumbered."

"I suggested *Clerks*." Sparky waves his hand in the air. "But was told it wasn't 'appropriate' for the little ones."

"Yeah, probably not." I laugh and tuck myself into a spot on the empty couch next to Sparky's.

The front door opens, bringing in a rush of cold, spring air. Trinity and Lilly stomp their boots out on the porch, then set them inside.

"Tin-it-ee!" Alexa yells, running over to them. "Illy!"

Chance rolls on his side and watches but doesn't join in. Lilly bends down to talk to him for a second quietly.

"Little dude's outnumbered," Sparky says. He points at Heidi. "Better hope that one's a boy."

Heidi scoffs and rubs her stomach. "Don't put pressure on my fetus."

"Eww," Sparky moans.

Trinity pulls a gagging face and throws herself on the couch next to me. "How are you feeling, Serena?"

"Better."

"Good." She reaches over and pats my leg.

Alexa toddles over to us and stops to tug at the laces of my boots.

"She's a shoe hound, watch out," Heidi laughs.

I glance down at the sparkling purple boots on Alexa's feet. "Oh my God, is she wearing her own little Dr. Martens?"

"Yes." Heidi grins. "Courtesy of Auntie Hope."

"Aun-tee," Alexa confirms with a big grin.

"That's so sweet." I swallow over the lump in my throat.

Swan eventually joins us, laying out a spread of snack foods on the coffee table—popcorn, pretzels, and fruit. Alexa settles next to me with a plate of apple slices and even offers to share them with me. Heidi lands next to her. Lilly stretches out on the blanket on the floor with Chance.

"Hi, Serena." Swan nudges Sparky into a sitting position and sits on the couch. "You want anything?" She nods to the coffee table.

"I'm good."

Lilly starts the movie. I watched it a bunch of times as a kid, but it's been a while. Somewhere in the middle, I end up dozing off.

"Wake up!" Alexa shouts.

"Shh. Let Serena rest," Trinity says.

My eyes pop open for the last few minutes of the movie. The kids have moved on to playing with a bunch of toy cars, zooming all over the living room.

"What do you want to watch next?" Lilly asks.

"No more cartoons, please," Sparky moans. "Unless it's *Snow White*. She's hot."

Swan squeezes her eyes shut for a second. "Why am I not surprised?"

"What? *Snow White*'s a classic."

"Okay. Hear me out," Swan says with a dramatic sweep of her hands. "*Snow White* would be the ultimate club girl."

"What?" Lilly turns toward Swan. "Why?"

"Think about it. She shows up to cook and clean for a bunch of scruffy ingrates."

"Oh my God." Trinity throws herself against the couch, laughing uncontrollably. "Too true."

"I feel attacked," Sparky says, throwing a cheese puff in his mouth and munching on it loudly.

"Honestly, and I know you don't want to hear this, Trinity." Lilly lifts her chin. "Belle's worse."

Trinity gasps. "Sacrilege."

"To be fair, all the men in Belle's life are shitty," Sparky says. "Like, the whole town makes fun of her because she likes to read. Gaston's a stalkerish douche, the Beast was cursed because he acted like an asshole to some lady, and her dad's a pathetic, needy wimp." Sparky jumps up, clearly agitated. "The dude lets a literal *beast* take his daughter as a hostage so *he* can go free." He throws his arms in the air, scattering cheese puffs everywhere. "Who does that?"

"Right," Lilly agrees. "Dad had one job—protect his kid—and he *failed*."

"He didn't just fail," Sparky argues. "He left her there knowing she'd end up the sex slave of a big ol' beast man."

"Yes," Trinity mutters, "*that's* the appeal."

I snort-laugh into my coffee mug and Trinity grins at me.

"You're all ruining my childhood," Heidi says. "And now I can't let my daughter watch *any* of these movies."

"Well," Trinity says, "the Beast has good qualities all along. He might be scary on the outside, but he learns to make sacrifices and step out of his comfort zone in order to make Belle happy."

"Aww," Heidi sighs. "That's true."

"All right, I'll give you that one," Lilly says. "But her dad still sucks."

"Agreed."

"Let's do *Cinderella* next," Swan says.

"I would *totally* do Cinderella." Sparky cackles into his bag of cheese puffs. "She's hot."

"Nope. She bugs me," Heidi says. "Because how is it true love when her prince needs her to try on a damn *shoe* to recognize her? I was so stressed out that someone else in the village would have the same shoe size before he got to her. A very suspect premise," she finishes in a teasingly haughty tone.

"Mommy!" Alexa squeals.

"What?" She pulls a wide-eyed silly face at her daughter. "It's true."

"That bitch could sew, clean, cook, charm all the critters, *and* run an entire household," Swan says. "She should've waited for a guy who at least recognized her in her street clothes."

"But she's basically a slave and abused by her family," I blurt. I hadn't planned to join in the conversation, but here I am, so I guess I'll run with it. "They make her live in the freezing cold attic with the mice. The prince offers her a way to escape."

Lilly nods quickly. "Yup. He's a nice dude, he's rich, a little dumb, but easy on the eyes. Back then, for a girl like Cinderella, he's a fantastic catch. *But* this is why women need to have their own income and way to make a living. So they don't *have* to settle."

I raise my hand and throw Lilly an air high-five. "Preach."

"No more." Heidi jumps up, wiping crumbs off her pants. "Lilly, *you* get to pick the next movie."

She raises her hands high in the air. "*Anastasia*. Every time."

"Ah, good one." Swan grins and says a few words in Russian—I think—to Lilly who nods.

Our attention's drawn to loud voices outside. The front door opens. Z, Murphy, and Teller stomp inside.

"Daddy!" Chance cries, jumping up and running over to Z.

I feel like an intruder and have to look away from the scene of happy toddlers excitedly greeting their loving fathers.

"They're all so nauseatingly adorable, right?" Swan whispers to me.

I flash a tight smile.

Wrath and Grayson stomp into the clubhouse next. I resist the urge to run to Gray. Wrath scoops Trinity up and steals her seat, setting her in his lap. "What're you up to?" he asks in between kisses.

"I had to defend *Beauty and the Beast* to these heathens." She points at Lilly who sticks her tongue out at her.

"We all decided Snow White was the most fuckable of all fairy-tale princesses," Sparky announces to everyone.

Teller scowls. "Super. Thanks for having that discussion around my *niece*, jackass."

"That's not...quite how the discussion went," Heidi says, casting a quick what-the-fuck frown at Sparky.

Grayson side-eyes his brothers as he approaches me. A relieved smile curves his lips. "Hey, buttercup. I'm glad you're down here today."

I stand and wrap my arms around his neck. "I missed you," I whisper.

He glances around. "Sounds like it was a good time." He peers over my shoulder at Sparky. "If not a *weird* discussion."

"We frequently dissect and critique popular culture," Sparky informs us.

"What were you watching?" Teller asks his sister.

"*The Lion King.*"

He slaps Murphy's arm. "You remember how many times she forced us to watch *The Little Mermaid* when she was little?"

"I did *not*," Heidi protests.

"Oh, yes you did." Teller grins. "I think that's why I have a thing for redheads."

"I'm sure that'll warm Charlotte's heart," Heidi jokes while she finishes picking up the blankets and cushions.

Swan invites everyone down to the dining room for lunch and almost everyone follows.

"I'll call you if I hear something," Wrath says to Gray.

"All right." Gray takes my arm. "You hungry?"

"I've been snacking all morning." I nod toward the coffee table of empty bowls and plates. "I should help Swan clear this, though."

"I got it," Trinity says, scooting out of Wrath's lap. "You're still recuperating."

"Thanks, Trin," Gray says to her. He tugs on my hand. "Come on."

Upstairs, in our room, he unbuttons his flannel shirt, hanging it neatly in the closet. "What's wrong, buttercup? You don't look…happy."

"I guess I'm still tired." I flick my wrist toward the door, not sure how to put my feelings into words. "Everything was a little overwhelming."

"I know what you mean. You want to take a nap? Get some rest?"

"Honestly, I kind of want to run by my apartment and pick up some of my things."

"We can do that."

Relieved, I step closer and wrap my arms around him.

---

IN THE TRUCK, I STARE AT THE LITTLE GREEN BUDS STARTING TO BLOOM on some of the trees we pass. "Spring might finally be arriving," I say.

"Hope we don't get another storm that kills everything off." Gray glances over at me. "You have an okay time hanging out with the girls?"

"Yeah, I had fun with them." My lips curve. "Alexa's so cute. I think we have the same taste in shoes."

He chuckles.

"Gray?" My voice strains with anxiety. "We've never talked about…I've never asked…do you, um, like kids?"

Silence.

"Like them? Yeah, sure."

Why am I doing this now? Today? Don't we have enough to worry about?

But like an idiot, I keep plowing ahead.

"Do you want some?" I clear my throat and force myself to ask directly. "Do you see yourself having children someday?"

"Someday? I don't know, buttercup. I can't see anything too far ahead right now, you know? Not until I get out of this rough patch."

*That's a no.*

I stare out the window.

A crushing weight of loss descends on me. But I'm not going to try to talk him into anything. That rarely works out well for anyone.

"Do you?" he asks.

"No, not now. Things are too up in the air with my job," I answer without turning away from the window.

"What are you talking about?"

"The night of the…attack. When I called you, Trish was right next to me. She heard me say your name and saw your name in my phone contacts." I let out a sad laugh. "She had even asked me earlier in the day how you were doing in treatment. I lied and told her I referred you somewhere else."

"Shit, I'm sorry." His hands squeeze the steering wheel tight. "What did she say?"

"Nothing. I was dealing with the paramedics and everything. But she made it clear she wants to talk about it when I'm better."

"What can I do to fix it for you?"

"Nothing. There's nothing you can do. She can fire me. Suspend me. I don't know."

I blow out a breath. "I'll worry about it in a day or two, Gray. It's not your problem."

He pulls the truck into a spot in front of my brownstone and shuts the truck off.

"Hey."

When I don't look at him, he reaches for me, gently touching my cheek. "Serena."

I finally turn.

"I'm sorry. I'll do whatever you need me to do, okay? You know the last thing I want to do is wreck your job."

Nodding, I sigh. "It's not your fault." A slight smile tugs at the corner of my mouth. "Well, maybe a little your fault." I reach over and poke him in the chest.

"Tell me if there's something I can do to help."

"I will."

Gray cautiously scans the street, up and down, before allowing me out of the truck.

The busted front door swings open easily. Gray moves slowly up the stairs, keeping me tucked behind him.

He stops and studies my door. Everything looks fine. Untouched.

Inside, it's chilly but no signs of any break-ins.

"Good." Gray says, searching each room. "Looks like your place is clean."

"Thank goodness." I hurry into my office and pack my laptop, tripod, camera, and chargers into their special backpack.

I set that on the couch and stop in my bedroom next. "How long do you think I'll stay at the clubhouse?" I call out to Gray.

"At least until we find this guy."

"Nothing yet?" I search through my closet. I don't need anything fancy for lounging around at the clubhouse. Jeans. I pull an old pair of Uggs out of their box and stuff them in a backpack. T-shirts, leggings, a few sweatshirts. Underwear, bras, pajamas.

Gray comes up behind me and slides the backpack out of my hands. "We can always come back. Or I can take you shopping for anything you need."

"Okay." I kiss his cheek. "Let me grab a few things from the bathroom and we can go."

My skincare routine has gone to hell the last few days. I pull my favorite serum and face wash out of my medicine cabinet.

A plastic rectangle falls into the sink with a plop that sounds louder than it should.

My pills.

*Oh my God.*

I haven't taken them since the day I was attacked.

All the popcorn and coffee I'd consumed earlier rises in my throat. Panic.

Absolute terror.

Not fifteen minutes ago, Gray made it pretty clear he doesn't want kids.

Tears fill my eyes.

I've been down this road before. The chances of getting pregnant should be slim.

But not once in my life have the odds ever worked in my favor.

I slip the pills in my pocket.

Then take a deep breath.

And another.

# CHAPTER FORTY-FIVE

## Grinder

As much as I hate disrupting her life, I like Serena at the clubhouse. Knowing she's safe, sleeping in my bed, and surrounded by brothers who won't let anyone near her.

I hate that I can't be there *with* her. Have to be home by ten like a fucking teenager. Fuck, I hadn't even had a curfew when I *was* a teenager.

*Maybe that's part of the problem.*

I chuckle under my breath. Christ, if I ever get the chance to be a dad, I'll be a nightmare of strict rules and cautionary tales. Anything to stop them from living with so many regrets.

Who am I kidding? Even *if* I knocked Serena up right this second, I'll be in my seventies by the time the kid's old enough to accept life advice from me.

I liked finding her downstairs hanging out with the old ladies and Sparky the other day. Sure, she looked uncomfortable as fuck but she made the effort and the girls all seem to accept her.

Weather's clearer today. I roll my shoulder as I grip the steering wheel. Might actually be able to go on the first run of the year with the club. Not that I'll be able to wear my cut or actually ride in formation *with* my brothers.

The club's gate rolls open as I approach. I guide the truck up the long driveway and park outside the garage. Dex waves to me from inside.

I'd offer to help, but I need to see Serena first. Inside the clubhouse, Sparky and Stash are sprawled out on the couches, laughing at whatever's playing on the big screen television bolted to the wall.

"Morning, Grinder!" Sparky calls out.

"Hey." I wave to them as I head up the stairs.

At my door, I stop and listen. Quiet.

Inside, Serena's curled up on the right side of the mattress. Like even in her sleep, she left space for me. I toss my coat on the chair and like a creepy fucker, lean over to watch her sleep.

So soft and gentle.

A bruise I hadn't noticed before mars the tender skin above her elbow.

How the fuck could anyone put their hands on her?

I stretch out on the bed behind her, trying not to jostle her awake. Her breath stutters.

"Gray?"

"Shhh. I didn't mean to wake you."

She sighs.

I move closer, pulling her against me, and rest my hand on her hip.

"Mmm." She snuggles her head into her pillow.

The soft scent of vanilla drifts toward me. Her shampoo or something. I inhale, finding peace in being next to her.

"Gray?" she whispers, turning to face me.

"Morning, buttercup." I touch her cheek and try not to flip out as I study the still-visible marks on her face. "How do you feel today?"

"Happy to wake up next to you for once."

*Ouch.* The only accusation in her tone is the one my own guilt places there. Still rubs at me. "Wish you were waking up next to me every day."

She slides closer, hooking her arm over my side. "I could stay at your place," she offers. "With you."

"No," I bite out. "You're safe *here*."

Someone bangs on our door. "Grinder!"

Serena sighs and climbs over me, jumping off the bed. I capture her hand. "Wait."

"I need to go to the bathroom."

I release her and she hurries across the room, closing the door behind her.

"Grinder!" The pounding starts up again.

I snarl and lunge off the bed, whipping the door open. "What?"

Jigsaw holds up his hands. "Easy, old man. Z sent me to get you. We're rolling out in twenty. Meeting with Chaser is going down at Remy's place."

"About fucking time," I growl. "I'll be down in a few."

He salutes me and turns around to bang on the door across from me.

The sound of the shower starts. My gaze narrows on the bathroom door, then the clock on the nightstand.

Steam billows around me as I open the bathroom door. I flick the switch for the overhead fan.

"Gray?"

"Who else?" I strip off my clothes and slide the shower door open.

Serena jumps and wraps her arms around her body.

I frown at her reaction. "What's wrong?"

"You startled me."

I step in and slide the door shut, reaching for her. "Come here."

"Don't you have to go?"

"I've got time. Come here and let me say good morning properly."

That finally unlocks her tension. She curls her arms around me, rubbing her slick, wet skin against mine. "That's better, buttercup."

She reaches between us and wraps her hand around my already hard cock, squeezing and stroking.

My thoughts fizzle and I groan. "That's not why I came in here."

"No?" She works her thumb against the most sensitive spot. My cock throbs, wanting inside her.

I dig my fingers into her hips and urge her to turn around. Her body resists. Her grip tightens. "I want to do this." She presses a kiss against my chest.

How am I supposed to say no? I groan and shift my hips forward, chasing her touch. I curl one arm around her and brace my other against the shower door. My gaze drops to her hand slowly sliding and giving a quick twist at the end. Over and over, until my vision blurs at the edges.

My climax builds to an almost painful degree. The urge to spin her around and bury myself inside her fights my body's need for immediate release. She kisses my chest again and my eyes open. She stares up at me, her eyes deeper than the night sky. Her hand squeezes a little harder, and I come in rough jerks against the cushion of her hip.

"Fuck," I groan, my knees weakening. I keep my arm wrapped around her so we both don't end up on the shower floor.

I breathe a long sigh of relief. My eyes blink open. The rush of the shower, the whir of the fan, everything returns to me slowly.

"Thank you, buttercup." I lean down and smash my lips against hers. She smiles against my lips.

After a second or two, she pulls away and turns toward the water.

"Let me do that." I grab the soap from her hand and lather it over her body.

"I was almost finished anyway," she protests. "Don't you have to go?"

Fuck, I'm supposed to be getting my head on straight for this meeting. "Yeah," I answer slowly. "But you know I'd rather be here with you, right?"

---

Rock, Wrath, Z, and I arrive at Remy's bar an hour before the meeting's set to take place.

Murphy, Teller, and Dex already got here a few minutes ahead of us. Murphy walks over to Rock's SUV to introduce Remy.

"Thanks for letting us use your place," Rock says, quickly shaking Remy's hand.

"Anytime." Remy lifts his chin at me. "Hey, Grinder." He nods to Wrath and Z. His eyes widen as Rooster's big, diesel pickup rumbles into the parking lot. Steer and Jigsaw should be with him.

"Come on inside." Remy sweeps his arm toward the one story, square shaped box of a building behind us. Inside, the place is nice. A warm, homey, unpretentious bar with wide-plank floors, a long gleaming L-shaped bar, a few booths along one wall, and a bunch of tables scattered in the middle. The far wall has a long table in the corner with a bench on one side and chairs on the other.

"That'll give you the most privacy." Remy points to the corner table. "Table isn't bolted to the floor or anything. Anyone starts shooting, you can just flip it over and take cover." He slaps Murphy's shoulder. "Right?"

Murphy slowly drops his gaze to Remy and holds out his fist to tap knuckles with him. "Yeah."

"Hopefully, there won't be any shoot-outs this afternoon." Rock scans the bar. It's one big open room. To our left, a short hallway with an Exit sign above it. "Restrooms that way?" he asks Remy.

"Yup. Exit too. Last door leads to the basement. It has *special accommodations* if you're in need of that today."

Murphy smirks.

Rock and Wrath walk through the bar, checking everything out.

"You close the place for us?" Z asks Remy.

"Nah, it's slow during the day. That's why it's just me right now. Bar's stocked though, so anything you want, let me know."

We all end up placing drink orders. More as a way to be able to drop a generous tip as a thank you, than to quench our thirst.

I take a seat at the table in the back. Rock slides in on my right, Z on my left.

Remy drops off our drinks.

Wrath settles his big frame at the corner of the bar where he can watch the door.

A few minutes later, Remy lifts his chin at me. "Black Escalade and a Mercedes G-Class just pulled into the parking lot."

"That's gotta be them," Wrath says.

A slight current of tension runs through all of us. Rock squares his shoulders and pushes the table out a few inches. Rooster moves closer to Z's side.

Sunlight punches into the bar as the door swings open.

Chaser swaggers inside slowly, slipping off his sunglasses and tucking them in a pocket of his cut. Two club brothers remain close to his back. One's about Wrath's size—I figure he's Chaser's SAA. Reminds me of the fucking Terminator the way he never stops scanning his surroundings. The other brother looks familiar but I don't remember his name.

Chaser doesn't so much as lift an eyebrow at all the extra Lost Kings inside the bar. It wouldn't surprise me at all if more of his guys were waiting outside or nearby just in case.

A taller but leaner character stays a few feet to Chaser's left. Not wearing Devil Demons colors, but inked from head to fingers. This must be the half brother.

Chaser nods to his entourage to take a seat at the bar where Wrath's stationed and approaches our corner slowly. His brother stops halfway and waits.

As MC protocol demands, since he called the meeting, Rock stands and greets Chaser first. Chaser shakes Z's hand, then Rooster's, and finally mine.

"Grinder." Chaser pulls me in, slapping my back. I return the friendly greeting. "Good to see you on this side, brother."

Time's been kinder to Chaser than it has to me. Still, up close like this, it's a shock to see he's aged at all. I kept picturing him as the cocky MC president's son in my head. Now, he's a stone-faced MC president, running his own club.

"How've you been?" I thump him on the back one last time. "How's Mallory?"

"Great. I know she's hoping to see you soon, too." He glances at Rock. "Once we get our business squared away."

Rock nods to the table we chose. Like any MC prez worth his patch, Chaser's not thrilled about taking the seat that leaves his back exposed. He lazily turns it to the side, pushing it against the wall before sitting and resting one arm on the table.

Rock, Z, and I sit across from him.

Rooster positions himself at the end of the table, so he's facing Chaser. Chaser's SAA moves in like a storm cloud to stand next to his prez.

Wrath's keen eyes shift between us and the other two Chaser brought with him.

"As much as I always enjoy a road trip, the weather's shit," Chaser says. "So, what am I doing here?"

Without saying a word, Rock slaps the drawing on the table and pushes it toward Chaser. "That look familiar to you?"

Chaser studies the picture then flicks his gaze toward Rock. "And this is…?"

"The guy who attacked my old lady had that tat on his hand," I explain.

"Looks an awful lot like the one on your brother's neck," Rooster adds, casting a glance in the brother's direction.

"*Half* brother," Chaser corrects. He lifts his gaze to me. "Who's your old lady?"

"No one you know."

He cocks his head and studies me closely, while I do the same.

He's a hell of a lot more even-tempered and thoughtful than I remember his pop being as we sit here and casually accuse his brother's crew of attacking my ol' lady. But just because I respect him, doesn't mean I'm going to tolerate any bullshit.

"Same guy paid me a visit at my apartment," I continue. "Do your *half* brother's minions take on side gigs for prison gangs?"

"Fuck no." Chaser lifts his hand and motions his brother to the table.

The brother glares daggers at Chaser. Maybe he doesn't like being hand-signaled to like a dog. Don't know, don't care.

Chaser flicks his fingers in the guy's direction. "Rock, Z, Rooster, you remember my *half* brother Quill. Grinder, this is Quill." Chaser's gaze narrows and he pins his brother with a hard stare. "Grinder's a long-time friend of *my* club."

Quill nods at me. "I must've missed you at Chaser's anniversary party, long-time friend."

*This cocksucker.*

I stand, placing my hands on the table and meet Quill's cold gaze. "I just got released from Pine Correctional. I think you have a few friends there you do business with?"

"Got no business inside." He pushes his hands out in front of him like he's rolling out a magic carpet of bullshit. "We leave *that* to the incarcerated."

I grunt and take my seat again.

Quill glances at Chaser before sitting across from me. "Why do you think my crew's involved?"

Rock hands him the drawing. Quill studies it but no emotions register on his face. "So?"

"Have you *not* looked in a mirror lately?" Rooster asks, rubbing his fingers over his throat.

Quill slides a lethal stare Rooster's way. Rooster meets it with a smirk and head tilt.

Rock taps the paper. "Everyone who works for your family has this ink."

"Not *everyone* who works for the family," Quill says. "They need to be at a certain level." He nods to Rock's inked hands. "I'm sure your MC has similar rules, yes?"

"The particular guy also had a red X at the corner of his eye." I tap my cheek.

Quill freezes. His left eyebrow lifts ever-so-slightly.

*Ah, that got a reaction.*

"Had a city accent," Z adds. "Bronx, maybe Brooklyn. Not Manhattan or Mexico where you grew up, right?"

I bite the inside of my cheek.

Quill's lips curl in lethal amusement. "You did your homework, Zero. Good for you."

"Is there anyone in your crew who would be looking to make extra money on the side?" I lean in closer before Z snaps and strangles this guy. "I know Big Chief. I don't picture you doing business with a guy like him long-term. It's too risky for the operation your dad built. The kid that came at me practically admitted it was unauthorized."

Quill's hard expression relaxes. A little ass-kissing seems to have worked. Too bad I can't stand the aftertaste.

"They can come at me all day long," I continue. "I don't give a fuck. But when they come after my girl, we have a problem. She's got nothing to do with any of this. She hasn't been able to go back to work since the attack."

"That's not right." Quill glances at Chaser, then back to me. "Chaser claims you're an important friend of his club. That makes you a friend of mine as well. I'll ask my guys." He slips a small notebook out of his pocket and a pen. "Give me the dates, times, and locations of the incidents."

*Aren't you thorough.*

I relay the information and he writes it all down in what looks like some kind of code full of lines and dots. I flick my gaze at Chaser who stares at the ceiling and shakes his head.

Quill stands and holds out his hand. "We'll contact you when we have information."

I shake his hand. "Appreciate it."

Quill will deliver. I feel it. He doesn't like being called out in front of his big brother. He's a man with something to prove.

Prison taught me the art of conquering patience. The waiting will be bitter, but revenge—when it finally arrives—will be sweet.

# CHAPTER FORTY-SIX

## Grinder

When we return to the clubhouse, Rock nudges my elbow and tips his head toward the war room. "I'd like to have a word with you."

"What's wrong?" I ask after he closes the door behind us.

"Nothing." He gestures for me to take a seat and rounds the table to take his own. "Want to chat, that's all. How do you feel about the way that went down?"

"Appreciated having everyone at my back."

"That's what we do, brother."

"Would've liked to ask Chaser more questions about this long-lost brother of his."

Rock snorts. "I don't think that topic is open for discussion."

"Yeah, got that."

"Besides this craziness, how's everything?"

"All right. I like working at Sully's place. Not sure I'm useful to him but he says he appreciates the help."

"Good." He spreads his hands in front of him and one corner of his mouth slides up. "I know it's not as glamorous as all the other opportunities we have to offer."

"Knock it off. It's honest work. That's all I need for now."

His smirk slips away. "Most of the club's business is on the right side now. Teller has things set up under a maze of corporations. We can find you something that can't be traced back to the club, if you're not happy there."

"What are my options?" I scoff. "Porn sets? Strip club? I'm too old for that shit."

He doesn't poke fun or seem insulted. "My shop's too small. Parole would see through that quick. Trin has her photography studio and I know she just lost Heidi as her assistant."

"I don't know dick about that stuff."

"There's Wrath's gym. Or Charlotte's law practice. It's wholly separate from the MC."

"And what exactly am I gonna do for her? Play private investigator? Answer the phones and do her filing?"

He ignores my sarcasm and continues. "Rooster's put together a security company for Shelby. But that's when she's on tour. He's throwing brothers work that way. Everyone seemed to have a good time."

Nah, that ain't how I want to spend my time. "As much as I'm itching to ride the wind again, I don't wanna do it for work. Chasing after some tour bus. Being held to a schedule instead of stopping to enjoy the sights." I slap my hand against the table. "I want to settle in one place. Finally put down roots."

"I understand." He taps his fingers against the side of the table. "How are things with Serena?"

I bristle at the question. "Why? You think I'm crazy for gettin' involved with her this soon after leaving prison? Or you worried she's too young for me?"

His expression remains calm and even. "Neither. I want you to be happy, that's all."

"She makes me happy. I wanna do the same for her."

"She seems to care about you a lot. Loyal girl. Smart, too. Did everything she could to protect you and keep you off the cops' radar."

*I hate like hell she was put in that position.* "I know."

"You gonna lock her down?" He smirks at the play on my last name.

"Cute, Prez." Christ it feels weird to talk about this with him. "Yeah, I want to propose."

He doesn't even blink. "When?"

"That's it? *When?* No cautionary advice?"

"You *want* someone to talk you out of it?"

"No." I roll my shoulders and stare straight ahead, avoiding his intense stare. "I'm not ready yet. I need to figure out this shit with Big Chief and I need to get Grillo to stop fucking with my life."

"We're working on that. He won't be on your back much longer."

"We both know he's involved in this somehow." I lift my gaze to his, staring right into his eyes. "If he's the reason Serena got hurt, he needs to die."

"Agreed."

I clench my fists. "I want to reclaim my life but it's like all these ghosts from prison and from my past wrapped themselves around me and won't be satisfied until they drag me back to hell." I hold my arms in front of me as if I'll find some evidence of the ghostly shackles straining to hold me down.

"You're not alone, brother." He reaches across the table and grips my forearm. "We all live with the ghosts of our pasts. But they don't have to define your present. Or follow you into the future."

## CHAPTER FORTY-SEVEN

### Grinder

Over time, I've mastered the art of patience. Focusing on the things I can control. Moving ahead. Biding my time. Only acting after thinking through all the consequences. Never reacting out of fear or any other emotion.

The two weeks we wait to hear from Chaser slowly chip away at my patience.

Finally, the call comes.

I meet Rock and Wrath in the war room, searching for the phone. "Where? What'd he say?"

"He wouldn't say anything over the phone," Rock says. "Asked to meet in the same spot as before."

"Already spoke to Remy and he's fine with it." Wrath claps my shoulder. "Let's roll."

"You trust this isn't a setup?" I ask Rock.

He slips a 1911 pistol into a holster under his cut. "As much as I trust anyone I don't share a patch with."

"Z, Rooster, and Jigsaw are meeting us there," Wrath says, adding a Glock to his holster.

Outside, Murphy and Teller jump into Wrath's truck. Rock and I climb into his SUV.

The ride seems longer than last time.

As we pull up to the desolate-looking bar, my gaze lands on Rooster's truck and several other black SUVs. "Looks like a fucking gangster funeral," I mutter.

Rock snorts. "That's exactly what it's about to be."

He backs into a spot next to Wrath's truck and we step out.

Remy meets us with a hefty length of sturdy metal chain over his shoulder. "This everyone who's coming?" he asks.

Rock quickly scans the parking lot. "All our guys are here."

Chaser's quick steps crunch over the gravel to meet us. No friendly handshakes this time.

"Everyone here?" Rock asks him.

"Yeah."

Remy holds up the chain. "I'm gonna close off the road so you don't get any surprise visitors. Behind the building is completely private. The basement's also available if you want it."

Chaser's eyes widen as he stares at Remy's stone-cold expression.

"Griff and I are going to head over to Zips," Remy adds, nodding to his buddy. "Unless you want us to stick around?"

"Nah, that's fine," I say. These two have done enough for us. No reason to drag them in further.

Remy gestures to Rock's truck. "You all should be able to drive around the gate easily enough. But there's a set of keys on the bar for the lock if you need it."

"Thanks." I thump both of them on the back.

After they leave, Chaser jerks his head. Rock and I flank him on either side as we walk around to the back of the building.

The multiple sets of boots crunching over the gravel behind us says our clubs are following at a respectful distance.

Behind the building, there's a wide concrete pad with a rusty metal drain in the center. Wrath reaches up and slaps a strip of thick, black tape over a security camera bolted to the roof.

A hint of grim amusement curls his lips. "Just in case."

Z, Rooster, and Murphy join Rock, Chaser, and me in a circle.

Wrath and Chaser's enforcer stand back a few feet. The rest of our two clubs form a loose perimeter around us.

"All right," Rock says. "Care to share why we're all out here settin' up like we're about to film a scene from an El Chapo biopic?"

Chaser narrows his eyes, apparently not amused by the comparison to the famous, incarcerated former cartel leader.

The roar of an engine echoes around the side of the building. Everyone starts reaching under their cuts, except Chaser. "Easy, that's Quill."

A black SUV with darkened windows backs up to the edge of the concrete pad and shuts off.

Chaser continues as if nothing happened. "You were right." He meets my eyes. "It was one of Quill's foot soldiers who came at you and roughed up your girl."

"Chaser," Rock says in a low, urgent tone. "You have to understand the gravity of this situation. We had your assurance nothing would change with your brother's crew running through our territory."

Chaser clenches his jaw. He's in a hell of a shitty spot. I'd feel bad for him if it wasn't *my* woman who was attacked. "From what I understand, it's like Grinder said. This guy took on some side action my brother didn't sanction." His gaze shifts to me. "Someone at Pine wanted you bad. Who'd you piss off before you left?"

"You kidding me?" I push into Chaser's space, not touching him but making it clear that's what's coming if he tries throwing the blame *my* way.

"Easy," Chaser says. "I gotta ask." His gaze shifts to Rock. "Our clubs share a long history." He tilts his head toward his brother. "I won't shit on that. Not for family. Or anyone else." His dark eyes land on me again. "You should know that better than anyone here, Grinder."

Nice, subtle reminder of all the ways his club helped protect me inside.

"He went after my girl," I snarl. "Scared her. *Hurt* her."

"We'll make it right." He raises his voice and glances over his shoulder at the SUV. "We'll make it right, won't we, Quill?"

Chaser's brother steps out of the vehicle and rolls over to us with the lethal grace of a lion on the hunt.

He stops at Chaser's side, shoulder-to-shoulder.

"I get that you don't have a reason to trust me." He glances at Chaser who nods for him to continue. "But my crew doesn't go after women. My guys know that."

"Obviously, they *don't*," I growl.

He stabs me with a murderous glare but takes a few seconds for a long, slow inhale and exhale. "We're still ironing out some issues since my father's death. Rio hasn't been...thrilled over certain recent structural changes."

"Seems you need to get your guys in line," Rock scolds. "Quickly."

Chaser clamps his mouth shut and glances down. Like he's trying not to laugh. Bet he gave his brother a similar lecture before this meeting.

Rooster steps closer to me. "Prez, you mind if I paint a picture here?"

Z's mouth quirks. "What's that, Rooster?"

Rooster locks eyes with Chaser, whose expression remains flat. "I haven't been patched-in as long as some of my brothers. But I've always known Kings and Demons had a good relationship."

Chaser's jaw tightens. "Yes, Rooster. I mentioned that about five minutes ago, if you were listening."

"I heard you. I wanted to emphasize this point for *Quill*." Rooster circles his finger in the air. "Our get-together is a courtesy. We're not the only MC in existence. If this shit went down somewhere else, you would've brought a war down on Chaser's club, not friendly chats at backwoods bars." He holds his hands up as a sign he's not trying to be disrespectful. "Just sayin'."

Z side-eyes his VP and barely hides his smirk. "Thank you, Rooster." He jerks his head for Rooster to fall back and keep quiet.

Quill's reaction is less amused. "I'm aware of the damage this incident caused. I want to make amends. Or I wouldn't be standing here."

I'm starting to hate this guy.

"Blood or cash." Wrath's low voice reverberates around our circle.

"I know how it's done," Quill sneers. "I didn't waltz into the life yesterday."

"As far as I'm concerned, you *did*," Rock says.

Quill raises his hand over his shoulder and snaps his fingers. The hatch of the SUV silently lifts. Two men dressed in black roll a third guy wrapped up in ropes out of the cargo area, then close the hatch.

"Got your boy rolled up like a Christmas goose, there, Quill," Wrath says.

Quill stares at Wrath and Chaser's enforcer. Neither of them move. Finally Quill stalks over and drags the *goose* across the concrete, throwing him into the center of our circle. He squats next to his foot soldier and rips the black bandanna away from his mouth.

"He's the one who came to visit me," I confirm. I note the red X tat and the lion on the hand.

He grins up at me from the ground. "Got mad respect for you, old man. Your woman's a sweet piece. Wish I'd been able to spend more time with her."

Either he doesn't really think Quill will discipline him or he has no fucks left to give.

Rooster pulls his piece and quietly hands it to me.

"Whoa, whoa," Quill holds out his hands. "Wait a second."

The doors of the SUV fly open and two guys jump out, guns drawn.

Chaos erupts with everyone pulling their weapons. Most of them seem to be aimed in Quill's direction.

Chaser raises his hand in the air. "We're on the same side."

As a show of good faith, Rock slides his pistol back in its holster. "Put 'em away."

Wrath's the last one to stand down.

Quill kicks Rio in the side. "Shut your mouth until further notice."

"I have a few questions." I lean down into Rio's face. "How'd you find Serena?"

"How'd *you* find her is the better question, grandpa."

This time, Chaser lands the kick to the guy's ribs. "Stop fucking around."

Rio hisses in a pained breath and glares at Chaser, then Quill. "Told you this arrangement was bullshit."

"Who told you about her?" I dig the tip of the gun in my hand into Rio's kneecap. "It's been a while, so I'll start low and move my way up, to get the hang of things," I warn him.

"Fuck! All right. All right. Your P.O. gave me her info."

I glance up at Rock, who nods.

"Why?" I ask Rio.

"I guess Big Chief needs someone on the outside who has access to folks with certain skill sets."

"No, why *me*?"

"Everyone inside says you're a *savage*," he says with wide-eyed respect. "Big Chief knew you'd get shit done. But you needed the right motivation. The deal was important."

Chaser kicks him again. "You mean the *deal* running goods through *my* territory."

"I don't know nothin' about that!" Rio yells. "The job was to convince the old dude to fall in line. If he didn't, then go after the girl."

"And then what?" I ask.

"Nothing. Big Chief figured after being locked up for so long, you were probably desperate for pussy, so you'd do whatever he needed with the right motivation."

I hang my head and choke down a pathetic laugh. The whole operation inside is doomed with Big Chief running things.

"Why's Grillo working with Big Chief?" I ask.

"Cash. He's got a kid with a hefty heroin habit and needs to put her in rehab."

Fuck, that's probably embarrassing for someone in law enforcement. No wonder he's such a prick.

Rio must be missing part of the bigger picture. "Why would Big Chief think turning Grillo loose on me was gonna motivate me to do his dirty work? If anything, I'd be *less* likely to get involved."

Rio blinks up at me. "Huh?

About the answer I expected from this joker.

"We good?" Quill asks me.

I stand and point the gun at Rio's head. "I got what I needed."

"No, no, no." Rio digs his sneakers into the cement and attempts to crawl away like a deranged inchworm. "You said if I told 'em everything, we'd be level!" he shouts at Quill.

"I lied." Quill shrugs but he presses his palm against the barrel of my gun, lowering it to my side. "I'll do the honors." He smirks at me. "Can't have a friend of Chaser's headed back to prison because of *my* crew's fuck up."

What this punk doesn't understand is I'd go back to prison for *life* if it kept Serena safe.

But there's no time to argue.

Quill pulls his Glock and points it at Rio's head.

"No, no, no!" The kid scrambles to his knees.

Quill pulls the trigger.

The deafening roar reverberates around us.

A shockwave of red slush explodes from Rio's skull, splattering the concrete. He topples over on his side, a slow halo of blood and brains spreading around his head.

I feel nothing except the irritation of not being the one to fire the kill shot.

# CHAPTER FORTY-EIGHT

## Serena

I STARE AT THE PREGNANCY TEST UNTIL I'M READY TO PUKE. *AGAIN.*

This can't be happening. *Again.*

I glance at my reflection in the mirror. *Why are you so fertile?*

Tears sting my eyes. I won't cry. I clench the stick in my hand and stare at those two miserable lines.

*These tests are wrong all the time.*

It's possible I screwed it up. I set the stick on the bathroom counter and march downstairs. The club installed lockers in the women's bathroom a couple of years ago. It was nice to be able to have a place to stick your purse or whatever.

What was even nicer—and it must have been either Trinity or one of the other women who came up with the idea and replenishes the supply—was the lockers are chock-full of the kinds of goodies every den of deviancy should offer to the women who visit seeking free, casual sex with dirty bikers.

Condoms—a wide variety of sizes, shapes, brands, and flavors. Single-use bottles of lube, individually wrapped vibrating cock rings, emergency contraception—*ha!*—tampons, pads, trial-sized bottles soaps, shampoos, toothpaste, travel toothbrushes and other toiletries. What I'm actually here for is in a lower locker.

Pregnancy tests.

I grab one of the pink boxes.

Paranoid about running into someone who will ask questions or report back to Grayson, I shove the box down the front of my pants and yank my sweatshirt over the bulge.

By the time I return to our room, I'm shaking. I run into the bathroom and slam the door. I rip open the box and yank out both sticks.

A few minutes later I'm staring at my original test and the two new ones.

*Three sticks. Six pink lines.*

What the hell am I going to do?

I should've confessed to Grayson the second I realized I'd forgotten my pills. Maybe swallowed one of those morning-after pills downstairs.

We're not married. We don't even live together. We haven't been a couple for long. How am I going to do this alone?

I rest my hand over my stomach. This time things are different. Even if Grayson gets angry with me or doesn't want to be involved, I'll be okay.

I'm *not* at the mercy of anyone else to take care of me.

*I have a job.* Well, I *had* a job. Trish let me go but promised she wouldn't report me for official disciplinary action. So, I still have my license. I'll be able to support myself *and* my baby on my own. I'm earning more money through my YouTube channel, so that will help with expenses too.

*I have an apartment.* But it's not a safe place for a baby. We can't stay there.

Shit.

How will he react? He made it pretty clear kids aren't in his current plan.

*Oh my God.*

*I'm* the one who told him we were good to skip the condoms. Swore to him I was on the pill.

Except, pills don't work when you get beat up in a parking lot, have to stay at the clubhouse for a few days and forget all about them.

Grayson was so sweet. So loving, the way he took care of me.

My toes curl, remembering the desperate way I woke up and wanted to connect with him after the attack. And so many times after.

He's going to think I tried to baby trap him on purpose.

My hands shake. The blood in my veins turns to ice.

No one is taking this baby away from me, no matter what. I can't go through that again. I won't.

No matter what, I'll protect this child.

# CHAPTER FORTY-NINE

## Grinder

Before leaving, the site, Quill retrieves a large black leather drawstring bag from the back of his SUV and hands it to Chaser, who hands it to me.

"Amends," Quill explains.

I can guess what's inside, but I pull the straps apart anyway and take a look. Bricks of cash, tightly bound together. "Thank you."

Quill nods. "Is this a fair settlement?" He glances from Chaser, to Rock, Z, Rooster, and then me. "Are we good?"

Rock tilts his head toward me.

"Yeah, I'm good," I answer. "Thank you."

"My brothers and I are vetting everyone in our organization again," Quill says. "We won't run into this problem in the future."

That's a big promise to make, but I'm tired of this guy and ready to get the fuck out of here, so I nod.

"Rock," Quill says. "Our arrangement still stands, yes?"

Rock glances at Z who nods. "Moving through our territory up to Canada. That's it, right?"

"Correct. We'll have cargo. But we're not looking to distribute anything in your region."

"Same rules we discussed before still apply," Rock says.

"Absolutely." Quill nods. "Thank you."

After his crew leaves, Chaser walks over to Rock's truck with us. He nods at the bag in my hands. "It's all legit."

As opposed to what? "Okay."

He holds out his hand to Rock who shakes it. "Thank you."

"Looks like your plate's full," I say when he holds out his hand to me.

"It never ends."

We talk for a few minutes—generic stuff, how's his dad, the family, riding. That sort of thing.

"I'll let you guys get on the road." Chaser lifts his chin. "Hey, Rooster, wait up a sec."

Rock watches closely while they have an animated conversation. Z joins them and Rock jerks his head toward the truck.

"What's wrong?" I ask.

"Nothing, why?" He slides his window down, watching the edge of the road carefully as he swings the truck wide around the closed gate.

Finally, we get on the highway. Can't wait to see Serena and let her know at least part of the problem has been handled.

"We still need to deal with Grillo," Rock says. "Before Big Chief finds someone else to do his bidding."

"Yeah, that occurred to me." I nudge the bag of money at my feet with my boot. "Why'd Chaser make a point to let me know the cash was *legit?*"

A grim smile twists Rock's mouth. "I think that's part of Quill's enterprise—counterfeiting money. Haven't been able to track down a lot of information about them, yet."

"You need to step light there," I warn.

"I'm aware." He flicks his gaze toward the bag. "We can wash that through Crystal Ball if you want. Z's got the laundromat down in Union too but, Christ that's a pain in the ass. You'll be swimming in quarters."

I reach into the bag and pull out one of the stacks, carefully flipping through the bills. "Actually, I think I know exactly what I want to do with some of it."

"More ink?"

"That too. But not today." I keep counting the bills. "What's the best jewelry store in the area?"

One corner of his mouth slides up. "I know a place."

A FEW HOURS LATER, WE RETURN TO THE CLUBHOUSE. DRIVEWAY'S FULL of cars. All the outside lights are on, illuminating the surrounding area.

Hope embraces Rock as soon as we walk in the door. He drops his forehead to hers and they share a few words. I move away to give them privacy.

Most of the guys from Downstate returned with Z, so it's a full house tonight. Both clubs celebrating together.

Z pulls me to his side when I try to pass him. "You feel good about this, G?"

"Good? Not really. Relieved I guess." I lift my chin at Rooster. "What was up with your whole 'let me paint you a picture' speech?"

He grins and strokes his hand over his beard. "What? I just thought I'd point out how Quill's fuck ups might screw with Chaser's MC if he's not careful."

"Jesus." Z gives Rooster a quick shove. "I got worried for a sec Quill might shoot you."

"I thought those crazy motherfuckers were gonna shoot *all* of us," Wrath says, draping his arms over Z and Rooster's shoulders. He squeezes Rooster hard enough to knock him off-balance. "Especially when you handed Grinder your nine, ya dick."

"What? The guy was being disrespectful." Rooster shrugs and smirks at the same time.

Trinity approaches us and raises an eyebrow at Wrath. "Come here, angel." He lifts her up and she wraps herself around him.

Rooster taps Trinity's shoulder. "Before you two maul each other. You seen Shelby?"

Trinity points toward the hallway. "She's coming."

"Serena with her?" I ask Trinity.

She frowns. "No, I haven't seen her all day, actually."

*Shit.* Did she hear the party going on and decide to stay upstairs? Is she sick? I pull my phone out and turn it on. Forgot to check it after the meeting.

No texts or voicemails from her.

I run into Lilly next. "Have you seen Serena?"

"No, not since last night." She tilts her head to the side. "Everything okay?"

"Yeah. Just worried about her."

Z wraps his arm around her and whispers something in her ear, then lifts his chin at me. "Everything all okay, G?"

"Gonna head upstairs to look for Serena."

"Don't stay up there all night."

"Yeah, yeah," I mutter. If Serena's not feeling well or she's too stressed to deal with the party, I'm staying by her side.

"Serena?" I push into our room, expecting to find her sleeping or reading.

No Serena.

No *sign* of Serena.

Bed's been made. Chair's empty. Desk is clear.

*What the fuck?*

Every last thing of hers is *gone.*

Not cleaned up, tidy, organized and put away.

*Motherfucking gone.*

I rip open the closet door. Her hangers—empty.

Yank out a dresser drawer—nothing.

Bathroom counter—*clear.*

Her brush, her pile of hair ties, all her fancy little bottles, colorful containers, and brushes that had started creeping over to my side of the bathroom sink are *gone.*

What the hell?

Why would she leave without telling me?

My gaze drops to the floor.

Trash can—*full.*

No need to dig through the trash. A bright pink and blue box sits right on top.

*Rapid Pregnancy Test. 99% Accurate.*

The big picture on the front explains it all.

*Two lines—pregnant. One line—not pregnant.*

The box is empty.

My heart pounds.

There's a pink box underneath the blue one. I pull that one out.

*Early Pregnancy Test. Clear Results Fast!*

Three white sticks are stuffed inside *that* box.

*Oh, buttercup. If you wanted to hide the evidence, you did a shit job of it.*

My hands shake as I lay all three sticks on the counter.

Three tests. Six lines, total.

This feels like visiting Rose again. Magnified by a thousand because the stakes are so much higher. I don't want to get my hopes up and be crushed. *Again.*

I scoop up the sticks and keep staring.

*Two lines—pregnant. One line—not pregnant.*

Someone knocks on our door.

I hurry to open it, with the tests still clutched in my fist.

Z's on the other side. "We're waiting on you, brother." He peers over my shoulder. "Serena coming downstairs—"

I shove the test sticks in Z's face. "Do these mean what I think?"

He backs up a step. His eyes widen. It takes him a minute to answer. "Yeah, but ours are never positive."

Shit, now I feel like an asshole.

"What's going on?" His concerned gaze lifts. "Are those Serena's?"

"They're not *mine.*"

His concern twists into confusion. "Where is she?"

"That's what I'm trying to figure out." I open the door wider. "All her shit's gone."

"Fuck." He slaps his hand over his mouth. "Brother, after what she went through…*before*…you think she got scared?"

*That's exactly what I'm starting to think.* "She knows I'd never hurt her."

"Yeah, but she's been through a lot. Maybe she panicked and ran." He clasps his hand over my shoulder. "You need to go find her, brother. *Now.* Don't let her get away."

Get away?

Serena can't run from me.

She's mine.

She's carrying my baby.

I warned her once that no matter how far or fast she tried to run, I'd catch her.

Obviously, she didn't believe me.

But she will.

Grinder and Serena's story concludes in<br>Throne of Scars (Lost Kings MC #20)

# THE LOST KINGS MC® WORLD

## By Autumn Jones Lake

Sometimes I'm asked where the stand alone books fit into the Lost Kings MC World. This is a loose, chronological reading order that might help!

### Suggested Chronological Reading Order

1. Kickstart My Heart (Hollywood Demons #1)
2. Blow My Fuse (Hollywood Demons #2)
3. Wheels of Fire (Hollywood Demons #3)
4. Renegade Path
5. Slow Burn (Lost Kings MC #1)
6. Corrupting Cinderella (Lost Kings MC #2)
7. Three Kings, One Night (Lost Kings MC #2.5)
8. Strength From Loyalty (Lost Kings MC #3)
9. Tattered on My Sleeve (Lost Kings MC #4)
10. White Heat (Lost Kings MC #5)
11. Between Embers (Lost Kings MC #5.5)
12. Bullets & Bonfires (Standalone)
13. More Than Miles (Lost Kings MC #6)
14. Warnings & Wildfires (Standalone)
15. White Knuckles (Lost Kings MC #7)
16. Beyond Reckless (Lost Kings MC #8)
17. Beyond Reason (Lost Kings MC #9)
18. One Empire Night (Lost Kings MC #9.5)
19. After Burn (Lost Kings MC #10)
20. After Glow (Lost Kings MC #11)
21. Zero Hour (Lost Kings MC #11.5)
22. Zero Tolerance (Lost Kings MC #12)
23. Zero Regret (Lost Kings MC #13)

24. Zero Apologies (Lost Kings MC #14)
25. Swagger and Sass (Lost Kings MC #14.5)
26. White Lies (Lost Kings MC #15)
27. Rhythm of the Road (Lost Kings MC #16)
28. Lyrics on the Wind (Lost Kings MC #17)
29. Diamond in the Dust (Lost Kings MC #18)
30. Crown of Ghosts (Lost Kings MC #19)
31. Throne of Scars (Lost Kings MC #20)
32. Reckless Truths (Lost Kings MC #21)

# ABOUT THE AUTHOR

Autumn Jones Lake is the *USA Today* and *Wall Street Journal* bestselling author of over twenty-five novels, including the popular Lost Kings MC series. She believes true love stories never end.

Her past lives include baking cookies, bagging groceries, selling cheap shoes, and practicing law. Playing with her imaginary friends all day is by far her favorite job yet!

Autumn lives in upstate New York with her own alpha hero.

www.autumnjoneslake.com

- facebook.com/autumnjoneslake
- goodreads.com/autumnjoneslake
- pinterest.com/autumnjoneslake
- instagram.com/autumnjlake
- bookbub.com/authors/autumn-jones-lake

Made in the USA
Columbia, SC
09 October 2024